all they
need to
know

all they need to know

A Novel

EILEEN GOUDGE

Published by Lake Union Publishing, Seattle

www.apub.com

Amazon, the Amazon logo, and Lake Union Publishing are trademarks of Amazon.com, Inc., or its affiliates.

ISBN-13: 9781662518126 (paperback)
ISBN-13: 9781662518119 (digital)

Cover design by Eileen Carey
Cover image: © Andreas Koslowski / plainpicture; © Chakrit Thongwattana / Getty; © Summit Art Creations / Shutterstock

Printed in the United States of America

For my beloved husband, Sandy

All They Need to Know

All they need to know,

> *Is that I've traveled on the wind,*
>
> *Carried along by tumbling woes,*
>
> *Wondering where it will end.*

Life cannot be trusted,

> *Any more than the wind,*
>
> *It mows down hearts and lives,*
>
> *And then, it begins again.*

But the wind blows through this endless blue,

> *Filled with dancing clouds,*
>
> *That move to allow the sunlight to,*
>
> *Shine where love abounds.*

> *—Karen Goudge Potter*

Beauty is truth, truth beauty—that is all

Ye know on earth, and all ye need to know.

—John Keats, from "Ode on a Grecian Urn"

1

Kyra sang as she drove, belting out "Midnight Train to Memphis" along with Chris Stapleton on the radio to keep from drifting across the centerline in her sleep-deprived state. She was somewhere in Nebraska and had been on the road for the past forty-eight hours since leaving New York, headed west. Destination unknown. Someplace where *he* wouldn't find her, if such a place existed. Her eyes were gritty from exhaustion, and her muscles twitchy from caffeine overload.

Almost out of gas, she was on the lookout for a service station when a glance in her rearview mirror showed the black SUV she'd noticed earlier was still behind her. Was it following her? Her voice dried up mid-note and fear snaked through her belly. If she were to become stranded by the side of the road, she would be a sitting duck. Spotting a sign with gas and food icons, she exited the freeway and felt the knotted muscles in her neck loosen when the black SUV disappeared from view.

It was ten on a Wednesday morning in September, the sun climbing in the sky and temps already in the eighties. The car she drove, a 2010 Ford Focus with over a hundred thousand miles on it, was a trade-in from the used-car dealership she'd stopped at in Buffalo. Its AC was nonfunctioning, and she sweltered in the midmorning heat, her T-shirt stuck to her skin where she'd sweated through it. Strands of her dark hair that had escaped her braid fluttered around her face in the hot air blowing in through the open windows. It smelled of fertilizer from the cornfields rolling past on either side of the road.

Finally, she came to a shabby building with two rows of gas pumps in front, advertised by its sign as Mel's Gas and Go. She pulled in at the first row of pumps, powered her windows up, and shut off the engine. Inside, she paid in cash for forty dollars' worth of gas, a bag of chips, and a large Coke. The store proprietor was just shy of unfriendly and didn't make eye contact, for which she was grateful. She'd kept her conversations with the people she'd met in passing to a minimum, in the hope that no one would remember her. Gray-haired and portly, with deep-set eyes above drooping jowls, the man wordlessly handed over her change along with the key to the restroom, at her request.

She'd filled her tank and was headed for the restroom when she was brought to a halt by the sight of a dumpster parked alongside the building. She couldn't see past it. Someone might be lurking on the other side; she could be walking into a trap. Uneasy, she glanced over her shoulder and saw a dark-blue Honda Accord she hadn't noticed before parked at the second row of pumps, its driver nowhere in sight. Her early-warning system pinged. Her heart rate accelerated and her chest tightened.

She'd been careful in covering her tracks. She'd traded her BMW for the beater she was driving, destroyed her credit cards, and paid in cash for her travel expenses to avoid creating a paper trail. The phone she was using, a burner, was for emergency calls only. But what if someone had been watching when she'd left home and tailed her? One of the cops, or the chief investigator at the DA's office, a former NYPD detective, who took orders from Rory? If so, what if they'd been instructed to detain her when no one was watching, by force if necessary?

A chill swept through her, despite the sun beating down and the hot pavement baking through the soles of her flip-flops. She was suddenly aware that she was in the middle of nowhere, not a soul in sight. Who would come if she called for help? Probably not the store proprietor, who didn't seem the type to get involved. She debated returning to her car and getting the hell out of Dodge, but she needed to pee and didn't know how long she could hold it or how far it was to the next restroom.

She proceeded with caution, watching for any movement in the shadows beyond the dumpster while casting glances behind her to see whether the driver of the Honda had returned. She saw nothing worrisome, and the only sound was the intermittent whoosh of vehicles passing on the road. But she remained vigilant, every muscle in her body tensed, prepared to bolt at the first sign of trouble.

She didn't expect to find trouble of the four-legged variety.

The first thing she noticed as she stepped past the dumpster was the RV parked in the weed-choked lot behind the building. The second thing she noticed was the dog chained to the metal steps to its entrance, a mixed breed with the black-and-tan markings of a German shepherd and the thick fur and curly tail of a Samoyed. A male, she saw when he sprang onto all fours as she approached. He wagged his tail like he didn't expect anything from her but was hopeful, anyway.

"Hey, buddy." He seemed friendly, but she extended her hand as she would with any strange dog, letting him sniff it. When he licked her fingers, she squatted down to pet him. He wagged his tail harder and pranced in place, his paws sending up puffs of dust. "Oh, you poor thing. Just look at you."

He appeared neglected, his fur filthy and matted, burrs stuck to it in spots. She could feel his ribs when she stroked his sides. There were oozing sores on his neck where the puppy collar he'd outgrown had chafed his skin raw. He had to be dehydrated, too; his water bowl was empty, and the area to which he was confined was devoid of shade. She felt a welling of sympathy mixed with anger.

"Who did this to you?" She suspected the store proprietor and presumed owner of both the dog and the RV.

The dog whined and licked her hand again. She stroked the fur on his head. "Not naming any names, huh? No matter. We just need to get you to someplace where you'll be taken care of." She planned to report the abuse to the appropriate authorities as soon as she got to her car, where she'd left her phone.

She took the empty bowl into the restroom and filled it with water after she'd peed and washed up. Watching the dog thirstily slurp the water in his bowl after she'd returned with it, she grew even angrier. What kind of person starved a helpless creature and left it chained up in the hot sun with no water? *The kind of person who'd beat a woman.* She shivered as her thoughts circled back to Rory.

She could hear the dog whimpering as she walked away. She stopped, and when she turned around, saw him straining at the end of the chain that held him tethered, trying to follow her. *Don't leave me,* his eyes seemed to plead. Something wrenched inside her. "Sorry, bud. I'd take you with me if I could. But don't worry, I'm sending help." Someone would rescue the dog; it just couldn't be her.

Kyra was in her car picking up her phone to make the call when she stopped. She remembered the one time she'd called 911 after Rory had beaten her. The responding officer had taken her statement and then promptly buried the incident report. What if she reported the mistreatment of the dog and the authorities failed to act on it? Or what if the dog was rescued, only to be placed in a shelter where he'd be euth-anized if he wasn't adopted within forty-eight hours? Both prospects were unacceptable. But what was the alternative? She could offer to take the dog off the owner's hands, but something told her his answer would be no. Which left dog theft as her only other option. If it was reported, the police would be looking for her. Even if she got away with it, a dog on board would slow her down and attract unwanted attention. Her survival depended on flying under the radar.

On the other hand, she'd already blown up her entire life. She'd walked away from a career she loved and was good at, left her home and her friends—all without a word to anyone. What was dognapping in comparison? Sure, it was risky, and she'd be saddled with the dog until she found him a new home. But in the end, she decided she couldn't turn her back on a fellow creature in need.

She drove her car around to where the RV was parked. She found the dog waiting patiently, like he'd never doubted she would return for him. He danced on all fours, his butt wriggling in his excitement as she unfastened the chain from his collar. She took it as a good sign when he didn't bolt. Instead, he looked up at her with his intelligent brown eyes as if awaiting further instructions.

"No barking, you hear?" she warned. "If we're gonna do this, it's gotta be a clean getaway."

He seemed to understand and followed her without making a sound as she hurried back to her car.

Kyra was opening the door to the driver's side when she spied the proprietor coming around the side of the building, carrying a bulging trash bag. She froze and placed a stilling hand on the dog's head, watching as the old man tossed the bag in the dumpster, hoping he wouldn't notice her.

No such luck.

He was turning to head back when he spotted her and yelled, "Hey! What do you think you're doing? That's my dog!" He began moving toward her at a surprisingly rapid pace for someone of his advanced age and girth.

Kyra dove into the driver's seat and saw a black-and-tan blur out of the corner of her eye as the dog sailed past her into the passenger seat. She slammed the door shut and hit the lock button a split second before a face, red and contorted with fury below a gray crew cut, loomed into view out the driver's-side window. The sight was followed by the sound of knuckles rapping against glass.

Panic fizzed in her veins. Her hands shook as she turned the key in the ignition. She slammed her foot down on the gas pedal and gave a cry of frustration when she heard the *ruh ruh ruh* of a flooded engine.

No, no, no, no. Her pulse raced. Sweat dripped from her brow.

Then came the sound of a booted foot kicking the door. The car rocked on its tires, each thud like a blow to her body, causing her to flinch. "Open up, goddammit! You're not getting away with this!" the old man shouted.

Memories of another time, another voice raised in anger, flooded her brain like the fuel flooding the engine. For a second, she sat frozen, then she took a calming breath and counted to ten. She turned the key in the ignition again. This time, the engine fired. "Thank you, Jesus," she murmured as she executed a three-point turn worthy of a stuntwoman filming a car-chase scene in a movie. She saw the old man leap backward out of the corner of her eye before she spun past him with a screech of tires.

Then she was tearing down the road, buzzing with adrenaline, wide awake where she'd been drowsy before. She didn't let out her breath until she was merging with the traffic in the westbound lane of I-80.

"We did it!" she cried. "We got away!"

Or did we? she wondered when she spied a highway patrol car in her rearview mirror after they'd gone another mile or so. It occurred to her the dog's owner might have snapped a picture of her license plate with his phone when she was making her escape. Her elation gave way to worry. Were the police looking for her? What if she was pulled over and arrested? The arrest would be recorded in the national police database, to which Rory, as a district attorney, had access. *Oh God.*

Her anxiety didn't lift, even after the patrol car passed her. Instead, the invisible band around her chest tightened, causing her airway to narrow. Her breathing became increasingly labored until it was like sucking air into her lungs through a straw. She grew lightheaded. Worried she would pass out at the wheel, she took the next exit and pulled over in the breakdown lane under the overpass. She powered her windows down, but the air that blew in, stinking of exhaust, didn't help.

She'd had her first panic attack a year ago. She'd feared it was a heart attack until the doctor at the ER who'd examined her had correctly diagnosed her symptoms. He'd given her a pamphlet with some breathing exercises to try in the event she suffered another panic attack. She'd had several since then, most recently after she was hospitalized in May of this year. The exercises had helped. What had helped the most was plotting her escape. Now she took slow, even breaths, holding every other one for the count of three, until gradually her breathing normalized and her head cleared.

You're being paranoid. You'll be long gone before you're wanted by the law in this county. If the dog's owner had even reported the theft. He might not have, lest the cops ask questions about what might have prompted it. *Former owner,* she corrected herself. Which reminded her: the dog needed a new home, and how was she supposed to find one while she was on the run?

She suddenly felt drained. For days she hadn't slept more than a few hours at a stretch. She'd been running on fumes. Now fatigue dragged at her eyelids and her limbs when she moved to start the engine. Doubts crept in. What made her think she could do this? Start over at the age of thirty-four with no job prospects and no money except the cash she carried? She couldn't get another teaching job outside New York. It would require her to get recertified, which would leave a digital footprint. There was no shortage of jobs for unskilled workers, but even if she limited her expenditures to the bare necessities, as she'd done when she was growing up poor, could she survive on a minimum-wage salary as an adult? On top of everything else, she had to find the dog a new home when she didn't even have a home of her own.

Kyra was pulled from her spiraling thoughts by a wet nose nudging her arm. She looked over at the dog, who stood with his forepaws planted on the center console, grinning at her and wagging his curly tail. "Easy for you. You won't be the one telling it to the judge if we're caught. For both our sakes, let's hope it doesn't come to that," she told him.

He cocked his head like he was trying to understand. He was trusting, unlike other dogs she'd known who'd been mistreated and who had become mean or cowed as a result. Despite his circumstances, he seemed eager to please and open to adventure. She admired his pluck and took heart from it.

"So what am I going to do with you? Any ideas? No? Oh well, we'll figure something out. What should I call you? You probably have a name, but you'll need a new one." She noted the black markings around his eyes in the shape of a mask. He looked like a furry Lone Ranger. "How about Ranger?"

He woofed his agreement.

"Ranger it is. It's a good name for you." Now, besides being partners in crime, they both had new identities. She was Kyra Smith, according to the fake driver's license she carried. Legally, she was Krystal Stanhope, and before that, she'd gone by her maiden name of Valenzuela. Smith was her father's name, though he wasn't named on her birth certificate. She'd never met the man; he'd walked out on her mom before she was born, and she'd only ever heard him referred to as "that no-good son of a bitch." But it turned out he'd been good for something, after all. A search of phone records in any area code in America would show dozens of Smiths. She could hide in plain sight.

One day, when she was divorced and free to do as she wished, she would have her name legally changed. If that day ever came. Meanwhile, she could run, but she couldn't hide indefinitely—or so she feared. Rory had access to resources the average person didn't, and an entire police force at his disposal. Which made him as dangerous from afar as when they had lived together.

But she couldn't dwell on that right now; she had more immediate concerns. "Now we just need to get you cleaned up," she said to her furry charge. "No offense, bud, but you stink." She eased back into traffic. Ranger stuck his head out the open window on the passenger side, sniffing all the enticing scents outside, his fur ruffled by the air blowing in. "But first, we need food. I don't know about you, but I'm starved." Her supper last night had been peanut butter on crackers, and she hadn't eaten since then. "What do you say, Ranger? You hungry for some breakfast?"

Ranger's head whipped around like he'd been answering to his new name since he was a puppy. It had probably been that long since he'd been properly fed, too, judging by his neglected state. Kyra could relate. Her mother wasn't as bad as Ranger's former owner, but she had seemed to view her parental responsibilities as optional, depending on her mood or whether she had plans that didn't include Kyra.

It hadn't helped, either, that they'd moved around a lot when Kyra was growing up, never staying in one place long enough for her to finish an entire school year at any of the dozen schools she'd attended, or form close friendships. Moves precipitated by her mom quitting or getting fired from a job, falling behind on the rent, and being threatened with eviction, in that order. They'd skip town, usually in the dead of night when those to whom monies were owed were sleeping, then it was on to the next town, where they'd stay at a campground or RV park until her mom found work and saved enough money to rent another place. There had been nights when they'd slept in her mom's car. Nights when Kyra had gone to bed hungry.

Between periods of homelessness, they'd lived in a succession of dives in sketchy neighborhoods. When they'd lived in Phoenix, the year Kyra was twelve, she had been caught in the cross fire when shots were exchanged during a fight that had broken out between rival gangs one day while she was walking home from school. She'd narrowly missed being struck by a bullet. The policeman who'd taken her statement had said, "Your guardian angel was watching over you, young lady." Maybe it had been true then, and maybe her guardian angel was watching over her now.

The problem was, she was married to the devil.

2

Kyra stopped at a 7-Eleven in North Platte, where she bought two breakfast burritos, one for her and one for Ranger. After they'd eaten, she drove to the nearest public library to search online for a local veterinary clinic that accepted walk-ins. An hour later, Ranger was pronounced in good health, apart from being malnourished and flea infested, by the vet who'd examined him. Better yet, he wasn't chipped. After a bath and a blow-dry, he looked like a different dog and didn't stink like roadkill anymore.

"Do you know of anyone who might want him?" she asked as she was leaving. She'd billed Ranger as a stray she'd picked up. "I can't keep him, but he's a good dog and deserves a good home."

She felt a pang at the prospect of giving him up. In the short time she'd known him, she'd grown attached, and he to her. When he wasn't glued to her side, he tracked her every movement with his eyes. She couldn't keep him, but he seemed to have no doubt as to whom he belonged.

"I can't think of anyone offhand, but I know of a shelter that will take him," said the kindly vet, a middle-aged man with salt-and-pepper hair.

"A no-kill shelter?"

"Of course," he said, as though any other kind was out of the question. He and Kyra were in agreement on that. "Melanie Byers, the woman who runs it, finds homes for all her dogs, and I imagine she'd have no trouble finding a home for this guy." He ran his hand over Ranger's newly fluffed and gleaming coat. "I can call her if you like. Oh, and no charge for today," he said, to her relief.

Minutes later, she and Ranger were pulling up in front of the shelter, housed in a whitewashed cinder block building just outside town, with an enclosed yard in front and fenced dog runs out back. Kyra was pleased to find it was clean and well kept inside. Each kennel had its own bedding and toys to keep the dogs from getting bored while they were caged. The director, Melanie, a short, round woman in her forties with a ready smile, said of Ranger, "He's a handsome fellow. And well behaved."

"Smart, too," Kyra said.

Melanie smiled down at him. "I'll know more after I've done a full assessment, but from what I've seen, he has the makings of a family dog. Either that or he'll make someone a wonderful companion."

Kyra felt torn when it was time for her to go. She hated leaving Ranger, even knowing he was in good hands and that he'd eventually go to a good home. He didn't make it any easier when he whined as she walked away. She stopped and retraced her steps, squatting down in front of him. She took his head in her hands and looked him in the eye. "It's gonna be okay, bud," she assured him. "You're going to a good home, where you'll be better off than you'd be if you stayed with me."

He barked his disagreement.

"None of that. You be good, you hear?" She hugged him, burying her face in the thick fur of his neck, which now smelled of shampoo, to hide her tears. When she drew back, he licked her cheek. He continued to whine as she walked away, and she felt as if her heart were being ripped from her chest.

Her tears were flowing by the time she reached her car. She started the engine and was about to shift into gear when she was stopped by a voice saying, *He has a home already.* Melanie must have thought so, too, because she didn't seem surprised when Kyra went back inside and announced, "I've changed my mind. I'm keeping him." Ranger had trusted her with his life when she'd been a stranger to him. She owed it to him, and to herself, to believe that it would all work out somehow.

With Ranger once again riding shotgun, she drove to the nearby PetSmart, to which Melanie had directed her, where she purchased dog food, a new collar, and a leash, along with other necessities. Her small pot of money, composed of the remaining funds from her checking account combined with the difference that she'd pocketed when she traded in her BMW for the beater she was driving—roughly $8,000 in total—had grown smaller with today's expenditures, but she had no regrets.

"It's just you and me from now on, bud," she said. "We're a team."

Ranger, trotting by her side as they exited the store, looked up at her as if to say, *I could've told you that.*

Two days later, she stopped at a pawnshop while passing through Reno, where she sold her diamond engagement ring and wedding band, and bought a gun. A Smith & Wesson .38. It was easy to operate, with less of a recoil than other guns of the same caliber, she was told. After dickering with the pawnbroker, she got it for a good price. Kyra wasn't a fan of guns and had never fired one, but a woman traveling alone never knew when she might need protection, especially a woman on the run. And this might be her last chance to obtain a gun legally without creating a paper trail. She'd been told that Nevada didn't require the purchase of firearms to be registered.

She crossed the California state line just west of Reno, then continued southwest on I-80 for another hour before taking the southbound fork at the junction in Auburn to State Route 49, which was the highway that ran north and south through California's storied gold country. She'd read about this area and its historic towns in the brochure she'd picked up at a rest stop, and decided to check it out. It was a tourist destination where a stranger wouldn't draw attention, but it was also off the beaten path. She could lie low and hopefully find a job that paid a living wage in one of those towns.

As she drove along the two-lane highway, the views alone sold her on the region. She passed grassy foothills dotted with oaks and scrub pines. The towns—originally gold camps founded by the forty-niners, according to the brochure—were charming and rustic, most of their businesses mom-and-pops.

She passed a sign that read GOLD CREEK, 12 MILES. A short way down the road, she stopped at a scenic overlook. While Ranger did his business, she took in the majestic mountains towering over a bucolic landscape of rolling hills painted in autumnal shades of ochre and sienna, and a wooded ravine below, through which a burbling stream ran. Dotting the banks of the stream in several spots, partially hidden by the surrounding foliage, were the ruins of abandoned mining operations, according to the brass plaque marking the site as one of historic interest.

The sun sparkled on the tumbling water; the air was cool and smelled of pine. The sense of desperation that had made her feel tightly wound, spurring her on while keeping her alert to danger throughout her cross-country flight, loosened its grip, and she felt at peace for the first time in days. Years, even.

The town of Gold Creek was straight out of a storybook. She stopped at the visitors' center just inside the town limits, where she snagged a map and some brochures. As she cruised the streets of the historic district, lined with quaint buildings that were a mix of brick and wooden construction built in different eras, she saw flowers blooming in window boxes outside storefronts and baskets that hung from the streetlights dotting the sidewalks. A leafy park sprawled over two blocks where the four main streets of the historic district intersected. Walkways wound through it, and a mosaic-tiled fountain splashed at its center. She imagined herself strolling through the park, or relaxing on a bench in a shady spot with Ranger on a summer day. The illusion that she'd traveled back in time was complete when she heard the clatter of hooves and saw a horse-drawn stagecoach make its way down the main drag. She was enchanted.

She parked and climbed from her car, Ranger leaping out behind her. She clipped his leash to his new collar, and they set off to explore.

At the corner of Sutter and Placer stood an imposing redbrick Victorian. The gilded letters stenciled on the frosted-glass inset of its door announced it as the offices of the Washburn County Sheriff's Department. She quickened her step as she passed by. She wasn't worried about being wanted for dognapping now that she was well outside the jurisdiction in which the crime had occurred, but she wouldn't put it past Rory to issue a BOLO on some trumped-up charge. Or he might have filed a missing person report. Someone in law enforcement might recognize her from a photo that was being circulated. It was a chilling thought.

She felt her stomach tighten when she spotted a man wearing the uniform of a sheriff's deputy emerging from the coffee shop opposite carrying a travel mug. She paused, waiting beneath the overhang of the shop next door as he crossed the street, headed toward the sheriff's office, and entered the building before she continued. Her paranoia, heightened by her bad experience with the Rochester PD, had made her extra cautious. Ranger, as if sensing her anxiety, stuck close to her side.

Catching her reflection in a shop window on the next block, she scarcely recognized herself as the bruised and battered woman she'd been six months earlier. She saw a woman in her thirties, dressed in a Hollister T-shirt and jeans, tall, with a lean—bordering on gaunt—frame and big eyes above sharply defined cheekbones. Her long, dark hair, plaited in a single braid, swung like a bellpull at her back as she walked. No one would guess she'd been abused. If they did, would they feel sorry for her, or would they judge her? See her as weak and pathetic? Any normal person would have fled after the first blow had been struck, and she'd stayed with Rory for years. Five long years.

She'd gotten away—that's what mattered, she told herself. And now, with any luck, she would get a fresh start. *Me and my shadow,* she thought, glancing down at Ranger with affection.

She turned right at the corner and climbed to the top of Signal Hill, presided over by the century-old iron bell tower, which was the tallest structure in Gold Creek. According to the bronze plaque affixed to its base, it had been used to summon the fire brigade in the days before telecommunications made it obsolete. At the bottom of the hill, she passed a building with a neoclassical facade—the town's original courthouse, which now operated as a museum—and a few doors down, a steepled church as picturesque as any she'd seen in New England. Another turn took her into the Garden District, so called because of its tree-lined streets of grand old homes on gorgeously landscaped double lots. Guided tours were given of some of its homes and gardens during the town's annual Pioneer Days Festival, held every year in May.

She wondered whether she would still be here next spring. She hoped so. Gold Creek ticked all the boxes on her wish list. It was picturesque, populous enough so she wouldn't stick out like a sore thumb, while at the same time, small enough so she wouldn't feel swallowed up like she would in a big city. It also appeared to be a dog-friendly town. Everywhere she went, she saw dog walkers. A bowl of water stood on the sidewalk outside every other storefront she passed, and outside the largest of the souvenir shops on the main drag, Mother Lode Mercantile, there was also a covered bin of complimentary dog biscuits. She paused to grab one for Ranger, who gobbled it up.

"What do you think, bud? Can you see us living here?" she asked him. "Of course, it depends on whether I can find work . . ." Preferably a job that paid off-book and didn't involve drug dealing, prostitution, or some other illegal activity. "Unless you have hidden talents I don't know about."

Ranger wagged his tail and grinned as if to suggest he had a few tricks he hadn't shown her.

Whether she stayed or went also depended on whether she could find affordable housing, which seemed a tall order, from the pricey listings she'd seen posted in the windows of the real estate agencies she'd passed. *One step at a time,* she told herself. *Starting with finding a place to stay tonight.*

On her way back to her car, Kyra stopped at the coffee shop she'd noticed earlier, which she saw, upon closer inspection, was in fact a combined bakery and café. Occupying the ground floor of a two-story built in the same style as the one opposite that housed the sheriff's department, but plainer, it was advertised by its sign in the shape of a cow that read COWBOY COFFEE. Its brick forecourt was scattered with café tables, where customers sat drinking beverages and nibbling on pastries.

She stuck her head in the door, calling to the purple-haired barista, "Okay if I bring my dog in?" The girl waved them inside. As Kyra waited in line at the take-out counter, she inhaled the mouthwatering aromas of house-made baked goods and fresh-ground coffee beans. In addition to coffee and pastries, the bakery café offered a menu of light bites for table service. When she got to the head of the line, she ordered the specialty beverage—a cinnamon latte—and a banana-nut muffin. She felt guilty for splurging on a fancy coffee and pastry, but after days of subsisting on fast food and convenience-store snacks, she'd decided to treat herself.

She sat at one of the tables outside, enjoying the sunshine as she sipped her latte and ate her muffin while watching the passersby on the sidewalk. She tossed the last piece of her muffin to Ranger, who caught and inhaled it, and was getting up to leave when her gaze was drawn to the upper floor of the building. Accessed by a cast-iron staircase, it housed four businesses, one of which was a tattoo parlor, with a retro neon sign that read RED INK TATTOOS. It gave her an idea. She'd never done any tattoo art, but she could draw. Perhaps the owner would hire her to create original designs. It was worth a try. She climbed the stairs with Ranger before she could change her mind.

The bell over the door tinkled as they entered. Inside, it looked more like an upscale art gallery than any tattoo parlor Kyra had ever seen. The exposed brick walls of the long, narrow space were covered with artwork, a mix of paintings and sketches. There was a cozy seating area by the window in front and a workstation in back, partially hidden behind a Japanese-style black lacquer trifold screen. A woman with short, curly silver hair, wearing khakis and a drab olive fleece top, stepped out from behind the screen.

"May I help you?"

Her welcoming smile instantly put Kyra at ease. "I hope so. I'm new in town and looking for work. I was wondering if you could use someone."

"You have experience with tattoo work?"

"No, but I can draw, if you need someone to do designs."

"Sorry, I wish I could help you, but I do all my own designs." She gestured toward the sketches on the walls. The subjects ranged from fairies and other mythical creatures to animals and birds and flowers.

"They're gorgeous." Kyra took a moment to admire them while she rearranged her features to hide her disappointment. "Oh well. I figured it was a long shot but thought I'd ask, anyway," she said, bringing her gaze back to the other woman.

"No harm in asking," said the owner warmly. "I take it you've worked as an artist?" She was a light-skinned Black woman in her midsixties, beautiful in the way of someone who had turned heads in her youth, with expressive dark eyes feathered with lines at the corners, and a mouth made for smiling. In her plain attire with no visible tattoos or piercings, she wasn't your average tattoo artist.

"I used to teach art at a private school, and I've sold some paintings in galleries." Kyra thought fondly of the Stoningham Academy. Located in the small community of Webster, fifteen minutes from Rochester, it had been her sole escape from the minefield of her homelife, on weekdays while school was in session, at least. She'd loved teaching. She'd loved her students, too—the artistically gifted and the untalented alike.

They'd been bright lights in her personal darkness, a daily reminder of a time when her life had seemed filled with promise. She had resigned via email on the day she'd left Rochester, citing a "family emergency" as the reason. She felt bad about that, but she'd had no alternative. She couldn't risk Rory getting wind of her plans.

"You should inquire at our local schools. They usually have job openings. I have a friend who teaches at the public high school, and she's always complaining about them being short-staffed."

"I'm afraid that's not an option," said Kyra with regret. The other woman eyed her curiously, and she felt compelled to add, "It's complicated." Fearing she'd aroused suspicion by failing to give a reason why she couldn't apply for a teaching job, she grew flustered. The teachers she knew who'd left the profession were either retired or disgraced. Since she didn't look old enough to have retired, it would be only natural to suspect that she'd been fired due to misconduct.

"It usually is," replied the other woman with a small shrug. "I'm Frannie, by the way. Frannie Le Vasseur." She stuck her hand out.

"Kyra Smith." They shook hands. "And this is Ranger." She glanced down at her dog, who was sitting politely at her feet, regarding Frannie. "Is it okay that I brought him in? I didn't think to ask."

"Well-behaved dogs are always welcome." Frannie bent to ruffle his ears, and he gave her his signature "Sammie" grin, for which the Samoyed breed was known. Kyra had been correct in guessing he was part German shepherd and part Samoyed, according to the vet who'd examined him.

"You wouldn't happen to know of an affordable place to stay that allows dogs?" she asked.

"Your best bet is the Pine Ridge Motor Lodge. It's good value and usually has vacancies this time of year. Just follow the highway south for a couple miles. You can't miss it—'the motor lodge time forgot.'"

"Sounds perfect."

"'Perfect' isn't the word I'd use to describe it, but it's clean and decent for the price, and dogs are allowed."

"I'm not picky. Thanks for the recommendation."

"Sorry I couldn't offer you a job."

"I appreciate you taking the time to talk to me, anyway."

Kyra was turning to go when the older woman said, "Listen, I'm having dinner with some friends tonight. If you don't have other plans, why don't you join us? One of them might know of something."

"Oh." Wary about being thrown in with a bunch of strangers, and worried about the cost involved, Kyra didn't jump at the invitation. "That's . . . nice of you, but I don't know what my plans are yet."

"My treat." Frannie seemed to have guessed part of the reason for her hesitancy.

Kyra felt her face warm. Growing up poor, she'd often been the recipient of charity. She remembered the time she'd been given a backpack stocked with school supplies as part of a church drive for needy children. She'd thanked the volunteer who'd given it to her, a middle-aged woman resembling Mrs. Claus, with her snow-white hair and rosy cheeks, and who'd replied, with an air of benevolence, "You're welcome, young lady. Never forget that you're a person, too." Like it had been in doubt. Kyra vowed then and there to never again be anyone's charity case if she could help it.

"It's nothing fancy," Frannie went on. "You can pay the next time." She wasn't being patronizing; she was genuinely kind. Kyra knew the difference, having experienced both. "And you can bring your dog. I'll clear it with my sister first. She owns the restaurant."

Kyra debated whether to accept the invitation. She didn't know whom she could trust. On the other hand, one of Frannie's friends might know of a job opening.

"Can I let you know?" she asked.

"Of course. You can call or text me at this number," she said, handing Kyra one of her business cards. "We eat early, and it's just downstairs, so you can meet me here after work if you decide to come."

"Cowboy Coffee is your sister's restaurant?" Kyra said in surprise.

"Yep. We co-own the building. It's been in our family for generations. When we decided to open our own businesses, I claimed the upstairs and divided it, taking one space for myself and renting out the others. Vanessa took the downstairs and turned it into the megachurch for java junkies and foodies that it's become."

"I'm a believer. I just ate the best muffin of my life there."

"Everything's made from scratch, and it's all great, which is why the lines are usually out the door. It was no surprise when it was named one of the top five bakery cafés in the West in *Sunset* magazine."

"Wow. Hopefully, I can join you tonight. I'll text you when I know my plans," Kyra said as she was headed for the door with Ranger. She paused, noticing a sign posted by the entrance that listed the various services offered by Red Ink Tattoos. "You do laser tattoo removal?"

"Yes, and I'm running a special this month." Frannie quoted a price well below the listed one, available only to Kyra, unless she missed her guess. "Is there a tattoo you'd like to have removed?"

Again, Kyra hesitated. She couldn't afford it even at the discounted price, but the opportunity to start over with a clean slate was tempting. "Do I need to make an appointment?" she asked at last.

"I can take you now if you have the time. Why don't you show me what you want to have done?"

Kyra turned around and lifted her T-shirt to show her lone tattoo: the name "Rory" in calligraphic script between a set of spread wings— like those of the fallen angel Lucifer, she imagined. The skin on her lower back burned where it was exposed, as it had when the tattoo was freshly inked. It had been Rory's idea for them to get matching tattoos, each with the other's name on it. She'd gone along only to appease him, knowing he'd be angry if she refused. Now hers seemed like a mark of her own weakness as well as his ownership. Tears filled her eyes. Tears of shame.

She heard Frannie say, "I can take care of that. It'll take a few sessions, but by the time I'm done, you won't know it was ever there." Kyra was grateful, both that she'd be rid of the tattoo and that Frannie hadn't commented on it. Nor, it became evident with her next words, was she judging Kyra. "Believe me, you're not the first person to regret a tattoo." Kyra nodded, swallowing against the lump in her throat.

The tattoo was the least of her regrets.

3

An hour later, feeling lighter after her first tattoo-removal session, Kyra drove to the Pine Ridge Motor Lodge. Located on a wooded ridge in the hills above Gold Creek, it comprised a dozen faux log cabins standing in a row beneath a canopy of pines. As Frannie had predicted, there were vacancies. Kyra requested the cabin at the end farthest from the office, which was the most private. Its decor was sixties era, and not in the style of a fun, retro makeover, but with the faded look of owners who couldn't afford an upgrade. But it was clean and comfortable enough, and best of all, budget friendly. After she checked in and unpacked, she took Ranger for a walk in the state park a short distance down the road. By the time she returned, she'd come to a decision. She texted Frannie, accepting her invitation to dine with her and her friends tonight.

Frannie texted her back: Great! Meet me here at 5.

She was walking through the door at Red Ink Tattoos with Ranger shortly before five.

"Be with you in a sec!" Frannie called from the back, where she was finishing up with her last customer of the day. She introduced them as he was leaving. "Kyra, meet Greg. Greg, meet Kyra." As she was in the habit of doing with strange men, Kyra assessed the skinny, bespectacled youth before deciding he wasn't a threat.

She admired his new tattoo as they shook hands. The head of a dire wolf, it adorned his right forearm and IDed him as a *Game of Thrones* fan. Having taught high school, she was familiar with the cult of *GOT*. "Nice tat."

"Thanks." He rotated his arm to examine Frannie's handiwork from every angle and seemed pleased with it. His gaze dropped to Ranger. "Nice dog. He kind of looks like a dire wolf."

"He does," she agreed. "Except he's not scary."

He bent to let Ranger sniff his outstretched hand. "What's his name?"

"Ranger. It's okay. You can pet him."

"Like the Lone Ranger?"

"Right." She noted with approval that Greg's knowledge of fictional characters extended beyond *GOT*.

"Cool."

"Just give me a minute to clean up and we'll head out," Frannie said as she turned the sign on the door from OPEN to CLOSED after seeing Greg out. She returned to her workstation and began spritzing every surface with disinfectant before wiping it down with a paper towel. "Have a seat." She gestured toward the sofa and chairs by the window. "I'm glad you could make it."

"Me, too. Thanks for the invite," Kyra said as she took a seat on the sofa.

"My friends are looking forward to meeting you. You'll like them," she said, as if sensing Kyra's skittishness. "Oh, and if anyone asks, Ranger's your emotional-support dog." Frannie winked, and glanced down at Ranger, who'd settled at Kyra's feet. He wagged his tail in approval.

"How many of you are there?" Kyra asked nervously. The larger the party, the better the chance that one of its members would know of a job opportunity. But it would also mean a greater risk of someone unwittingly disclosing her whereabouts to Rory or one of his minions.

"Four, including me. Suzy and I have been best friends since kindergarten. Marisol is the daughter of another friend, who passed away—I've known her since she was a baby. Jo, I met by chance. She came to me for a tattoo. We hit it off, and we've been friends ever since. We call ourselves the Tattooed Ladies Club, but it's more figurative than literal. None of us is what you'd call circus-sideshow material."

"Why the name, then?"

"Long story."

"I'd love to hear it."

Frannie told the story while she finished cleaning up. "It began with a bet between my two oldest friends, Suzy and Althea. Suzy planned to get a tattoo for her sixtieth, and Althea bet she'd chicken out. They agreed the loser would pick up the tab the next time the three of us met for dinner. Suzy being Suzy, she not only won the bet but also mooned us and everyone else at the restaurant when she showed off her tattoo: a pear with a bite taken out of it, on her butt. It set the tone for the evening. We all drank too much and got silly, like when we were schoolgirls together. I suggested we make it a standing date, and from then on we met for dinner once a month, same time, same place. Sadly, Althea's no longer with us," she said, her face creasing with sorrow, "but after she died, her daughter, Marisol, took her place at the table. Jo became a member a couple years ago."

"They sound like an interesting bunch," Kyra said. And a tight circle of friends. Would it be awkward with her tagging along? More importantly, if she were to take them into her confidence, could she trust them not to blab to anyone who might come sniffing around, asking after her?

"It'll be a fun evening. I can promise you that much, even if nothing comes of it job-wise. Shall we?" she said as she grabbed her coat and purse after she'd finished cleaning and straightening up.

The bakery café downstairs was bustling when they arrived, every table filled and customers waiting in line at the takeout counter. Other customers were checking out the merchandise displayed in the antique pie safe by the entrance—coffee mugs, T-shirts, and ball caps with the Cowboy Coffee logo, along with its packaged house-blend coffee beans. As Frannie led her and Ranger through the crowded dining area to the table in back reserved for their party, Kyra took in the original heart-pine flooring, pressed-tin ceiling, and rustic-contemporary decor, which she hadn't had a chance to fully appreciate when she'd visited before. Cowboy accoutrements—colorful woven saddle blankets; fancy braided lariats; and vintage tin spatterware, like you might find in a cowboy camp—adorned the walls between blow-up black-and-white photos from rodeo events.

"That's Vanessa's late husband, Buck, when he was a rodeo champion." Frannie paused to point to a photo of a man in a cowboy hat riding a bucking bronco. "Cowboy Coffee is named in his honor."

"There you are. About time," said a stylish blonde seated at their table, wearing a cropped pink jacket with black polka dots and designer jeans. She looked to be around Frannie's age, with fewer wrinkles than Frannie and hair that was professionally colored. "What, did you get stuck in traffic?"

Frannie smiled and rolled her eyes. Being as her workplace was upstairs, she probably had the shortest distance to travel of any of them. "Blame it on my client who showed up late for his appointment. Guys, this is Kyra. Kyra, meet the gang."

A chorus of voices called out greetings.

"Who's your date? He's a cutie," said a thirtysomething woman, short and curvy, wearing a jean jacket with a collection of slogan buttons pinned to the front over a Virginia Woolf T-shirt. She had a smile that lit up her face. Lively brown eyes sparkled behind her funky zebra-striped glasses.

"This is Ranger." Kyra bent to stroke his head.

"Her 'emotional support dog,'" said Frannie, making air quotes.

Kyra was thinking she could use the support right now. She felt shy suddenly, like when she'd been the new girl at the schools she'd attended when she was growing up. She'd had trouble making friends then, but tonight she was welcomed warmly by the other women and drawn into their midst despite herself.

Ranger made the rounds, getting petted and fussed over, while Frannie made the introductions. Suzy, the stylish blonde and self-described "fashionista grandma," was the owner of the Shear Delight hair salon on King Street. The short, curvy woman was Marisol, who managed her family-owned bookstore, Buckboard Books. Kyra recalled passing by it earlier; there had been a cat curled up and asleep on a stack of books in the front window. Marisol's late mother, Althea, she learned, had immigrated to this country from the Philippines and married Marisol's father, Duncan Macgowan, whose great-grandmother had founded the bookstore. She had the brown skin and eye shape of her Filipina heritage; the sprinkle of freckles across her nose and natural red highlights in her black hair were from her Scottish father. Jo, a wedding photographer, looked like a character from a children's book illustration, with her wide blue eyes fringed with pale lashes and long strawberry-blond hair parted down the middle—a cross between Alice from *Alice in Wonderland* and Pippi Longstocking. She was the youngest of the group and the only one wearing a wedding ring.

"Nice to meet you all. Thanks for including me." Kyra took her seat at the table between Frannie and Suzy, and Ranger assumed his Sphinx pose at her side. Could the others tell she was nervous? She threaded her fingers through Ranger's collar, calmed by his presence.

"Kyra's new in town," Frannie said when their server had come and gone after taking their orders. "We met when she stopped by earlier, looking for work."

"You're hiring?" Suzy seemed surprised.

"No, but I thought one of you might be or know of someone who is."

"What sort of work are you looking for, Kyra?" asked Marisol as she helped herself to a cheese straw.

"Anything." Kyra felt her face go hot. Too desperate? She reached for her glass of water and took a gulp. "I used to teach art, but . . . um, I don't anymore, and it's tough to make a living as an artist."

"Tell me about it," Frannie said. "Why do you think I became a tattoo artist? I earn more in a year doing body art than I ever did selling paintings. Plus, my work is a traveling gallery, you might say. It's always attracting new customers. But you must have other skills. Have you ever worked retail?"

"I worked at a shoe store when I was in college." Kyra didn't mention that it had been a part-time job or that she'd left after six months when the store's owner, a married man, started coming on to her.

"I usually hire extra help in the summers and around the holidays, but business is slow this time of year," said Marisol with regret as she nibbled on her cheese straw.

"I'd hire you in a hot minute if I could afford it. My husband and I are saving up to buy a house," explained Jo. Kyra detected the hint of a Texas twang in her voice. "I could use an assistant."

"You're buying a house? That's exciting," Kyra said.

"It will be if we ever get there." Jo sighed. "At the rate we're going, our girls will probably be grown before we've saved enough for a down payment. It's always something. The latest was a new pair of glasses for Jess after she fell down on the playground at school and broke her old ones. Jess is my eldest," she explained to Kyra. "She's five. Her sister, Emma, is three."

Kyra was surprised to learn Jo was a mom of two. She didn't look much older than her former students at the Stoningham Academy, with her willowy figure, dressed in clothes a teenager might wear: holey jeans and a smocked, embroidered peasant blouse. Only when she spoke did she seem her real age. She sounded like a mom, the kind who provided firm guidance while never letting her children forget for an instant that they were loved. The opposite of Kyra's mother, in other words.

"Do you do hair, by any chance?" asked Suzy hopefully. "One of my stylists, who's also a reservist in the National Guard, was recently deployed. I'm in desperate need of someone to replace her."

"I'm afraid not," Kyra said. "I can't remember the last time I got a haircut, even." She fingered the end of her braid self-consciously.

"Stop by my salon and I'll fix you up." The gold bracelet Suzy wore sparkled with reflected light as she raised her glass of Diet Coke to take a sip. "And if you don't think it's beneath you, which I'd understand if you did, I could use someone to wash hair and sweep up. It's only part-time. I can't afford full-time help at the moment. Is that something you'd be interested in?"

"Yes!" Kyra brightened. "And no, it's totally not beneath me." She'd take any job at this point.

"In that case, you're hired. It's minimum wage, but you'll earn extra money in tips. Can you work mornings?" Kyra nodded. "Perfect, and that'll leave you free to look for other work in the afternoons."

"When do you want me to start?" Maybe she could arrange to be paid in cash. She'd speak to Suzy about it later.

"How about Monday morning? We open at nine. Mornings are usually our busiest time, so you'll work from nine to noon. Come a few minutes early and I'll show you the ropes. Oh, and your 'emotional support' dog is welcome," she added, looking down at Ranger with wry amusement.

"I should warn you, he sheds."

Suzy laughed. "Honey, it's a hair salon. No one would even notice."

"So, Kyra, where are you from, and what brings you to Gold Creek?" Jo asked.

"I'm from New York. I was ready for a change, and there's almost no chance I'll run into my ex here. Bad breakup." She kept it vague.

"I hear you," said Marisol with a knowing shake of her head. If she was like other single women in their thirties, she'd weathered her share of breakups.

"In fact, if anyone you don't know should ask about me . . ." Kyra felt a clutch of fear at the thought. "I'd appreciate it if you didn't say anything."

"Your ex is the stalkerish type, huh?" said Suzy.

"Something like that." *And so much worse.*

"My lips are sealed."

"I'm not in the habit of giving information to random dudes unless it's a book they're looking for," said Marisol.

"I'm a vault," said Jo, hand to her lips miming the turning of a key in a lock.

Frannie said nothing. She didn't have to. Kyra trusted her implicitly. From the moment they'd met, it had seemed as if they'd known each other for years. Maybe they'd been friends in another life.

Just then, their food arrived, along with a beef patty on the house for Ranger, who gobbled it up before the women had picked up their forks. Kyra had ordered the bacon and spinach quiche, same as Frannie, which was delicious.

Talk turned to other subjects. Suzy proudly showed photos from her twin granddaughters' ballet recital. Marisol reported that her father was recovering from his recent gallbladder operation. Jo gave a progress report on her three-year-old's potty training.

"Sean and I have been letting her run naked around the house, hoping she'll get the idea. But whenever she has to go, she demands that we put her diaper on. At this rate, she'll still be in diapers when she graduates college." Jo shook her head and took a bite of her sandwich. She'd ordered the roast beef with bacon jam, which was as big as her head. How did she stay so slim, eating like that?

"Oh, there's Gertie!" Frannie waved to someone who was passing—a woman with a shock of white hair styled in a kind of cockatoo's crest, and candy-apple-red glasses that matched her cowgirl boots.

She paused to greet them. "Hi, ladies! What are y'all up to?"

"The usual. Solving the problems of the world one bite at a time." Frannie brandished a forkful of her quiche. "You?"

"The usual murder and mayhem."

"Gertie's a forensic artist," Frannie told Kyra.

"Really? You mean like a police sketch artist?"

"As we're commonly known," said Gertie. "Or, as we say in the business, we draw lines to stop crimes."

Kyra was intrigued. "I've never met a forensic artist before."

"Gertie, this is my friend Kyra Smith. Kyra, this is Gertie Naylor." Frannie introduced them, and Ranger popped his head up from below the table, tail wagging, eager to meet the newcomer. Gertie obliged by offering her hand for him to sniff. "Kyra used to teach art. Right now she's looking for temporary work until she finds something permanent. You wouldn't happen to know of any jobs?"

"Ever done any bookkeeping?" Gertie asked Kyra. "Being as crime doesn't take a holiday, I never seem to find the time to balance my books, or even hire a replacement for my accountant who retired."

"I've never worked as a bookkeeper before, but I'm good with numbers." Growing up, she'd had to be. Her mom had spent what little money they had like she expected more to appear magically when they ran out. From a young age, Kyra had learned to balance a checkbook, do the math in making a budget, and calculate unit pricing in her head when she shopped in grocery stores.

"Beggars can't be choosers, and I need all the help I can get. Can you start right away?"

"Yes, but only in the afternoons. I'll be working mornings at Suzy's salon."

"No problem. You can make your own hours. Call me and we'll work out the details." Gertie handed her a business card from her purse.

Kyra couldn't believe her good fortune. Things were looking up.

When they were done eating, Vanessa, the owner and Frannie's sister, brought dessert. "Beignets, made from an old family recipe," she announced as she placed a heaping platter on the table.

The scent of fried dough dusted with sugar wafted toward Kyra, causing her mouth to water, even with her belly full. She'd never eaten a beignet before, although she'd been told they were sold on every street corner in New Orleans, where Frannie had mentioned her family was from originally. She wondered whether the sisters were of Creole descent. They looked alike, except Vanessa was stout where Frannie was lean and wore her curly silver hair long, gathered into a bun.

"Bless you," murmured Jo as she helped herself to a beignet.

"Damn you," said Suzy.

"I'll take that as a compliment," said Vanessa with a laugh.

"Why don't you join us, sis?" Frannie asked.

Vanessa shook her head with regret. "Maybe another time. I have trays coming out of the oven any minute and my new kitchen help to supervise. Enjoy, ladies!" she called as she hurried off.

"Thanks again for including me . . . and for everything," Kyra said when the women were saying their goodbyes outside after supper. "It was great meeting you all." She'd arrived in town not knowing a soul, and she now had four new acquaintances, one of whom had given her a job. She'd expected to feel like an outsider. Instead, the Tattooed Ladies had welcomed her into their midst.

As for Ranger, he now had four new sources of treats and head scratches.

What would they think if they knew the truth? whispered the voice in her head. She'd told them she was seeking a fresh start, which was true, but she hadn't told them the full story. They didn't know she'd been in an abusive relationship for years. She'd been married to the devil, yes, but she'd allowed his abuse to continue. At first, she'd stayed because she'd loved her husband and believed him when he promised to get help. Once she realized he was never going to change, she'd stayed because she'd feared the devil she didn't know—the even uglier side of him that would be revealed if she tried to leave and he caught her—more than the devil she knew. Also, because his gaslighting had caused her to doubt herself. It had taken a beating so severe it had left her hospitalized with multiple injuries, including a ruptured spleen, before she finally fled for her life.

A "bad breakup"? That was putting it mildly. More like a living nightmare.

She felt a pang, knowing she'd never be part of this circle of friends if she couldn't be honest with them. Friendships didn't grow in the dark, and existing friendships withered in the dark. She'd discovered the latter when her oldest friend, Mia, whom she'd known since college, had drifted away after one too many canceled lunch dates. Each time Kyra had canceled, it had been because she couldn't bring herself to face Mia with bruises or a black eye. Mia would have seen through any excuse she might have given about how she'd gotten those injuries. She would have urged her to get help and to press charges. She wouldn't have understood why Kyra felt stuck. After Mia stopped calling, it had been a relief in one sense, but Kyra mourned the loss of their friendship. She'd forgotten until tonight how much she'd missed the company of other women.

"See you on Monday," Suzy called with a waggle of her fingers as she headed off to her car.

"Don't be a stranger." Jo hugged Kyra in parting.

"Drop by the bookshop when you get a chance," said Marisol.

"Did you find a place to stay?" Frannie asked as she and Kyra lingered in front of the building after the others had left.

"Yes. I booked a cabin at the Pine Ridge, as you suggested," Kyra told her. "You were right—it's seen better days, but it beats sleeping in my car." Frannie's eyebrows went up, and Kyra feared she'd revealed too much. "Not that I've actually slept in my car," she added. Not recently, anyway. She didn't count the few times she'd pulled over to take a short nap during her cross-country trip.

"Glad to hear it. But if you ever need—"

Frannie's phone rang before she could finish the sentence. She excused herself to take the call. "Hey, Chaz. What's up? . . . Oh God. What happened? Is she all right?" From her words and the stricken look on her face, it was bad news. "Okay, I'm on my way. Tell her . . . Never mind. I'll tell her myself."

"Everything okay?" Kyra asked after she disconnected.

"That was the sheriff's office. My daughter . . . I have to go." Frannie started walking.

Kyra hurried after her. "Is there anything I can do?" She recalled Frannie mentioning a grown daughter during dinner, who'd been injured in an accident, from what Kyra had just overheard. Poor Frannie.

Frannie paused to look at her. "Thanks, but no. You should go. We'll catch up later."

"I want to help. Really."

"You don't know what's involved, and trust me, you don't want to know."

Kyra couldn't leave her, not when she was in the middle of a crisis. Frannie had helped her out. How could Kyra abandon her? "I'm coming with," she insisted. "Whatever it is, you shouldn't have to deal with it alone."

When Frannie didn't answer right away, Kyra feared she'd overstepped. She wasn't a friend; she was merely an acquaintance. Had the call come before the others left, one of the Tattooed Ladies would have accompanied her to the ER, if that was where she was headed. *Who am I but some stray she took in and fed? Besides, I don't need this. I have enough problems of my own.*

She was surprised, and secretly pleased, when Frannie said, "Okay. But don't say I didn't warn you."

4

Kyra was even more surprised when she found herself heading toward the building across the street with Frannie instead of the ER. Clearly the emergency involving Frannie's daughter wasn't a medical one. Was she the victim of a crime? Or had she been arrested? Whatever awaited them at the sheriff's office, it could spell trouble for Kyra if someone there recognized her.

Her footsteps faltered. Panic swirled in her stomach. She was tempted to bail, but what excuse could she give for doing so? Besides, Frannie needed her. Fighting to control her panic, Kyra continued.

The exterior of the Italianate building, distinguished by its decorative brickwork and carved stone pediments, gave way to the interior of a modern-day law enforcement agency as she entered. Past the reception desk was an open-plan office where a dozen or so uniformed personnel sat at desks, each in their own modular cubicle, working on a computer or talking on the phone. The staticky sound of voices talking over a two-way radio emanated from somewhere in the building.

Kyra tensed as a pair of uniformed officers stepped from the elevator to her right, headed for the door. She feared she'd be recognized as the subject of a BOLO alert or missing person report. Ranger had no such worries; he greeted the passing strangers with a grin, tail wagging. One of them paused to give him a smile and a scratch on the head, saying, "Hey, pooch. Nabbed you, did they?"

Kyra felt a chill go through her, as if he'd been speaking to her. Once again, she fought the urge to bolt. She reached for Frannie's hand, and when she felt the older woman's fingers tighten around hers, it strengthened her resolve. She was relieved when the uniforms continued without showing any sign of recognizing her.

"I'm here to see Deputy Fuentes. He's expecting me," Frannie informed the gray-haired desk sergeant. A minute later, an athletic-looking man with black hair and salt-and-pepper sideburns, wearing the khaki uniform of a deputy, strode from the back into the reception area, sparing Kyra and her dog only a cursory glance, to her relief. From the hug they exchanged, he and Frannie were old friends.

"Where's Hannah? Is she all right?" Frannie asked.

"She's in lockdown." He held a hand up to still the words forming on Frannie's lips. "She's fine, but she seemed disoriented when she was brought in. I didn't want her wandering off before you got here."

"So she's not under arrest?"

"Not at this time, no." The phrasing of his answer suggested a previous run-in with the law, or perhaps more than one. Whatever the reason Frannie's daughter had been brought in, it couldn't be good.

"You said she assaulted someone? Who?"

"Woman by the name of Mallory Chambers. She claimed to know you."

"She's the receptionist at my dentist's office. She knows Hannah, too. What happened?"

"According to Ms. Chambers, she approached Hannah on the street after noticing she was acting strange. She asked if she needed help, and Hannah pushed her, hard enough to knock her down."

Frannie gasped, growing pale. "Was she hurt?"

"A scraped knee and some bruises is all."

"Why did Hannah push her? Did she say?"

"No. She's not talking. The good news is, Ms. Chambers declined to press charges."

"Bless her. She's a kind soul. I'll send her flowers to thank her."

"That would be a nice gesture," he agreed.

Tears filled Frannie's eyes. Kyra fished a clean tissue from her purse and handed it to her, and Frannie gave her a weak smile. "Hannah isn't normally violent. You know that," she said to the deputy.

"Maybe she was confused. I'm sure it wasn't intentional." He spoke as a friend, not a police officer.

Kyra was impressed by his sensitivity in handling the situation. It was a reminder that there were good cops.

"So what now?" Frannie asked.

"I can release her into your custody or have her transferred to Washburn Medical for a psych eval. Your call."

"I'll take her," she said. "She can stay with me until I get her living situation sorted out."

"She's not still at Caring Village?"

"No. She moved out a few weeks ago. She was staying with a friend, last I heard. She didn't tell you?"

"She wasn't making a whole lot of sense when I questioned her." They exchanged a loaded look. "I'm sorry, Frannie. I know this hasn't been easy for you."

Frannie nodded, her expression one of weary resignation. "Thanks, Chaz. And thanks for giving me the heads-up instead of . . . you know."

"Sure. Anytime."

Frannie turned toward Kyra. "Chaz, this is my friend Kyra Smith. Kyra, this is Deputy Chaz Fuentes. He's an old family friend."

"Nice to meet you," Kyra said as they shook hands. She felt another flutter of unease, but relaxed somewhat when the deputy didn't look at her like he thought he might know her from somewhere.

"Sorry we're not meeting under better circumstances," he said, and Kyra murmured that she was so sorry, too. Poor Frannie. "Wait here while I get Hannah," he said to Frannie.

After he left, Kyra said to Frannie, "It's going to be okay." She didn't know that it would be. It was just something you said. Frannie nodded distractedly but seemed comforted by her presence.

The deputy returned shortly with a disheveled-looking woman in her late forties, a younger version of Frannie with big dark eyes and curly raven hair threaded with silver that fell past her shoulders. She wore jeans, raggedy at the knees and riding low on her bony hips, and an oversize hoodie.

Frannie hugged her. "Honey, are you okay?"

"I'm fine, Mom."

"What happened?"

"Nothing."

"It wasn't nothing. You attacked Ms. Chambers. What on earth possessed you to do such a thing?"

"I didn't *attack* her."

"You pushed her and she fell."

"It was an accident. I thought she was someone else."

"Who?"

"No one you know."

"Did you think you were defending yourself against this person?"

Hannah frowned, either because she was annoyed or because she was trying to remember the details of what happened. Kyra suspected it was the latter. As a teacher, she was trained to spot the signs of a mental disorder. In her experience it was most often drug induced, and involved those students who'd used drugs recreationally or habitually—but with some, it was due to brain chemistry, as appeared to be the case with Hannah. "I don't know, Mom. Do we have to talk about it now?"

"Fine. We'll discuss it later," said Frannie, seeming to realize the conversation was going nowhere. "In the meantime, let's get you sorted out. Do you have a place to stay?"

"No. I was staying with my friend Remy, but he got kicked out of his place, so we both had to leave. Can I stay with you?"

"For now. Tomorrow I'll call Rhonda at Caring Village and see if they can take you back."

"I'm not going back there." A stubborn look settled over Hannah's face.

"Why not? I thought you liked it there. Did something happen?"

"Nothing happened."

"Then why did you leave?"

"It was because of their stupid rules."

"Rules, or just the rule requiring you to take their meds?" Hannah's silence confirmed her mother's guess, and Frannie went on, "Honey, this is what happens when you go off your meds. You get confused, like when you mistook nice Ms. Chambers for someone who was out to get you. You *need* your meds, Hannah. I know you don't like taking them, but it's not optional."

"I'm not crazy," she insisted.

"No one said you were. That's not a word I would use, or that any-one else should use. But you do have a mental disorder, and there's no shame in that. You can stay with me on one condition: that you take your meds. It's non-negotiable," she added when Hannah opened her mouth as if to protest.

Hannah shut her mouth, but from the stubborn set of her jaw, she remained unconvinced. "Fine," she said, as though she were agreeing to Frannie's terms only because she had nowhere else to go.

"Good. Now come meet my friend Kyra."

Kyra was aware of Frannie watching her closely as she made the introductions, like she was accustomed to other people reacting to Hannah in ways that marked her as different, even lesser than. Kyra knew what it was like to be viewed as lesser than. In elementary and high school, she'd been one of the kids in the free-lunch program who'd worn clothes from Salvation Army stores. She didn't know which had been worse: the kids who'd shunned her and made fun of her or the kids who'd been nice to her solely because, as one girl in her ninth-grade class, Jill Mathers, had put it, "It's what Jesus would do." The former had been honest in looking down their noses at her, at least. In any case, she would never want anyone else to feel bad because they were different.

She smiled as she shook Hannah's hand. "Nice to meet you, Hannah. I'd know you anywhere. You look like your mom. You have her eyes."

5

Hannah greeted her shyly, murmuring a few polite words before she dropped to her knees to greet Ranger. "Who's a good boy?" she cooed, her face, which had been closed a minute ago, now open and glowing. "Yes, you. You're a good boy, aren't you? I know, I like you, too. I wish I could take you home with me." Ranger responded by washing her face with his tongue, which Hannah allowed, giggling. She was clearly a dog lover and seemed like a nice person. Kyra was looking forward to getting to know her as well as Frannie. Until recently, she would have told anyone who asked that she preferred her own company to that of others, but the people she'd met since she'd arrived in town were living proof that she didn't always know what she needed or what was good for her.

"Sorry, he's spoken for," she said with a laugh. "His name's Ranger, by the way."

Hannah looked up at her, smiling. "Ranger. Cool. Can you bring him for a visit sometime?"

"Great idea. How about one day next week? Come for dinner," said Frannie, leaping at the suggestion.

"I'd love to," said Kyra, surprising herself once again.

"Soon as you're settled in, we'll make a date."

Frannie thanked Chaz, signed a form, and they left.

Ranger, as if sensing she needed a friend, stuck close to Hannah's side, and when they were outside, she asked, "Would it be okay if I walked him?"

"Sure," Kyra said, and handed her the leash.

"Thanks for coming," Frannie said as they strolled to their cars, Hannah walking ahead of them with Ranger.

"I don't know that I was much help," Kyra said.

"You were there. That's what matters."

"I'm glad." She'd benefited as well. Visiting the sheriff's office had put to rest her fear that she was wanted by the law. No one there had paid her any mind. "Hannah seems to have bounced back," she observed with a nod in her direction. The animated woman being towed by Ranger on his leash was nothing like the subdued and addled-seeming person whom she'd first met.

"She usually does."

"What does she take medication for, if you don't mind my asking?"

"Hannah is schizoaffective." Frannie's tone was matter of fact, but Kyra sensed her statement contained a world of hurt and a history of episodes like today's that had landed Hannah in custody.

"I'm sorry." Kyra had heard of the disorder but didn't know much about it other than that it had some of the same aspects as schizophrenia, such as paranoia and a tendency toward delusions, both visual and auditory. She felt for both mother and daughter. "It must be difficult for you as well."

"It certainly makes life interesting."

"As in the Chinese curse, 'May you live in interesting times'?"

"Exactly." Frannie gave a smile that didn't reach her eyes. "She functions normally when she's on her meds, but as you may have guessed from our conversation earlier, she doesn't always take them. When she's unmedicated, she hears voices and doesn't always know the difference between what's real and what isn't. That's what led to her attacking Mallory. Is it horrible of me to say I'm glad it was Mallory and not someone else?" *As in, someone who might have pressed charges,* Kyra thought.

"Not at all," she said.

"I owe her. I owe you, too."

"Me? I didn't do anything. Besides, you already bought me dinner."

"Fine. We're even, then." Frannie cast her a dry smile. "And thanks for being so nice to Hannah."

"Why wouldn't I be?"

"Not everyone is."

"That's their problem. Hannah is sweet."

"That, she is. Confused at times, but she has a good heart." They passed under a streetlight, and in its glow, Frannie's expression was one of tenderness mixed with worry. She hugged Kyra goodbye when they reached her Jeep. Kyra tensed reflexively before sinking into the older woman's warm embrace. It was like coming home to something she hadn't known she was missing. "Good night, and sleep tight." Words a mother might use, if you had a mother to tuck you in at night.

"I'll probably be asleep before my head hits the pillow," Kyra said. "It's been a long day."

"I'll bet. Good luck with your job search."

"Thanks to you, I'll be earning money until I find a permanent job."

"You can thank Suzy and Gertie for that. You'll enjoy working for them, in case you have any doubts. Suzy's salon is a jewel box, and Suzy and Jasmine—her other stylist—are its jewels. The customers are nice, too, at least the ones I've met. I'll pop in on Monday to see how you're doing."

"Great! See you then."

Kyra and Ranger arrived at their cabin at the Pine Ridge Motor Lodge shortly after nine. Furnished with a knotty-pine bed and dresser, on which sat an old box television set, it was a dump compared to her riverfront home in Rochester, which had seemed like a fairy-tale castle until she discovered her Prince Charming was not who he seemed. But she wasn't noticing the room's worn carpeting or the sun-bleached plaid drapes and bedspread. All she saw was a safe haven. Ranger conducted a thorough inspection, sniffing every nook and cranny, then, satisfied that no further action was required on his part, hopped onto the bed and curled up. Kyra lay down next to him.

"We're safe, bud," she said as she stroked his thick fur. "For tonight, anyway."

She fell asleep before she could change out of her clothes and into her pajamas. She slept soundly and awakened the next morning to pale light leaking through the curtains. She'd been dreaming that she was still at home, in bed with Rory, and for a disoriented second she thought the dream was real. With a strangled cry, she bolted upright, suddenly wide awake, her heart pounding. A pair of eyes in a furry face glittered in the shadows pooled below the bed. Ranger. Awareness flooded in, followed by sweet relief: she was alone with her dog and in no present danger.

Ranger nudged her foot, which was dangling over the edge of the mattress, with his nose. "Okay, bud, I can take a hint," she told him.

She got up and took him outside to do his business. Wearing the clothes that she'd slept in, she and Ranger headed for the park where they'd gone for a walk the day before, and spent the next twenty minutes or so hiking one of its trails as the day broke and the surrounding forest gradually revealed itself. The sun had risen by the time they returned. She fed Ranger and showered while he ate. Breakfast for her was a protein bar washed down with a small carton of orange juice. It was all she could manage with her stomach in knots.

With the break of day, her worries had returned. Money being the most pressing among them. She had enough to last for the next couple of months if she stayed at the motel, where she was paying the weekly rate, and kept her other expenses to a minimum. But she might run out before she found permanent work. What then? She couldn't survive on what she'd earn working two part-time jobs.

Best get cracking, then. The voice in her head sounded suspiciously like Mrs. Babbs, Kyra's homeroom teacher the year she'd attended John Wayne Elementary in Dripping Springs, Texas. Mrs. Babbs, who'd taught school for four decades and buried two husbands, had had no patience for slackers.

Kyra spent the rest of that day and the following one conducting an online job search when she wasn't pounding the pavement in town. In addition to working retail, she'd done some waitressing when she was in college. But at the shops and eateries downtown where she inquired, no one was hiring. She was told to come back in the spring, at the start of the tourist season, when business typically picked up. She tried not to be discouraged. It was early days yet. Meanwhile, it wasn't as if she was unemployed.

Monday morning, at half past eight, she headed back into town with Ranger for her first day of work at Shear Delight. She wore her nicest jeans, a clean shirt, and her warmest jacket. The sun was shining, but it was cold enough for her breath and Ranger's to form frosty plumes in the air as they walked from her car—parked two blocks away in the municipal parking lot—to Suzy's salon. Located on a narrow side street off the main drag, it was housed in a single-story stucco building painted cream, with a deep-green trim and sporting a pink-and-green-striped awning over the window and entrance. The sign on the door read CLOSED when she arrived, but Suzy answered her knock.

"Hi. I'm not too early, am I?" Kyra asked. "You said to come early."

"You're right on time." Suzy flashed a welcoming smile. She looked like she'd stepped from the pages of a fashion magazine, wearing a multihued jacket in jewel tones over a teal shift that brought out the blue of her eyes and pink ballet flats. "Coffee? I was just about to make some."

Kyra shrugged off her jacket as she entered. "Why don't I do it? That's what I'm here for." She was eager to make herself useful. She bent to unclip Ranger's leash from his collar, and he set off to explore.

"You're not on the clock yet," said Suzy.

"Good thing I'm not a clock watcher."

Suzy beamed her approval. "Good to know. Come, I'll show you where everything is, and then I'll walk you through your duties."

"Wow." Kyra paused to look around her as Suzy led the way to the door in back with an EMPLOYEES ONLY sign over it. The color scheme of the interior reflected the exterior. The walls were painted cream with dark-green trim, and the antique sofa and chairs by the window were upholstered in striped-green damask. A row of three full-length, gilt-framed mirrors faced the stylists' stations along one wall. Black-and-white-checkerboard flooring and rose-colored drapes with polished-brass tiebacks completed the look of a La Belle Époque Parisian boudoir. This was what Frannie had meant when she called it a "jewel box." It smelled pleasantly of hair products and the pink roses in a vase on the reception desk. "What a gorgeous space. I love what you've done with it."

"You should have seen it before I renovated," Suzy said. "You're looking at six months of my blood, sweat, and tears. Not to mention every cent I could scrape together or borrow from the bank. Some people thought I was crazy to go into debt. I was newly divorced at the time, with two young children and a deadbeat dad for an ex. But I'd dreamed of opening my own salon ever since I graduated beauty college and started working as a hair stylist. A place where my customers would feel pampered from the moment they walked in. When a woman is in beautiful surroundings, she feels beautiful."

"I imagine every woman who comes here leaves feeling gorgeous. With a great haircut," she added.

"Speaking of which, why don't I trim those split ends for you?" Suzy fingered the end of Kyra's braid.

Kyra hesitated. "Now? I was going to . . ."

"Coffee can wait. Have a seat." Suzy pushed her into the chair at one of the stations, and Ranger settled at Kyra's feet. Suzy fastened a pink-and-green nylon cape around Kyra's neck and loosened her hair from its plait so it spilled over her shoulders and down her back. "Oh my God. Your *hair*. I know someone who'd pay good money for it if you ever decide to go short."

"I wasn't planning on it." Although it was something to consider if she got desperate enough.

"Nor should you. What's a Disney princess without her long, flowing locks?"

45

Some princess. Her happily ever after had been a horror show. Kyra pushed the thought from her mind. "Beautiful flowers." She motioned toward the vase of roses reflected in the mirror.

"They're from my son. He sends me flowers every year on my birthday and Mother's Day. Or rather," she amended, her expression clouding over, "his wife does and puts his name on the card."

Kyra knew from their conversation at dinner the other night that Suzy had two grown children, a son and a daughter, with children of their own. Her son, Adam, a successful restaurateur, lived in Seattle; and her daughter, Christina, an attorney, was in DC. From Suzy's remark, and the troubled look on her face now, her relationship with her son was not all that she might have wished it to be.

"Happy belated birthday," Kyra said.

"Thanks," Suzy said, shaking off her funk. "Though the less I think about being a year older, the better."

They were interrupted by the rattle of a key in a lock. Kyra watched in the mirror as a young woman—statuesque, with a pretty face framed by dark hair braided in an elaborate weave—entered. "Hey, boss!" she called to Suzy, peeling off her jacket. "*Brrr.* It's cold out. Where did summer go?"

"It went with the tourists." Suzy introduced them. "Kyra, meet Jasmine, my goddaughter and chief stylist. Jasmine, meet Kyra. I hired her to work mornings, washing hair and sweeping up."

"Praise the Lord," said Jasmine with a grin as she flipped the sign from CLOSED to OPEN. "Kyra, you're a godsend. Does this mean we can go back to taking breaks?" she asked Suzy.

"*Morning* breaks. We'll both be doing double duty in the afternoons until we find someone to replace Morgan. You have a problem with that, take it up with HR," she said when Jasmine made a face.

"I had your job when I first started here," Jasmine told Kyra as she hung her jacket on the coatrack by the door. "Aunt Suzy hired me when I was still in beauty school. I worked my way up from there."

"And she's worth her weight in gold." Suzy beamed at her protégé.

"You bet your ass." Jasmine turned her attention to Ranger, who'd gone over to greet her, bending to ruffle his ears. "Who's this? We have a store dog now?"

"His name's Ranger, and he belongs to Kyra," said Suzy as her scissors flashed, snipping Kyra's split ends.

"Suzy said it was okay to bring him," said Kyra.

"He sure is hairy. Bet he gets hot in the summer with all that fur."

"He's not one to complain." Kyra remembered when she'd found him chained up in the hot sun, dehydrated and half-starved, his fur matted and infested with fleas, and it made her mad all over again.

When Suzy was done trimming her hair, Kyra followed her into the employees-only area in back, which held Suzy's office, a tiny bathroom, a supply closet, and, in one corner, a sink and countertop with a mini fridge below and a shelf above, which held a row of mugs. A coffee maker and electric teakettle stood on the countertop, along with a canister of coffee, coffee supplies, and boxes of tea bags. Kyra followed Suzy's instructions on how to operate the coffee maker, and while the coffee was brewing, Suzy showed her where everything else was and described her duties.

At one point, Kyra got up the courage to ask, "Would it be possible for you to pay me in cash? I, uh, haven't opened an account with a local bank yet, so . . ." She trailed off, heat rising in her cheeks.

"No problem," Suzy answered. Kyra got the feeling she hadn't bought her excuse about not having a bank account, but she didn't question it, for which Kyra was grateful. She silently blessed Suzy.

The morning saw a steady stream of female customers. One of Kyra's duties was to give the customers a shampoo and rinse, which she found she enjoyed. She took her time with each one, massaging her scalp between sudsing and rinsing her hair, giving her the full treatment. She knew how much a kind gesture or a gentle touch could mean to someone who might be going through a rough patch or just having a bad day. Every kindness she'd been shown when she was at her lowest had meant the world. The customers seemed to enjoy getting the spa experience for the price of a haircut from their moans of pleasure, and they tipped generously, an unexpected bonus.

Frannie stopped by at one point, as promised. "How's your first day going?" she asked.

"So far, so good." Kyra paused as she swept up hair clippings. "I think I've gotten the hang of it."

"She's doing an awesome job!" Suzy raised her voice to be heard above the humming of dueling hair dryers. Both she and Jasmine were with customers. "Who knew she had magic fingers?"

"Best shampoo ever!" piped the middle-aged brunette at Suzy's station.

Kyra warmed at the praise. "It's not magic. I just take my time."

"Whatever you're doing, keep it up," said Suzy. "It's good for business. I had three customers today ask if they could book a shampoo and blowout between haircuts."

Kyra beamed, happy to know she was making a difference.

"Did you get with Gertie yet?" Frannie asked her.

"We spoke over the phone. I'm meeting her this afternoon to go over the work she wants done."

"Excellent. Gertie's a pistol, but she's a straight shooter. You two should get along just fine."

"Any advice? I want to make a good impression."

"None that would apply to you. When someone has a problem with Gertie, nine times out of ten, it's a man. She doesn't take kindly to mansplaining or being talked down to because she's a woman. Though from what I've observed, she has the men she works with well trained."

Kyra smiled at the image of the white-haired scrap of a woman she'd met bossing around the male employees at the sheriff's office. "How's Hannah?" she remembered to ask as Frannie was leaving.

"Good, or so she says. But she's taking her meds, which is good, even though I have to watch to make sure she does it. I'm hoping I can convince her to go back to Caring Village once she's stabilized."

"Is that like a residential facility?"

"It's actually a group home, and one of the nicer ones. It's in a big house in a quiet neighborhood with shops nearby, about a fifteen-minute drive from here. There are never more than half a dozen residents at any given time, so it was like one big family whenever I visited. Hannah had friends there. And the staff is lovely. Everyone was surprised when she left."

"But not you?" Kyra guessed.

"No." Frannie sighed. "I've been through this with Hannah before. She gets an idea in her head and . . ." She trailed off with a short shake of her head. "I've found it's best to take it one day at a time with her."

"Tell her I said hello."

"Will do. This morning she asked when you were coming for supper. How about this Friday, if you don't have other plans?"

Kyra hesitated. When she'd accepted Frannie's invitation, she'd been caught up in the moment. Now she wondered if it was such a good idea. The closer she got to Frannie and the other Tattooed Ladies, the harder it would be to keep secrets from them. And if they were to learn the details of her "bad breakup," what would they think? She couldn't bear the thought of being pitied or judged. Which was why she'd kept her fellow faculty members at the Stoningham Academy at arm's length, even the ones she'd been friendly with. But the time she'd spent with the Tattooed Ladies, and today with Suzy and Jasmine, had made her realize how starved she'd been for the company of others. Now, like a flower turning toward the sun, she turned toward the friendship that was being offered.

"Sounds good," she said.

"Great! Dinner's at six. I'll text you the address."

She got off work at noon and stopped at Mother Lode Mercantile on her way back to her car, where she bought a bag of popcorn from its old-timey popcorn machine. She ate it while seated on the bench on the covered walkway in front, sharing it with Ranger. Her next stop was Buckboard Books across the street. A two-story built of sandstone in the Edwardian style with arched casement windows, gables, and a front bow window, it looked like a bookshop you might see on a cobbled back-street in London. Inside, books filled shelves that lined the walls and divided the space, where they stood in rows. More books were displayed on the antique tables scattered throughout. A staircase, which was roped off, led to the upper floor. Oriental rugs covered the hardwood floor in some spots, and in the cozy reading nooks tucked here and there, customers sat in overstuffed chairs with their heads buried in books. The air smelled of old woodwork and new books. And, faintly, of cats. Ranger watched with interest as a tabby cat wandered past, ignoring him. A marmalade cat snoozed in one of the reading nooks.

Ranger, spotting a familiar face, began pulling on his leash, towing Kyra toward the romance section, where Marisol was shelving books. Marisol's face lit up when she saw them. She wore a Dr. Seuss–themed T-shirt with jeans and red Converse high-tops. The T-shirt went with *The Cat in the Hat* tattoo on her forearm. "Kyra, hi! Is this a social visit, or is there something I can help you with?"

"I just stopped by to say hello." Kyra couldn't afford to buy a book. She would be getting her books from the public library for the foresee-able future. "I also wanted to check out your bookshop. What a great place!" she said, looking around her. "It looks like it's been here forever."

"Not quite, only for the past hundred or so years."

"Has it always been in your family?"

Marisol nodded and slid another book into its place on the shelf she was restocking. "Founded by my great-great-grandmother Millicent and named after the buckboard wagon she used to peddle her wares door-to-door before then. She was quite the trailblazer, I'm told, and a tough cookie. According to family lore, she once fended off a masked bandit with her shotgun. Another time, she delivered a baby along with books when she happened to arrive as her customer was giving birth. She's also said to have delivered lifesaving medicine during a cholera epidemic. I don't know how much of it is fact and how much is fiction, but it makes for good stories."

"Even if only half of it's true, she sounds like an amazing woman." Kyra wondered about her own ancestry. She knew only that her maternal grandfather, whom she'd never met, was Mexican. "I read somewhere that this is the oldest bookstore in Washburn County and the second oldest in the state."

"Right. I just hope I can pass it on to the next generation if I ever have kids," Marisol said with a sigh. If she was single and childless, it didn't appear to be by choice. Maybe she hadn't met the right person yet. "Anyway, I'm glad you stopped by. You, too, Ranger." She bent to stroke his fur, which he seemed to take as an invitation to jump on her. He planted his forepaws on her pant legs, tail waving. Marisol indulgently ruffled his ears. Kyra, not wishing to encourage bad habits, reprimanded him, and he dropped back onto all fours with a guilty look.

"Sorry. He sometimes forgets his manners."

"No worries. Can I get you something to drink? Coffee? Tea? Water?"

"No, I can't stay, but thanks." Kyra was due at Gertie's shortly.

"Listen, why don't we do lunch one day this week?"

"Sure, but maybe a bag lunch in the park? I'm on a tight budget until I find a permanent job."

"In that case, let's make it dinner. I'll cook. Have you ever had *kare-kare*?"

"No, what's that?"

"Traditional Filipino curry dish. Do you like spicy food?"

"Love it."

"My mom used to make it." A look of sadness passed over her expressive face. "So, what day is good for you?"

Once more, Kyra gave in to the gravitational pull of the Tattooed Ladies. "I'm free every evening this week except Friday." They settled on Wednesday of that week. "Can't wait! Just tell me what to bring, and text me your address."

"No need to bring anything. As for my address, you're looking at it." She pointed toward the staircase. "I'm the proverbial shopkeeper who lives above her shop. Which might explain my nonexistent love life. I have no life outside work. The male company I keep these days is strictly the fictional variety."

"You could do worse." Kyra spoke from experience.

"That's my problem in a nutshell." Marisol studied the cover of the paperback novel in her hand depicting a bare-chested hunk and buxom blonde in a clinch. "How can a mere mortal compete with the likes of Rhett Butler and Mr. Rochester, Atticus Finch and . . . and Noah in *The Notebook?*"

"I don't think I've read that one."

"You should. It's good, even if it was written by a man. It's here somewhere. Ah, there it is." She plucked a copy of *The Notebook* from a lower shelf—the movie tie-in edition—and handed it to Kyra.

Kyra pretended to show an interest before handing it back. "I saw the movie, so I know how it ends."

Marisol bent to scoop up a black cat that had wandered into view. As she stroked its fur, it purred loudly while casting a baleful eye at Ranger. "Meet Black Bart. He's named after the notorious outlaw, who's rumored to have holed up here in Gold Creek at one point during his reign of terror."

"How many cats do you have?"

"It varies from week to week, but we currently have eight." Marisol explained that her bookshop partnered with a local feline shelter, where the cats lived when they weren't wandering the stacks at Buckboard Books in search of their future owners. "So far it seems to be working. You wouldn't believe how many customers come for a book and end up falling in love with a cat."

"What about the customers who are allergic?"

"They tend not to linger." Her gaze dropped to Ranger, who was eyeing Black Bart warily. "I see he has a healthy respect for cats. Smart dog. Some of our canine visitors have gotten their noses scratched after they got a little too curious. Which is why we keep dog treats on hand to distract them." She extracted a Milk-Bone from her pocket and tossed it to Ranger, who gobbled it in two bites.

"You're doing a good thing."

"Yeah, except I'm too young to be a cat lady. I'm not even forty, for crying out loud. Maybe if I had a boyfriend . . ." She trailed off with a shrug.

"You looking?"

"At the moment, I'm taking a break. The local singles scene is . . ." She made a face. "If it's not someone I've known since they were snorting milk out their nose in second grade, it's someone who's only interested in a hookup. But then, I grew up in this town. You might have a different experience."

"I'm not looking, either."

"Too soon?"

"Way."

Marisol's brown eyes behind the bedazzled glasses she was wearing regarded Kyra curiously. She seemed to be waiting for Kyra to provide more details of the "bad breakup," which she'd alluded to previously. When Kyra offered none, she said, "Well, you'll know when you're ready."

Try never. "I'm in no rush."

"Excuse me, miss, do you have any books on tropical fish?"

Kyra glanced over at the child who'd spoken, a little girl with red pigtails.

"I sure do. Come with me." Marisol disappeared with the child into the warren of shelves in back. She could hear them chattering, Marisol's adult voice carrying above the child's softer voice. "Do you have a fish tank? You do? Awesome! What kind of fish are in it? *Oooh,* I love angelfish."

She'd make a good mom, Kyra thought.

She lingered in the romance section, with its row after row of novels promising happily ever afters. She wondered how many of their readers ever experienced the kind of love depicted in their pages. More likely, they'd been disappointed in love or gotten their hearts broken at some point. Or they'd been broken by someone they'd once loved, as she'd been. Her gaze fell on a book displayed face-out on the shelf in front of her. Its cover, showing a man and woman strolling hand in hand on a deserted beach at sunset, seemed to mock her. She felt her gut twist as the memories rushed in.

She and Rory had first met at the opening of a group show featuring the works of up-and-coming artists, of which she was one, at a small art gallery in Tribeca, two days before her twenty-third birthday. She'd been two years out of college, working temp jobs and selling her paintings at street fairs on weekends to support herself. The show was her first, and she'd been both proud and nervous. *You deserve this,* the angel on her shoulder had whispered. *Impostor,* the devil on her other shoulder had mocked.

The devil was usually right, in her experience. Her future had seemed bright when she'd attended Fordham University on a full scholarship. She'd been praised by her professors and told she was "going places." But in the real world, that of the fiercely competitive New York art scene, she was but an asteroid drifting in the galaxy in her relative anonymity, while the rising stars made names for themselves. She hadn't gone any further than the street fairs where she'd sold some of her paintings, and then the gallery in Tribeca where the group show she was in was being held.

She'd been working the room, doing her bit to chat up the guests in the hope of making a sale, when she'd noticed a man, in a tailored gray sports coat worn over a collared pink shirt, standing in front of her painting—on which there was now a red sticker showing that it had been sold, she'd been delighted to see. He was studying it as he sipped from the glass of wine in his hand. He was somewhere in his thirties, medium height with an athletic build, and handsome—the kind of handsome she had only ever seen in movies and on TV. He wore his blond hair short on the sides and longer on top. His features were irregular in a way that made his good looks interesting rather than cookie cutter.

He must have sensed her staring at him, because he turned his head to look at her. A look of frank appraisal, which left her feeling hot and quivery inside. His eyes were an unusual shade of blue, so pale they were nearly transparent, fringed with dark lashes. The eyes of a gray wolf, she would later liken them to.

She wasn't in the habit of approaching strange men; usually, it was a case of them coming on to her and her discouraging their advances. But she found herself drawn to him as if by a magnetic force.

"What do you think?" she asked as she sidled up to him, gesturing toward the painting, a landscape of Sheep Meadow in Central Park that she'd painted one day at sunrise when it was deserted.

He didn't disappoint. "Best in show, in my opinion. You're very talented."

"How did you know it was mine?" She was embarrassed to have been caught fishing for compliments. It wasn't something she normally did. In the art world, it was considered the mark of an amateur. It could lead to getting one's hopes crushed by someone else's brutally honest opinion.

"The gallery owner pointed you out after I asked whether the artist was here tonight. I would have introduced myself, but you were talking to someone, and I didn't want to interrupt. You beat me to it." A single dimple appeared on one side of his mouth when he smiled. His gaze traveled over her, and he seemed to like what he saw.

She wore her one good outfit, the "little black dress" that was an essential of every single-in-the-city girl's wardrobe and made her legs look a mile long.

"I'm flattered. If you're interested . . . in the painting, that is, I could show you some of my others. This one's sold, as you can see."

"I know. I bought it."

"You? Oh my God, and here I've been babbling like an idiot." The heat in her face intensified.

"Not at all. I'm glad I snagged it before someone else did." He held her gaze for a beat or two, long enough to spark a one-woman heat wave that had her perspiring, before he went back to studying her painting. "I already have a spot picked out for it. I plan to hang it over my living room fireplace."

Flustered, she blurted out the first thing that popped into her head. "You have a fireplace?" The only residences in New York City she'd seen that boasted fireplaces were owned by wealthy patrons of the arts who hosted receptions for up-and-coming artists, a few of which she'd attended. The closest thing to a fireplace in the cramped fourth-floor walk-up in Alphabet City she shared with her housemate, Kate, was the electric heater they used when the building's furnace was on the fritz.

"It came with the house."

"You're renting an entire house?"

"I own it, actually."

"Here in the city?"

"No. I live in Rochester. I'm only in town for the weekend. I saw the sign outside advertising tonight's opening as I was passing by on my way to my hotel and decided to check it out. I'm glad I did."

"What brings you to the city?"

"Business."

"Does it involve collecting art?" She wondered if he was an interior designer.

"Not even remotely."

"Oh? What line of work are you in?"

"I'm the district attorney of Monroe County."

She stared at him in surprise. "Seriously? You're the guy who gets the bad guys locked up?"

"I try. I don't always succeed."

"Well, I'm sure the good folk of Monroe County sleep easier at night with you keeping it safe." She was mildly appalled to find herself flirting with him. Normally, she didn't flirt. It wasn't her style.

"I like to think so."

"*And* you own a house with a fireplace. Lucky you."

"I'd be even luckier if you would agree to have dinner with me tonight." He gave her a heated look that caused her to tingle from head to toe and rendered her momentarily speechless.

"I don't even know your name," she said when she recovered her wits.

"It's Rory. Rory Stanhope." When he shook her hand, the electric thrill that shot through her was like being zapped by a Taser, if the sensation of being Tasered were a pleasant one. He wasn't wearing a wedding ring. Even better. She had a strict rule against dating married men. "Now that we've been formally introduced, what do you say? Will you have dinner with me, Krystal?"

Had she told him her name? She couldn't remember. Staring into his mesmerizing eyes, she couldn't think straight. "I'd love to," she said, and watched his face light up as if she'd granted his fondest wish.

"I was hoping you'd say that."

"What if I'd said no?"

"Either way, you'd be having dinner with me."

"Oh? And why is that?"

"Because when I want something, I usually get it. I'm not one to take no for an answer."

She wondered what he saw in her. She was aware that men found her attractive, but she was sexually inexperienced compared with the fellow artists her age whom she hung out with. Too busy earning a living and taking classes on the side to have a boyfriend—she was studying for her master's in education so she could support herself as a teacher if she failed as an artist. Rory Stanhope was older and more sophisticated than the men she'd dated, most of them starving artists like herself whose idea of a romantic evening was splitting a pizza and having sex afterward. She imagined the women he dated were glamourous and accomplished. In other words, nothing like her.

"Why me?" she blurted out, then immediately regretted revealing her insecurity.

"Besides the fact that you're beautiful and talented? That. What you just said."

"What?"

"You're not full of yourself like some women I know, which is refreshing. In fact, you're the kind of woman I could easily fall in love with." His words and the smile playing over his lips acted on her like a drug. She suddenly felt woozy. "Which means you have to promise to be gentle with me."

"Why wouldn't I be?" she asked.

"If I fall in love with you, you might break my heart."

"Or you might break mine."

He took her hand again, this time to give it a reassuring squeeze. "I promise to always be gentle with you, Krystal."

Now, in the cozy bookshop, Kyra felt an urge to call out a warning to her younger self as she might to the girl in a movie who was about to walk down the dark alley or get a ride from the shifty stranger or enter a room where danger lurks: *Don't go there.* Because she knew how this particular movie ended. She knew the handsome stranger with the hypnotic eyes was not who he seemed.

The first time he'd hit her was when they were on their honeymoon in Jamaica. Afterward, he'd seemed as shocked as she'd been by the blow he'd struck in a fit of jealousy after falsely accusing her of flirting with one of the hotel staff, and sick with remorse. He'd claimed it had never happened before and swore it would never happen again. After her shock wore off, she'd forgiven him.

For the next six months, he'd been a model husband, and the terrible incident in Jamaica came to seem like a nightmare she'd had. Until he'd hit her again. It became a cycle over the next five years. There would be periods of calm disrupted by sudden, violent fits of rage followed by tortured apologies, with the calm periods growing ever shorter in duration with the passage of time. By the end, every day had been a minefield to cross, with her trying not to say or do anything to set him off. Until one day she'd realized there was nothing she could have said or done differently to alter the collision course she'd been on since the day they'd first met. *Love,* she thought now, *is for readers of romances and the lucky few who get to experience it.* She was neither.

She became aware of a warm body pressing against her leg, and when she glanced down, saw that Ranger had moved in close, like he sensed her distress. He looked up at her with worried eyes, and in that moment she felt more connected to him than ever before. The smartest decision she'd ever made, she thought, was to rescue him from his former owner rather than leave him to an uncertain fate. They'd rescued each other, as it turned out. "I'm okay, bud. Everything's okay." She squatted down to put her arms around him, burying her face in his thick fur. "No more bad guys." As she said it, she hoped it was true.

A short while later, Kyra pulled up in front of a Queen Anne–style home in the Garden District with more curlicues and furbelows than a Victorian ball gown. She hadn't expected the down-to-earth police sketch artist she'd met at Cowboy Coffee to live anywhere this grand. Either Gertie Naylor had family money or a rich husband, or crime paid, in her case. If it was the latter, she was the best paid artist Kyra knew.

She stopped Ranger before he could bound out after her. "Sorry, no dogs allowed." She wasn't sure whether that was the case, but from the look of the place, it was a safe bet. "I know, hard to believe, but not everyone loves dogs," she said when he cocked his head to give her a quizzical look. "The lady of the house might change her mind about hiring me if you left muddy paw prints on her floor."

She cracked the window on the passenger side and then headed up the front walk. Brick pavers laid in a herringbone pattern and bordered by flower beds curved in a path through a lush garden. There was a columned portico over the entrance, which boasted a stained-glass fanlight above a solid oak door. She used a brass door knocker in the shape of a lion's head to announce her presence. Gertie appeared a minute later, in high-waisted jeans, a two-toned Western-style shirt, and fancy cowgirl boots—today's pair purple with paisley stitching, like she'd been wearing when they'd first met.

"Thank heavens you're here," she greeted Kyra, pushing a hand distractedly through her cockatoo's crest of silver hair. She seemed agitated. "When can you start?"

"Um. I thought I was here to discuss the work you needed to have done?" Kyra said, momentarily thrown by the unexpected greeting.

"Sorry, I'm getting ahead of myself. There's been a development. Since we last spoke, I found out I'm being audited by the IRS. So you see, I'm in a pickle."

"Oh no." Kyra had never been audited, but she could imagine how scary it was, from all the times stern-faced enforcers from collection agencies had come knocking at their door when she'd lived with her mom. Usually, it had been her fending them off while her mom ducked them. "I'm sorry."

"Not as sorry as I'll be if it turns out I owe them money. The sooner you get started, the better."

"I can start right away if it's okay to bring my dog in. I don't like leaving him in the car."

The lines of tension in Gertie's face eased, and she broke out in a smile. "Bless you. And yes, of course, your dog is welcome if he's well behaved."

"He is." Usually.

"I remember him. A mixed breed, if I'm not mistaken. Like my Charlie."

"Charlie?"

"My dog. He went over the rainbow bridge last year. It was his time—he was fifteen—but nothing prepares you. My friends are urging me to get another dog, but none could replace my Charlie. Maybe in time . . ."

Kyra returned to her car. When she opened the door, Ranger sprang out, shook himself, and looked up at her as if to say, *What took you so long?* She'd been gone for less than five minutes. "Missed me, did you?" she said to him. He responded by forgetting his manners and jumping up on her, tail wagging.

From the trunk of her car, she grabbed the tote that held her valuables, those she hadn't sold—her laptop, the few bits of jewelry she owned that weren't worth much, and remaining cash—which she took with her everywhere she went, for security reasons. A child could bust the flimsy lock on the door to her cabin at the Pine Ridge. They were ushered inside, and Gertie led the way down a short hallway to a large, formal parlor with an ornate marble fireplace and crown molding that had been converted to a home office. In the center opposite the fireplace was a moss-green velvet sofa flanked by a pair of chintz easy chairs, and a coffee table. To the right was a grouping of office furniture—a drafting table, computer desk, and a row of filing cabinets. To the left stood a round table with six chairs and a whiteboard.

"Can I get you some coffee or tea?" Gertie offered.

"No, thanks, but I'd love a glass of water, and some for my dog, if you don't mind."

"You got it."

Gertie left the room, and while she was gone, Kyra checked out the sketches pinned to the corkboard that covered one wall. Portraits of men and women—mostly men—dozens of them arranged in rows, rendered in pencil. They were simple, rudimentary, some might say, compared with the portraits Kyra had drawn, with minimal details and shading and an absence of facial expression.

"Those are suspects in criminal cases I've assisted with."

Kyra turned to find Gertie crossing the room, carrying a glass of water in one hand and a dog bowl in the other. She handed Kyra the glass and placed the bowl, filled with water, on the rug in front of Ranger, who drank from it. Kyra sipped her water and went back to studying the sketches.

"Were any of them caught?" she asked.

"Let's just say they don't call me Gertie Nail 'Em for nothing." She winked, her green eyes sparkling behind her candy-apple-red glasses. "First impression?" She motioned toward the rows of sketches.

"They're . . . skillful."

"Hogwash. They're crap. Artistically speaking, anyway. But artistry tends to get in the way with forensic art."

"Why is that?"

"The goal is to develop a likeness of the suspect, not draw something like you might see in an art gallery. Accuracy before artistry. And I must be doing something right, because in eighty percent of the criminal cases I've assisted with, the sketch I drew of the suspect resulted in an arrest."

"Impressive. So you weren't exaggerating when you said you draw lines to stop crimes."

"It goes beyond catching criminals. A positive ID of a suspect can mean the difference between a guilty or an innocent verdict in the cases that go to court. It's usually not like you see on TV, with a murder weapon surfacing at the zero hour or an eyewitness pointing a finger at the defendant from the witness stand. Sometimes it comes down to the police sketch, which is why accuracy is key."

"How accurate can it be if you've never laid eyes on the subject?"

"That's where it gets tricky. You're relying on someone else's memories in developing a sketch of a suspect, often someone who's traumatized. First, you need to gain their trust. If they don't trust you, they tend to become rattled or uncooperative. Either way, they won't be much use to you."

"It can be hard to trust when you don't know who you can trust." Gazing at a sketch of a suspect, Kyra saw a different face in her mind's eye—handsome, with the eyes of a gray wolf. She shuddered. When she brought her gaze back to Gertie, the older woman was regarding her curiously.

"Yes," she agreed. "Which is why I tread gently when I'm interviewing someone, especially someone who's experienced a recent trauma." Kyra was relieved when she changed the subject. "I understand you're an artist. Maybe you'd be interested in taking my course. Twice a year, in the spring and fall, I teach a three-week course in forensic art. This year's fall course starts next week."

Intrigued, Kyra asked, "What would it involve?"

"Classes are held Mondays through Fridays from one to three. It's never more than a handful of students. I limit enrollment to keep the classes interactive. I still have a couple slots open, if you're interested."

"What are the chances of it leading to a job? Assuming I'm any good at it."

"Some of it depends on where you live and if you're willing to travel to take assignments in other places. There are only so many jurisdictions in this country that employ forensic artists. But a number of my former students have found jobs in the field, and some are quite successful. Speaking for myself, I have more work than I can handle."

"Really? I never would've imagined Gold Creek was a hotbed of crime."

"It's not, but our local sheriff's department secures all of Washburn County, which covers thousands of acres and includes other towns, townships, and one fairly populous city. Many of the calls they respond to are in Pine City. I've also assisted with criminal cases in other jurisdictions on occasion, sometimes across state lines. And in one case, across an international border, when I was hired by the Royal Canadian Mounted Police. As an independent contractor, I charge by the hour, so it can provide a good living."

"It must if you can afford to live in a house like this one."

Gertie laughed. "Not that good. This house belonged to my husband's parents before he inherited it. We just pay the cost of the upkeep, which is never-ending with these white elephants. But our combined incomes allow us to live comfortably and go on trips. If we ever get around to taking one. We've been talking about going on a cruise since our youngest was in college, and she's a wife and mom now, which'll tell you how long it's been. Maybe after Larry retires . . ."

"What about you? Do you have any plans to retire?"

"No, but lately I've been thinking it's time I slowed down. First, I'd need to find someone who can take on some of my workload."

"You don't know of anyone?"

"No one local. But I always have an eye out for talent. Who knows? I might find it among this fall's crop of students. It could even be you." She gave Kyra an encouraging pat on the back.

The more Kyra thought about it, the more excited she became. Forensic art would be the ideal career for her, one for which she was uniquely suited. She had training as an artist and could relate to people who'd been traumatized, as she'd been. And if she could earn enough to support herself, sharing Gertie's workload, it would both banish the wolf at her door and allow her to utilize her existing skill set.

"How much for the course?" she asked.

"Five hundred dollars."

The stated sum acted as a pinprick bursting her bubble. It might as well have been $5,000. Kyra didn't have that kind of money to spend on a course, even one that might lead to future employment. The operative word being "might." Still, she hated to pass up what could potentially be the opportunity of a lifetime.

"I'm not sure I'd have time now that I'm working two jobs," she said with regret.

"You can make your own hours working for me, if that helps any. My date with the devil—excuse me, the IRS auditor—isn't until the middle of next month, which gives us some wiggle room."

"To be honest, money is an issue, too," she admitted. "I just relocated to Gold Creek, and until I find permanent work, I need to stick to my budget."

"I hear you," said Gertie with a sympathetic grimace. "I was your typical starving artist before I stumbled into forensic art. According to my teachers in school, I was a budding Picasso. But in the real world,

I was just another artist trying to make a buck. The market for a pretty picture to hang on someone's wall is limited, I discovered."

Her words struck a chord with Kyra. She might have been describing Kyra's own experience as an artist.

"Crime, on the other hand"—Gertie reached to smooth a bent corner on one of her sketches, that of a beady-eyed, scruffy-cheeked bad guy from central casting, with her thumb—"pays. In my profession, at least. It's a daily occurrence, and there's no shortage of criminals, which means there's usually enough assignments from local law enforcement in any given year to employ two forensic artists."

"It's something to consider." Kyra was tempted. Her visit to the local sheriff's office with Frannie had given her a fresh outlook on law enforcement after her bad experience with the RPD. But working in law enforcement would entail a certain amount of risk. Rory might get wind of it through his connections.

"Tell you what," Gertie said. "I'll waive the fee for the course in exchange for you whipping my books into shape in time for my audit. You'd be doing me a huge favor, actually. Otherwise, I could be forfeiting more in back taxes than any money I earn from teaching."

"I'm happy to do the work, but since you're paying me, I can't see how it's a favor."

"That's because you, being a millennial, are used to records being stored digitally, whereas mine—fair warning—are mostly paper receipts and invoices stuffed into shoeboxes, in no particular order. I'm a dinosaur. So you see, you really would be getting me out of a bind."

Kyra considered it. She'd vowed to never again accept charity after the free school lunches and meals at soup kitchens she'd eaten, and the winter coats from coat drives she'd worn, but what Gertie was proposing wasn't charity. They'd be helping each other. As for her working in law enforcement, it might be weeks, or even months, before she was qualified to do so. Enough time for an abuser to have moved on to his next victim. She didn't know if that would be the case with Rory, but she knew if she allowed her fears to dictate her every move, she would never be free of him.

"It's a deal," she said.

◆　◆　◆

Gertie produced a stack of ledgers and boxes filled with receipts, and got Kyra settled in at the desk in her home office. After Gertie left the room, Kyra got to work, while Ranger found a sunny spot by the bay window to curl up in. It wasn't as bad as it had looked at first glance; the records from before Gertie's previous bookkeeper retired were in good shape. It was the subsequent two years' worth of spotty records and jumbled receipts that presented a challenge. But she soon developed a system. She created an Excel spreadsheet on the desktop computer, into which she entered columns of numbers, and organized the receipts into piles, according to dates and whether they were for tax-deductible expenses. Her job at Suzy's salon, however pleasant the environment, wasn't intellectually stimulating. It felt good to exercise her brain. She'd always been good with numbers, whether it was because her right brain was as developed as her left brain, as one of her teachers in school had suggested, or because she had to be in order to survive. Her mother's habit of shoving bills into drawers and forgetting about them—until a creditor called or came knocking, their utilities were shut off, and she was served a notice of eviction, usually in that order—had forced Kyra to grow up early. She'd begun managing her mom's finances around the time she'd learned to do long division when she was in fifth grade. By the time she'd left home to go to college, she'd become the main bread-winner as well, having worked after-school and summer jobs from the age of fourteen, babysitting and dog-walking, and later busing tables and washing dishes in restaurants.

When Kyra looked up again, the shadows of late afternoon stretched across the parquet floor. Time to call it a day. The sun was setting, the sky streaked with gold and crimson above the horizon, as she drove back to her motel with Ranger. She hadn't eaten a proper meal all day, and her stomach was growling. When she spotted the neon sign of the roadside tavern up ahead, which she'd passed on previous trips to and from town, she impulsively pulled into its parking lot. The Redbird Tavern looked like it catered mainly to the drinking crowd, but she could probably get a decent meal there. Her mouth watered at the prospect of a juicy burger and fries.

"Just this once," she said to Ranger, although he seemed to have no objection to her splurge if it meant him getting fed, too. "We earned it today." Tomorrow she'd go back to pinching pennies.

She climbed out of her car, and Ranger bounded out the driver's side after her. She grabbed her tote and headed for the entrance. She stepped into the dimly lit interior, which smelled of stale beer and ciga-rette smoke from the days before smoking was banned. A bar stretched along one end, with booths lining three of its four walls and tables in the center. The dozen or so patrons, blue-collar workers stopping on their way home from work from the way they were dressed, sat drinking beers at the bar, some watching the football game in progress on the flat-screen above it. Kyra took a seat at one of the two-tops, and Ranger settled at her feet. The male bartender, who looked to be in his thirties, short and bandy-legged with a shaved head, came over to take her order. He cast a disinterested glance at Ranger. If dogs weren't allowed, he didn't comment on it.

"Two burgers to go, one plain, just the meat and bun, and the other with fries and all the fixings," she ordered. "Oh, and what's the password for your Wi-Fi?" The place had Wi-Fi, according to the sign by the entrance.

He gave her the password, and after he left, she logged on to the network on her laptop, killing time checking her notifications while she waited for her food. She'd set Google Alerts to notify her of any men-tions of either Krystal Stanhope or Rory Stanhope online, in the hope that it would provide advance warning of any search being conducted for her, whether physical or virtual. So far, there had been nothing worrisome.

At one point she looked up and saw someone enter through the door to the parking lot. A tall man, built like a lumberjack and dressed like one, in jeans and a checked flannel shirt, and work boots. She guessed him to be in his midthirties, He had thick reddish-brown hair that grew in a dozen different directions and a neatly trimmed beard. He resembled the bearded figure of the Brawny paper-towel logo. *An off-duty cop?* She wondered when he paused inside the entrance to do a visual sweep. His gaze landed on her briefly, causing her to grow uneasy—Had he recognized her?—before moving past her.

She was distracted by a notification popping up on her laptop screen. She clicked on it, and saw it was a video of a news broadcast from the local NBC affiliate in Rochester. She put her earbuds in, hit "Play," and was jolted by a shock of recognition when a familiar figure appeared on the screen. Rory. A blond female reporter was interviewing him on the steps of the Monroe County courthouse in connection with a criminal trial he was prosecuting, involving the murder of a prominent citizen. Kyra was as spooked by the sight of him, and by the sound of his voice, as if he'd just walked into the bar.

"Excuse me, miss, is this seat taken?"

She started at the voice coming from beside her. She pulled out her earbuds and turned her head to see a scrawny man with dirty-blond hair pulled back in a scraggly ponytail standing beside the vacant chair at her table. Elk River Gun Club, it said on the front of his T-shirt. A pentagram was tattooed on the hand resting on the back of the chair. In his other hand he held an open beer bottle.

"I'm expecting someone," she told him.

He ignored her, dropping into the vacant chair. "Who, your boyfriend?" She caught a whiff of beer on his breath. The one he was drinking apparently wasn't his first of the evening. "How about I hold his place for him till he gets here? Pretty lady like you shouldn't be drinking alone."

She glared at him. "I'm not drinking, and as I said, I'm expecting someone."

"What's his name? Maybe I know him."

"I don't think so. Now, will you please leave, or do I have to call management?"

He gave a coarse chuckle. "The management? Lady, this ain't exactly the Ritz, in case you hadn't noticed."

She heard a low growl, and when she glanced down, saw Ranger standing on all fours with his hackles up, like he did when he sensed a threat. He fixed their uninvited tablemate with a hard gaze. *Good boy.* She placed a hand on his head. "I should warn you, my dog is trained to attack on command."

"That so?" He appeared unconcerned. "Name's Jed. What's yours?"

He extended his arm to give her a fist bump, and she recoiled as if from a thrown punch, reacting as automatically as a soldier fresh from a battlefield hitting the floor at the sound of an engine backfiring.

His expression soured. "Jesus, lady. What's your problem? I was just trying to be nice."

"I—" she started to say, then broke off. She didn't owe him an explanation.

"What, you think you're too good for me?"

Before she could respond, she heard another voice say, low and threatening, "Dude, you hard of hearing or something? The lady asked you to leave." She registered the masculine hand, sprinkled with red-gold hairs, clamped over the shoulder of her harasser before her gaze traveled up and up, taking in the broad torso and bearded face of the man she'd noticed earlier. *Scrawny Man, meet Brawny Man.*

Scrawny Man, with a violent twist of his body, broke free from the other man's grip and leaped to his feet. The sneer on his face withered as he took in the sheer size of his opponent, whom he seemed to recognize. "You," he said. He glared at him and then sloped off, muttering, "Whatever. I can do better."

"Hope I'm not interrupting anything," said Brawny Man with a dry twist of his lips.

She watched as Scrawny Man joined two other equally disreputable-looking men at the bar before bringing her gaze back to Brawny Man. "Never saw him before in my life."

"Best steer clear of him. Jed's bad news."

Duh. Tell me something I don't already know. "He didn't seem like he was a fan of yours, either."

"That's because I arrested him once."

"You're a cop?"

"I was. Coop Langston." He extended his arm, and she automatically shook his hand. As she did, a jolt of attraction shot up her arm and spread through the rest of her. *Whoa. Where did that come from?* She couldn't remember the last time she'd been physically attracted to a man.

She didn't give him her name. Instead, she asked, "What did you arrest him for?"

"Domestic battery. His wife pressed charges."

Kyra shuddered. She was still shaken from the one-two punch of watching the video of Rory immediately followed by her encounter with Scrawny Man. Now she was learning that the guy who'd been hitting on her was a wife beater. Why her? Could he smell it on her, or was the word "victim" written on her forehead in invisible ink that only would-be perpetrators could read?

Then there was Coop Langston, whom she had no reason to trust, although she wasn't getting any danger vibes from him. He was an ex-cop, and the one time she'd trusted a cop to do right by her, he'd betrayed her trust. For all she knew, Coop's intentions were no more honorable than those of the creep he'd rescued her from.

"Figures," she muttered.

"That's a good-looking dog you've got there. What's his name?" he asked, his gaze dropping to Ranger. Who didn't seem bothered by the bearded stranger.

"Ranger."

Coop bent to greet him. "Hey, Ranger. You don't look so ferocious to me."

Ranger confirmed this by licking his extended hand after giving it an exploratory sniff. Coop scratched him behind his ears, and he promptly rolled over onto his back. Ranger seemed to recognize him as the alpha male of the two, which annoyed Kyra, though she couldn't have said why.

"Mind if I sit down?" he asked, straightening after he'd given her dog a good belly rubbing. "I promise I'm not hitting on you," he added as if he'd read her mind.

"Neither was the last guy, according to him."

"The difference is, I'm with someone."

"You don't want to keep her waiting, then."

"He, actually. My brother." He pointed toward a man at the bar who was talking with the man seated next to him. Casually dressed and in his thirties, with the same thick red-brown hair as Coop. "He ran into an old friend he hasn't seen in years, so I thought I'd keep you company while they catch up. In case Jed gets any more big ideas. But if you want me to leave, just say the word."

"Suit yourself," she said with a shrug.

He sat down. "Can I buy you a drink?"

"Thanks, but I'm not staying. I'm just waiting on my order."

As he sat down across from her, his huge frame seemed to invade her personal space, even with the table acting as a barrier between them. His shoulders were as broad as crossbeams, his biceps the size of Easter hams. He signaled to the bartender, who came over to take his order.

"Hey, Doug. How's it going?" he greeted him, and the two men knocked knuckles. "How's Cat? She must be about ready to pop."

Doug grinned. "Any day now. We can't wait to meet Savannah. Or Serena. We haven't decided on a name yet."

"You have a preference?"

"I don't know, man. I don't got a say."

"Happy wife, happy life?"

"More like the pregnant lady gets whatever she wants. What about you, Coop? When are you gonna settle down and start making babies?"

"I was married once, remember? Marriage isn't for everyone."

"Maybe you just haven't met the right woman yet." Doug the bartender cut a sideways glance at Kyra, to her horror. She was relieved when Coop ignored the comment. The bartender took the hint and said, "What can I get you?"

"The usual."

The bartender left and returned shortly with a glass of something fizzy poured over ice and topped with a wedge a lime. He placed it in front of Coop. "Here you go. Gin and tonic minus the gin."

Kyra studied Coop's face as he sipped his drink. He wasn't handsome in the traditional sense, but he had a certain rugged appeal. His nose looked to have been broken at some point earlier in his life. His facial hair had more red in it than the hair on his head. His eyes were the warm brown of sun tea brewed on a back porch.

"So, what brings you to Gold Creek?" he asked.

Startled by his question, she asked, "What makes you think I'm from out of town?"

"Saw you pull in earlier while I was taking a call outside. Noticed the New York plates on your car."

Damn. She mentally kicked herself for forgetting to swap her New York plates for California plates after she crossed the state line. With any luck, she would find a used set at a junkyard where they wouldn't ask questions. Then another, more troubling thought occurred to her. "Were you following me?" He might work for Rory, if Rory had hired him to track her down.

His gaze sharpened. "Why? Do you have reason to believe you're being followed?"

"No," she lied.

He studied her with his cop's eyes, as if trying to decide whether to believe her. "If you suspect you're being targeted, you need to report it. I can also arrange for someone at the sheriff's department to escort you home."

"That won't be necessary," she replied stiffly. The last thing she wanted was a police escort.

He kept his gaze leveled at her until it became clear she wasn't going to offer any further information, and then he rose, picking up his drink. "Okay, then. If you change your mind, I'll be sitting over there." He gestured toward his brother, who sat alone now at the bar, watching them with an amused expression that suggested Kyra hadn't misread Coop's intentions toward her. "Pleased to make your acquaintance, Ranger." He gave her dog a last pat on the head before saying to Kyra, "Nice chatting with you. Enjoy the rest of your evening."

Kyra felt a pang of misgiving, regretting her rudeness. Maybe he really was a nice guy; Ranger seemed to think so. And if he'd hoped to get lucky by coming to her rescue, could she blame him? She was, after all, a woman alone in a bar. She imagined most women he approached were only too happy to give him their phone number or go home with him. Men like him didn't usually have to work at it. It wasn't his fault that she wasn't like most other women.

"Look. I'm sorry if I—"

She was interrupted by a voice calling, "Hey, asshole." She turned to see that it was Jed who'd spoken. He was still seated at the bar with his friends, emboldened by their presence, apparently, as he scowled at Coop. "Your girlfriend know you're a killer? Does she know you shot an unarmed man?"

6

Kyra watched the color drain from Coop's face. "Is it true? What he said?" She jerked her chin in the direction of Jed.

Coop didn't deny it. He just stood there looking at her, his jaw tight.

She gave a humorless laugh and slowly shook her head. "Of course. I should have known." The mere fact that she'd been attracted to him ought to have been a red flag. The last man who'd had a similar effect on her, and whom she'd made the mistake of marrying, had turned out to be a monster. Was she subconsciously drawn to men like the smooth talkers her mom used to bring home after nights out at bars? Men who had eventually revealed their true colors as users or abusers, or both. Maybe she'd been warped by what she'd witnessed when she was growing up.

"It's not what you think," he said tightly.

"What I *think* is that you pretended to come to my rescue when you're as bad as he is." She cut a glance at Jed, who seemed to be enjoying the show along with his friends and the other people at the bar who'd turned around to watch, a smirk on his lips. "Isn't that how men like you snare their unsuspecting victims? I understand Ted Bundy was popular with the ladies."

Okay, so maybe that was going too far, she thought. The aforementioned killing might have been accidental, or there might have been extenuating circumstances. The torment she saw reflected in his eyes suggested the killing had been anything but cold-blooded. But she was too rattled by the events of that evening, and by Coop's comment about her New York plates, to react in a rational manner.

She stuffed her laptop into her tote, then stood. Her food arrived at that moment, boxed to go, and she snatched it up along with her tote. "Come, Ranger," she ordered, and headed for the door with her dog, with the haste of someone exiting a burning building. Regardless of whether Coop meant her harm, he was still a danger, with his high-voltage handshake and smoking body clad in denim.

The next day, she was at work at Suzy's salon when Jo unexpectedly blew in through the door, carrying a toddler on one hip and leading a little girl of around five by the hand. The toddler had her mother's strawberry-blond hair, the older girl a mop of dark curls. "Can I leave the girls with you for a bit?" she asked Suzy, sounding frantic. "I wouldn't ask if it wasn't an emergency."

"What happened? Are you okay?" Suzy was instantly alarmed.

"I'm fine. It's Sean. He passed out at work and was taken to the ER. I just got off the phone with his business partner. I need to be with him." Only then did she seem to notice that Suzy and Jasmine were both with customers. "Oh, but I can see you're busy. I'm sorry, I shouldn't have asked."

"I'll take them," Kyra volunteered before Suzy could respond.

A look of relief washed over Jo's face. "You're sure it's no trouble?"

"Not at all, if it's okay with the boss." She paused as she was sweeping hair clippings into a pile with the broom in her hand, looking to Suzy.

"You don't even have to ask," said Suzy as she brushed dye over a piece of hair belonging to her customer before wrapping it in a square of foil. "Why don't you take them to the park? It's a nice day, and you can turn them loose in the playground."

"You guys . . ." Jo looked like she was about to cry.

"Any idea why Sean passed out? Is he sick?" asked Jasmine.

"Not that I know of. He's been a little off lately, and he's been getting these headaches, but he didn't think it was serious."

"Go," said Suzy with a shooing motion. "Call as soon as you have news."

Jo brought the girls over to meet Kyra. "Jess, Emma, this is my friend Kyra. You're gonna stay with her while Mommy takes care of Daddy." The older girl hung back, seeming shy, while the younger one didn't object when she was transferred from her mother's hip to Kyra's.

"Hi, Emma. Aren't you a cutie?" Kyra said to the toddler, whose big blue eyes regarded her curiously before she turned her attention to Ranger, who'd wandered over to check out their small visitors.

"Doggie!" She squealed with delight and reached toward him. Ranger grinned up at her, tail wagging.

"I want to go with you, Mommy," whined Jess.

"I know, sweetie, but I can't take care of you and Daddy at the same time. I won't be long," Jo assured her.

Jess's eyes filled behind the purple-framed glasses she wore. Her lower lip wobbled.

Kyra, seeing the need for quick intervention, lowered Emma onto the floor, where she could reach Ranger to pet him, and squatted down so she was eye level with the older girl. "Hi, Jess. I'm very glad to meet you. I'd love to take you and your sister to the park to play if that'd be okay with you. Would you like that?" The girl stared at her gravely before giving a slow, shy nod. Kyra beamed at her. "Good choice. Because it's too nice a day to be indoors. Do you like dogs? My dog loves to play fetch. When we get to the park, do you think you could find a stick for him to fetch?" The girl nodded again. "Perfect. Did you know if you play with a dog, he'll be your friend for life?"

"Mine, too!" crowed the little one.

"Yes," Kyra agreed. "And if it's okay with your mommy, we can stop for ice cream on the way as a special treat. How does that sound?"

The older girl blinked back her tears, and a smile edged its way onto her face, melting Kyra's heart. She, too, had been shy as a child and could relate. "Mommy, can me and Em have ice cream?" Jess asked.

"May I," Jo corrected. "And yes, you may. Thanks for doing this," she told Kyra. "And thanks for . . ." She nodded toward Jess, who was petting Ranger along with her sister. "You won't have any problems with Emma—she's not the least bit shy, as you can see—except possibly a smelly diaper change." She handed Kyra the diaper bag slung over her shoulder with a look of apology.

"I think I can handle a poopy diaper," Kyra said. "Go be with your husband, and don't worry about the girls. I've got this."

Jo embraced her—with a short, fierce hug of gratitude—then bent to hug each of her daughters. "Girls, you be good. Mommy will be back as soon as she can. I love you both." With that, she hurried off.

"You're earning your Girl Scout merit badge today!" Suzy called to Kyra as she headed to the door with Ranger and the girls a minute later.

"I want to play, too! Can I come?" Jasmine mock-whined.

Kyra treated each of the girls to a baby cone at the Gold Nugget Ice Cream Parlor, and they set off for the park down the street. The sun was shining, not a cloud in the sky, and the air was pleasantly cool. As soon as they got to the playground in the park, Emma toddled over to the swings, demanding to be pushed, while Jess made a beeline for the slide, accompanied by Ranger.

Pushing Emma on her swing while keeping an eye on Jess, Kyra wondered what had possessed her to volunteer to care for two little kids. She used to babysit when she was a teenager but hadn't spent much time around little kids since then. Nor did she have any of her own. Even when she was a child, she hadn't played much with other children. She and her mom hadn't lived in any one place long enough for her to get to know the other kids in the neighborhood well, and she'd made few friends at the schools she'd attended. She'd planned to have a child with Rory until he'd shown his dark side. How could she have brought a child into that toxic situation? If she needed further proof that she'd made the right decision, she'd received it when Rory, in a fit of rage after discovering she'd secretly been using birth control while they'd been supposedly trying for a baby, beat her to within an inch of her life.

Listening to Emma's peals of delight with each push that sent her sailing higher into the air, while watching Jess go up and down the slide, Kyra felt a tug of yearning. It was sad to think that she might never be a mom. Never experience moments like this one with a son or daughter of her own. Choosing to become a single parent wasn't an option. Having been raised by a single mom who'd done a lousy job of it, she couldn't see herself going that route. If she ever had a child, they would have two parents, and given that she'd vowed never to let another man into her heart, what were the odds?

She wondered idly what her mom was up to. They hadn't spoken since Kyra had called from the road to inform her that she'd left Rory. Typical of Mom, she'd urged Kyra to reconsider. She'd asked questions like *Has it really been so bad?* and *Why not try couples counseling instead?* That had set Kyra's teeth on edge. At the time, Mom had been living in Reno, sleeping with her married boss from the casino where she worked. Knowing her, she'd moved on to "greener pastures" since then, which in her case meant a new job and a new boyfriend in another town. Kyra supposed she ought to check in with her, let her know she was all right. Mom didn't have her new number—Kyra didn't trust her not to leak it to Rory—so she had no way of reaching her except via email.

I'll get around to it eventually.

Kyra was distracted from her thoughts when Emma commanded, "Down."

She unbuckled and lifted Emma from her kiddie seat, and then followed as she toddled off to join her sister. Ranger ran in circles around the girls while they played, herding them as his ancestors had with sheep. To the casual observer, they might have appeared to be a family. Kyra briefly allowed herself to imagine she was the mom of these two adorable children, and their dad was . . .

Coop Langston? She was jerked from her reverie by the image of the big blue-jeaned cop whom she'd met last night at the Redbird Tavern and privately dubbed Brawny Man. What was *he* doing in her fantasy? Maybe it was because she hadn't been able to stop thinking about him, or maybe it was because she recalled the bartender asking him when he was going to settle down and start a family. Whichever, Kyra didn't want him invading her thoughts, nor did she expect to cross paths with him again.

After the girls tired of playing on the slide, Kyra organized a hunt for a stick the right size to play fetch with Ranger. Jess immediately took charge, bossing around her little sister as she examined and rejected each of Emma's finds until she found what she deemed to be the perfect stick. Ranger, who was always up for a game of fetch, kept the girls entertained chasing after the stick again and again until it was time for them to go, after Suzy had texted to let Kyra know Jo was en route.

On the way back to the salon after a diaper change, they stopped briefly at Mother Lode Mercantile, where Kyra bought each of the girls an inexpensive souvenir they'd picked out. Jess selected a piece of rose quartz for her rock collection, and Emma a rubber eraser in the shape of a horse.

Jo showed up with her husband minutes after Kyra returned with Ranger and the girls. A tall man in gray cords and a navy sweater, with curly dark hair and eyes the color of melted chocolate like his eldest's, Jo's husband was so attentive to his wife and daughters, you'd never know he'd just come from the ER if not for the bandage on his forehead. He held the door open for Jo as they entered and then scooped his daughters into his arms when they came running to him, kissing them each.

"Are you okay?" Suzy asked him. "You gave us quite a scare."

"I'm fine," he claimed.

"Really. Then what's with the bandage?"

"This?" He fingered the bandage on his forehead as if he'd forgotten it was there. "It's nothing. Just a little bump where I hit my head when I fell." He lowered the girls back onto their feet and straightened.

"It wasn't 'nothing,'" Jo said, frowning. "You passed out!"

"Do you know what caused it?" asked Jasmine.

"Low blood sugar, or possibly anemia, according to the ER doc," Sean said. "We'll know more when I get the results from the blood work. In the meantime, I made an appointment with my internist, and I imagine she'll want to run more tests. Personally, I think it was a combination of stress and sleep deprivation." He explained that he and his business partner had been working around the clock, getting ready to launch their new app. He turned toward Kyra as she approached. "You must be Kyra. Hi, I'm Sean," he said, smiling warmly at her as they shook hands after Jo had relieved her of the diaper bag she carried. "Thanks for taking such good care of the munchkins."

"It was my pleasure," Kyra told him. "Your girls are precious, and we had fun playing at the park. Anytime you need someone to watch them in a pinch, I'd be happy to do it if I don't have other plans."

"Girls, can you say thank you to Miss Kyra?" Jo prompted.

"Thank you, Miss Kyra," said Jess.

"Fank you, Kee-ya," Emma lisped.

It warmed Kyra's heart when they each hugged her goodbye. Emma threw her arms around Ranger next and whispered something in his ear, which Kyra could have sworn he understood from the way he pricked his ears and wagged his tail.

"Nice meeting you, Kyra. And thanks again," Sean called as they were leaving.

Watching them go, Sean holding Emma cradled in one arm, Jo holding Jess by the hand, with her other hand wrapped around Sean's, Kyra felt another tug. They were a beautiful family. A beautiful couple. College sweethearts who'd gone on to marry and were still madly in love, it was plain to see.

Kyra remembered when she'd felt that way about Rory. He'd seemed perfect for her, but it had been an illusion. Would she ever know true love? First, she'd have to learn to trust again, an unlikely prospect, given that she'd sooner walk over a bed of live coals than risk getting burned by another man.

"What a week, and it's only Tuesday!" exclaimed Suzy later when she and Kyra were in her office. Kyra had stayed after work to eat lunch with her, at Suzy's invitation—she'd ordered takeout from Cowboy Coffee. Jasmine had gone out, so it was just the two of them. They sat on either side of Suzy's desk, Ranger at Kyra's feet, poised to catch any scraps that might fall in his direction. "I don't know when we've been busier, thanks to you and your magic fingers. I should rename this place the Shear Delight Salon and Spa." She speared a lettuce leaf in her salad with her plastic fork.

Kyra smiled. "Then you'd have to offer a full menu of spa treatments, and my 'magic fingers' don't extend to Swedish massages and facials." She fed a piece of cheese from her turkey-and-Swiss sandwich to Ranger before she took a bite.

"You do enough. I just hope the work isn't too boring for someone of your gifts."

"Not at all. If there's one thing I can say about working here, it's that it's never boring." The Shear Delight Salon, Kyra had discovered, was the "women's room" of Gold Creek, where gossip and confidences were freely exchanged. Today, one of the customers, a fortyish aerobics instructor named Renee, had confided to Kyra, while Kyra had been shampooing her hair, that she had a married lover. Kyra had been shocked, not by the admission—her mom had had more than one married lover that she knew of, and Kyra had known other women, fellow artists, who weren't discriminating in who they slept with—but by Renee's naive belief that her lover would eventually leave his wife for her.

"Good to know. But I'm well aware it's only a matter of time before you move on to a better job. Which I'm all for, though I'll hate to lose you. Speaking of which, how's the job search going?"

"Actually, there's been a development on that front. Not a job, per se, but it might lead to one."

"Do tell." Suzy leaned forward eagerly. She wore a gold sweater dress with a wide leather belt, in which she looked camera-ready, with her blond hair falling in soft waves around her flawlessly made-up face.

"I enrolled in Gertie's fall class. She's planning to slow down when she can find someone worthy to share her workload with. I figured I'd give it a shot. If I'm any good, she might pick me."

"Wow. That would be amazing."

"It's a long shot." Gertie might pick someone else.

"You can draw. It's just a matter of learning how to draw in a different style."

"There's more to it than that. It also involves people skills."

"Which you have."

"I do?" Kyra had never thought of herself as someone with people skills, despite having worked as a teacher. It had been one thing to teach a subject she was passionate about or help her students realize their potential. It was another to make small talk at parties, which she'd always found mildly excruciating.

"You're a good listener, and you don't judge."

Because I know what it's like to be judged. "I may have some stiff competition."

"Maybe, but my money's on you," Suzy said with a wink. "And if Gertie does pick you, she'll eventually retire, and you'll become her successor."

Kyra took another bite of her sandwich, contemplating her future as she chewed. She was buzzing with excitement, and reminded herself she had a long way to go before she could even be considered for the job. She changed the subject. "What about you? Do you think you'll ever retire?"

"Ha! Maybe in fifty years or so, if I live that long. And I'll thank you not to do the math." Suzy plucked an olive from her salad and popped it into her mouth. "You're only as old as you feel."

"Well, you don't look a day over forty."

Suzy grinned and made a swirling motion with her hand that encompassed her face as she said, "Trust me, this doesn't come naturally. It takes work. And if I'd stayed married to Wayne, I'd look twice my age."

"How long were you married?"

"Fifteen years. We were high school sweethearts, and then I was a teen bride after I got knocked up."

"Did you divorce him because of his drinking?" She recalled Suzy mentioning that her ex was an alcoholic.

"More like I woke up and smelled the coffee. I thought I was managing his drinking," she explained, "until I started going to Al-Anon meetings and learned there's a name for people like me: enabler. I was part of the problem, you see. I divorced him soon after. Best decision I ever made, apart from the fact that my son blamed me for the divorce and still does." Her expression clouded over.

"How old were your kids when you got divorced?"

"Adam was nine, and Christina was fourteen. Adam idolized his dad, so he took it hard when Wayne moved out."

Kyra felt bad for Suzy; it seemed so unfair. She'd never met either of her kids, but she couldn't imagine Suzy being anything other than a loving mom. "What about your daughter?"

"She knows the score. Both my kids saw their dad drunk enough times to know he was no angel. But only Adam blames me for cruelly kicking his dad to the curb when he was at his lowest, the way he sees it. In hindsight, I probably should have told them that Wayne was also cheating on me."

"He cheated on you?"

"With more than one woman that I know of. But I didn't want to bad-mouth him to our kids, so I spared them that detail."

"Did he ever hit you? Your ex?"

Suzy regarded her thoughtfully, and Kyra worried Suzy had guessed she had a personal reason for asking. "No. Wayne's a drunk, but he's not a mean drunk. He tends to wax sentimental when he's been drinking. Most famously when he suggested we 'give it another go,' as he put it, while he was giving his toast at our daughter's wedding in front of her other guests. I was mortified. Christina was furious. And Wayne, as usual, was clueless." She rolled her eyes and gave a wry laugh.

"At least he's not bitter."

"No. I'll give him that. He knows it was his fault that we split up."

Suzy forked a piece of tuna from her salad and brought it to her mouth. "What was it with your ex? Booze, women, gambling, or all of the above?"

"None of those things, actually." Suzy seemed to be waiting for her to provide more details, but Kyra held back; it was too awful, and her own part in it too embarrassing. She said simply, "It was a toxic relationship." Which she had stayed in long after a stronger person would have left. She might still be with Rory if circumstances hadn't forced her to flee. Hot shame washed through her.

Suzy seemed to sense her discomfort and let her off the hook, saying, "Sore subject, huh? I didn't mean to pry. I tend to overshare, but that's just me. Really, some things are best kept in their box."

The problem is, they don't always stay in their box.

"You doing okay out at the Pine Ridge?" asked Frannie when they were washing up after supper on Friday.

"You mean the Bates Motel?" Kyra joked as she dried the pot Frannie had just washed.

"That old place is still in business?" Hannah walked in carrying dirty dishes from the table. "It was a fossileum when I was a kid, and it doesn't look to have been updated since then."

"It's not that bad," Kyra said. "Even if I expect to be stabbed every morning when I'm in the shower."

Hannah snickered, and she and Frannie exchanged an amused glance. Seeing them together in this relaxed setting, sharing a mother-daughter moment as Frannie scrubbed a pot at the sink and Hannah loaded the dishwasher, no one would have guessed Hannah suffered from a mental disorder, or that their lives had ever been disrupted by it.

Kyra was enjoying herself, and the evening had been a success. Frannie's cabin on Brambleberry Lake, an A-frame built of logs on a stone foundation, located roughly ten miles from town on the north shore of the lake, with both mountain and lake views, was rustic in style but had all the comforts of modern living. For dinner, Frannie had served homemade Moroccan lamb stew with couscous and roasted vegetables, and apple crumble for dessert. Kyra had eaten two helpings of the stew. A home-cooked meal was a treat after her steady diet of mostly packaged and fast food in the week prior. And this was her second one this week; she'd eaten dinner at Marisol's on Wednesday, where they'd feasted on the traditional Filipino dishes Marisol had prepared.

"Something tells me your fortunes are about to improve." Frannie tipped her a wink and handed her another pot to dry.

"Do you know something I don't, or do you have a crystal ball?"

"Neither, but when you told me you'd signed up for Gertie's course, I knew something good would come of it."

Kyra felt her stomach take a dip and regretted that second helping of stew. "What if I suck at it? Even if I don't, Gertie might pick someone else to partner with."

The course wasn't scheduled to begin until Monday of the following week, but she was already second-guessing her decision to sign up for it. Would her time be better spent searching for an existing job? She didn't share Frannie's confidence. Forensic art seemed more like sorcery than any art form she'd practiced. Even if it led to a job, it might be a case of being careful what you wish for if Rory's connections in the law enforcement community extended as far as the Washburn County Sheriff's Department. She felt a slither of unease at the thought.

You're getting ahead of yourself. If Gertie were to pick her, it could be months before she'd be qualified to work in the field. A lot could happen during that time. Rory could move on. Or he could drop dead.

"Think positive." Frannie reached over to give Kyra a pat on the shoulder.

"If you become a police sketch artist, would that make Ranger a police dog?" asked Hannah. Ranger, who was patrolling the kitchen in search of dropped crumbs to snarf up, trotted over to her at hearing his name. Hannah offered him a dirty bowl to lick before placing it in the dishwasher. He thanked her by licking her on the cheek, causing her to giggle as she pretended to push him away.

"I don't think it works that way, but I imagine he'd like that."

"I bet he'd be good at catching bad guys."

"You wouldn't know looking at him now," she said, smiling as she watched him give Hannah another sloppy kiss, "but I think you might be right. Hopefully, we'll both get the chance to prove ourselves."

"First we need to find you a place to live," said Frannie, moving on to more practical matters.

"I've been looking," said Kyra, "but the rentals I've seen advertised are more than I can afford."

"There might be ones that haven't been advertised yet. I'll ask around."

"Mom knows a ton of people," Hannah said.

And I'm lucky enough to be one of them. Where would she be without Frannie and the other Tattooed Ladies? Frannie had asked her to dinner with her and her friends when she'd been a stranger, new in town. Marisol had cooked her a meal. Jo had called that morning to invite her over for Sunday brunch, to thank her for babysitting her girls. Suzy had given her a job, and every day was a party at Suzy's salon. In the short time she'd known them, her new friends had adopted her. Despite her initial reservations, Kyra had come to trust them and rely on them.

"I can use all the help I can get," she said. "But don't go to any trouble. You've done enough already."

"Nothing anyone wouldn't do for a friend," Frannie said, handing her the last pot to dry. "Besides, it's no trouble. I'll make some calls. We can't have you getting stabbed in the shower, now, can we?"

7

"The pen may be mightier than the sword, but it's no match for the power of the pencil in the hand of a forensic artist." Gertie, standing at the head of the class in her uniform of high-waisted jeans, a Western-style shirt, and cowgirl boots, looked like a modern-day Annie Oakley minus her six-shooter.

There were four students in this year's fall course, not counting Ranger, who'd been permitted to attend: three women including Kyra, and one man, ranging in age from early twenties to midforties. They sat at the round table in Gertie's home office, their eyes on their instructor as she went on.

"But it takes more than a pencil to catch criminals. Because in this business we rely on others to do our job. By that, I mean witnesses and victims, who are generally unreliable. Some are unsure about what they saw, or they can't recall. Some make false claims, usually because they're protecting someone else. Some are just plain ornery. It's your job to calm any jitters, spot the falsehoods, and earn their trust so you can work together as a team in developing a sketch of the suspect."

"What if they didn't get a good look at the suspect?" asked Nate. A recent college grad, he resembled Buzz Lightyear with his blond crew cut and jock's physique. The two things he'd excelled in at school were sports and art, according to him. After a knee injury cost him his shot at pro ball, he'd decided to pursue a career in forensic art. He'd confessed to being a true-crime-show junkie.

"It happens," Gertie said. "But often when a witness claims they didn't get a good look at a suspect, or they have sketchy recall of a particular event, they saw or remember more than they know. Memories are like data on a hard drive. As everyone who's ever deleted a document or email in the mistaken belief they're getting rid of incriminating evidence knows, data can usually be retrieved."

Gertie turned and wrote something on the whiteboard behind her: *The way out is in.* "That's a quote from the Buddhist monk Thich Nhat Hanh. Make it your mantra. Your job as a forensic artist is to become the eyes of your witness by getting into their head and retrieving any buried memories they might have."

"What if it's someone who's traumatized?" asked Staci. "I was raped once when I was in college. When the police questioned me, I was in shock and probably not making much sense. I couldn't have described my rapist if my life depended on it." A twentysomething with spiky dyed-red hair and ear gauges, she published an e-zine, its target audience hard-core feminists like herself.

Kyra flashed on the one time she was raped, and not by a random attacker. She felt sick to her stomach, recalling it—the hands whose touch had once made her shudder with pleasure causing her to recoil in horror. It was its own circle of hell being raped by one's husband, she'd discovered.

"You were raped? Oh my God, how awful!" exclaimed Ashley. Kyra was startled, thinking Ashley had read her mind before realizing the comment was directed at Staci.

Ashley, a commercial artist before she became a stay-at-home mom, was looking to reenter the job market now that her kids were both in school. Short, with a round face framed by blond hair she wore chin length, she might seem like the average soccer mom if you didn't know she was pursuing a career in forensic art.

"I'm sorry that happened to you, Staci." Gertie regarded her with compassion, pausing a beat as if out of respect before she went on. "To answer your question, it's more common than not for victims of violent crimes to be traumatized, which can affect their recall of a particular event. They need to be handled with care. Always keep in mind there's a human being involved, not just a crime."

"The cop who interviewed me acted like he thought I was partly to blame because I'd been drinking that night," Staci said with disgust, tears glittering in her eyes. "It was like being raped all over again."

Kyra knew the feeling. When the RPD cop who'd responded to her 911 call failed to act on it after she'd pressed charges against Rory, she'd felt victimized twice over. Her heart went out to Staci.

"Sad to say, your experience isn't unique. Law officers in general have a lot to learn when it comes to handling victims like yourself with sensitivity," said Gertie with a rueful shake of her head. "I once interviewed a nineteen-year-old college student who'd been raped at knifepoint. By the time I got to her, after she'd been to the ER and the police had interviewed her, she'd all but shut down. I knew if I didn't get her to open up, we'd lose our one shot at getting her to identify the suspect."

"What did you do?" Kyra asked.

"I talked to her. Not about her rape but about other stuff. I asked about her family, her interests, what kind of music she liked. I brought her a blanket and a cup of tea when I noticed she was shivering. I was with her for over an hour, just two women chatting, before I felt she was ready to be interviewed. She not only cooperated but also was able to identify the suspect from the sketch I'd drawn."

"Did they catch the guy?" Staci asked with an intensity that matched her fierce gaze.

Gertie crossed the room to the corkboard on one wall where her sketches were displayed, each one paired with a mug shot. She pointed to a sketch of a white middle-aged man with a large nose and deep-set eyes. It was a close match to the corresponding mug shot. "You're looking at him. Lucky for us, a match was found in the system. He was a serial rapist with a long criminal record."

Nate pumped his fist. "Dude, you rock! Ms. Naylor, I mean," he corrected himself, blushing.

"Thank you, Nate." Gertie directed a dry smile at him. "Call me biased, but I do believe I have the best job in the world. Who else can boast that they catch bad guys with a pencil?"

Her words struck a chord with Kyra. But it wasn't just about catching bad guys, she thought. It was also about empowering victims by giving them a role and a voice in bringing their perpetrators to justice. Imagine if she could make a difference in the lives of others like herself who'd been victimized and felt powerless as a result! If she could help them, it might help her to move forward.

She reined in her excitement, reminding herself that it remained to be seen whether she had the makings of a forensic artist.

"Speaking of bad guys," Gertie continued, "some witnesses might seem more like suspects. Some even have criminal records. Addicts, prostitutes, drug dealers, registered sex offenders, you name it—I've seen them all. You need to check your judgment at the door and acknowledge their worth, even if their one good deed in a lifetime is coming forward as a witness. No one likes to be disrespected, whether they're a law-abiding citizen or a convicted felon. If you're looking down on them, they sense it. Then you're dealing with a witness who's unco-operative at best, hostile at worst."

"I don't know that I could look a sex offender in the eye," Ashley said. In her high-collared shirt, sitting up straight with her face pinched in disapproval, she resembled a prim schoolmarm. "I have *children*."

"In that case, you might want to rethink your career choice." Gertie leveled a cool look at her, which caused Ashley to blush and sink lower in her seat.

Kyra recalled the two men she'd encountered at the Redbird Tavern the other night. She didn't know which one was worse: the alleged wife beater who'd harassed her, or the accused killer who'd "rescued" her. Why did she always seem to attract the wrong kind of man? Was it some weakness of character they could spot, like a predator in the wild spots the weak or lame in a herd? And, much to her annoyance, the attraction had been mutual in the case of Coop Langston.

Gertie went on to discuss the different methods used in forensic art. She was one of the handful of working forensic artists who still sketched freehand. Most used a software program to create composite sketches digitally. In rural jurisdictions where law enforcement agencies lacked the funds to employ a forensic artist, the most commonly used method was Identi-Kit, a computer program developed by the FBI that didn't require highly specialized training. All the above methods were considered valid. Gertie had stuck with hers because, as she put it, "If it ain't broke, don't fix it." She ended the day's session by conducting a mock interview with Staci playing the role of witness. An interview that was far gentler in its approach than the real one described by Staci.

"Your homework assignment for this week," Gertie announced as she was wrapping up, "is to develop a sketch of someone you've never met from someone else's description of them. It's due on Friday."

"A sketch of a suspect?" Nate asked hopefully.

"Before I turn you loose on the bad guys, let's start with family and friends." Gertie regarded him as one might an overexcited puppy needing to be brought up short on its leash.

"Can it be more than one person?" asked Ashley.

"By all means. The more you practice, the better."

Kyra was eager to get started. All she needed was someone to interview, and she knew just the person to ask. She stopped at Red Ink Tattoos on her way home, after putting in several hours on Gertie's books. Frannie was finishing up with a customer when she walked in with Ranger.

The customer, a man in his mid to late forties with the look of a seasoned road warrior and arms sleeved with tats, broke into a grin when Ranger went over to greet him and Frannie. He scratched Ranger behind his ears. "Hey there, pooch. You up next? Looking to get a tat on your belly, maybe?"

"How was your first day of class?" Frannie asked after the man had paid and left.

"I want to be Gertie when I grow up," Kyra said, and Frannie laughed.

"Don't we all."

"The question is, do I have what it takes? Today I learned there's way more to it than meets the eye. You have to try to get into other people's heads and see what they saw. How does anyone do that?"

"I don't know, but Gertie and others like her have mastered the art, and you will, too."

"I'm not so sure."

"I had doubts about my abilities, too, when I was training to become a tattoo artist."

"You did? But you're so good at it." Frannie was not only a gifted painter, but she was also much sought after as a tattoo artist. She didn't do any advertising apart from the sign posted outside, but her work advertised itself. She'd had customers come from out of state and as far away as Canada.

"I wasn't always. Which is why I practiced on pigs' ears back then instead of humans. Pig skin is the closest in texture to human skin. Also, a dead pig doesn't get mad when you mess up."

"Speaking of practice, I could use your help with my homework assignment for this week."

"Count me in," said Frannie after Kyra had described the assignment. "Why don't you come over tomorrow evening? I'll see if the girls can join us. The more the merrier, right?" She sent a group text to the other Tattooed Ladies, inviting them to her house for cocktails and a practice session with Kyra the following evening at six. Within minutes, they had all accepted the invitation.

Kyra marveled at the change in her circumstances in the short time since she'd arrived in town, jobless and knowing no one. Now she had two jobs, an exciting career opportunity, and friends.

Friends who don't know the real you, whispered the devil on her shoulder. They knew her as Kyra Smith. They'd never met Krystal Stanhope. They'd never seen her with a black eye or bruises, or listened to her excuses about how she'd gotten them. Had they known her then, she would have been seen as an object of pity, someone in need of their protection. They might have taken her under their wing, but she wouldn't have been one of them, not in the way she was now. Kyra was of two minds. Part of her wanted to come clean, while another part of her wanted to just be one of the girls.

"Did Hannah get the job?" she asked as they were leaving after Frannie had locked up for the day. Hannah had mentioned at dinner the other night that she'd applied for a job at the Walmart in Pine City.

"Yes, except it's not the cashier position she applied for," Frannie said as they descended the stairs to the street. "She'll be stocking shelves to start with. But she can work her way up from there if she sticks with it."

Something in her voice made Kyra say, "You sound like you're worried she won't."

"There have been times Hannah was unable to work because of her mental illness, so her résumé has gaps in it. But she's worked in retail before. She'll be fine as long as she keeps taking her meds."

"Isn't it a condition of her staying with you?"

"Yes, but there's nothing to stop her from leaving."

"Where would she go?"

"Who knows?" Frannie turned to face her when they reached the bottom of the stairs. She looked worried, haggard almost, with the surrounding shadows deepening the hollows of her eyes. "She still refuses to go back to Caring Village. The last time she went AWOL, she wound up on the streets."

They were standing in the forecourt of the building, which served as an outdoor dining area for the patrons of Cowboy Coffee at the other end, where it was enclosed by planter boxes. The sun had dipped below the mountaintops to the west. At the Whiskey Barrel across the street, happy hour was in full swing. Kyra heard mingled voices and the tinkle of the converted saloon's player piano. She shortened Ranger's leash when she noticed him staring intently at a standard poodle passing on the sidewalk with its owner. He'd been known to go rogue where another dog was involved.

"What did you do?" Kyra asked.

"The same thing I always do. I went and got her, and brought her home. But I don't always know where to find her."

"That must have been scary for you, not knowing where she was or if she was all right."

"You have no idea." Frannie's gaze turned inward briefly. "She's been in and out of psychiatric facilities, and on and off the streets, since she was eighteen."

"How old was she when she was diagnosed?"

"Fourteen. Before then, I'd noticed she'd become moody and withdrawn, but I'd chalked it up to adolescence. It wasn't until I got a call from the principal at her school one day, about an incident Hannah had been involved in, that I got my first clue it was more serious than I'd imagined. She'd been caught burning her textbooks in a trash can on campus. Needless to say, I was shocked and mystified. When I spoke to her about it, Hannah said the voices in her head made her do it. I took her to a psychiatrist to find out what was wrong with her, and he diagnosed it as schizoaffective disorder."

"Oh, Frannie, I'm so sorry." Kyra's heart ached for her friend. She wasn't a parent herself, so she could only imagine what it was like for Frannie.

"There's no known cure, only management of the symptoms," Frannie went on, her voice matter of fact. "But as with anything life throws at you, you learn to cope. And it's worse for Hannah."

"What about her dad? Is he in the picture?"

"Not to speak of. He moved out when she was fifteen. Six months later, he remarried and started another family with his new wife. His normal family," she added in a voice laced with sarcasm.

"Does Hannah still see him?"

"Now and then. They're not close."

Kyra's own problems seemed small compared to Frannie's and Hannah's. She wasn't the parent of a child with an incurable illness, nor was she mentally ill. "I never knew my father, and the best I can say about my mother is that she was there . . . some of the time. Hannah's lucky to have one parent she can count on."

Frannie gave her a weak smile. "I'll be there for as long as I'm able, but I'm not getting any younger."

"Sixty is the new forty, or so I hear."

"According to Suzy, anyway. Speaking for myself, I've earned every one of these gray hairs." She fingered her cap of silver curls. "Although," she admitted, "there were days when it seemed like too much to bear. The first time Hannah was an inpatient in a psych ward, when she was seventeen, I was so worn out by then, I had half a mind to get *myself* admitted. The 'rest cure,' it was called, back when Dad used to go away to a sanitarium for weeks, sometimes months, at a time."

"When was this?"

"From the time I was little until . . ." She trailed off, the creases in her face deepening as though the memory of a family tragedy was too painful to discuss. "He was diagnosed with depression, though I suspect it was a misdiagnosis. He had many of the same symptoms that Hannah does. They say mental illness runs in the family. I've been dealing with it in one form or another for most of my life."

There was no trace of self-pity in Frannie's voice, but she sounded tired. The kind of tired that can't be cured with a night's rest or even a vacation. She also seemed stressed. Kyra wished there was something she could do to make it better. Then it came to her. A small thing when compared with the many kindnesses Frannie had shown her. But it was something, and something was better than nothing.

"Are you in a hurry?" she asked.

"Not especially. I'm headed home, but I don't have any plans for the evening. Why?"

"I know of something that would relax you."

"A margarita?" Frannie cast a wistful glance in the direction of the Whiskey Barrel.

"What I have in mind doesn't involve alcohol."

"Okay, I'll bite. What do you have in mind?"

"Come with me and I'll show you."

They headed off down the street with Ranger leading the way—he was familiar with the route by now. Arriving at her destination, Kyra let herself in with her key and punched in the code to disarm the alarm system. It was after hours, Suzy's salon deserted. Kyra directed Frannie to the shampoo station in back, composed of a reclining chair positioned in front of a deep sink, below a shelf on which stood bottles of shampoo and conditioner. Minutes later, Frannie was reclining in the chair with her neck resting on the folded towel Kyra had placed on the edge of the sink, her head tipped back while Kyra worked suds into her hair and massaged her scalp with slow, circular strokes.

"This," Frannie said, with her eyes closed and her lips curved in a contented smile, "is heaven."

8

Late the following day, Kyra drove with Ranger to Frannie's for the gathering she was hosting that evening. It was dark when she pulled into the driveway at ten to six. She was the first to arrive, apparently; the only other vehicle parked in the driveway was Frannie's Jeep. She climbed from her car, and Ranger bounded out after her. Her breath misted in the cold air as she headed up the front path, carrying her tote, which tonight held her art supplies along with her valuables.

"I'm not too early, am I?" Kyra asked when Frannie greeted her at the door wearing a long corduroy skirt in chocolate brown and a red V-neck sweater that brought out the color in her cheeks.

"Not at all. Come on in. Hannah's out for the evening, but the girls should be arriving any minute," Frannie said as she ushered her inside and led the way to the great room, where a fire crackled in the fireplace and a spread was laid out on the coffee table—an assortment of cheeses and crackers, some kind of dip with chips and crudités, and empanadas like the ones sold at Cowboy Coffee. "What can I get you to drink? Wine, beer, or the hard stuff? I also have sodas if you prefer nonalcoholic."

"I'll take a club soda if you have one, since I'm working tonight."

Frannie crossed the room to the oak sideboard that served as the bar tonight. She was pouring soda into an ice-filled glass when the doorbell rang. She handed Kyra her drink and went to answer it.

Kyra took a seat by the fire, and Ranger settled at her feet. The great room, with its open-beamed ceiling and stone fireplace, was both grand and cozy, with views of the lake through its floor-to-ceiling windows. Outside, the dark waters of the lake glittered with reflected moonlight. She heard voices drifting from the front hallway, and then Frannie reappeared with Suzy and Marisol.

"Hello! Hello! What did we miss?" Suzy wore a floaty silk tunic in a multicolored, swirly pattern, slim black pants, and purple suede ankle boots. "Oh, drinks. Yes, please. Why don't you get that? I can mix my own," she said to Frannie when the crunch of tires outside announced another arrival.

"I'll take a glass of white while you're at it," said Marisol as she flopped down on the sofa next to Kyra.

"Coming right up." Suzy poured a glass of chardonnay for Marisol and mixed a gin and tonic for herself.

Marisol was a throwback to the sixties tonight, wearing bell-bottoms and a loose-fitting shirt, possibly from the vintage clothing store that she shopped at and had told Kyra about when they'd had dinner together at her place. "Hey, girl," she greeted Kyra. "Yeah, I see you, too," she said to Ranger when he popped his head up to grin at her. She dug a dog biscuit from her voluminous tapestry shoulder bag and tossed it to him. He caught it with his teeth and ate it in two bites.

"The gang's all here!" Frannie's voice called a minute later.

Kyra turned around to see her entering with Jo, who looked as if she'd been blown in by a gust of wind. Her cheeks were flushed, and pieces of her red-gold hair had escaped her messy bun. "Hi, everyone! Sorry I'm late. Emma threw a tantrum as I was leaving. Is that wine I see? I could use a glass. Or two. No, better not, or I won't be in any shape to drive home. A wine spritzer, maybe?"

"How about a Shirley Temple with a splash of gin?" suggested Suzy.

"Perfect."

When they were all gathered in front of the fire with their drinks, Frannie raised her glass in a toast. "Here's to helping launch Kyra's new career!"

There was a chorus of "cheers" and the clinking of glasses. Kyra blushed, feeling self-conscious. What if she turned out to have no talent for forensic art? Her "new career" might fail to launch despite her and her friends' best efforts. How embarrassing would that be?

"I wouldn't have missed this for the world," said Jo. She'd removed her sneakers and sat with her legs tucked underneath her in the over-stuffed chair to the right of the sofa, sipping her Shirley Temple. "Even if I had to resort to bribing the girls so they'd let me out of the house without a fuss."

"With what?" Marisol asked as she helped herself to an empanada.

"Waffles. Fortunately for their dad, who's cooking tonight, they don't discriminate between Eggos and homemade." She wore jeans and a sweatshirt that said WEDDINGS ARE NOT FOR WUSSES.

Kyra turned toward Jo. "How's your husband? No more fainting spells, I hope."

"No, thank God, though he's still getting headaches," she reported. "I told him it'd be *me* going to the ER with a heart attack if he gives me another scare like the last one."

"He had us all worried," said Suzy. She scooped up some of the dip with a celery stick and popped it into her mouth.

"Did he see his doctor about his headaches?" asked Marisol.

Jo nodded. "She doesn't know what's causing them. She said it could be migraines. She prescribed some medication, but wants him to see a neurologist if his headaches persist. I'm sure it's nothing," she said, but the troubled look she wore belied her words.

"Kyra, tell us more about this homework assignment of yours," said Suzy when talk circled back to the reason for tonight's gathering. "It sounds intriguing."

Kyra felt her nerves kick in again. "We're supposed to draw a sketch of someone we've never seen—or more than one person, in this case—from someone else's description of them. Which, frankly, I'm not sure I can pull off."

"It's been done before," Frannie reminded her.

"Not by me. I trained as an artist, but I'm an amateur at this. Which is why I need your help. I need each of you to think of someone to describe. Someone I've never seen, which should be easy since I know almost no one."

"Does it matter who it is?" asked Jo.

"It can be anyone, as long as you have a photo of them. I'll need to show it for comparison."

"Living or deceased?" Frannie topped a cracker with a wedge of Brie and placed it on a napkin, passing it to Jo, on her left, before helping herself to one.

"Makes no difference."

"Can it be a fictional character?" joked Marisol.

"Why? Do you have one in mind?" Suzy arched an eyebrow at her.

"Atticus Finch. He's in my top five."

"Does he look anything like Gregory Peck?" asked Frannie.

"The actor?" said Jo around a mouthful of cracker and cheese.

"Yes. He plays the part in the movie."

"They made a movie of *To Kill a Mockingbird*?"

Frannie rolled her eyes and muttered, "Kids these days."

"Who wants to go first?" Kyra reached for her tote on the floor at her feet and pulled out her sketch pad and pencils.

"I will," said Frannie.

"My person is my grandmother, CeCe," she began, leaning back in her chair and sipping her white wine with a faraway look on her face. "Long gone, may she rest in peace, though her memory lives on in the goodies made from her recipes that are sold at Cowboy Coffee. Everything

Vanessa and I know about cooking and baking, we learned from CeCe. She also taught us everything we needed to know about life."

"She sounds like a wonderful role model," Kyra observed.

"She was. She practically raised us."

"Were your parents alive then?"

"Yes, but they weren't always able to care for us. Our father was . . ." Frannie gave a small, helpless shrug, and Kyra recalled what Frannie had told her about him. "He had a nervous condition, and Mother couldn't cope with raising two children on her own when he was away at the sanitarium. We stayed with CeCe during those times. Hers was my real home, as far as I was concerned."

Kyra's thoughts drifted to her own family. She'd never met any of her relatives. Her mother was estranged from her family, and if her father or any of his extended family was still living, Kyra wouldn't know. She knew only that her maternal grandparents owned a farm in Nebraska, where her mom had grown up. Her grandfather had emigrated to this country from Mexico with his parents when he was a small boy, and they'd settled in the Midwest, where he'd eventually met and married his wife. God-fearing folk who attended church every Sunday, they held themselves and others to a high moral standard, according to her mom. When Mom was sixteen and pregnant with Kyra, they'd given her an ultimatum: either she give the baby up for adoption or find another place to live. Mom had moved out and kept her baby—probably the only unselfish choice she'd ever made. She still called her parents occasionally but hadn't visited them since she moved out. Kyra suspected she stayed in touch so she could hit them up for loans when she needed money. Mom also had a brother, Stuart, who was older than she was, and with whom she'd had no contact since she left home.

"I used to love visiting you at your grandma's," Suzy said to Frannie. "It was like the gingerbread house in 'Hansel and Gretel' minus the witch. We had such fun exploring all its nooks and crannies."

Frannie produced a photo album and showed Kyra a picture of the house, a two-story wooden structure with a covered balcony wrapping around the upper floor, distinguished by its decorative ironwork. "It was built by CeCe's great-grandfather Henri in the style of the home he'd owned in New Orleans before he emigrated to Gold Creek in the 1800s. He and his wife were this town's first Creole settlers. It's still standing, if you'd care to visit sometime. CeCe bequeathed it to the Gold Creek Historical Society. She left the building that once housed our family mercantile store to Vanessa and me."

"And look what came of it," said Jo. "If you hadn't opened Red Ink Tattoos, I wouldn't have met you, or become a Tattooed Lady." She told the story, for Kyra's benefit, of the day she'd gone there to get a tattoo with which she'd planned to surprise her husband on their anniversary that year. She pulled up a pant leg to reveal the tattoo, a heart wreathed in roses, inscribed with both her and her husband's initials and the word "Forever" above her right ankle.

Kyra thought of the tattoo she'd had removed by Frannie over the course of several sessions. She reflected on how different her own experience had been from Jo's. Jo's tattoo symbolized what she wished to remember; hers had symbolized what she wished to forget. What she couldn't erase, like she had her tattoo. She wondered again if she'd ever know the kind of love Jo and her husband shared.

She pushed the thought away to focus on the task at hand. "How would you describe your grandmother? Was she short or tall, thin or heavyset?" she began, using the interview technique she'd learned from Gertie.

"She was short, and what they called 'pleasantly plump' in her day, like all the women on my father's side of the family," Frannie said. "I got my height and build from my mother's side."

"What color was her hair?"

"Black with gray streaks in it when I knew her. It tended to frizz in damp weather like mine does. She usually wore it pulled back in a bun."

"What color were her eyes?"

"Dark like mine."

Kyra produced a scrapbook from her tote filled with photos she'd cut from magazines and pasted onto its pages—men and women of different ages and physical types. "Reference photos," Gertie called them. It had been today's class project. Gertie had asked them each to create a scrapbook from the stack of old magazines she'd brought to class for that purpose, to be used as a visual aid when they conducted interviews. Kyra flipped to a page in her scrapbook and showed it to Frannie.

"Which of these two women looks the most like your grandmother?"

"That one." Frannie pointed to the woman on the left.

When she'd formed a rough mental picture of her subject as described by Frannie, Kyra began to draw. At first she was self-conscious, aware that she was being watched, but she soon became immersed in the process. Her hand flew over the page as if it had a mind of its own as she sketched.

It had been this way as far back as she could remember. She had only to pick up a pencil or paintbrush to enter a magical realm where her troubles and worries ceased to exist. When she was in school, she'd sketched to occupy herself and keep from feeling lonely when she'd sat alone in the playground during recess. When she lived with Rory, her art—both the practice of it and teaching of it—had been her refuge, to which she could escape for periods of time to keep from losing her mind.

She paused occasionally to show Frannie more reference photos and ask about specific physical characteristics. Did her grandmother's nose, ears, or mouth look more like this or that person's? Was her chin rounder or more square? When she showed Frannie the finished sketch, her nerves flared again. Had she succeeded in capturing her subject's likeness, or had she failed miserably?

She got her answer when Frannie gasped and said, "Oh my God. It's *her*. It's CeCe."

Kyra released her pent-up breath and felt the tight muscles in her neck loosen. When Frannie showed her a photo of her grandmother, Kyra was relieved and gratified to see that the smiling, round-faced older woman in the photo resembled the woman depicted in her sketch. It wasn't a perfect match, by any means, but close enough to have her thinking she might be onto something.

◆ ◆ ◆

Marisol was up next. "I don't know this person well," she began. "But he seems interesting."

"Who is he, and how do you know him?" Suzy asked.

"He works as a guide for Gold Creek Tours, and Buckboard Books is one of the stops on his tour. His name is Cal."

"Young, old, or somewhere in between?" Kyra flipped to a blank page in her sketchpad.

"Young. He just graduated college."

"How would you describe him?"

"Young."

"You said that already."

"Am I repeating myself?" Marisol grimaced as a telltale blush bloomed in her cheeks.

"Uh-oh. She's in lur-ve." Jo grinned and popped the cherry from her drink into her mouth, making it seem suggestive somehow.

"Shut up," Marisol said, tossing a throw pillow from the sofa at her, which Jo ducked, laughing. "He is cute," she admitted. "In a goofy kind of way."

"Goofy how?" asked Kyra.

"He has big eyes and hair that sticks straight up on top like a cartoon character's. An adorable cartoon character," she added. "He claims it grows that way and that he doesn't use any hair product."

"My daughters would love him," said Jo. "But then, they're into SpongeBob SquarePants."

Kyra guessed the man in question looked nothing like SpongeBob SquarePants from Marisol's description and from the dreamy-eyed look on her face. "What color is his hair?" she asked.

"Somewhere between blond and brown. Sun-kissed, you might say."

"What color are his eyes?"

"Blue, like Daniel Craig. And he has the cutest dimples."

"Girl, you've got it bad," observed Suzy from across the room as she mixed herself another gin and tonic. She'd come with Marisol, who was the designated driver tonight, so she was free to imbibe.

Marisol groaned, burying her head in her hands. "I know. It's pathetic. I'm practically old enough to be his mother."

"But you're not his mother," Jo reminded her.

"Which means he's fair game," agreed Frannie. She and Suzy might differ in their approach to aging—Frannie believed in growing old gracefully, while Suzy was fighting it all the way—but they were both liberal-minded. Neither seemed to have a problem with a May–December romance, whether it was an older man/younger woman or a younger man/older woman.

"Life would be dull if I only dated men my age." Suzy returned to her seat by the fire, carrying her drink. "Besides, women your age are at their sexual peak, which makes you the perfect match for a twentysomething."

"The men you date don't live with their parents."

The room fell quiet as the others processed Marisol's startling statement. The only sound was the crackling of flames in the fireplace and the tapping of Ranger's claws against the hardwood floor as he went to investigate a noise outside. He stood at the window with his ears pricked as if he was following the movements of a nocturnal creature in the darkness beyond what only he could see.

Frannie was the first to respond. "Well, I can see how that might be a problem."

"Technically, he doesn't live with them." Marisol absently helped herself to another empanada and bit into it like someone stress-eating. "He's staying at their vacation home here, which they rarely use except in the summers. And it's just until he figures out what's next for him.

106

He'd planned to start law school in the fall but was having second thoughts, so he's taking a gap year."

"In other words, his parents aren't likely to walk in on you in bed with their son," said Suzy, rattling the ice in her drink before taking a sip.

Marisol nearly choked on the mouthful of food she was swallowing. "We're not having sex! God."

"More's the pity." Suzy shook her head.

"I don't know if he's into me, or if he's into older women, even."

"Only one way to find out. Why don't you ask him out for coffee or drinks?" Frannie suggested.

"Maybe I will."

Kyra's thoughts wandered to Coop Langston, and she frowned. Why was she still thinking about him? Must be all this talk of romance. He was the first man to generate any sexual heat in her since her marital bed had gone cold—regrettably, given what she'd later learned about him. A picture formed in her mind of his large, muscular figure, its upper half stretching the fabric of his shirt and its lower half packed into his snug-fitting jeans. She quickly dismissed it, although she couldn't delete the memory of him from her mental file folder, and got back to the business at hand.

"Does this look anything like Cal?" she asked when she showed her finished sketch to Marisol.

Marisol studied it and then pulled out her phone, scrolling to a photo of a smiling man posed against a backdrop of shelved books, holding a tabby cat in his arms. Early twenties with big blue eyes, blondish hair that stuck straight up like bristles on a broom, and dimples. "You tell me."

He looked enough like the man depicted in her sketch to reassure Kyra that her first effort hadn't been a fluke. "My sketch probably wouldn't get him arrested, but it does look a bit like him," she said.

The other women came over to take a look. "Oh, he's adorable!" exclaimed Suzy.

"And *way* better-looking than SpongeBob SquarePants," declared Jo.

"And he seems to like cats," observed Frannie as she peered at the photo.

Marisol moaned. "I know. I am so screwed."

◆ ◆ ◆

"My person is my mom," said Jo when it was her turn. "And only because you've met my husband."

"Are you and your mom close?" Kyra asked. She was always curious about other people's relationships with their mothers. Maybe because her relationship with her mom was unusual, to say the least.

"No. I mean, yeah, I love her. She's my mom. But . . . she's a former beauty queen, and I was the girl who attended her senior prom as the photographer for the school paper and not as someone's date. I deprived her of the precious moments other mothers and daughters enjoy, such as shopping for a prom dress, not to mention photos of me all dolled up posing with a date. Need I say more?"

"At least she didn't embarrass you in front of a date," Kyra said.

She recalled her own senior prom, which she'd attended with her friend Connor, who'd also been her lab partner in biology. She'd been mortified when her mom had flirted with him after Connor arrived to pick her up. What saved it from becoming her Most Embarrassing Moment Ever was Connor, who was gay but still in the closet then, finding the humor in the situation. He'd said dryly, when they were on their way to the prom in his car, *Imagine how disappointed she'd be if I slept with her.*

The other women alternately laughed and groaned in sympathy after Kyra had told them the story. "Your mother sounds like she might have personal boundary issues," said Frannie, putting it mildly.

"More like she's perpetually seventeen, in her own mind, anyway." Becoming a mom when she was a teenager had had the opposite effect on her that it did on most teen moms. Instead of forcing her to grow up faster, it had resulted in a case of arrested development.

"Once a beauty queen, always a beauty queen. That's my mom's motto," said Jo as she spread cheese on a cracker and popped it into her mouth.

"What does she look like?" Kyra asked Jo, flipping to a blank page in her sketchbook.

"Like she did when she was competing in pageants—from a distance, anyway—thanks to the miracles of Botox and plastic surgery and her daily beauty regimen. With big hair. Mama is five foot three, according to her driver's license, but in heels with her hair done, she's closer to six feet."

"Good God," exclaimed Suzy. "My customers would scream bloody murder if I did that to them."

"That's because they're not in Texas, where no self-respecting woman would be caught dead in public with flat hair. The ladies of my mother's set, at least. They never leave home without a canister of hair spray tucked in their purse for emergency touch-ups. I once saw an actual dead woman in her coffin who looked like she was wearing one of Dolly Parton's wigs. Apparently, it was her last wish to be buried looking like she did in her wedding photos from the sixties when beehive hairdos were in style." The twang in Jo's voice grew more pronounced as she spoke of home.

Suzy burst out laughing, and the others joined in, even Kyra, who couldn't recall the last time she'd enjoyed a good laugh. In that moment, in the company of these smart, generous, funny women, she felt like she belonged.

By the time Kyra was done with her sketch, the logs in the fireplace had burned down to embers. She showed it to Jo, who studied it and drawled, "Well, butter my biscuit and pass the gravy. Add a tiara, erase a few of those age lines, and I could be looking at Miss Crockett County of 1978."

Suzy went last. It was no surprise when she chose her son as her person. Kyra knew from their previous conversations that Suzy's relationship with her son was strained, and that it was a source of heartache for her. Suzy recounted a recent incident in which her son had blown off a planned family outing to go fishing with his dad instead while he was visiting with his family this past July.

"I don't get it," she said, shaking her head. "Wayne's a half-assed father when he's sober, and a piss-poor excuse for one when he's drunk. Why am I the bad guy?"

"It's because Adam's secure in your love, and he's still chasing his father's," said Frannie, who usually had words of wisdom to impart about any life problem.

"You're probably right, but that doesn't make it any easier," said Suzy with a sigh.

You only hurt the ones you love. The refrain from a song Kyra had heard somewhere popped into her head. Its words were never truer than in her case. Rory had professed his love to her, and maybe he did in his own mind, but it was a twisted love.

"Lord in heaven!" exclaimed Suzy a short while later as she studied the sketch Kyra had drawn of her son. "It's like I'm seeing a ghost! Or, rather, my ex when he was Adam's age."

Kyra grew excited. Twice, or even thrice, might be a lucky streak, but hitting the mark—or close to it—four times in a row must mean she had the makings of a forensic artist. "He must've been handsome."

"He was before drink robbed him of his looks. When we were in high school, all the girls were crazy about him. Probably a few besides me were steaming up the windows of his Camaro with him, but I was the only one foolish enough to get knocked up. Which," she added wryly, "is what can happen when your boyfriend tells you he's 'shooting blanks' and you believe him."

Marisol gasped. "He told you that?"

"After the first time we did it that night. Probably he believed it, too. Sex education back then wasn't what it is now." Suzy shook her head and took another swig of her drink. "But I have no regrets. My marriage was a disaster, but how could I regret my children? I just wish Adam would forgive me."

"Forgive you for what? You did nothing wrong," said Frannie, frowning.

"I wasn't a perfect mom."

"Show me a parent who is." Frannie got up to toss another log on the fire and paused as her gaze fell on a photo on the mantel of a younger, joyful-looking Hannah blowing out the candles on a birthday cake. Her expression turned wistful. "We do the best we can, and we get what we get."

Kyra considered her own parents. Her father, who had taken off before she was born, never to be heard from again, and her mother who, if she had done the best she could, it hadn't been good enough. Kyra couldn't imagine any of the Tattooed Ladies bailing on a family member who needed her or shirking her familial duties. Hearing their stories tonight, her admiration for them had grown. They were survivors, each in their own way. Frannie had survived the mental illnesses of both her father and daughter, and she and Suzy had both survived their bad marriages. Marisol had survived her mother's death and disappointments in love. Jo had survived her mother's disappointment in her.

The fact that Kyra had survived her own marriage was nothing to be proud of. She wasn't strong like these women, any one of whom would have left a husband who raised a hand to her before he could do it again, and probably called the cops. What would they think if they knew her story?

It was a little after nine when the party broke up. The dirty dishes and glasses were loaded into the dishwasher, and the leftovers stowed in the fridge. There were final visits to the powder room and then a scrum at the front door as arms were wrestled into coat sleeves and goodbyes exchanged.

"When you're done with it, could I have the sketch you drew of my mom?" Jo asked as she was leaving. "I'd like to give it to her. It would make her day."

"Of course," Kyra said, pleased to be asked.

"If you breathe a word about Cal to anyone, I'll have to kill you," Marisol said to Kyra as she helped a slightly inebriated Suzy with her coat. "If anyone asks, tell them he's a friend of a friend."

"A friend with benefits." Suzy giggled, and after a few failed attempts, managed to insert her arm into the coat sleeve Marisol was holding up.

"Mind out of the gutter," scolded Marisol. She zipped Suzy's coat and steered her toward the door, pausing to say under her breath to Kyra, "I should be so lucky."

"Don't worry, your secret is safe with me," Kyra assured her. She was good at keeping secrets.

Kyra was the last to leave. She was headed out the door with Ranger when Frannie said, "Oh, I almost forgot—I have a lead on a place. My friend Shirley's son keeps a travel trailer on his property that he might consider renting out. Any interest?"

Kyra stopped with her hand on the doorknob and felt a pulse of excitement. "Definitely."

"I figured as much, so I asked Shirley to speak to her son about it. Of course, I don't know what kind of shape it's in. Even if he's willing to rent it out, you might decide it's uninhabitable once you've seen it."

"It couldn't be worse than the Bates Motel, where I store my perishables in an ice chest and I'm kept awake at night by the people next door either having loud sex or watching the porn channel with the volume turned up. If it's affordable and dogs are allowed, I won't mind if it's only semihabitable."

"It's out in the country where the four-legged critters outnumber the human populace, so I don't imagine a dog would be a problem. As for whether it's affordable, you'll have to speak with Shirley about it. That is, if she gets the go-ahead from her son. He's out of town right now."

"Will you let me know as soon as you hear back from her?"

"Of course, and hopefully it'll be good news."

Kyra broke into a grin and bent to stroke Ranger's head. "You hear that, bud? We may have found ourselves a home."

9

On Friday, Kyra presented her homework assignment in class. She went last after Ashley, Staci, and Nate had given their presentations, and her stomach was in knots as she stood at the whiteboard, to which she'd taped her four sketches along with the comparison photos. After the brutal criticism her classmates had received from Gertie, she was bracing herself for more of the same.

Gertie didn't pull any punches with her, either. "They're good," she said as she studied Kyra's sketches. Her furrowed brow, below her cockatoo's crest, suggested it hadn't been a compliment. "Too good."

Kyra was confused. "What did I do wrong?"

"You did a decent job of capturing the likenesses of your subjects, but when I look at your sketches, they tell me the artist was focusing more on drawing a pretty picture than on the goal. What's the goal of a forensic artist in a criminal investigation?" she asked, addressing the class.

"To create a visual by which to identify the suspect," Ashley piped up.

"That is correct. Thank you, Ashley. Mine wouldn't win any prizes"—she motioned toward her own sketches of suspects pinned to the corkboard on the opposite wall—"but they got the job done."

The criticism stung, but Kyra swallowed her disappointment. "I'll try to do better next time. Or worse," she corrected herself, provoking laughter from her classmates and a smile from Gertie. "I guess I lost sight of the fact that it's about catching bad guys, not impressing art critics."

"The only opinion that matters is that of the witness or victim who gives a positive ID, or not. You won't see any of my sketches hanging in a gallery or museum. In a post office on a wanted poster, more like. But knowing I helped take bad guys off the streets is the best feeling in the world."

"I'll remember that in the future," said Kyra, making a mental note to focus more on the goal than her craft from now on. If Gertie was being hard on them, she told herself, it was to prepare them for a day when they might be employed as forensic artists. There were no do-overs in Gertie's profession.

Kyra stayed after class to work on Gertie's books. An hour later, she was preparing a suspense account report of unclear expenses when her phone rang. It was Frannie. "Good news," she said. "My friend spoke with her son, and he's willing to rent out his trailer if you and he can agree on terms."

Kyra felt a surge of excitement. "Great! When can I see it?"

"Can you meet her there in twenty minutes? Her son's still out of town, but she's authorized to act as his proxy."

"I'm on my way," she said as she exited her program and powered down the desktop. "What's the drive time from town?"

"About fifteen minutes, so you should be fine if you leave now." Frannie gave her the address along with Shirley's phone number, ending with "Good luck. Call me afterward and tell me how it went."

"I will. Thank you. I don't know how I can ever repay you."

"Don't thank me until you've seen it. It might be worse than the Bates Motel."

As she drove to the address on Old Post Road with Ranger, Kyra hoped she wouldn't get lost. She was in unfamiliar territory, where some of the roads she passed were unmarked. Nor was she using GPS; until she could afford to replace her burner with a smartphone, she was relying on a road map to navigate. According to the footnotes on the map, the road she was on, which wound through the rural area east of town, had been the route used by the Pony Express, thus its name. The views were of wooded stretches broken here and there by buildings or fields where cows and horses grazed. The sky was gray, with rain in the forecast. The temps had been falling steadily over the past week, along with the leaves from trees. That morning, Kyra had awakened to frost on the ground.

It was a few minutes after three thirty, and just under fifteen minutes since she'd set out, when Kyra turned onto a gravel drive where there was a mailbox painted with the address of her destination. It led to a two-story, white clapboard farmhouse on a spacious lawn shaded by a mature oak at one end and enclosed by a white picket fence. Beyond stretched a grassy field. Snow-capped mountains rose in the distance. She parked and climbed from her car, while Ranger powered down the window on the passenger side with his paw and leaped out—his latest trick, which he'd taught himself, clever dog that he was. Ranger set off to explore, while Kyra took in her surroundings. She noticed a clearing at the far edge of the field, beyond which a creek ran, partially hidden by the trees that grew along its banks. A travel trailer stood at its center—a vintage Airstream, if she wasn't mistaken. The teardrop model, in silver. It was smaller than she'd expected: a tiny home.

"Not exactly the Taj Mahal, is it, bud?" she said to Ranger when he returned. "On the plus side, it's off the beaten track, where there are more squirrels than people, from what I can see. No one would find us here." She hoped.

Five minutes later, a blue Subaru Forester came rattling down the drive and parked at the end. A diminutive older woman hopped from the driver's seat. Pale-blue eyes creased at the corners. Curly red hair threaded with gray. She wore a tan Carhartt jacket and carried a collapsible umbrella. "Sorry I'm late," she said. "Couldn't find the darn key. But I've got it now." She produced a key ring from her coat pocket, then extended her other hand. "Hi. I'm Shirley. And you must be Kyra."

Kyra shook her hand. "Nice to meet you. And no worries, I just got here myself."

"Hope you didn't have any trouble finding it. Cell service can be spotty in this neck of the woods, and first-time visitors tend to get lost if they're relying on their GPS."

"I used a road map."

Shirley's eyes widened in surprise. "Fancy that, a millennial who knows what a road map is."

Kyra imagined she would be even more surprised, shocked even, if she knew the reason she was using one. "Your son owns all this?" she asked, looking around her.

"All thirty-four acres. Before that, it belonged to me and my husband. We sold it after Ed retired and we decided to downsize. Bit of a drive from town, but the peace and quiet make up for it. And the views. Imagine waking up to this every morning." She spread her arms wide as she looked around her.

"Gorgeous," Kyra agreed.

Shirley's gaze dropped to Ranger. "Fannie didn't mention you had a dog."

Kyra grew worried. "I hope it's not a problem."

"Not at all," Shirley assured her, bending to greet Ranger. "Unless he runs afoul of a skunk; then it'd be your problem. Plenty of those around here, along with badgers, possums, rabbits, coyotes, and deer. The deer eat everything the bunnies don't. Some call them pests, but I prefer to think of them as neighbors who can be annoying at times." She led the way along the south side of the building to where the tended grounds gave way to the tall grass of the field. "Frannie tells me you're new in town," she said as they followed the path to the clearing, Ranger racing ahead of them.

"Yes. I relocated from back east."

"I hope you're finding it to your liking."

"Very much so."

"I was born and raised in Gold Creek, so you could say I'm biased, but there's no better place to live, in my opinion. It's got it all—scenic views, mountain air, and a mostly law-abiding citizenry."

It began to rain. Shirley unfolded her umbrella, holding it high in an effort to keep them both dry. "Here we are. Casa Grande, as my son calls it," she said when they reached the clearing. Kyra's heart sank. The Airstream looked even smaller up close than it had from a distance. Its outdoor space, however, was large enough to hold a picnic table and a set of four Adirondack chairs arranged around a fire ring, with room to spare. Firewood was stacked underneath the trailer at one end. The creek burbled through the trees beyond. "No one's used it for a while, so it could probably do with a cleaning and an airing."

Shirley unlocked the door and stepped aside to let Kyra in. "Stay," Kyra ordered when Ranger tried to follow her, lest he dirty the floor with his muddy paws. Inside, a thick layer of dust coated every surface. The air smelled stale and musty. The interior was compact—cramped, some might say. It held a two-burner cooktop and microwave; a mini fridge, sink, and a pair of upper and lower cabinets, separated by a foot of countertop; a platform bed and bathroom the size of a phone booth; a small table with bench seating; and a cushioned bench that served as a sofa. It wasn't ideal, but she'd made do with more primitive accommodations during those times she and her mom had been between addresses. Once it was aired and scrubbed, it would be livable. The only question was whether she could afford it.

"It's perfect," she announced when she emerged. "Perfect" was a generous description, but it was an improvement over the Bates Motel, and the setting was lovely. She could see herself drinking her coffee outside in the mornings, listening to birdsong, and sitting by a campfire at night. "How much?"

"I haven't a clue. It's never been rented before. How does five hundred sound?"

"A week?"

"A month."

Kyra couldn't believe her ears. The quoted sum was a fraction of what the cheapest listings she'd seen advertised rented for. "Do you need to check with your son first? He might want more for it."

"Well, he left me in charge, so I'm making a command decision. And seeing as how you're a friend of Frannie's, you get the family rate. The place is just sitting empty. Not like he planned to do anything with it."

"I'll take it," she said before Shirley could change her mind. "I can pay in cash. First, last, and security?"

"Why don't you just pay for the rest of this month? You can work out the details with my son when he gets back from his trip."

Kyra was relieved and grateful to learn she wouldn't have to spend a chunk of her remaining money on rent. Unless her new landlord had other ideas. "When do you expect him back?" she asked.

"Sunday."

"Oh. I was hoping to move in right away. Should I wait until he gets back?"

"That won't be necessary. I'll let him know to expect you. Meanwhile, I'll have someone hook you up." She pointed toward the generator on a concrete pad tucked behind the trailer. "Welcome to the neighborhood." Shirley grinned and handed over the key before they headed back. "Watch your step." She steered Kyra away from a hole in the ground a few feet ahead of them. "Rabbits. Something to keep in mind if you plan to put in a garden come spring."

Would she still be here then? Kyra wondered. She hoped so; this town had come to feel like home. But if she couldn't find permanent work, or if Rory tracked her down, she would have no choice but to move on. Either possibility was all too real. Good-paying jobs were scarce, especially for someone who couldn't work in her chosen profession, and Rory had the resources to track her down. And the determination. *I'll never let you go,* he'd once told her, and she didn't doubt he'd meant it. She felt a cold finger of dread brush over the back of her neck at the thought.

When she reached her car, she retrieved her tote from it, from which she pulled the zippered pouch that held her remaining cash—a little over $3,000. She paid Shirley, who scribbled a receipt on the back of a shopping list she'd dug from her pocket, and handed it to her.

"Nearest market is Wheeler's, at the crossroads of 49 and Gold Creek Road. You can't miss it," she said as she was climbing into her SUV. "Trash pickup is on Tuesday mornings. If you need anything or have any questions, give us a holler—Ed and I are just down the road."

"Thanks. I will," Kyra said. "And thanks for everything." Mainly she was grateful for the good deal on the rent, which she hoped Shirley's son would honor. He might decide to charge her more, in which case she'd either have to fork it over or find another place to live in the absence of a signed lease. The thought made her nervous. She could only hope her new landlord was as nice as his mother.

She got in her car, and as she opened the door to the driver's side, Ranger leaped in. It was growing dark by the time they arrived back at the Pine Ridge, so she waited until the following morning to pack up her things and check out. She drove to her new home with Ranger, stopping at Wheeler's Market on the way, where she picked up some basic provisions, dog food, and cleaning supplies. A mom-and-pop establishment with a row of gas pumps in front and a sign in the window advertising bait and tackle, she found it was surprisingly well stocked for a country store.

She spent the rest of the morning scrubbing the trailer inside from top to bottom. Moving in was a cinch in comparison. When she'd fled Rochester, she'd brought only what she would need. She'd left behind most of the contents of her walk-in closet filled with expensive clothes, shoes, and accessories that Rory had selected for her because he'd wanted her to look the part when they appeared in public together or entertained. The stuff she carried, which filled two suitcases and several cardboard boxes—a half dozen changes of clothing, including an outfit suitable for job interviews; her art supplies; and a handful of mementos such as her engraved "Teacher of the Year" plaque from two years ago and a hand-painted ceramic mug one of her former students had made for her—required no more than three trips to and from her car. By the time the last box had been carried inside and unpacked, it was lunchtime.

She fed Ranger and made a bologna sandwich for herself, which she ate outside at the picnic table. It had stopped raining and the sun had come out. Through the trees that grew along the creek, she could see water tumbling over rocks. The burbling of the creek and chirping of birds were the only sounds she heard.

After she ate, she set out with Ranger to explore, taking the path that followed the creek, headed south. She hadn't gone far when she came to a spot where the creek deepened and widened to form a swimming hole. Hot and sweaty from her labors, she couldn't resist. She removed her sneakers and jeans, and leaving Ranger to chase tadpoles in the shallows, waded in. She was in up to her thighs when the sandy bottom suddenly dropped away and she was plunged into deep water so cold it made her gasp. Pushing away the wet strands of hair covering her eyes, she began swimming back toward the creek bank.

"It's okay, boy! I'm fine!" she called to Ranger when he began paddling toward her like he thought she might need rescuing. Satisfied that his mistress was in no danger of drowning, he turned back. He sprang onto the creek bank when he reached it and vigorously shook himself off, sending water droplets spraying from his fur. A minute later, Kyra was stepping from the water onto dry land.

"Not the best time of year for a swim."

She froze, hearing the voice, and watched warily as a male figure emerged from the shadows of the trees higher up on the creek bank. Tall and bearded, wearing gray cords and a navy fleece vest over a checkered shirt. Coop Langston.

"You," she gasped. "What . . . what are you doing here?"

"I could ask you the same question," he said in a mild tone, bending to give Ranger a scratch behind his ears when he ran over to greet him. "Are you aware you're trespassing on private property?"

"I live here. And what's it to you, anyway?"

"This happens to be my property."

She stared at him in shock. "*You're* Shirley's son?"

"One of them—she has four. You've met my mom, I take it."

"Yes, when I was here yesterday. She showed me your trailer."

"Ah yes. Mom told me. You must be my new tenant."

"Kyra Smith." She gave him her name. No point in withholding it now. "And you're Coop."

"You remembered." He smiled slightly, as if there was some significance in her remembering his name. "Saw your car in the driveway when I pulled in but didn't recognize it. You changed your plates."

After he remarked on her out-of-state plates on the night they'd met, she'd bought her unregistered California plates at a junkyard, where she'd paid in cash and no questions were asked. She hadn't expected to see Coop Langston again. Kyra didn't respond, and was relieved when he made no further comment, though she was aware of his cop's eyes studying her.

"For the record, I wasn't sneaking up on you," he went on. "I was just coming over to introduce myself. Didn't know we'd met already."

"Me either." Obviously. "You weren't due back until tomorrow." An accusatory note crept into her voice.

"I decided to come home a day early. Should I have checked with you first?" he replied with a sardonic lift of his brow.

She grew flustered, and stammered, "N-no. It's just . . . I wasn't expecting company."

"Yeah, I can see that." His eyes traveled over her, and she became aware that she was standing there in her wet T-shirt and underwear. "What do you say we continue this conversation after you've changed into some dry clothes?"

She hastily pulled on her jeans and sneakers and headed back to the trailer with Ranger and her new landlord. When they arrived, she went inside to change. She emerged a few minutes later wearing dry clothes, with her damp hair hanging loose around her shoulders, to find a fire blazing in the fire ring, Coop tending it. The air smelled pleasantly of woodsmoke. She looked for Ranger and spotted him in the field, his curly tail waving above the tall grass as he chased after a butterfly.

"Thought you might like to warm up after your swim," Coop said.

"I didn't plan on going for a swim, but thank you," she replied stiffly. She sat down in one of the Adirondack chairs and stretched her hands toward the fire, its heat warming her chilled fingers.

He fetched another split log from the stack underneath the trailer and tossed it onto the fire before lowering his huge frame into the chair next to her. "So, now that you know who your landlord is, are you having second thoughts about renting from me?"

"Why would I?" she asked, rather than giving him a direct answer.

"I don't know, but the last time I saw you, you were running like you couldn't get away from me fast enough."

"I was spooked."

"By what Jed said?" She nodded, and waited for an explanation. But all he said was, "I'd be happy to refund the money you paid if you're worried about renting from an accused killer."

Kyra considered it. But she wasn't getting any creepy vibes from him, nor did she know the circumstances of the alleged killing. It might have been an accident. Besides which, where would she go if she left? Affordable housing in Gold Creek was as scarce as the gold that had once lured prospectors to this region by the tens of thousands more than a century ago and was now all but tapped out.

"I'm not. If it's okay with you, I think I'll stay," she said. "I'm sorry if I was rude before."

"Apology accepted. I don't blame you for being mistrustful. You didn't know me, and it pays to be cautious with strange men."

"That was before I met your mom."

He laughed. "If you knew her like I do, you'd be more scared of her than you were of me. My brothers and I lived in fear of invoking her displeasure when we were growing up. When we stepped out of line or mouthed off, she came down on us like a ton of bricks. Inside that tiny body of hers is a tiger."

"I could see that." Kyra had sensed a tough streak underneath Shirley's kindly demeanor. "Speaking of your mom, she mentioned she and your dad used to own this property. Did you grow up here?"

"Yep. In some ways it's like I never left, except now I own it."

"Do you live here alone?" She recalled him mentioning he wasn't married.

"I do."

"It's a lot of house for one person," she observed, gazing across the field at the white clapboard two-story.

"I was married when I bought it. My wife and I got divorced soon after." His tone was matter of fact, but Kyra sensed it was a painful subject. "She moved back to Montana, where she's from originally."

"I'm sorry."

He shrugged. "It's been eight years. Plenty of time to get over it."

Some things you never get over. "But you didn't consider selling and buying a smaller place?"

"No. This is home. There are times I feel like a penny rattling around in a jar, but between my parents and brothers and their wives and kids, all of whom live in the area, there's usually at least one family member dropping by on any given day. And we still celebrate our family occasions at the house."

"I can only imagine. I don't have any siblings. Everything I know about big families comes from watching TV." Kyra used to wish she had siblings when she was younger. Of course, she'd wished for a lot of things back then. "Must be nice."

"Sure, but when I was a kid, I'd have given anything for a room of my own. I shared one with my two older brothers, and all four of us shared a bathroom. I recall some epic battles, and there was always somebody banging on the door to the bathroom, accusing whoever was in it of hogging it." He chuckled and shook his head at the memory. "We gave our parents ample cause to crack the whip."

"Was your dad as strict as your mom?"

"No. He worked as a deputy sheriff, but Mom was the law at home."

"Your dad was a cop?"

"For thirty years before he retired. I used to go on ride-alongs with him when I was a kid."

"So you followed in his footsteps when you became a cop."

"Yep. Runs in the family. My younger brother is a highway patrol officer."

"What kind of work do you do now?"

"I'm a therapist. I specialize in the treatment of PTSD."

That surprised her. "How does a former cop become a therapist?"

"In my case, by getting fired from my job."

"You were fired?"

"Technically, I resigned. I was dealing with some personal issues at the time, and when I realized I could no longer uphold the oath I'd taken when I became a cop to protect and serve, I turned in my badge and service weapon. I went back to school and got my master's in clinical psychology."

Kyra wondered if the personal issues to which he'd alluded had had something to do with the killing he'd been accused of. "Why did you decide to become a therapist?"

"I wanted to help others like myself. Most of my clients are law enforcement and ex-military. PTSD is an occupational hazard, as you might imagine. Us tough guys tend to avoid dealing with our emotions, which can cause problems after experiencing a traumatic event. I have clients who blew up their marriages, lost their jobs, and in some cases their freedom, before they finally sought treatment."

"And you're able to help them?"

"The ones who want to be helped. I should also mention that I work from home, so if you notice frequent comings and goings, those would be my clients. In case you suspected me of being a drug dealer."

"Good to know," she replied dryly.

Eileen Goudge

"So, what's your story, Kyra Smith?" He turned toward her, and as his tea-brown eyes met hers, she felt a physical jolt go through her, like she had when they shook hands on the night they'd first met. It left her feeling rattled.

"Like most stories, it's of interest only to those involved," she said.

"That sounded like a deflection."

"That's what a therapist would say, but you're not my therapist."

"Fair enough. I'll go with an easy question, then. What do you do for a living?"

"I taught art at a private school before I came here. At the moment I'm working temp jobs while I look for something permanent."

"Do you have a husband or boyfriend? Or girlfriend?"

"None of the above." Kyra tucked her left hand under her thigh before remembering that she'd sold her wedding band and diamond engagement ring. Her reflexive move wasn't missed by Coop. She saw him glance down and was relieved when he didn't comment on it. "It's just me and Ranger."

Ranger had returned from explorations and now lay between them, facing the fire with his head resting on his forepaws. He lifted his head at hearing his name, and Coop gave him a scratch behind his ears.

For a minute, he and Kyra sat together in companionable silence. She still didn't trust him entirely, but after meeting his mom and getting to know him a bit, she'd softened toward him. She sneaked glances at him, wondering what it was about him that made him attractive. She normally wasn't attracted to men with facial hair. Maybe it was his eyes. Cop's eyes, yes, but they seemed kind.

"Well, I'll let you get back to it," he said finally, and rose. "Need any help moving in?"

"All done, but thanks."

"If you run low on firewood, there's more in the woodshed." He pointed in the direction of the house. "Just don't leave any fire that's burning unattended. Wildfires are a danger in these parts. Oh, and if you have laundry, feel free to use my washer and dryer. Door is usually

126

unlocked, but I'll give you a key, just in case. I believe that about covers it unless you can think of anything else."

"I'll need your Wi-Fi password. You do have Wi-Fi, don't you?"

"I do. We're not entirely cut off from civilization out here in the boonies."

She stood and pulled out her phone. She gave him her number, and he texted her the Wi-Fi password. "Thanks," she said, tucking her phone back into her pocket. "One more thing . . ." She hesitated to warn him of the danger she might be in, but she also knew she owed it to him, as her landlord. "If anyone should come nosing around asking after me, you don't know me."

His gaze sharpened. "Anyone in particular you're worried about?"

"It's just that the guy I was with before, he, um, didn't take it well when I broke up with him. If he decides to look me up, it could get . . . unpleasant."

"Has he been stalking you? Did he threaten you?"

"No," she answered truthfully. Though if Rory hadn't threatened her recently, it was because he had no way of contacting her, not because he wasn't capable of it.

Coop clearly wasn't buying it. "Kyra, if you're in danger, I need to know."

"I'm not, and if I were, I'd tell you." She wasn't in any imminent danger, at any rate. At least, not as far as she knew. It was the thought of the unknown that sent a chill slithering down her spine.

She was distracted by a low growl. She glanced down and saw that Ranger had lifted his head from his paws and was staring at something, or someone, hidden in the foliage on the opposite creek bank, his ears pricked and his hackles up. The tiny hairs on the back of her neck stood up. "What is it, bud?"

The next thing she heard was a scream.

10

She froze, her heart climbing into her throat and her chest constricting. The next thing she knew, she was doubled over with her hands on her knees, struggling to get enough air into her lungs. "Can't . . . breathe," she gasped out. She grew lightheaded. Black spots swarmed across her field of vision.

"It's okay, honey," she heard a voice say through the roaring in her ears and wheezing sounds she was making. "You're okay. You're having a panic attack, is all. Now, I want you to take a deep breath and let it out nice and slow. That's it. In . . . out. In . . . out. Keep it up. You're doing great."

Gradually, the steel band around her chest loosened. Air trickled and then flowed into her lungs. Her vision cleared. She looked up into a pair of concerned brown eyes in a bearded face. Coop.

She straightened, and a thought popped into her head. *Did he just call me honey?* She was still woozy, and when he put his arm around her waist as if to steady her, she felt a tingling sensation where he was touching her like she got when feeling returned to an arm or a leg that had gone numb.

"Better?" he said.

She nodded. "Sorry. I don't know what came over me. I heard a scream, and . . . What in God's name *was* that?"

"Sounded like a mountain lion."

"You have mountain lions here?"

"Uh, yeah, being as we're in the mountains. But sightings are rare, so you're not in any danger."

"Do you know of anyone ever being attacked by a mountain lion?"

"Not in these parts, and they aren't known to attack humans unless they're threatened or protecting their young. That said, you'd be wise to stay out of the woods after dark. We have bears, too."

"I have no intention of wandering in the woods after dark." It wasn't just a question of what might be lurking there, but whom. She felt a wet nose nudge her hand and bent to stroke the silky fur on Ranger's head, reassuring him she was okay. "Sorry for freaking out on you," she apologized again.

"It's not the first panic attack I've witnessed. It's fairly common among people with PTSD. That's how I know how to talk someone through it. Was that the first time you've had one?"

"No. It's happened a few times before."

The first time was a year ago. She'd been at the supermarket where she shopped and had spied a couple having an argument. She'd been too far away to hear what they were saying, but from the man's red face and pinched lips and the woman's defensive body language, it was clear that it was heated. Kyra had stopped short, and she must have blacked out for a second or two because the next thing she remembered was sitting on the floor with her head pressed to her knees and her chest in a vise. When she looked up, she saw to her horror that she'd attracted an audience. A balding middle-aged man wearing the red vest of a store employee came over and crouched down in front of her, asking if she was all right or if she needed him to call an ambulance. She was mortified.

"Do you remember what triggered it those other times? Did something frighten you or make you anxious?"

The last time was after I stole someone's dog and was afraid that I was wanted by the police. Which was the least of my worries because I'm also on the run from my abusive husband.

"Not that I recall," she lied.

"Some of my clients who are prone to panic attacks have found it useful to keep a record. After each episode, they make a note of what they were doing and how they were feeling before it happened. That way, they can see a pattern emerge and know to avoid certain triggers. You should try it."

"Maybe I will."

"Would you feel safer if you stayed up at the house tonight? You can sleep in one of the guest rooms. Your dog is welcome, too."

Kyra was tempted to take him up on his offer, but she shook her head. She might sleep easier if she stayed the night at Coop's, but she might also do something she'd regret, like kiss him. And she was still recovering from the last man she'd kissed, and later married. "Thanks, but I think I've caused enough trouble for one day. Starting with accusing you of trespassing on your own property."

He smiled. "I accused you first, so that makes us even."

"That's generous of you. Most people would think twice about renting to someone who'd been rude to them."

"I wouldn't know, being as I'm new at this whole landlord thing."

"Speaking of which, do you need me to sign anything?"

"You mean like a lease?" She nodded, and he continued, "I'll draw one up, but it doesn't have to be binding. It can stipulate that you're free to leave at any time without penalty. Would that suit you?"

"Yes, thank you. So we're good?"

"We're good." His gaze lingered on her, causing the tingling sensation she'd experienced a minute ago to return, spreading from the roots of her hair to her toes; then he turned to head back to his house.

In the days that followed, she avoided Coop and suspected he was avoiding her as well. Whenever their paths happened to cross, they'd pause to exchange pleasantries and any news that was pertinent, but those exchanges were brief and impersonal. The rest of the time, she saw him only in passing or from a distance. Once when she was returning from town, she'd come upon him chopping firewood in his backyard. She'd paused as she was coming around the side of the house, transfixed by the sight of him, in his jeans and T-shirt, swinging his axe, the muscles in his powerful arms rippling with his movements. The spell was broken when he caught her staring at him. He stopped and waved. She waved back and continued on her way, her face—and other parts of her body—on fire.

She'd noticed he had a lot of visitors. Some were friends and family members. Some were clients. The former came and went by the front entrance, the latter by the entrance to his practice, located at the rear of the building. One day when she was home, reading a book on criminology she'd borrowed from Gertie, she heard Ranger bark, followed by a knock at the door. She wasn't expecting any visitors, so her first instinct was to stay out of sight in case today's was of the unwanted variety. When she peeked through the curtains, she was relieved to see it was Shirley, holding a covered plate.

"I hope you like chicken pot pie," she said, handing Kyra the plate after she opened the door.

"Love it." She lifted a corner of the foil covering the plate and inhaled the tantalizing aroma of the still-warm pie. "If it tastes as good as it smells, I'm in for a treat. Thank you. It was sweet of you to think of me."

"I was bringing some to Coop, so I just brought extra."

"Would you like to come in?"

"Another time. I have to run. How're you doing? You settling in okay?"

"Yes, thank you." Her tiny home was growing on her. It was cramped but comfortable, and its outdoor space and views made up for the amenities it lacked, especially now with the fall leaves at their peak. She drank her coffee outside in the mornings and ate her meals at the picnic table, weather permitting. She took Ranger on long walks, tramping all over the property and down the country road beyond, often returning with wildflowers she'd picked, or wild raspberries she'd harvested, along the way. At night, she fell asleep to the murmuring of the creek and the calls of nightjars.

"Judging from the roses in your cheeks, I'd say country living suits you. My son treating you okay?"

"He's been the perfect gentleman." Kyra wanted to snatch the words back as soon as they were out of her mouth. She'd made it sound like there was something going on between them.

Shirley must have thought so, too, from the twinkle in her eye, but all she said was, "You like chili?"

"I adore it." Growing up in the Southwest had given her a taste for spicy food.

"Next time, I'll bring you some of my smoky beef chili."

"That would be lovely, but don't feel you have to—"

"It's no trouble at all. When I cook, I usually make enough to feed an army. Force of habit from when I was cooking for a family of six. If I didn't spread the wealth, it'd go to waste. Enjoy," she said, and left.

In the coming days, Kyra was kept busy between her two jobs and her coursework, which was intensive and covered everything from basic drawing techniques to police procedure and the role of the forensic artist in a modern-day criminal investigation. She took copious notes in class, listened to podcasts on the subject, and read the books and articles on the assigned reading list. During the third and final week of the course, Kyra, Nate, Staci, and Ashley conducted mock interviews like they would in the field, with volunteers acting the parts of the witnesses and victims.

When it was her turn, Kyra was thrown into a mild panic when her "victim," a petite brunette named "Linda" with more piercings than Staci, stated at the outset, "I didn't get a good look at him. His face was in shadow." Her story was that she'd been mugged at knifepoint outside the nightclub where she worked as a cocktail waitress when she was leaving to go home at around midnight on the night in question. But if she hadn't seen her assailant's face, Kyra had little to go on.

Then she remembered something Gertie had said. *Memories involve vision, taste, hearing, touch, and smell. If any of the five senses are blocked or impaired in someone while they're witnessing a crime, it can cause gaps in their memory of the event after it's occurred. It's your job as a forensic artist to find ways to fill in those gaps.* Maybe Linda had seen more than she remembered.

Before she began her interview, Kyra did a Google Earth search, which showed the parking lot of the building where the mugging had taken place. "Linda, when you were assaulted, do you recall seeing any vehicles come into or out of the parking lot during that time?" she asked. She knew from Linda's statement she'd been in the parking lot of the building at the time, just outside the service entrance.

"I don't remember," Linda said. "But if anyone had witnessed the attack, wouldn't they have intervened?"

"Not necessarily. They might not have had a clear view, or they might have been reluctant to get involved. But if a vehicle *had* been entering or exiting the parking lot during that time, its headlights would've been on at that hour, in which case, the parking lot would've been partially lit."

"Right. That makes sense."

"Also, it was a Saturday night, at a time when nightclubs are typically at their busiest, so it stands to reason there would've been at least one driver entering or exiting the parking lot while you were being mugged." She paused to allow Linda to process this before asking, "Did you notice anything about your mugger's appearance? Was he short or tall, fat or thin?"

Linda consulted her script. "Short and kind of stocky."

"Did he have any scars, marks, or tattoos?"

"I don't know. It was dark."

"But maybe not fully dark. If a passing car was shining its headlights, you might have noticed if, say, he was wearing glasses or he was balding."

"Maybe."

"Did you notice anything else about him? Something you might have felt or sensed rather than seen?"

"Like what?"

"Like a boner," called Staci from her front-row seat.

"Eww," said Ashley, looking disgusted.

Nate guffawed.

"I was thinking more of facial hair," said Kyra, barely managing to keep a straight face.

"Come to think of it," Linda said, "I thought I felt something tickling my cheek when he had his face pressed against mine, holding the knife to my throat." She gave a theatrical shudder.

Now we're getting warm.

"Like a beard or a mustache?" Kyra prompted.

"More like a mustache."

After Kyra gleaned what she could from Linda, she got to work developing a sketch of the suspect: a man in his mid to late twenties with wide-set eyes in a bulldog face, framed by dark shoulder-length hair and distinguished by a mustache. When Gertie produced a mug shot for comparison, Kyra was pleased to see that its subject bore more than a passing resemblance to the man depicted in her sketch.

"Excellent interview technique, Kyra," Gertie praised her. "It's a reasonable assumption that the parking lot of a popular nightclub would typically see some comings and goings at that hour on a Saturday night. In which case, the attack wouldn't have occurred in complete darkness, and Linda here, whose real name is Donna, by the way . . . Thank you, Donna"—she motioned toward Donna/Linda, who stood and took a bow—"might have seen more than she remembered."

Kyra warmed at the praise. "It was something you said that gave me the idea. When you told us it was our job to fill in any gaps in the memories of the people we interview. In this case, I began by determining whether there *was* a gap, or if she really hadn't seen her mugger's face."

"Good thinking. If this had been an actual criminal investigation, your sketch would've gotten the suspect nabbed."

"I didn't make him too pretty, did I?"

Gertie studied her sketch. "I think it's safe to say no one would want this fellow hanging on a wall in their home."

Kyra took it as a compliment and smiled at the irony. Back in the day, if she'd been told any of her drawings or paintings wasn't fit to be displayed, she would have felt like a failure.

Friday of that week was the last day of the course. After reviewing the material they'd covered over the past three weeks, Gertie gave a speech commending everyone's efforts and wishing them well in their future endeavors. After class was dismissed, Kyra stayed behind to do some more work on Gertie's books. She was sitting down at her desk when Gertie made a surprising announcement.

"Kyra, I wanted you to be the first to know: I'm retiring at the end of this month. I didn't say anything in class today because it hasn't been publicly announced yet." She perched on a corner of the desk. She wore her uniform of jeans and a Western-style shirt, and today her lipstick matched the red boots she had on.

Kyra was stunned. "Wow. I don't know what to say. You said you were planning to slow down, but . . . retirement?"

"It's sooner than I expected, but my husband is retiring, and it seems like the right time for me, too."

"But you're too young to retire!"

Gertie smiled. "Bless you, darlin', but the date on my birth certificate says otherwise. I'm not getting any younger, and I'd like to do some traveling and see more of my grandchildren before I die."

"How will the sheriff's department manage without you?"

"That's what I wanted to talk to you about. I'm recommending you as my successor."

"Me?" Kyra stared at Gertie in disbelief. "But I don't have any experience."

"Not in the field, but neither did I when I first started out. Most of what I know, I learned flying by the seat of my pants. And you've proven to my satisfaction that you have what it takes."

"What about the others? They're good, too."

"Nate shows promise, but he's green. He lacks the qualities that are essential in this job and that you possess: maturity and empathy. Something tells me you've experienced trauma in your life. Just a guess, and it's none of my business, but I noticed you had a strong reaction when we were discussing the Foster case." She referred to a case they'd discussed in class involving a young woman who'd been beaten and stabbed by an unknown assailant, later identified as her ex-boyfriend.

Because I know what it's like to be brutalized by someone who professes to love you. Kyra didn't think Gertie would be shocked to learn of her history of abuse—she must have heard it all in her line of work—but she had no wish to go there, so she neither confirmed nor denied Gertie's suspicion.

"The same could be said of Staci. Why didn't you choose her?"

"She has empathy, but she's not at your level in terms of her skills. Nor is Ashley. Which leaves you."

"I don't know what to say."

"No need to say anything, but I'm hoping you'll apply for the position."

"I appreciate the opportunity, but can I think about it? Or do you need an answer right away?"

Kyra's stomach churned with a swirl of emotions. She was at once elated and panic-stricken. She'd imagined herself easing into it over time, if given the opportunity, working in partnership with Gertie until she got up to speed. She'd be tossed into the deep end if she took over from Gertie now. Was she ready for that? Even if she were, did she dare? Working in law enforcement would mean a greater risk of Rory discovering her whereabouts. The longer it was delayed, the more time for him to move on and find someone new to obsess over. *It's too soon,* she thought, terrified.

"Of course." Gertie's voice intruded on her thoughts. "But don't take too long. I spoke to the sheriff about you, and he would like to schedule an interview before he interviews other candidates."

"I'll let you know by Monday." Kyra gave a crooked smile. "One thing's for sure. No one could ever replace you."

Gertie chuckled. "I don't know about that. Right now, I'm just an old broad who's ready to start tackling her bucket list." She slid from her perch, opened a desk drawer, and pulled out two business cards, handing them to Kyra. "Here are the numbers for the sheriff's office and my attorney, Drew Halliday. Drew can file the necessary paperwork to get you licensed as an independent contractor. You'll also need a website. I can recommend a web designer if you don't have one already."

"That's assuming I get the job."

"I have faith in you." Gertie's eyes twinkled behind her candy-apple-red glasses. She bent to pet Ranger, who'd wandered over from his sunny spot by the bay window to see if she had anything for him, too. She fished a liver treat from her pocket and tossed it to him—he had her well trained—and he wolfed it down. "I'll miss seeing you both around here."

"We're not going anywhere so fast. I still have another day's worth of work."

"After which, you can start cataloging my sketches for my archives, if you're looking to pick up extra work. Although," she added with a knowing smile, "something tells me you won't be doing temp work for much longer."

Kyra was still in a quandary when she left two hours later. She was excited about the opportunity that had been presented to her. If she seized it, she could be making a comfortable living doing a job she loved, one that would allow her to stay in Gold Creek, and making a difference in the community. As for the risk involved, when would it ever be safe for her to come out of hiding? Six months, a year, five years from now, or maybe never? The fact was, she had no way of knowing, and was she going to spend the rest of her life living in fear? Hadn't Rory controlled and terrorized her for long enough?

As she drove home, her mind traveled back in time.

"No one will ever love you like I do," Rory said as he knelt before her.

She caught herself before she could voice the thought, *God, I hope not.* He was penitent now but might get angry again if she didn't watch out, and she couldn't take any more. She brought her hand to her cheek, which was tender and swollen where he'd struck her. It throbbed, but she wasn't in pain; that would come after the numbness wore off. Right now, she was still in shock.

She shivered, feeling chilled. The bed on which she sat might have been an ice floe. His voice seemed to come from far away as he went on. "Baby, I'm so sorry. I didn't mean to hurt you. It won't happen again. I'll make sure that it doesn't. You were right when you said I needed professional help. I realize that now, and I promise to make an appointment with that therapist you found."

That's what you said the last time, and the time before. In the three years they'd been married, she'd lost count of the number of times he'd hit first in a fit of rage and begged forgiveness afterward. It had become a familiar pattern. And he had yet to get professional help. "Okay," she said. What else could she say?

"I'd never hurt you on purpose. You know that, don't you?" He gently traced with his fingertip the bruised flesh under her right eye, which was puffy and would be swollen shut come morning. "When I saw that son of a bitch, Hanratty, flirting with you at the party, I lost it."

They'd gone to a New Year's Eve party that evening at the home of one of Rory's cronies in the state justice department. The "son of a bitch" to whom he'd referred, State Supreme Court Judge Clark Hanratty, had been among the guests in attendance. Unlike the other judges she knew, who were all ancient, Hanratty was relatively young and attractive, though not her type. She'd met him on previous occasions, and he'd struck her as an egotistical bore. While they'd been talking at the party, he'd seemed less interested in anything she'd had to say than in boasting about his accomplishments. Rory had had a different take on what he'd observed from across the room. To listen to him talk, Hanratty had practically had his tongue down her throat. He'd lit into her when they were on their way home from the party. By the time they arrived, he'd worked himself into a rage.

Now his eyes that had blazed with fury minutes before were filled with remorse. "I shouldn't have taken it out on you. I don't know what comes over me sometimes. It's like one minute I'm myself, and the next I'm . . . Jesus, I've become my dad, haven't I?" His voice broke, and his features twisted. He bowed his head, the picture of contrition. "I swore I'd never be like him."

She didn't say anything. She'd forgiven him in the past, even wept for the defenseless boy he'd been when his father used to beat him. She wasn't so forgiving anymore, but her heart softened toward him despite herself. She couldn't get the picture of that poor little boy out of her head.

"I need—" She broke off.

He cupped her head between his hands, looking into her eyes. "What do you need? Anything, baby."

"I need to get away." She cringed at the pleading note that crept into her voice. She shouldn't have to ask for her husband's permission. "Just for a few days. To . . . to clear my head." Her friend Nina from work owned a cabin in the Poconos, and she'd offered to let her use it.

A crease appeared between his brows. "Why? You don't think I'll give you the space you need?"

She swallowed the hysterical laugh that bubbled up her throat. When had he ever given her space to think—or breathe, even? "It's not that," she lied. "I just think it would be good for me. For us."

"How could it be good for us to be apart? Look, I know I messed up. It won't happen again, I swear." When she didn't respond, he went on, an edge of desperation in his voice. "You believe me, don't you? Say you believe me."

"I believe you," she said in a flat voice. "But I still think I should go away."

"I have a better idea. Why don't we go away together? Someplace warm with sandy beaches. How about that resort in Jamaica we stayed at when we were on our honeymoon?" She suppressed a shudder. Had he forgotten what had happened on their honeymoon? What he'd done to her? "As soon as this trial is over, we'll pick a date and I'll book the hotel and flights." He was referring to the criminal case he was prosecuting. The defendant, Glenn Severs, a software executive, was charged with the murder of his wife, who'd gone missing nine months earlier and was presumed dead. Rory was confident of a guilty verdict despite the absence of a body, murder weapon, or any physical evidence that implicated the defendant. He had reason to be. He usually won.

"We . . . we could do that," she said. "But first I'd like to go away by myself. Just for a little while."

His frown deepened. "That's what my mom said when she left my dad, that it would just be for a little while."

When Rory was thirteen and his brother was ten, his mom had moved out and filed for divorce. She'd promised her sons she would return for them as soon as she found a job and a place to live. Meanwhile, Rory's father, a successful attorney with deep pockets, had sued for full custody and won despite her allegations of abuse. Rory had never forgiven his mother for what he saw as her abandonment. It didn't matter that she'd fought for custody, or that she'd continued to see her sons on the days she'd had court-ordered visitation. The fact was, she'd left him in the care of his abusive father.

"That was different. I'm not leaving you." She didn't dare. There was nowhere she could go, she'd become convinced, where he wouldn't hunt her down. He was like a pit bull when it locked its jaws on something, and as a district attorney, he had resources the average person didn't. She might well end up missing and presumed dead, like Glenn Severs's wife. But if she got away for a little while, maybe she could figure something out. Come up with a plan for a permanent escape.

He smiled, as if it hadn't occurred to him she might actually leave him. Wasn't everyone always telling her how lucky she was to have such a handsome and devoted husband? Other women were always coming on to Rory. She wished one of them would succeed in turning his head, but as far as she knew, he'd been faithful to her. For what it was worth. "Good. Because I plan to spend the rest of our lives proving to you that I'm the man you deserve. We'll start over, put the past behind us. Go on that second honeymoon. In the meantime . . ." He rose to his full height, and she saw to her horror that his expression had shifted from sorry to sultry. He bent to kiss her, and frowned when she stiffened and drew back. "Come on, baby. Let me make it up to you." He placed his hands on her shoulders and attempted to push her onto her back, his eyes heavy-lidded with desire.

She resisted. "Not now. Not like this," she whispered.

"You want it, too. I can tell. Don't play hard to get."

Oh God. How could he *not* see her panic? Was he blind, or simply determined to have his way with her? "No. Really. I . . . I'm not in the mood."

"Relax, and leave the driving to me." He gave a throaty chuckle. As if it were a sex game they were playing. He climbed onto the bed and straddled her, using the weight of his body to push her onto her back. She felt his erection pressing against her thigh through his pants. *Dear God.* She lay stiffly beneath him as he murmured against her neck, "I'm never letting you go. Baby, I love you."

The memory washed over Kyra like a storm surge swirling with bits and pieces of debris. She felt dirty and a little sick to her stomach reliving that awful night. She gripped the steering wheel as she drove. She was also angry. Angry at Rory for forcing himself on her, and angry at herself for submitting. If she'd fought back, he might have hurt her worse, but she'd have had her self-respect, at least.

"Maybe I've been looking at this all wrong," she said to Ranger in the passenger seat. He swiveled his head around to look at her, ears pricked. "I've been focusing on what I stand to lose instead of what I've lost already." Rory had taken so much from her—her innocence, her trust, and on that night, her freedom to say no. Was she also going to let him rob her of the opportunity Gertie had offered?

It was getting dark by the time she pulled into the driveway at Coop's. She parked and climbed out of her car while Ranger performed his trick of opening the window on the passenger side and leaping out. They were making their way past the house to their trailer when Ranger unexpectedly changed direction and went streaking through the open gate to the yard and up the front path before she could stop him. He ignored her when she called, "Ranger, come!" By the time she caught up with him, he was sitting on the porch outside the front door barking to announce his presence to whoever was inside. The door swung open. Kyra froze, staring at the huge form filling the doorway.

"Coop. Hey," she said when she recovered. "Sorry to disturb you. Seems Ranger decided to pay you a visit when he saw your gate was open."

He smiled. "My fault for forgetting to latch it. But you're always welcome," he said to Ranger as he bent to greet him. "Both of you," he added, his eyes meeting Kyra's when he straightened.

"He doesn't know it's impolite to drop in on people unannounced."

"Tell that to my family members," Coop replied with a chuckle. He wore jeans and a gray fleece pullover, what she thought of as his mountain-man look. During office hours he wore business attire, chinos and a collared shirt. "Actually, I'm glad you dropped by. I was hoping to have a word with you."

"Oh? If it's about yesterday, it won't happen again. I didn't see your truck in the driveway when I was coming over to do my laundry, so I assumed no one was home. I should've knocked before I let myself in." Instead, she'd walked in on Coop in the kitchen making himself breakfast. His brother Liam had borrowed his truck, she learned. Coop hadn't seemed bothered by the intrusion, but she'd been embarrassed. After stammering an apology, she'd left. "Again, I'm sorry."

"No worries. You're welcome to use my washer and dryer anytime, though if you come in again without knocking and find me in my underwear, you'll have only yourself to blame," he teased.

"Do you usually cook in your underwear?"

"Sometimes. You know what they say, if you can't stand the heat—"

"Get out of the kitchen," she finished for him.

"Or get undressed." His eyes sparkled, and his lips curved in a playful smile.

She laughed. "Now *that* would be an eyeful."

He was flirting with her. Worse, she was flirting back. *This has to stop.*

"But, just so you know," she went on, so there would be no misunderstanding, "I plan to knock in the future."

"Duly noted."

"So, what was it you wanted to talk to me about?"

"Nothing special. I just wanted to check in with you, see how you're doing. Whenever I see you, one of us is either coming or going. We haven't had a chance to have a proper chat. Would you like to come in?"

"Thanks, but I should really—"

"Or we could sit on the porch. It's such a nice evening, and this might be our last chance before the cold weather sets in." Before she could demur, he grabbed a jacket and stepped outside, walking over to the pair of wooden rockers to his right. She followed, drawn by his magnetic presence, which she found difficult to resist. When they were both seated, Ranger curled up between them, watching the sun set below the mountaintops to the west, he said, "Never gets old."

"No, it doesn't." Realizing she was looking at Coop and not the view as she said it, she tore her gaze from him.

"Everything okay at Casa Grande? No issues to report?"

"Nope. All good."

"No bear or mountain lion sightings?"

"Don't even." She shot him a warning glance. "The only danger is that I'll become spoiled with your mom bringing me meals. I don't know which was tastier, her chicken pot pie or her beef chili. It's a toss-up."

He grinned. "Wait'll you try her lasagna. I guarantee it'll be the best you've ever eaten."

"I look forward to it, but I hope she doesn't feel obliged to feed me just because I'm living on your property."

"It probably has more to do with the fact that you live alone. She's been bringing me meals since I got divorced. She seems to think I'd waste away otherwise. The irony is that Angela, my ex-wife, wasn't much of a cook. I did most of the cooking when we were married."

"Does your mom know that?"

"No doubt, though she never said anything to me about it. Nothing escapes Mom. If she didn't deliver meals back then, it was probably because she didn't want my wife to feel insulted."

"Well, I have no objection if she wants to feed me. I've been so busy between my jobs and the course I was taking, I haven't had time to do much cooking, or anything else for that matter."

"How's it going with the course?" he asked. She'd mentioned to him in passing that she was taking Gertie's course.

"Today was the last day, actually."

"Ah. So, what's next?"

"I may have a job prospect."

His expression grew animated. "Really? That's great!"

She hesitated to give details. Her friends would have been the first to know of her opportunity if she hadn't run into Coop first. But she was bursting with her news, and he was here. "Can you keep a secret?"

"Depends. Does it involve a crime?"

"In a way, but not the way you might think. Gertie Naylor is retiring, and she wants me to replace her."

He stared at her in surprise, then broke into a grin. "Wow. That's huge. But why is it a secret?"

"She hasn't announced yet that she's retiring. Also, I haven't decided yet whether to apply for the position."

"Why wouldn't you? Sounds like an incredible opportunity."

"It's also a huge responsibility. I've never worked in the field before. I'd planned on taking it slow, maybe partnering with Gertie while I learned the ropes. If I get this job, I'd be plunged into the deep end."

"It was the same with me when I became a cop. You'll learn, like I did. Or is there another reason you're hesitating?" He seemed to see past the wall she'd erected around herself, which made her nervous.

"It's complicated."

He was quiet for a minute as if he was waiting for her to elaborate, as she imagined he did with his clients in giving them space to share what was on their mind, or come to their own conclusions. "What are you afraid of, Kyra?" he asked finally. His voice was soft, but she winced as if from a shout.

"Who said I was afraid?"

"Call it a cop's intuition. You were a teacher, and now you're working odd jobs while contemplating a career change. You're also living off the grid, driving a car with unregistered plates."

A guilty flush spread across her cheeks. "How did you . . . ?"

"I had one of my buddies at the department run your tags. You didn't think I'd rent to just anyone, did you? Your story had some holes in it, so I also did a background check. I didn't find any outstanding warrants. In fact, I couldn't find anything at all online about a Kyra Smith the same age as you who used to be teacher and who matches your description. Which suggests it's not your real name. The only people I know of who are living under assumed names are either bail jumpers, in WITSEC, or wanted in connection with a crime. Which are you? More to the point, *who* are you?" His tone was even, but his eyes seemed to burn into her.

"I . . ." She stopped, swallowed hard, and said, "Are you asking me to leave?"

"No. I'm asking you to trust me."

She saw nothing in his eyes to suggest that he was untrustworthy, but she held back, nonetheless.

"What aren't you telling me, Kyra?"

She didn't know how to respond. How could she tell him about her past without making herself look bad? In her mind, it was a tale as tangled as a spiderweb, with no beginning or end. "It's a long story, and I'd rather not get into it," she said at last. "But I swear I'm not in any trouble with the law." That she knew of, anyway. She might be wanted for dognapping. "Nor am I in witness protection."

"Is it about your ex? Is he the reason you're living under an assumed name?"

She was tempted to confide in him. But even if he could be trusted to keep her secret, telling him about her past could jeopardize her position, or any good opinion he might have of her. "How about we leave it on a need-to-know basis? I promise to apprise you of any developments that might affect you."

"Is that a polite way of saying it's none of my business?"

"No. I'm saying it's *my* business that no one else needs to be dragged into. Can I trust you not to say anything?" She studied him, her muscles tense, and a breath caught in her lungs. She didn't relax until he nodded and she knew it would be okay. He wasn't going to rat her out or evict her.

She stood to leave, and as if by some unspoken agreement, he rose to escort her home. As they crossed the field together, with Ranger leading the way, Kyra mulled over the day's events, from Gertie's startling announcement to her chat just now with Coop. Strangely, she felt better after talking to Coop. She trusted him not to reveal what he'd learned from his background check, or rather, what he hadn't learned. And he seemed to trust her to fill him in when she was ready. Now, if only she could find the courage to seize the opportunity to take over for Gertie when she retired.

◆ ◆ ◆

By Monday morning, she'd come to a decision. Before leaving for work, she called the sheriff's office and asked to speak with him. She was put on hold, and then a woman's voice came on the line. "Sharon Anderson. I'm the sheriff's personal assistant. How may I assist you?"

Kyra was intimidated by the scary-sounding woman. After she stated her business, she was put on hold again and then told, "The sheriff can see you in his office tomorrow morning at nine thirty if that's convenient."

"Yes. I'll see him then. Thank you."

After she disconnected, she shared her news with the Tattooed Ladies via a group text. She'd already told them about being tapped as Gertie's replacement, and had received a stream of congratulatory messages and thumbs-up emojis in response. Frannie called to personally congratulate her. Kyra reminded her she hadn't gotten the job yet and didn't know whether she would. When she arrived at the salon a short while later, Suzy gave her a hug that was so animated, with her hopping up and down and swaying from side to side, it could have passed for a dance move.

"Take all the time you need," she said after Kyra had asked for time off for her interview tomorrow. "We'll manage without you, won't we, Jazz?" she called to Jasmine.

"Long as nobody's expecting any spa treatments." Jasmine pointed the comb she'd been running through her customer's hair in Kyra's direction. "You've spoiled our customers rotten."

The customer, a petite woman named Danielle who was one of their regulars, and who swore nobody in Washburn County could do Black hair like Jasmine, perked up at the mention of spa treatments. "Damn, and I was hoping for one of those hot-stone massages I've heard about. Closest I ever get to a spa treatment these days is when I take a bubble bath after I've put my little ones to bed."

"I look like a damn masseuse to you?" demanded Jasmine, and Danielle laughed.

Later, when they were getting coffees in back, Kyra said to Suzy, "If I get the job as Gertie's replacement, I'm not sure I can go on working for you. I hate the thought of leaving you in the lurch."

Suzy was more than understanding. "We both knew it was only temporary, and much as I hate to lose you to the hotbed of crime that is Washburn County"—she made air quotes around the phrase "hotbed of crime"—"I'm tickled pink for you." She stirred a spoonful of Splenda into her coffee.

"I haven't gotten the job yet," Kyra reminded her.

"You will. I have a good feeling about it."

"We'll see." Kyra's nerves kicked in again, and her hand shook as she poured coffee into her mug.

"I believe in you, sweetie. I've seen what you can do." Suzy motioned toward the sketch Kyra had done of her son, framed and hung on the wall above her desk, which was visible through the open door to her office. "Now you just have to believe in yourself."

Easier said than done. Kyra was nervous about her interview for more reasons than one. Starting with the fact that she needed to come clean with the sheriff before she could even be considered for the job. No law enforcement agency would hire someone without doing a background check, which, in her case, would reveal what Coop had uncovered: that the woman he knew as Kyra Smith didn't officially exist. The sheriff might not be as willing as Coop had been to take her at her word when she told him she wasn't involved in anything illegal.

The following morning, as she was getting dressed for her interview, she said to Ranger, "What do you think, bud? Am I doing the right thing, or am I asking for trouble?"

He looked up at her with his head cocked to one side like he was trying to understand and wished he had an answer for her. Earlier, they'd gone for a walk, from which he'd returned looking like a fuzzy sock covered in lint from the dryer, with all the burrs and foxtails that were stuck to his fur. But after she'd picked his fur clean and given his coat a good brushing, he looked like a show dog.

She went back to studying her reflection in the mirror. Her hair was coiled in a bun at the back of her head. She wore her one good outfit: the black pencil skirt, teal silk shirt, and heels she'd brought from Rochester. She looked presentable. No one would guess she was a nervous wreck inside.

She straightened her shoulders and tilted her chin up. "Screw it. What doesn't kill you, right?"

It was a cold, blustery October day. As she drove to town with Ranger, fallen leaves scuttled across the road, and fluffy clouds sailed across the sky above, blown by the wind. Her first stop was Suzy's salon, where she dropped Ranger off. "Sorry, bud," she said when he whined in protest, "I can't take you with me. You stay here and keep the ladies company until I get back."

Suzy held on to his collar so he wouldn't try to follow Kyra, calling out, "Good luck!"

Kyra arrived at the sheriff's office at twenty past nine, carrying sample sketches she'd drawn in a portfolio tucked under one arm. She announced herself to the desk lieutenant, and a few minutes later, a trim woman with straight, silver hair worn chin length strode into the reception area from in back. The scary-sounding woman she'd spoken with on the phone, no doubt.

"Sharon Anderson," she said as they shook hands. Her tone was as brisk as her handshake. "The sheriff is expecting you. If you'll come with me . . ."

Kyra followed her through the maze of modular cubicles in the open-plan office, occupied by uniformed personnel working at their desks, and down a short hallway that led to the administrative offices. The one at the end had SHERIFF KURT MCNALLY stenciled in gold letters on its frosted-glass inset.

"Enter!" a man's voice called from inside after the assistant knocked.

She opened the door and poked her head in. "Ms. Smith is here to see you, sir."

"Send her in."

Kyra stepped inside. The office held a vintage oak desk, with two visitors' chairs facing it, and a nubby griege sofa against one wall, flanked by a bookcase on one side and a row of filing cabinets on the other. Sunlight poured through a pair of double-hung windows behind the desk, where a man with a boxer's build and sharp blue eyes below a full head of coal-black hair shot with iron sat at the desk, looking at something on his computer. He wore the khaki uniform of his office and radiated an air of authority when he rose, extending his arm across the desk to shake her hand.

"Sheriff McNally. Thanks for coming in."

"My pleasure, sir."

"Can I have someone bring you something to drink? Coffee or tea?"

"No, thank you. I've had my coffee already."

"Have a seat." He gestured to the visitors' chairs opposite the desk.

Kyra sat down, smoothing her skirt over her knees. She recalled an expression used by her mom's boss, LouBeth Hunnicutt, at the road-house in Bisbee, Arizona, where Mom had worked the year Kyra was ten. "I'm as jumpy as a frog on a griddle," LouBeth would say about everything from getting her period to an impending visit from the county health inspector. That was just how Kyra felt right now. Jumpy as a frog on a griddle. Her hands shook and one of her legs was jittering. Could she trust the sheriff? Would he believe her story? Would he still want to hire her after he'd heard it?

"I spoke with Gertie, and she told me you're interested in taking over for her after she retires," he began. "She'll be leaving some mighty big shoes to fill. Think you're the one to fill 'em?"

"I believe I am, sir," she said with more confidence than she felt.

"Gertie thinks so, too. According to her, you're the most promising student she's had in years. Our mutual friend Frannie speaks highly of you as well."

"You know Frannie?" Kyra was surprised to hear it, though she probably shouldn't have been. Frannie seemed to know everyone in town.

"We go way back. She used to babysit me when I was playing cops and robbers with my toy pistol. She bossed me around then and still does, truth to tell. She warned me to go easy on you, or else."

Kyra smiled at the image of Frannie bossing the sheriff, and she suddenly didn't feel as nervous. "I brought samples of my work if you'd like to see them." She passed her portfolio across the desk to him.

"Impressive," he said as he leafed through her samples before handing the portfolio back to her. "I understand you have a degree in fine art. What got you interested in forensic art?"

"Gertie. I didn't know much about it before I met her. Once I took her course, I was hooked."

"Have you ever worked in law enforcement before?"

Kyra took a deep breath and let it out slowly in an effort to calm the butterflies in her stomach. "Sir, before we go any further, there's something you need to know." She paused, smoothing her sweaty palms over her skirt. Her heart was pounding. "My legal name is Krystal Stanhope. Kyra is short for Krystal. Smith was my father's name, though it's not listed on my birth certificate. If you were to run a background check"—as Coop had—"you would find that Kyra Smith doesn't exist."

The sheriff studied her across his desk, appearing more curious than surprised by her admission. Maybe because he'd seen and heard it all in his three terms as sheriff and the years he'd worked as a deputy before that. "I can think of only two reasons why someone would have an alias: either because they're on the run from the law or they're attempting to defraud someone else. You don't strike me as either a criminal or a con woman, Ms. Smith. So why are you living under an assumed name?"

"It's because of my husband. If he knew where I was, I wouldn't be safe."

The sheriff's gaze sharpened. "Has he threatened you?"

"Not recently, but he has in the past."

"Are you saying he was physically abusive?"

She nodded and laced her fingers together in her lap to stop her hands from shaking. "I never pressed charges, though I tried to once.

When I followed up the next day, I was told the officer who'd responded to my 911 call was unavailable. I left a message, but he never got back to me. Later, I found out there was no record of an incident report being filed. No recording of my 911 call, even."

"What did you make of it?"

She hesitated, aware of whom she was talking to. Sheriff Kurt McNally wore the khaki uniform of his office rather than police blues, and his jurisdiction was a continent away from the police department in Rochester, but cops stuck together in her experience. She didn't know any who'd crossed the "blue line." Then she remembered the nice deputy who'd handled the incident involving Frannie's daughter with sensitivity. Coop was another one—a former cop, he was doing good work helping other cops who suffered from PTSD. Maybe Sheriff McNally was one of the good guys.

"I think the report was buried, sir. On account of who my husband is."

"Is he in law enforcement?"

"He's the district attorney of Monroe County in New York. His name is Rory Stanhope."

"Ah." He nodded in understanding. "But you could've gone to the state police. Why didn't you?"

"I wasn't trusting of law enforcement after what happened. Also, Rory has friends in high places. The only reason I'm telling you is so you wouldn't think I was a fugitive from justice if you ran a background check."

"Most fugitives would know better than to apply for a job in law enforcement."

"Good point." She smiled thinly.

He was quiet for a minute, seemingly troubled about what she'd told him. She grew worried. Was he judging her? How could he not? Hadn't she judged the women like her whom she used to see on the news? Women who'd stayed in abusive relationships and paid the price, losing custody of their children, or their lives in some cases. She used to think, *Why don't they leave? Why do they put up with it? Where is their self-respect?* She hadn't imagined such a fate could ever befall her. Until it did.

The only difference between her and those women she'd seen on the news was that no one had died, and she'd gotten away in the end.

When the sheriff spoke again, his words came as a surprise and a relief. "I have a wife and two daughters. If any one of them were harmed by someone, I'd probably react first as a husband or father before I remembered I was an officer of the law, and I'd be lying if I said otherwise. I wish for your sake, Ms. Smith, someone like me had been there for you when needed it."

Her eyes filled. "So you believe me?"

"Why wouldn't I?"

"I can't prove my allegations. He'd claim they were false, if you were to confront him. And he'd have you convinced of it. He almost managed to convince me I was imagining things." When he hadn't been beating her, he'd been gaslighting her. Pretending conversations she recalled word for word had never taken place, or that she'd gotten her "dates mixed up" after they'd made plans and he'd failed to show up. Over time, it had caused her to question her own reality. "It's what he does, and why he's successful at it. He has the highest conviction rate of any district attorney in the history of Monroe County. He's known for getting juries to deliver a guilty verdict on the basis of circumstantial evidence alone."

"I'm not so easily fooled. I can usually spot a liar, whether he's in prison orange or a suit and tie. But I have no cause to make inquiries about your husband if he was never charged with any crime."

"No, but if he were contacted in connection with a background check, it would put me at risk." She was mortified when she felt a tear trickle down one cheek and quickly knuckled it away. "No one knows about any of this except you, not even Frannie." She felt a pang, thinking about how open Frannie and the other Tattooed Ladies had been with her. She didn't like keeping secrets from them.

"Anything we discussed today stays in this room," he assured her. "Subject to revision should a change in circumstances warrant it, of course. If he threatens you again, I want to know about it."

Overcome, Kyra started to choke up again, and swallowed hard before replying, "Of course, and thank you." She hesitated before she got up the courage to ask, "Will you still consider me for the job?"

"I'm interviewing other candidates, but yes, Ms. Smith, you're still in the running. From what Gertie told me and from what I've seen of your work, you're more than qualified. Also," he added with a smile, "I don't want to get on Frannie's bad side, or she might send me to bed without my supper."

Kyra was giddy with a mix of relief and excitement. As she was escorted from the building by the sheriff's assistant minutes later, she thought, *He called me Ms. Smith.* That made it official, if not by any government-issued form of identification. Krystal Stanhope was no more.

◆ ◆ ◆

She stopped at Red Ink Tattoos across the street on her way back to Suzy's salon. Frannie was busy with a customer but waved her inside. The customer, a purple-haired girl wearing earbuds, was tapping on her phone. She glanced up at Kyra as she approached and then went back to her texting.

"I won't keep you," Kyra said to Frannie, raising her voice to be heard above the buzzing of the tattoo gun. "I just wanted to thank you for putting in a good word with the sheriff. I didn't know you knew him."

"Since I was in high school and he was in kindergarten. I used to babysit him."

"So he said."

"Did he tell you I used to threaten to confiscate his toys when he misbehaved? He was a little hellion back then. I like to tease him that if he hadn't become a cop, he'd have ended up on the wrong side of the law." Frannie chuckled as she shaded in a detail on the Celtic cross that she was tattooing on the skinny leg stretched out on the footrest of the adjustable chair in her workstation. "How'd the interview go?"

"He's interviewing other candidates, but I think I have a shot."

"You're a gifted artist and you've got the right instincts. *And* you're Gertie's choice, which I'm sure carries a lot of weight. Relax, kiddo. You've got this." Frannie flashed her an encouraging smile.

"I hope you're right."

Frannie stepped on the foot pedal below the chair, and the buzzing of the tattoo gun ceased. The only sounds then were the muffled thuds of bodies hitting the mats in the karate dojo next door. "There you go, all set," she said loudly to the purple-haired girl, who removed her earbuds and examined her tattoo. She seemed pleased with it.

"Awesome! Wait'll my mom sees it. She'll freak."

Frannie suddenly looked uneasy. "Didn't you say you were over twenty-one?"

"I just turned twenty-two. And don't worry, the driver's license I showed you isn't a fake one. But you'd think I'm still twelve from the way Mom treats me. I wasn't allowed to get my ears pierced or wear makeup until I was fourteen. When I was in college, I was the only kid in my dorm with a curfew. Not," she added with a sly smile, "that it stopped me from staying out as late as I wanted."

At least your mom cares enough to give you a curfew. Growing up, Kyra had been the one looking after her mom, not the other way around, as was the natural order. She'd done the shopping, cooking, and cleaning when she hadn't been running interference with bill collectors and angry landlords. She'd even gotten rid of her mom's low-life boyfriends who'd moved in by threatening to call the cops on them, correctly guessing they were involved in some criminal activity or other. When they'd handed out the manual on parenting, Mom must have been absent that day.

"How's life in the country?" Frannie asked after her customer had paid and left.

"It's growing on me, and Ranger's in dog heaven. His new favorite activity is terrorizing the rabbits and squirrels unless they're only taunting him. If he ever caught one, he probably wouldn't know what to do with it."

"Speaking of which, your new landlord is quite the catch."

Kyra's heart beat faster at the mention of Coop, but she feigned indifference. "That may be, but, unlike my dog, I'm not doing any chasing. Our relationship is strictly business."

Frannie kept her head down as she cleaned and tidied her workstation. "Then I guess it wouldn't interest you to know he broke up with his last girlfriend a few months ago, and hasn't seen anyone since."

"He mentioned he was divorced. He didn't say whether he was currently in a relationship. Not that it's any of my business." Though, naturally, she'd wondered. She imagined he got a lot of interest. The thought caused her to frown. Why should she care? His love life was no concern of hers.

"Did he tell you why he got divorced?"

"No, why did he?"

"It's not my place to say. You should ask him."

"It's really none of my business," Kyra said, though she was curious. She was grateful when Frannie changed the subject.

"You doing anything tonight?" Frannie asked as she crumpled the disinfectant wipe she'd used to clean the tray that held her instruments when she was working on a customer and tossed it in the trash.

"Nothing special, why?"

"I'm meeting Suzy for drinks at The Press." She named the wine bar down the street from Suzy's salon. "You're welcome to join us."

"I have a better idea. Why don't you both come to my place for supper instead? I'll invite Jo and Marisol, too," Kyra said.

Frannie's eyes lit up. "Great idea! I'm dying to see your new place."

"It's tiny. It would be crowded with two people. Five would be a clown car. But the forecast isn't showing any rain, so we can eat outdoors. I'll light a fire to keep us warm. We'll do a weenie roast."

"Perfect. What can I bring?"

"Let me check with the others first, and I'll let you know. Shall we say sixish?"

Kyra texted the others, and by the time she got to Suzy's salon, all four of the Tattooed Ladies had accepted her invitation. She was excited, and also anxious. She couldn't remember the last time she'd had friends over for supper. In the past she'd hosted dinner parties for Rory's cronies and the big donors to his campaign when he'd been running for reelection, but seldom for friends. She'd worried she wouldn't be able to fake it with her friends like she could with strangers and casual acquaintances. They might have seen through her bright hostess patter or spotted the bruises on her neck and arms that makeup and dim lighting couldn't hide, and asked questions. But tonight's gathering would be different because she planned to come clean about her past. Emboldened by the sheriff's reaction when she'd told him, she'd decided it was time her new friends heard her story.

Kyra supplied the hot dogs and fixings, and borrowed a set of folding lawn chairs from Coop. Her friends brought the rest. Frannie contributed the wine; Suzy a tub of coleslaw and an economy-size bag of potato chips; Marisol the non-alcoholic beverages along with plastic cups and utensils, and paper plates. Jo brought the makings for s'mores, and her camera to capture the occasion for posterity.

After the wine was poured, when they were all seated around the fire, Ranger sacked out at Kyra's feet, Frannie proposed a toast. "Here's to the new forensic artist of the Washburn County Sheriff's Department."

The others joined in, while Kyra protested, "I haven't gotten the job yet."

"When will you know?" Marisol looked like a baby llama, bundled in her off-white, pulled-loop wool jacket.

"Soon, I would imagine. Gertie plans to retire at the end of this month, and the sheriff will need to hire someone to replace her by then, if not before." Kyra felt a flutter of anxiety as she spoke.

"The fix is in," said Suzy, stylish as usual in dark-rinse designer jeans and an expensive-looking shearling jacket.

Eyeing her heeled suede boots, Kyra wondered how she'd managed to cross the field in them without twisting an ankle.

"Or so I hear," Suzy added, sliding her oldest friend a glance.

"I don't have a crystal ball," said Frannie, "but I know the sheriff thinks the world of Gertie and respects her opinion. Anyone she chose as her successor is a shoo-in. Also," she added with an impish smile, "Kurt knows he'd never hear the end of it from me if he didn't hire you."

"Who else is in the running?" asked Jo. In firelight, wearing a puffy pink jacket with her strawberry-blond hair pulled back in a high ponytail, she might have been on a Girl Scout camping trip.

"I only know of two candidates," Kyra said. Her former classmates Ashley and Nate had both applied for the position after Gertie's formal announcement that she was retiring. "But I imagine there are others, some with years of experience." The market for forensic artists was finite, with only so many jurisdictions in the country.

"Maybe, but they don't have Gertie's seal of approval," said Frannie.

They roasted hot dogs on skewers over the fire and ate them with the fixings and sides that were laid out on the picnic table, while seated around the fire. Ranger had been fed earlier, but it didn't stop him from making the rounds, begging for handouts. After they'd eaten, the women complained that they were too stuffed to eat another bite, but somehow they found room for dessert.

They were toasting marshmallows for s'mores when Marisol made a surprising announcement. "Cal and I met for coffee."

Suzy's eyebrows shot up. "You went on a date with Cal?"

"It wasn't a date. It was coffee."

"Your idea or his?" Frannie asked. She wore khakis and a sweatshirt in a jungle-camo print that might have caused her to blend into her surroundings if she'd been the retiring sort. Frannie was the opposite of retiring. Her cap of silver curls gleamed in the firelight, and her face was animated.

"His. He wanted to talk to me about something."

"What, the lonely nights when he lies awake thinking about you?" Jo teased.

Marisol rolled her eyes. "He's thinking of applying to film schools, and he wanted my advice."

"Has filmmaking always been his dream?" Kyra asked. Noticing that her marshmallow had caught on fire, she blew on it. It was still edible, she decided. Ranger agreed after she tossed it to him.

"I think it has more to do with him not wanting to go to law school than wanting to become a filmmaker."

"What did you advise him to do?" Frannie placed her toasted marshmallow on a graham cracker and topped it with a square of chocolate and another cracker.

"I told him he should follow his passion wherever it takes him."

"Especially if it takes him to your bed," Suzy said with a sly chuckle.

"I wish." Marisol sighed. "After he goes back to school, I might never see him again."

"You never know," said Jo. "When Sean and I first met, I didn't think I'd see him again."

"You mean it wasn't love at first sight?" Kyra was surprised. "You two seem so perfect for each other."

"Long story short, we met in college at a gay-straight alliance mixer. I went with my roommate, Carmela, and Sean went with his dormmate, Reggie, both of whom are out and proud, so we each assumed the other was gay. It wasn't until I bumped into Sean months later when I was with the guy I was seeing at the time that we discovered we were both wrong. We've been together ever since."

Their love for each other had radiated from them like an aura whenever Kyra had seen them together. Even after ten-plus years of marriage and two kids, they were like honeymooners. Kyra hadn't known a love like theirs was even possible, and given her disinclination to get involved with anyone, she'd probably never experience it. The thought of what she might be missing out on made her sad.

"You and Sean were meant to be." Marisol heaved another sigh and then took a bite from her s'more. "I'm just one of the stops on Cal's tour."

"He wouldn't have asked for your advice if that were true," Frannie pointed out.

"Okay, so he values my opinion, but does he want to jump my bones?"

"Why don't you give him something to look at the next time he stops by?" suggested Suzy.

"Wear something sexy, you mean? I'd have to raid your closet, and nothing would fit," Marisol said, licking chocolate from her fingers.

"I'll take you shopping, then. You won't recognize yourself after I'm done with you."

"I'm not sure Cal would, either." Marisol sounded dubious.

Jo got out her Nikon and began snapping photos. When Kyra noticed the camera aimed at her at one point, she ducked out of the frame. "No pictures." She held her hands up in front of her face.

"Camera shy?" Jo asked.

"I just don't want any pictures of myself ending up on social media." *Where my husband might see them.*

"I get it," said Marisol. "Which is why, if you go on my Insta page, you'll see a ton of cat photos and very few of me. If a cat looks fat in a photo, it doesn't care."

"I'd never post a photo of someone without their consent," Jo said in her defense.

"Good, because then I'd have to kill you," said Suzy.

"You guys." Jo shook her head in despair. "You're both gorgeous, and I bet neither of you has ever taken a bad photo. As for you . . ." She turned to Kyra. "You could be a model with those cheekbones."

Kyra didn't see herself as model material, or even especially pretty. Her nose was too long, her mouth too wide, and her body had more angles than curves. But the conversation had provided her with the opening she'd been seeking. All evening she'd been waiting for the right moment to come clean. Now her heart began to pound as she gathered her courage. She was opening her mouth to tell her friends the reason why she didn't want any pictures of herself on social media when Frannie spoke.

"Kyra, just think of how far you've come since you first arrived in town. You were out of work, didn't know a soul, and now you're part of this community with two jobs *and* an exciting career opportunity. Not to mention a home with a view. All in two short months. You're an inspiration, my dear."

Kyra swallowed the words she'd been about to speak. How could she follow up Frannie's glowing tribute by revealing the ugly truth about herself? She wasn't an "inspiration," she was a fraud, hers a cautionary tale: *Make the wrong choices and you could end up like her.* A victim.

"I couldn't have done it without all of you," she said brightly. "Now, who wants another marshmallow?"

After her friends left, she lingered by the fire while Ranger kept watch for nighttime marauders. Last night, he'd alerted her to a raccoon raiding her trash can. Tonight, when his ears pricked up at the approach of what sounded like either a person or a large animal in the darkness beyond the clearing, Kyra felt a prickle of alarm. But the bark he gave was one of welcome rather than warning.

It was followed by a familiar voice calling, "It's just me." A minute later, Coop stepped into the light.

"Party's over." Her words and dry tone belied the thrill he'd sparked in her with his arrival. He looked sexier than any man had a right to, in his jeans and lumberjack boots, with his hair tousled as if he'd run his fingers through it.

"I know. I saw your friends leave. Mind if I join you?"

Maybe it was the two glasses of wine she'd drunk, which had her in a relaxed mood, but she found herself gesturing toward the empty chair beside her. "Would you like something to drink? There's some wine left. Help yourself." She nodded in the direction of the leftovers on the picnic table.

"I don't drink, but thanks. I'm in AA," he explained when she raised a questioning eyebrow.

"Oh." She was surprised to learn he was a recovering alcoholic. She wondered if his drinking in the past was what had led to him quitting his job as a cop. "There are bottled water and sodas, too."

"I'm good." After paying Ranger the attention he clearly believed he was due from the way he was prancing and grinning at their guest like a four-legged court jester, Coop sat down next to her, stretching his long legs out in front of him. "You and your friends seemed to be having a good time tonight."

She grew worried. "Were we making too much noise?"

He laughed. "You wouldn't ask if you'd ever been to one of my family gatherings. Between the crying babies, the older kids making a ruckus, and the adults all talking at once, they tend to be noisier than a zoo at feeding time."

"You all seem to get along." From what she'd observed, his was a close-knit family. She'd met his dad and two older brothers in passing on separate occasions when they'd visited, and Shirley was a frequent visitor.

"We do, for the most part, though if my brothers and I are on good terms now, it's because they were smart enough to marry amazing women and have kids that I adore, as I frequently remind them."

"When I was a kid, I used to wish for a baby brother or a sister," Kyra said. "This was before I was old enough to realize it would've been just another life for my mom to screw up like she did mine."

"She did a number on you, huh?"

"She's not the maternal type. Which, by the way, she would be the first to admit."

"Was your dad in the picture?"

"No. I don't know if he's even still alive. He and my mom were both sixteen when she got pregnant. From my mom's description, he reacted the way most sixteen-year-old boys would to the news that they were going to be a father. In short, not well. He was out of the picture before I was born."

"What about your extended family? Are you close with any of your relatives?"

"If any are living besides my mom, I haven't met them. My mom's parents kicked her out after she told them she was pregnant, and her older brother sided with them. All I know about my dad's family is that they moved out of state around that time, never to be heard from again."

"Where did you grow up?"

"All over the place, mainly the Southwest. We moved around a lot."

"Because of your mom's job?"

"In a way, except it wasn't because of job transfers. Each time she quit or got fired from a job, she'd fall behind on the rent; then it'd be on to the next town and a new job wherever she could find work."

His face creased in sympathy. "Must've been tough on you."

Tough. That was one word to describe it, though she would have chosen a different word: "lonely." "I didn't have many friends, being the perpetual new kid in school. The few that I had at each school were social outcasts like myself. I sometimes wonder whether we hung out together because we genuinely liked each other or to form a buffer against the bullies. Probably some of both."

"That explains your trust issues."

"If by that you mean I'm cautious with other people until I get to know them, then yes, I suppose so."

"Yet you still don't trust me."

"I trust you." *To a point.*

Her measured response prompted a skeptical look from him. "Then why haven't you told me what you're running from? All I know is that it has something to do with an unnamed ex about whom you've told me nothing. I don't even know *your* real name."

She froze, her heart thumping, like when he'd caught her half-dressed down by the creek. She felt naked then. Vulnerable. Now he was peeling away her protective layers one by one, getting closer to the ugly truth at her core, which she couldn't admit even to her friends. How much should she tell him, if anything? He already knew or suspected more than she was comfortable with. And what did she know about his past besides the fact that he was a divorced ex-cop and recovering alcoholic?

"I'm not the only one with baggage." She narrowed her eyes at him.

"The difference is, I've been transparent with you."

"You haven't told me if what that creep Jed said about you is true. Did you kill someone?"

A shadow of some emotion passed over his rugged face, there and gone in an instant. "Yes. I was involved in a fatal shooting when I was a cop."

"What were the circumstances?"

He was quiet for a minute. There was just the crackling of the flames and the hoot of an owl from somewhere in the darkness. When he spoke again, his voice was as flat as his expression. "That night, my partner and I responded to a report of a burglary at Kessler's Pharmacy. It was still in progress when we arrived on the scene. One perp fled, and I gave chase while my partner cuffed the other one. I had my gun drawn, and when I finally got him cornered and saw him reach into his pocket for what I thought was a weapon, I ordered him to freeze. He ignored me, so I fired at him. I didn't shoot to kill, so help me God.

I shot to disable, like I'd been trained to do. But the bullet nicked his femoral artery. He . . ." His voice caught. "He'd bled out by the time paramedics got to him."

"God. How awful."

He nodded as he stared into the flames. "He was nineteen. Never been in trouble with the law before. Later, I learned the only thing on him was his phone." She saw a muscle twitch in his clenched jaw.

It was a horrific tale, one that might cause someone who didn't know the details to jump to conclusions. A dark night. A boy in a hoodie. A cop in hot pursuit. But Kyra saw a terrible tragedy where someone else might see a travesty. She felt only pity for those involved. "So that's what Jed meant when he called you a killer."

"The boy was a cousin of his. That's why Jed hates me, besides the fact I arrested him for assaulting his wife. I don't blame him for that. He couldn't hate me more than I hate myself for what I did."

"But you said it was an accident."

"It was. And according to the findings of the IA investigation, I was innocent of any wrongdoing. It was ruled a justified shooting. Doesn't change the fact that someone's dead because of me."

"Is that why you quit your job?"

"Let's just say it was a contributing factor. That, and my drinking. I was sick about what had happened. Distracted at work. Couldn't sleep without having bad dreams. So I did what any alcoholic would do: I numbed my pain with booze. I was what you might call a functioning alcoholic, but my drinking got out of control after the shooting. When I wasn't drunk, I was hungover. My wife threatened to leave me if I didn't get clean. My partner, Nadia, confronted me, and I was given several warnings by my supervisor. Only reason I wasn't fired was because of my dad. He'd worked at the department for thirty-five years. I've known Sheriff McNally since I was a kid."

"He seems like a good guy." Whatever the outcome of today's job interview, she'd always be grateful to the sheriff for treating her with kindness and respect.

"He is, and a good friend. He gave me more chances than anyone who'd screwed up as much as I had deserved until he had no choice but to give me an ultimatum: either resign or be fired. I chose to resign."

"Was that when you got sober?"

"You would think, but it doesn't usually work that way. I'm what we call in the program a 'low-bottom drunk.' Took more than a few knocks, including my wife leaving me, before I hit bottom."

"I'm sorry," she said. She'd never had a problem with alcohol but knew what it was like to be in the grip of something over which it seemed you had no control. With Coop, it had been the monkey on his back. In her case, she'd felt trapped by her situation and insecurities. "I'm sorry about the boy who died, too. Thank you for telling me."

"At least now you know you're not living next door to an axe murderer."

"I never thought that."

"Really." He challenged her statement with a raised eyebrow.

"Your mom doesn't seem like the mother of an axe murderer."

"You mean it wasn't my charm or good deeds that won you over?"

"That, too," she said, smiling at him.

They sat together in companionable silence for a little while longer, listening to the crackling flames until the fire had burned down. Finally, Coop stood and stretched. "I should go. It's getting late."

"Past my bedtime." An early riser, she was usually in bed this time of night. After her long and eventful day and the wine she'd drunk, she was more tired than usual. She stood. "Thanks for stopping by, and thanks for . . ." Her voice trailed off. How could she express appreciation for his honesty without making herself look bad? He'd been open with her, and she hadn't returned the favor.

"In AA we call it a 'share,'" he supplied. "Thanks for listening, and for not judging me."

"I'm in no position to judge."

He eyed her as if he was waiting for an explanation. When she offered none, she could tell from his expression that she'd disappointed him. "Be sure to put the fire out before you turn in," he said, turning to go.

She felt something twist in her chest. "Coop?" she called as he headed back to the house, and possibly out of her life in any meaningful way. He'd bared his soul, and she'd given him nothing in return. She couldn't leave it at that. He stopped and turned around. "It's Krystal. Krystal Stanhope. My real name."

He nodded, and his expression softened. "Nice to meet you, Krystal."

11

The next few weeks passed without incident. Kyra continued working mornings at Suzy's salon and afternoons at Gertie's, where she'd finished the bookkeeping and begun cataloging the hundreds of composite sketches representing Gertie's forty-year career. Meanwhile, she waited anxiously for word from the sheriff about the job as Gertie's replacement. Gertie had postponed her retirement until the middle of November to give him enough time to interview all the candidates.

The call came on a Wednesday morning in November when Kyra was at work.

"Ms. Smith? This is Sharon Anderson, calling from the sheriff's office. Will you please hold for the sheriff?" said the clipped voice of the sheriff's assistant before her boss came on the line.

"Ms. Smith. Sheriff McNally, here. I'm calling about the job. It's . . ."

The rest of the sentence was drowned out by the sound of hair dryers and ladies chattering in the background. She moved from the salon proper into the employees-only area, stepping into Suzy's office, where it was quieter. "I'm sorry, sir. Could you repeat that?" she asked, her heart pounding.

"I said the job is yours if you still want it."

Her heart swelled, and a grin spread across her face. "Yes. Absolutely. Thank you, sir."

"Don't thank me. You earned it."

"When do you want me to start?"

"You can work that out with Gertie. She'll be on board to supervise until you get up to speed. In the meantime, why don't you come in and we'll discuss terms?"

They arranged to meet the following day at his office at two o'clock. Kyra rushed back into the salon to tell Suzy and Jasmine her news after she disconnected. They were both thrilled for her.

"Congratulations, sweetie!" said Suzy as she expertly twirled the brush in her hand around a piece of the chestnut mane she was blow-drying—belonging to a fashionably attired older woman with the preternaturally smooth skin of someone who'd had face work done. "You deserve it. And much as I hate to lose you, I'll sleep easier at night knowing you're helping to keep our community safe."

"You can put those magic fingers of yours to work catching criminals," called Jasmine from her station, where she was braiding her customer's hair.

"I'll miss working with you guys." Kyra felt a tug of regret at the thought of leaving them. In the short time she'd worked at the Shear Delight Salon, it had come to feel like home, and these two wonderful women felt like family, with Suzy as the cool mom and Jasmine as the sister she never had.

"We'll miss you, too," said Suzy, sounding a little sad.

"Especially when I'm listening to customers bitch about how I'm not as good as the last shampoo lady," said Jasmine.

Kyra laughed.

"It's only until I find a suitable replacement," Suzy assured Jasmine. "You'll still see us," she said to Kyra. "We're not going anywhere. And Ranger can stay on as our official greeter if he needs a job."

"Thanks, but I have a feeling his people skills will be needed where we're going." She would be interviewing people who'd been traumatized, and who better to provide comfort than a dog? She herself had benefited from Ranger's calming influence on more than one occasion when she'd been stressed. Hopefully, she could get permission from the sheriff to bring him along on her assignments.

After lunch, she headed over to Gertie's with Ranger to finish cataloging her sketches; she had a couple more days' worth of work before she was done. Gertie served tea and biscuits in the sunroom off the kitchen, as she'd gotten into the habit of doing before they started work. Kyra thanked Gertie for all her support and for giving her the opportunity to become her successor when she retired.

"Did you know the sheriff planned to hire me?" she asked before she sipped her tea.

"Goodness, no." Gertie helped herself to a biscuit. She broke it in two and fed half to Ranger, who was sitting in front of her, looking up at her expectantly. "I may work for the department and go to the same church as him, but I'm not privy to the sheriff's plans. That said, I like to think my recommendation carried some weight. The rest was your doing. You obviously impressed him in your interview."

"I pray his—and your—faith in me will be rewarded." Kyra wished she had the same faith in herself. "He said you'd be supervising me until I get up to speed. Is that still the plan?"

"Yes, barring unforeseen circumstances."

"Good. Because I'm not ready to fly solo."

"By the time I retire and start tackling my bucket list, you will be. Trust me."

"What if I'm not?"

"If you have any questions, I'll only be a phone call away."

"So when do I start? The sheriff said I should discuss it with you."

"That, I don't know, being as crime has its own timetable. It's predictable only in one sense: just as we know rain will fall, we know crimes will occur. It's only a matter of when and where. All I can tell you is that when the next call comes from the sheriff's office, it'll be your number they're calling. I'll be on hand merely to provide any guidance that might be needed."

Kyra swallowed her anxiety and nibbled on a biscuit. It tasted like dust in her mouth.

The following afternoon, she met with the sheriff at the appointed time to discuss the terms of her contract. She learned that she was to receive a monthly retainer of $2,000, and for any services rendered beyond those covered by that sum, she would bill at the standard hourly rate of $200 per hour. She felt as though she'd won the lottery. Now there was only one last piece of business to discuss . . .

"Sir, would it be all right if I brought my dog to work with me?" she asked as the meeting was wrapping up.

"You have a dog?" The sheriff looked up from the paperwork he was shuffling into a pile on his desk.

She nodded. "He's not a licensed therapy dog or anything, but I think he'd be an asset. I'll be working with people who've been traumatized. He can sense when someone is anxious, and he's there for them if they need a furry friend to calm their nerves. I didn't teach him to do it. He does it instinctively. He's the most empathetic dog I've ever known, and smarter than most humans that way."

The sheriff smiled. "That's true of most dogs I've met. When our girls were babies, our family dog, Jet, usually knew when they needed a diaper change or a feeding before my wife or I did."

"So is that a yes?"

"Sure, why not? We have a fine tradition of K-9 officers here at the department. Your dog would be a member of the team. And I'd be interested to see if you're right about his therapeutic value."

Kyra was walking on air when she left.

Her next stop was the offices of Halliday, Greer & Kapur. Drew Halliday, the attorney Gertie had recommended, was a distinguished older man with a crest of silver hair nearly as impressive as Gertie's. Kyra hired him to draw up and file the necessary paperwork to form an LLC in the name of Smith Sketch Services, of which she was the sole executive. It would have its own tax ID number, which was of critical importance in her case because it wouldn't leave a digital footprint that could be traced back to her. As an independent contractor, she was free to work for any law enforcement agency who wished to retain her services; there were nine in Washburn County alone, including the police departments of its towns and cities. However, she'd decided to limit her work to the Washburn County Sheriff's Department. The criminal cases it investigated generated enough assignments to provide a good income for a forensic artist, according to Gertie. Also, Kyra didn't know who in law enforcement she could trust besides Sheriff McNally.

That night, Kyra slept soundly for the first time in weeks. No bad dreams about sleeping in her mom's car or going hungry. She would never be homeless or go hungry again, God willing. She could even afford the occasional indulgence—a fancy coffee from Cowboy Coffee, a scoop of Chocolate-Honeycomb Chip from the Gold Nugget Ice Cream Parlor, a paperback from Buckboard Books—and, more importantly, buy a smartphone and start saving for a reliable set of wheels.

But even as she celebrated her good fortune, Kyra remained conscious of the fact that her new life in Gold Creek could end in a moment with a knock at her door. If Rory were to discover her whereabouts, she'd have two choices: leave and look for another place to live—where he wouldn't find her—or stay and fight for what was hers. It was between the devil and the deep blue sea, in other words. She didn't know which had the better odds for survival.

The following morning at ten, she was at work when she got the call—her first assignment. She immediately phoned Gertie, who was there to meet her when she arrived at the sheriff's office with Ranger.

"You've got this," she said, as if she'd sensed Kyra's nervousness.

Deputy Fuentes, whom Kyra recalled from her first visit to the sheriff's office, escorted them to the conference room where the interview would take place, briefing them on the case along the way. It involved an armed robbery that had occurred at a convenience store in Pine City at approximately one that morning. The suspect's face was hidden by the ball cap he wore in the footage from the store's CCTV cameras, thus the need for a forensic artist. On the plus side, the witness, a store clerk who'd been on duty that day—a twenty-two-year-old Bangladeshi man named Rashid—was able to provide enough details for Kyra to work with when she interviewed him.

She was reminded of something Gertie had said in one of her class lectures. *Witnesses fall into two categories: passive and nonpassive. The former is less traumatized; therefore, the event they witnessed isn't as embedded in their consciousness. The latter has experienced a greater degree of trauma, and as it's human nature to remember the best and worst that's happened to us, they tend to have total recall.* Rashid fell into the second category. The store clerk was so shook up he kept lapsing from English into his native tongue, but from the details he recalled, the holdup was seared into his memory. After he identified the suspect from the sketch Kyra had drawn of him, a match was found in the system: a convicted felon and repeat offender wanted in connection with other robberies.

"Good work, Kyra," Gertie said as they were leaving after Kyra's sketch had been logged as evidence. "You asked all the right questions, and you got the witness to relax enough to answer them."

"That was mainly due to Ranger."

Gertie smiled and dropped her gaze to the dog, who was keeping pace with them. During the interview, he'd gone over to sit beside the agitated witness, which seemed to calm him. "You two make a great team."

"You hear that, bud?" Kyra said to him. "It's all about teamwork." Ranger grinned up at her, tail wagging.

"You also made a good choice in continuing with the interview when the witness was struggling with his English instead of pausing it until a translator could be found."

"I made a judgment call. I wasn't sure if it was the right one."

"It was. I don't know of any Bengali translators working in this area. It might have been a day or more before one was found, enough time for a witness's memory to become fuzzy."

"I just hope the suspect is caught."

"Thanks to you, there's a good chance he will be. All in all, I would say you're off to a good start."

Kyra was called into the sheriff's office twice more that week, both times with a successful outcome in the form of a positive ID. She was thrown into a panic, nonetheless, when Gertie announced on Monday of the following week that Friday would be her last day. She and her husband had booked a cruise through the Greek islands, and they were leaving on Saturday. After that, Kyra would be on her own. What if she crashed and burned flying solo in her mentor's absence?

"You're ready. You know what to do," Gertie assured her. "And remember, I'm just a phone call away if you have any questions or concerns."

Kyra still felt nervous at the thought of Gertie not being physically present. Good thing her friends were there for her, of which she was reminded in the days that followed. Jasmine gave her a gift certificate to Fur Elise, the pet shop down the street owned by her friend Elise, which also offered dog grooming. Suzy told her she could continue working at the salon for as long as she needed between assignments at the sheriff's office. Frannie gave her a travel mug from Cowboy Coffee for when she went on late-night and early-morning calls. Jo and Marisol took her to lunch one day.

On Friday, Kyra attended an author event that Marisol was hosting at Buckboard Books. They were chatting after the author's reading when Marisol remarked, "By the way, I saw one of your sketches on the news today." She was referring to the one Kyra had drawn of the suspect in a recent burglary, which had been made public with the suspect still at large. "Have they caught the guy yet?"

"No, but a caller to the tip line said he looked like the guy who was renting the apartment down the hall from her. Too bad he was gone, along with the stolen goods, by the time the police showed up."

"The elusive type, huh? Sounds like someone I know." Marisol's gaze shifted to her love interest, Cal, standing in line with the other attendees who were waiting to get their copy of tonight's featured book signed. A bestselling mystery writer, the author looked like a sweet little old lady, but her reading tonight had revealed a mind filled with dark and twisted imaginings.

"Cal's wanted by the police?" Kyra teased.

"If he is, it's for stealing my heart." Kyra groaned at the cheesy line, to which Marisol responded, "Corny but true." Wearing a pink circle skirt and indigo cardigan sewn with jet beads from the vintage clothing store where she shopped, she looked like she'd come from a fifties sock hop.

"Does he know, or is he still clueless?"

"I've put out subtle signals."

"How subtle are we talking?"

"Subtle enough so he either hasn't picked up on them or he did and he's letting me save face by pretending he didn't."

"The direct approach might work better."

"What works for Suzy wouldn't work for me. I'm the fun friend a man might take to a party but wouldn't take home afterward."

"Since Cal lives with his parents, that might not be an option, anyway."

"I told you, he doesn't actually live with them, but I take your point."

"Why don't you invite him to stay for a drink tonight after you close up shop?"

"*Hmmm.*" Marisol gnawed on her lower lip, frowning, as she considered it. "All right. I'll do it." She broke into a grin and nudged Kyra in the ribs with her elbow. "Hey, you're not half-bad at this."

"What?"

"Giving advice to the lovelorn, especially for someone who's sworn off men."

Maybe there's hope for me yet, Kyra thought.

As she was leaving with Ranger a short while later, carrying a signed copy of the featured book—which she'd bought to support both its author and Marisol—she was pleased to see Marisol deep in conversation with Cal. She hoped her friend took her advice and that it worked out for her.

Over the next couple of weeks, she and Ranger became regular visitors at the sheriff's office. She was surprised to learn that the number of incidences of violent crime in Washburn County was, on average, higher than in some rural counties. This was due to the fact that its most populous community, Pine City, like most cities, saw its share of gang-related activity and drug trafficking in addition to the usual robberies, assaults, rapes, and domestic disputes. As a result, Kyra was called in at all hours of the day and night, and she soon became acquainted with the majority of the department's thirty-eight deputies and fourteen nonuniformed employees. They welcomed her into their midst, and little by little, their kind gestures and friendly overtures chipped away at her initial reserve.

Ranger became the department's unofficial mascot. There was always someone to give him a scratch behind his ears, and he knew every pocket and desk drawer where a treat might be hidden. Soured by her bad experience with the police in Rochester, Kyra saw a different side of law enforcement at the Washburn County Sheriff's Department. She saw it in action during her fifth visit.

That day she'd interviewed the witness to a gang-related shooting, a young man whom she suspected, from his glassy eyes and twitchy limbs, was high on drugs. He'd grown increasingly agitated and hostile over the course of the interview, until finally he erupted, accusing her of trying to trip him up. He lunged toward her across the table. Startled, she froze, and when she heard Ranger give a sharp bark, she wished she hadn't tied him up. She'd been afraid the hostile-seeming witness would provoke him and get bitten; it hadn't occurred to her that her dog wouldn't be able to protect her. Luckily, her liaison officer, Deputy Fuentes, was on hand and reacted quickly. He had the man face down on the floor and in handcuffs before she could catch her breath or make a move.

"Did they teach you that at the ninja academy?" she said after the witness had been removed by another deputy. Shaken from the incident, which had brought up some bad memories, she didn't want him to know how deeply it had affected her. "I don't think I've ever seen anyone react so quickly."

Deputy Charles "Chaz" Fuentes, a twenty-two-year veteran of the department and married father of three, was in his late forties with graying hair, but he was as physically fit as any rookie fresh from the police academy. He and Kyra had become friendly in the weeks they'd worked together, and she appreciated that he'd never hit on her, as some of the other men in the department had. He was also a dog person. It was Fuentes who'd suggested she get Ranger certified as a therapy dog after observing him in action. She'd taken his suggestion and contacted a local trainer who offered a six-week course for dogs and their handlers. She'd enrolled Ranger in the next available course, scheduled for January.

Fuentes grinned and made a show of puffing up his chest. "I'm not as quick as I was when I was younger," he said, "but when it involves one of our own, I'm a superhero."

"Is that what I am? One of your own?"

He seemed surprised by her question. "Why do you ask?"

"I don't wear a uniform. Technically, I'm not even an employee of this department."

"Kyra." His expression grew serious, and he placed a comradely hand on her shoulder, looking her in the eye as he spoke. "There isn't one of us who wouldn't take a bullet for another, and that includes you."

She nodded, her throat thick with emotion. Hearing his words, she felt secure for the first time in her life. In that moment, she went from seeing her colleagues as potential threats to seeing them as allies.

◆ ◆ ◆

Kyra was so busy with work that she didn't see Coop again until the second week in November. It was a Monday, cold and overcast, with snow flurries in the forecast. There was still snow on the ground from the previous weekend's snowfall in the shady spots where it hadn't melted. She'd just gotten home from work and was playing fetch with Ranger, who had energy to burn after being cooped up all day. At one point, as he was fetching the ball from the undergrowth along the creek bank where she'd accidentally tossed it, she noticed that he was limping.

"What is it, bud? Did you step on something?" She squatted to examine his paw and was horrified to discover a fishhook embedded in it and not a sticker, as she'd imagined. She stroked his silky head, holding him still with her other hand as he whined and tried to lick his bleeding paw. She felt his pain as if it were she who was hurting. "It's gonna be okay. The vet will fix you right up," she reassured him while struggling to control her panic. How was she going to get him to the vet in town when he couldn't walk without making his injury worse and he was too heavy to carry? The distance from her trailer to her car was roughly half the length of a football field.

Desperate, she phoned Coop. "It's Ranger. He's hurt. I need your help."

"On my way," he said. Two minutes later, he was at her side, kneeling to examine Ranger's injury. "It doesn't look to be in too deep," he said as he gently palpated the pad of the paw impaled with the fishhook. Ranger whined like he was in pain but seemed to trust that Coop was trying to help him. "I think I can get it out without hurting him any worse, if you'll allow me."

Kyra hesitated. Did he know what he was doing? What if he made it worse? On the other hand, the vet was twenty minutes away. Twenty minutes in which her dog would suffer and an infection might set in.

"I'm certified in first aid," he told her. "It was a job requirement when I became a cop. First responders sometimes have to treat injuries at accident and crime scenes. I've cleared blocked airways and applied compression packs to stop bleeding. Trust me, this is a piece of cake in comparison."

She agreed to it, albeit reluctantly, and he lifted Ranger into his arms. Her fifty-pound dog might have weighed no more than a feather duster from the swiftness with which Coop moved as he carried him across the field to his house and into the downstairs bathroom, with Kyra following. She spread a towel over the tile floor of the bathroom, and Coop gently lowered Ranger onto it.

"The first aid kit is upstairs. I'll be back in a sec," he said, and left the room. He reappeared in record time, carrying the first aid kit, a bottle of hydrogen peroxide, and a pair of heavy-duty wire cutters.

She stroked Ranger's fur as he lay with his head on her lap, whining, while Coop performed the extraction. After disinfecting the wound, he gently pulled the fishhook out by its straight end, which he'd clipped with the wire cutters so as not to do further damage by pulling it out by its barbed end. He spoke to the patient in soothing tones all the while. "Hang in there, dude. I know it hurts, but it'll be over before you know it, and you'll be chasing squirrels again in no time."

Ranger endured his ordeal bravely and without snapping at his angel of mercy, like she had seen some injured dogs do. Afterward, he washed Coop's face with his tongue to show his appreciation.

Coop laughed and ducked his head to escape the lashing. "Yeah, I love you, too. Now, hold still."

Witnessing the scene, Kyra felt her heart melting like a Popsicle in July.

"Has he had his tetanus shot?" Coop asked when he was done, the injured paw cleaned, dressed, and covered with a plastic bag secured with adhesive tape. Kyra answered in the affirmative. "Good. Less chance of an infection. But you might want to have the vet take a look at him, just in case."

"I plan to do just that. And thank you. This makes twice that you've come to the rescue."

"Least I could do," he said gruffly. "I can't help feeling partly responsible. My brothers and I used to fish in the creek when we were kids. There's a good chance that fishhook is one of ours."

"Even if that's true, you came through today."

"Consider it a benefit of having a resident landlord."

They both rose at the same time, Coop lifting Ranger in his arms as he did. Their gazes locked. Time seemed to stop, and the tight space they were in shrank farther. She could smell his woodsy scent and see the flecks of gold in his tea-brown eyes. In the silence, she could hear the sound of her own breath and, for a dizzying moment, thought he was going to kiss her. Which he might have if they hadn't been separated by fifty pounds of dog. And from the heat prickling on her skin and the pounding of her heart, she would have let him. Instead, the moment passed and they stepped into the hallway.

As they headed back across the field to her trailer, Ranger rode in Coop's arms, seemingly none the worse for his ordeal, and Kyra walked beside them on shaky legs. She was at once grateful to Coop and guarded in his presence. She recalled the night they'd met. The sparks that had flown between them then and today, she thought, could easily grow to become a wildfire if she wasn't careful.

12

Two days later, she was called into the sheriff's office early one morning while it was still dark out. She'd been awakened from a sound sleep, but by the time she arrived with Ranger shortly after seven, she was wide awake. Ranger's wound was healing nicely. She'd removed the bandage and plastic bag that had covered his injured paw, and he trotted alertly at her heels, like a K-9 officer reporting for duty. She entered to the usual cacophony of phones ringing, two-way radios squawking, and mingled voices issuing from the "pool," as the open-plan office was generally referred to.

She was greeted by Fuentes in reception. This week, he was working the day shift, which ran from six to two, but was pulling a double today, having just come from the scene of a multiple-vehicle accident involving injuries that had all county units deployed in the early hours of the morning.

"What have you got for me?" she asked as they made their way through the pool toward Fuentes's desk.

"Twenty-eight-year-old female victim, name of Hailey Peterson. She was assaulted by an unknown assailant while she was out jogging earlier." Fuentes briefed her on the case.

Kyra suppressed a shudder. "How bad was she hurt?"

"Bad enough, but the assault doesn't appear to have been sexually motivated, so it could've been worse."

Thank God for small blessings. "The assailant?"

"He fled before she got a good look at him."

"I don't suppose any witnesses have come forward," she said hopefully.

"None so far, but we're canvassing the neighborhood. The neighbor who called it in, and who was with Ms. Peterson when the first responder arrived, didn't witness the attack." He stopped when they reached his desk, pulling a folder from the stack of case files on top of it. He handed it to Kyra. "It's all here, such as it is."

A quick perusal of the file confirmed her worst fears. Unless she got lucky, this case would likely remain unsolved. "According to this," she said as she handed back the file, "you're looking for a Caucasian male somewhere between the ages of eighteen and eighty with no distinguishing features."

"The proverbial bushy-haired stranger," he agreed with a downturn of his mouth. "But you might have better luck than Higgins." Deputy Dale Higgins had been the first responder who'd taken the victim's statement. "He described her as 'unresponsive' when he interviewed her."

"Probably because she was in shock."

"Well, she seemed to have recovered enough to be interviewed when I spoke with her. Head-wise, that is. She's pretty beat up."

Kyra didn't need to be told. She'd seen the photos that had been taken at the ER and that were in the file. The photos, however, didn't prepare her for the visual when she entered the conference room where the interview was to take place and saw the woman seated at the long table that dominated the room. She was thin, with dirty-blond hair pulled back in a ponytail, wearing a light-blue tracksuit. She might have been pretty, but it was hard to tell with the bruising and swelling that disfigured her face. One eye was swollen shut. A row of stitches on her lower lip was crusted with dried blood. A bandage covered her right ear. Kyra stopped and stifled a gasp. She was remembering when she'd last seen a similarly battered face. It had been looking back at her in the mirror.

She shivered, remembering that day in May of this year. She'd been rushed to the ER the night before with multiple injuries from a beating so severe, she nearly died. The surgeon who'd operated on her to remove her ruptured spleen had told her afterward she was lucky she'd survived "the accident." It was the first she learned of the spin her husband had put on it. When she returned home after being discharged from the hospital ten days later, she found a newer-model BMW parked in their garage in place of her old one, which Rory had wrecked to back up his story, she discovered. As soon as she recovered enough to travel, she'd fled one day while he was at work, taking just the clothes on her back, what she could carry in her car, and the money from her checking account.

Images flashed through her head like slides in an old-time slide carousel projected upon a screen: She saw a fist coming at her. She saw Rory's face contorted with fury. She saw herself lying on her side on the living room floor, curled into a protective ball while she was kicked repeatedly. She remembered thinking, in her disassociated state, *I really need to vacuum under the sofa more often.*

Her stomach twisted, and she tasted bile at the back of her throat. She took her time in unclipping Ranger's leash from his collar, in an effort to collect herself. Ranger pressed up against her as if he sensed her distress, and she paused briefly to lay her hand on his head in wordless communion.

She sat down across from the other woman, and Ranger assumed his Sphinx pose at her side. Fuentes took his place at the head of the table, where he could observe without his presence being a distraction.

"Hi, my name is Kyra." She introduced herself but didn't offer her hand. Physical contact, even something as innocuous as a handshake, wasn't always welcomed by victims of violent crimes, she'd learned on the job. "I'm the forensic artist who'll be working with you today. It's Hailey, right?"

The other woman nodded.

"Nice to meet you, Hailey. First, I want you to know how sorry I am about what happened to you," she went on. "It was horrific, and I apologize in advance for making you go through it again. But if you'll bear with me for a little while longer, I could use your help in developing a sketch of your attacker."

"I didn't get a good look at him," she said.

"Our minds can play tricks on us after a traumatic event. You might have seen more than you remember."

"I already told the police everything I know. Not him." She inclined her head toward Fuentes, wincing as if even that micro-movement had caused her pain. "The other one."

"My questions may be different from the ones Deputy Higgins asked you."

"Different how?" she asked nervously.

"Don't worry. It's not like a test in school. There are no right or wrong answers, and it's okay if you don't know the answer to a question." Hailey shrugged, which Kyra took as consent to proceed. "Before we get started, would you like anything to eat or drink? Coffee or tea? Or maybe a candy bar. I'm sure if I ask nicely, Deputy Fuentes would get you one from the vending machine." She glanced over at him, and he smiled. It was part of their routine in getting nervous interviewees to relax.

"No, I'm good. How long will this take?"

"It depends. Some interviews take longer than others, but I promise to make it as quick as possible so we can get you home." Was it her imagination, or had Hailey flinched at the mention of home? "You can pet him if you like," she said when Ranger went over to greet Hailey. "He's friendly."

"Is he a police dog?" She let him sniff her hand before petting him.

"No, though he might disagree. Ranger takes his job very seriously."

"What's his job?"

"He helps calm people who are stressed, which helps me do my job better."

Right now he was working his magic on Hailey, who smiled when he placed his head on her knee. "He looks like a German shepherd, only hairier," she said as she stroked the thick fur on his neck.

"He's part shepherd and part Samoyed. He gets his thick coat from his Samoyed ancestors. They were used to herd reindeer in Siberia, where it snows in winter, so they'd have needed all that fur to keep them warm."

"He reminds me of a dog I had when I was a kid. He was a mixed breed, too. A Heinz 57, my dad called him."

"What was his name?"

"Rufus. He was a good dog." She smiled at the memory and then winced and touched her lip where it was stitched as if it hurt to smile. Kyra felt sorry for her. She remembered when it had hurt to smile, although she hadn't had much to smile about back then. "He loved to play fetch. He never got tired of it."

"Ranger, too. It's his favorite game."

"Dogs. They're so dumb."

They exchanged a laugh, and Kyra was glad to see they'd formed a connection.

She bent to pull her laptop and art supplies from her tote on the floor at her feet. The latter was composed of a Strathmore nine-by-twelve-inch sketch pad; boxes of pencils, a mix of lead and charcoal; a battery-operated pencil sharpener; and Wite-Out for adding highlights, a trick of the trade she'd learned from Gertie. She didn't use colored pencils. Colors in a sketch might confuse a witness—if, for instance, the subject's hair color was depicted as blond instead of light brown, or their eyes were depicted as green instead of blue—and result in a negative or false-positive ID. Colors also tended to degrade when a sketch was reproduced.

She powered up her laptop. "Shall we begin?" she asked Hailey, who nodded but still seemed nervous. Kyra smiled at her encouragingly before she proceeded. "Hailey, when you were assaulted, was there anything about your attacker's appearance that stood out?"

"No. Like I said, I didn't get a good look at him. It all happened so fast."

"Where were you at the time?"

"I was jogging in my neighborhood. I like to go early when no one else is around."

"About what time was this?"

"Fiveish? It was still dark out, but it's a safe neighborhood, so I don't worry—or I didn't—about being attacked. Anyway, I was headed home after I ran my loop when I heard footsteps behind me. I got scared and picked up the pace, but then I felt hands grabbing me before I could get away."

"Did you see the person who grabbed you?"

"Not at first. He came at me from behind."

"What happened after that?"

"He punched me in the face, and then he took off." She grimaced and touched her face where it was swollen on one side.

"Was that when you saw him? When he punched you in the face?"

"Yeah, for a couple seconds, but it was dark. I couldn't see very well."

Kyra felt an answering twinge in her own face, like the pain from a phantom limb she'd heard described by amputees, recalling her own healed injuries. But something about Hailey's statement seemed off.

"Was his face covered?"

"No."

"Did you notice anything unusual about his features or the shape of his face? Anything that stood out?"

Hailey shook her head. She was visibly tense, so Kyra went with an easy question next. She would circle back to the subject of the suspect's facial characteristics when Hailey was more relaxed.

"Was he short or tall, thin or heavyset?"

"He was tall and built. You know, like he worked out at the gym."

"Did you notice any scars, marks, or tattoos?"

"No."

Kyra clicked on a folder on her laptop, and rows of thumbnail images, arranged in pairs, appeared on the screen. Unlike the reference photos in the scrapbook she'd used previously, which had been cut and pasted from magazines, these images had been culled from the police database and the internet. Some were mug shots; others were Facebook profile photos of random men, with photos of male celebrities sprinkled in. The men were different ages, ethnicities, and body types. She clicked on a photo of a pair of images to expand it and turned her laptop so that Hailey could see its screen.

"Hailey, which of these two men would you say looks most like your attacker?"

Hailey studied the images and shook her head. Kyra struck out with the next three photo pairings she showed her as well. She didn't score a hit until the fifth pairing. Hailey pointed to the man on the left. Blond and blue-eyed, he appeared to be in his mid to late fifties and had a prominent chin that made his long face look like a boot. "That one."

"What color was his hair?"

"Um. Brown, I think?"

"How much or little hair did he have?" Kyra showed her another pair of photos. Both men were approximately the same age, one with a receding hairline, the other with a full head of hair. "More like the man on the right or the man on the left?" She knew better than to ask any questions that might plant a suggestion in the mind of an interviewee, such as, *Was he bald?*

Hailey pointed to the man with the receding hairline.

When Kyra had gleaned enough detail to form a rough mental picture of the suspect, she reached for her art supplies and got to work. She sketched the rough outlines of the man's face and added hair. As she gradually filled in features, she paused here and there to ask additional questions. She suspected Hailey was hiding something. She'd seemed evasive when she was answering the questions, and her story didn't add up. What was she hiding, and why? Kyra had her own theory.

"Hailey, does this look like the man who attacked you?" she asked when she showed her the finished sketch.

"Yeah, that's him," Hailey said after giving it a cursory glance.

"Would you recognize him if you saw him in a lineup?"

"I guess."

"You don't sound too sure."

"I'm sure."

"Could it have been someone else who attacked you?"

"I don't know. Maybe." She cast a furtive glance at Fuentes, as if to gauge his reaction, which confirmed Kyra's suspicion.

"Could it have been someone you know?"

"No. I told you, I never saw him before," Hailey insisted.

"So you say, but your story doesn't add up. According to your statement, you didn't return home at any point after the attack, yet I noticed the clothes you're wearing don't have any bloodstains on them. That tells me you were wearing different clothes when you were attacked. You also claim you only caught a glimpse of your attacker before he fled, but from what I can see of your injuries, they're consistent with multiple blows. That suggests he took his time working you over, in which case, you'd have gotten a good look at him. What are you not telling us, Hailey?"

Out of the corner of her eye she saw Fuentes give her a WTF look. She was overstepping. She didn't have the authority to challenge Hailey's statement. But he didn't intervene, either because he was curious to know where she was going with this or because he trusted her. Probably some of both.

Hailey froze, a look of panic flashing across her face. Kyra felt for her. She'd been in her position. She'd lied, more than once, to protect her abuser. She was flooded with shame at the memory. But right now she had to stay strong, for Hailey's sake, if she couldn't or wouldn't help herself.

"Here's what I think really happened, and correct me if I'm wrong," she went on. "I think you were home when you were attacked. I think your attacker is someone known to you, and that you were protecting him when you lied to the police. Was it your husband who attacked you, Hailey? Did he cause your injuries?"

Hailey absently twisted the gold band on her ring finger. Her tell. "Why are you asking me these questions?" Visibly distressed, she didn't even seem to notice when Ranger nuzzled her hand.

"You're not in any trouble," Kyra assured her. She resisted the urge to go easy on her, leaving it to Ranger to offer comfort. What Hailey needed was a dose of reality. *If someone had given me the push I needed, I might've gotten away sooner.* "I only want to help, but I can't help you unless you tell the truth. So I'm going to ask you again, was it your husband who caused your injuries?"

Hailey stared at her mutely, the red flags on her cheeks and guilty look in her one good eye a dead giveaway. She looked like a kid who'd been busted for telling a lie but was sticking to her story.

"Would you care to revise your statement, Ms. Peterson?" Fuentes asked.

"No," she mumbled, and Kyra's heart sank.

"You're sure about that?"

"Yeah. Can I go now?"

"You're not under arrest. You're free to leave at any time."

Kyra, seeing her one chance to help Hailey slip away, grew desperate. She tried a different tactic. "Your husband should be here any minute to pick you up," she said. "He called to say he was on his way." She was lying. She didn't know if Hailey's husband had been contacted or if a ride had been arranged for Hailey.

She knew her hunch was correct when Hailey said in a panicked voice, "I don't want him to come."

"Why not? You don't think he'd be concerned about you?"

Hailey said nothing as a range of emotions played across her battered face: fear, anger, despair, uncertainty, and the tiniest flicker of hope. Kyra's heart ached for her. She'd experienced those same emotions and been similarly paralyzed. She stared at Hailey, wordlessly compelling her to confess. It worked.

"He did this to me. Gareth. He beat me," she burst out.

The air in the room felt suddenly charged. Out of the corner of her eye, Kyra saw Fuentes sitting at attention, his gaze pinned on Hailey. Picking up on the tension in the room, Ranger abandoned his efforts to get Hailey's attention and returned to Kyra's side. She stroked his head absently.

"It's okay, Hailey." She spoke gently. "You did the right thing by telling us."

"I'm sorry I lied." Hailey swiped at the tears trickling down her cheeks.

"It's okay. I understand, and I promise you're not in any trouble. You lied because you were afraid if you told the truth, it would make your husband angry, and he might hit you again. Isn't that right?"

Hailey nodded, sniffling. "I wasn't gonna say anything, but then I went out and ran into my neighbor Geneva as I was coming home, and she called the cops. Things kind of snowballed from there."

"Why don't you tell us what really happened?" urged Fuentes.

She hesitated, then began in a halting voice, "Gareth works nights. He usually lets me sleep in, but this morning he woke me up when he got home from work. He started accusing me of shit I didn't do, like he always does when he's in one of his moods. I denied it, of course, because it was total bullshit. You can see how *that* went." She touched her face again, grimacing. "Later after he fell asleep, I got cleaned up and went for a walk. Just, you know, to clear my head. I ran into my neighbor Geneva as I was passing her house on my way home. Today's trash-pickup day, and she was putting her trash cans out. She saw my face and was like, 'Oh my God. What happened to you?' So I made up the story about being attacked by some rando. I didn't want her to know it was Gareth. What would she have thought?"

"Probably that he deserves to be locked up," growled Fuentes. From the look of disgust he wore, he wouldn't fail Hailey the way Kyra had

3443334844

been failed by the RPD cop who'd buried her report to protect her abuser who was also his superior. But she had to take that first step; no one could do it for her. Kyra extended her hand across the table, palm up. Hailey regarded it as she might a suspicious package that could contain a bomb before hesitantly placing her hand in Kyra's. Their eyes met above their conjoined hands. Kyra silently willed Hailey to do the right thing and save herself.

"Do you wish to press charges, Ms. Peterson?" Fuentes asked.

Hailey shook her head. "God, no. Gareth would kill me."

"He can't hurt you if he's in lockup."

"Yeah, but what about after he gets out?"

"I can have a judge issue a restraining order."

"That wouldn't stop him."

"He won't stop if you stay with him," Kyra said. "The next time— and there *will* be a next time—he might hurt you even worse." *Believe me, I know. It happened to me, and I almost died as a result.*

"I'm scared," Hailey said in a small voice.

Fuentes rose and walked over to stand beside Kyra, presenting a united front. As he faced Hailey across the table, he looked more like a kindly father than a cop, despite the uniform he wore. "I know of a shelter where you could stay until you get back on your feet. It's called Stepping Stones. You'd be safe there. The woman who runs it is like the Secret Service. Say the word and I'll make the call. I can also have someone drive you home and wait while you pack a bag, then drive you to the shelter."

Hailey looked tempted. "How can I be sure Gareth won't find me there?"

"What have you got to lose?" Kyra said.

Hailey didn't answer right away. Kyra could almost hear her thinking, *Do I dare? What if it only makes things worse? What if I can't make it on my own? What if I'm not good enough . . . smart enough . . . strong enough?* The same tapes that had played in Kyra's head before she finally found the courage to leave her husband. "I . . . I'd like to press charges," she said at last.

Kyra resisted the urge to pump her fist and give a shout of triumph. It would have been inappropriate under the circumstances. She'd have to settle for seeing Hailey's abuser brought to justice.

She got her chance sooner than expected. She and Ranger were being escorted from the building by Fuentes, after Hailey had left, when she saw a scruffy-faced man in handcuffs coming toward them down the hallway, being led to booking by a uniformed deputy, cursing and threatening to sue the department. Gareth Peterson, presumably. She said to Ranger, "Who says there's no justice?" He looked up at her, wagging his tail. "Whoever it was, they were wrong."

"Anyone ever tell you you'd make a good cop?" Fuentes asked.

"Why? Do you know of any openings?" she replied lightly.

"Maybe, if I decide to take early retirement, which I probably should after the way I bungled that one." He shook his head in disgust as they watched Gareth Peterson pass by, still cursing and muttering threats. "I can't believe I didn't catch the inconsistencies in her statement."

"You didn't take her statement. That's on Higgins."

"Yeah, but I'm his supervisor."

"Who's working a double shift after coordinating operations at the scene of a five-car pileup. You're only human, Chaz."

"Don't remind me," he said with a rueful twist of his mouth. "What made you suspect she was lying?"

"Besides the clothes she was wearing, you mean? She seemed evasive when she was answering my questions."

"This is why we call you the Witness Whisperer."

"Who?" She paused to look at him in confusion.

"Those of us who've had the pleasure of working with you." This was the first Kyra was learning of her moniker, and it made her smile, even if it was over the top. "I may have started it. I had my doubts that anyone could replace Gertie, and I always admit when I'm wrong. You've proved a worthy successor."

"I learned from the best."

"It's more than that. Today, I could've sworn you were a mind reader, the way you connected with the victim."

"I'm not a mind reader," she said as they continued.

"Then you must have some personal experience in that area."

He gave her a questioning glance, causing Kyra to grow uncomfortable. She should've known he'd suspect something, witnessing her emotional appeal to Hailey, which could only have come from someone who had either been married to an abuser or had grown up in an abusive home. She debated whether to confide in him. She trusted Fuentes not to repeat anything he was told in confidence. But she couldn't bring herself to do it. Here at the department she was known for her successes, not her past failures. She was the Witness Whisperer, according to Fuentes. He would see her differently if he knew her story, and might treat her differently, as Sheriff McNally did. The sheriff was never less than professional in his dealings with her, but she'd noticed an excess of courtesy, a gentleness in his tone when he spoke to her that was absent in his interactions with other members of the department. With Fuentes, there was none of that. He and her other colleagues didn't know her as a victim or see her as someone to be pitied or handled with care. They saw her as a valued member of their team. She meant to keep it that way, so she told the truth but not the whole truth.

"Let's just say my mom didn't always keep the best company."

13

It was noon by the time she arrived home after a stop at Wheeler's Market to pick up a few things she needed. It had been raining off and on all morning, and the sun had finally come out. As she headed for her trailer, Ranger racing ahead of her down the path, the droplets of moisture clinging to the tall grass of the field glittered like diamonds. Inside, she made a fresh pot of coffee, poured herself a cup, and sat down at the kitchen table to drink it while she browsed on her laptop. She checked for any mentions of Krystal Stanhope on social media. She saw that she'd been tagged in a Messenger group thread comprised of four of her former colleagues at the Stoningham Academy.

> **Nina Pelletier:** Anyone heard from @KrystalStanhope? She's not answering my calls or texts. I haven't heard from her since she left. And where did she go, anyway? She didn't say. Something about a family emergency????

Nina, who'd taught math at the academy since Carter was in office, had been Kyra's closest friend at work. "A young person in an old person's body," as she described herself, Nina was an energetic woman with a thatch of frizzy Einstein hair to match her head for numbers. Kyra used to secretly wish that Nina was her mother. She felt bad about quitting her job and skipping town without letting Nina know, but she'd had no choice. Any communication with friends from back home would be dangerous if Rory was searching for her. He could be tapping their phones and monitoring their internet activity, for all she knew.

> **Patrick Noonan:** Same. @KrystalStanhope, if you're someplace far away where there's no internet, getting boned silly by a secret lover, I want all the details. Spill, girlfriend! I promise not to tell your hubby.

Patrick was head of the drama department at Stoningham. A former actor who'd most notably played Polonius in a Broadway production of *Hamlet* in his youth, he'd given up acting to become a teacher and lived with his husband, Roger, a local caterer. Patrick made an art of camp and was one of the few people who could make her laugh, even when she'd been at her lowest, like when he'd remarked about one of his more flamboyant friends, "He opens his mouth and a purse falls out."

> **Gabrielle Loiseau:** Maybe she's in WITSEC?

Gaby Loiseau—Madame Loiseau to her students—taught French at the academy. In her late forties, divorced with a daughter in college, she'd grown up in rural Maine and had been to France only once but spoke fluent French. A foodie, she'd introduced Kyra to all the good French restaurants in their area. Kyra had eaten the best french onion soup she'd ever had in her life at a hole-in-the-wall bistro in Webster that Gaby had taken her to. She still dreamed about that soup.

> **Cora Crawford:** Or she met with foul play????

Cora was the school secretary and an avid mystery fan. A stereotypical spinster, she'd read every Agatha Christie and Rex Stout novel and was addicted to the mystery series she watched on the British streaming channels she subscribed to. Kyra used to enjoy listening to Cora's lively Monday-morning recaps of the shows she'd binge-watched on BritBox or Acorn over the weekend.

> **Patrick:** OMG. LET'S NOT GO THERE @MissMarple-Maven. Not everyone who goes missing ends up in a shallow grave, hacked to pieces. Do you know if she was even reported missing?
> **Nina:** I spoke with her husband. He told me she was taking care of her sick mom in Reno, and he didn't know when she'd be back. Which is weird because she once told me she and her mom weren't close. Also, when I asked for her mom's number, he said he'd text it to me but never did. Something's fishy.

Kyra shook her head in disgust. Her "sick mom"? What a joke. If her mom was sick and lived nearby, Kyra might have looked in on her, but she would never in a million years take an extended leave of absence from work and travel thousands of miles to nurse her. Maybe if she was dying, but that was more than Mom would do for her.

> **Patrick:** I agree, but why would he lie?
> **Gabrielle:** Why does anyone?
> **Cora:** It's usually the husband.
> **Patrick:** OMG. Do you know who he IS? He's a DA! He puts criminals behind bars!

Takes one to know one, Kyra thought. What would the people who worked for him and the voters who'd elected him—not once, but twice—think if they knew the sordid truth about Rory? The only difference between him and the criminals he prosecuted was that Rory had never been charged.

Cora: So? It's not always the drunken slob in the wifebeater. Death Row is full of guys who go to work every day and church on Sundays.
Patrick: Before or after they were incarcerated?
Nina: People, she's not DEAD. Jeez.
Cora: We don't know that for a fact.

Kyra felt sick about ghosting her work friends. They were worried about her, although none but Cora seemed to suspect she'd met with foul play, and Cora watched too much TV. The good news was that it appeared her current whereabouts were unknown to them, which meant she'd succeeded in covering her tracks. With any luck, Rory wouldn't discover where she was, either.

When she checked her email, she saw she had a message. It was from her mom. Who else? Mom was the only person to whom Kyra had given her new email address after she'd deactivated her account associated with Krystal Stanhope. As she clicked on the message, she expected to be hit up for a "loan," as was usually the case when her mom contacted her. Loans that were never repaid.

Subject: Greetings from Arizona

Hey, baby.

How are you? I'm fine. I moved since we last spoke. I'm living in Sun City now working at an old folks' home if you can believe it. I'm the new recreational director (Don't fall off your chair laughing) and the youngest person here by a couple of decades. The pay is shit, but the job comes with free room and board and access to the pool and gym, so it could be worse. And who knows? I might meet some rich old

fart and get him to marry me without a prenup. Think
Daddy Warbucks with a bum ticker. LOL.

What's new with you? Where are you living now? I
think I'm entitled to know, as your mom, even though
you told me not to ask. Drop me a line when you get
a chance. Or better yet, call me. It's been ages.

Hope to see you again sometime before I grow chin
whiskers. If I ever meet my Daddy Warbucks, I'll
invite you to the wedding.

xxoo

Mom

Kyra rolled her eyes at that last part, but at least her mom wasn't
asking her for anything. Also, she had expressed motherly interest in her
daughter's welfare for a change. She fired off a quick reply.

Subject: RE: Greetings from Arizona

Hi Mom,

Glad to hear you're doing well. I'm fine. I'm in a good
place. I'll call when I can.

Xx

Your daughter

She was careful not to reveal anything that would give away her
location. She didn't trust her mother to not leak it to Rory. Mom always

did what was best for Mom, with no thought or care as to how it might affect someone else. Also, she'd been impressed by Rory the one time they'd met. It wouldn't take much coaxing on his part to get Mom to spill, especially if he offered her money in exchange for information.

Minutes after she hit "Send," a new message popped up in her inbox. She felt her blood run cold when she read the address and subject line: MISSING YOU. *Oh God.* How had he gotten her new email address? Then the penny dropped: from Mom, of course. She must also have forwarded to Rory the email Kyra had just sent in reply to hers—the timing of his email was suspicious. Unless . . .

She had a sudden, chilling thought. Had one of the investigators at the DA's office—or "cyber goons," as she called them—hacked into her system on Rory's orders? Her hand shook as she clicked on the message.

Subject: MISSING YOU

My Darling Krystal,

Please don't delete this unread! First and foremost, I want you to know I don't blame you for leaving me, and I'm truly sorry if I made you feel as if you had no other choice. What I did to you was unforgivable, and you have every right to be angry. I have no excuse. The only thing I can say in my defense is that the man you married, and who loves you with all his heart, is who I really am, not the man who behaved despicably toward you. Baby, you're the best thing that ever happened to me, and if I didn't always show it, it was only because I didn't feel worthy. I may seem like I have it all, but on the inside I'm still the kid who was beaten by his dad and told he was worthless. But that's my problem, not yours. I should've listened when you begged me to get help. Instead I let my stubborn pride get in the way.

You might be surprised to learn I'm seeing a thera-pist. Not the one you found but someone who came highly recommended. Sheila Barnes. She's great. She's helped me to see where I went wrong and how to fix it. All I ask of you is that you allow me to show you that I'm a changed man. I want to make things right with us, and I hope and pray you'll find it in your heart to give me that chance. I understand if you're not comfortable meeting me, but I'm hoping we can talk on the phone at least.

Don't give up on me—and on *us*—because of the mistakes I made in the past! I'll do whatever it takes to win you back, and I swear I'll never, ever hurt you again. I love you, baby. We belong together. Till death do us part, like we vowed on our wedding day.

Yours always,

Your loving husband

Till death do us part. A trickle of ice water ran down her spine as she read those words. She folded in on herself, hunched over with her arms wrapped around her middle, as she once had when protecting her soft spots from her husband's blows. Her heart raced. The invisible band around her chest tightened, constricting her breathing. *He knows where I am. He's coming for me.*

She was distracted from her spiraling thoughts by a rough tongue licking her hand. She glanced down to see Ranger looking up at her, his expressive brown eyes seeming to communicate, *I've got you.* Her tension eased, and she stroked the silky fur on his head. "I know you do, bud."

Her panic ebbed, and she was able to think it through logically. She'd slipped up in giving her mom her email address but had been smart enough not to share any other personal information with her. The one time they'd spoken in recent weeks, Kyra had made the call from a burner phone. She used the smartphone she'd recently purchased at the T-Mobile store in town strictly for work calls and communicating with the people she knew here. Also, if he'd known her whereabouts, Rory would have paid her a visit rather than email her. She was safe . . . for the time being.

If he could see her now, would he even recognize her? She wasn't the naive and malleable woman he'd married. Nor was she the broken woman she'd been before she summoned the courage to leave him. She'd clawed back some of her dignity and carved out a new life for herself. She'd found a place to call home, where she'd also found her calling, and where she had the support of her friends here and her colleagues at the Washburn County Sheriff's Department.

And Coop. She hadn't been able to stop thinking about him or their near kiss the other day when she'd been at his house. They probably would have kissed if he hadn't been holding Ranger at the time. Part of her regretted that they hadn't, but what she wished for right now was the comfort of his arms around her. For a sweet moment, she imagined it before she pushed away the image to focus on the present.

She got up and lifted the hinged lid of the bench seat where she'd sat, retrieving from the storage compartment underneath the burner she'd purchased along with her new smartphone to replace the one she'd tossed. She removed its packaging, plugged it in to charge, and punched in her mom's number.

"Hello?" said a high, breathy voice when her call was answered. Her mom sounded more like a teenager than a grown woman.

"Did you give Rory my email address?" she asked without preamble.

"I'm fine, thanks for asking," her mom said snippily. "Nice of you to call and check up on your mother."

"Just answer the damn question."

She heard splashing noises in the background, like someone swimming in a pool. She pictured her mom lounging poolside in a bikini. She could still rock a bikini at the age of forty-nine, and pull it off when she lied about her age to the younger men she dated. Kyra was weirdly proud of that fact. They might have been poor when she was growing up, but her mom had been the envy of the other, less pretty class moms at the schools she'd attended, from the way they'd looked at her.

"Yes," she admitted. "But only after the *third* time he called. He was begging. The poor guy was in tears. I felt sorry for him. What was I supposed to do?"

"You could have told him no."

"Honestly, I don't see why you're making such a big deal of it."

"I didn't ask your opinion, Mom. I asked that you respect my privacy. Which you failed to do. Did he offer you money in exchange?"

Mom would sell her soul for walking-around money. She also liked to brag about her wealthy and important son-in-law. How could her daughter give up such a prize? So they had problems. What couple didn't? When Kyra had told her she was leaving him and why, she'd urged Kyra to stay and work it out.

The rules are different with men like Rory. When some drunken bum gives you a black eye, you call the cops. When it's your rich husband, you suck it up and get a nice piece of jewelry out of it.

Kyra had resisted the urge to snap, *If he's so great, why don't you marry him yourself?* Mom wouldn't have gotten the sarcasm. The sad truth was, she *would* marry him if she could.

"What? No. How could you think that? I would never—"

"How much?"

She quit protesting and whined, "What was I supposed to do? You left me high and dry."

"Well, just so you know, you're not getting another dime from me." In the past, Kyra had found it easier to write a check than listen to a litany of woes whenever her mom had needed an emergency cash infusion.

"Fine, I won't ask."

Kyra rolled her eyes. "Like I haven't heard that before."

"I mean it. And I'll pay back what I owe you as soon as I'm back on my feet."

Which would be never. "You seem to be doing all right for yourself."

"I'm getting by, but I'm not sure how much longer I'll be able to keep this job."

"You haven't met your Daddy Warbucks yet?"

"Ha ha. The only guy close to my age is the manager, and he's a dick."

Of course, he was. Mom had burned through as many bosses as she had boyfriends. Whenever she was fired from a job, it was usually because she'd either messed up at work or things had gotten messy because she'd slept with her boss, or a combination of the two. "Did you date him before you discovered he was a dick?"

The brief silence at the other end confirmed her suspicion. "I thought he was different from the others. It's why I left Reno. Ben offered me this job and made certain promises. I thought he was The One."

She sounded so defeated, Kyra felt a tug of sympathy despite herself. Her mom had a history of bad relationships, but it wasn't always her fault. Some of the men had seemed nice before they'd shown their true colors, and some of it was just bad luck. "Sounds like you're better off without him."

"Not if I lose this job."

"You'll find another one if this one doesn't work out," Kyra said in a gentler tone.

Any sympathy she felt for her mom dried up with her next words. "Easy for you to say. You don't know what it's like. I never had it easy."

Eileen Goudge

"Like I did?"

"You didn't have a kid to raise. You had opportunities I didn't."

"I created my own opportunities." She'd studied hard in school to get her college scholarship. Even with her full ride at Fordham, she'd had to work part-time jobs to earn enough money to pay for any extras. When she was doing her postgrad, she'd worked temp jobs in New York City to augment her meager earnings from selling her paintings at street fairs. True, she didn't have the responsibility of raising a child, but nor had her mom, one might argue. More often than not, Kyra had been home alone when she wasn't in school from the time she was old enough to feed herself.

Mom changed her tune. "I know, and I'm proud of you, baby."

"Don't be. I messed up big-time when I married Rory."

"Was it really so bad?"

"You have no idea. You shouldn't even be speaking to him after what he did to me."

"Just because you're mad at him, it doesn't mean I have to be."

"He *beat* me, Mom."

"Yes, I know, and it must've been awful for you if it was as bad as you described. But he's sorry. You should have heard him on the phone. He was sobbing. Couldn't you at least talk to him and hear what he was to say?"

"There's nothing he could possibly say that I'd want to hear or that would change my mind."

"If you'd just—"

"Bye, Mom. Nice talking to you."

"I'm sorry!" her mom's voice bleated before she could end the call. "I should've respected your privacy."

"Damn right."

"No need to rub it in. I said I was sorry."

"Apology accepted. I have to go now."

"Wait! You still haven't told me anything. Where are you living? Did you find another teaching job?"

"Nice try, Mom."

"What? I'm not allowed to ask how my daughter is doing?"

"You can ask, but don't expect an answer."

"I ask only because I care! I love you, baby." Her voice cracked.

"I know, Mom, and I love you, too." Despite everything, she did. There had been some good times with her mom. She was selfish, irresponsible, and didn't know the meaning of the term "age appropriate," but when Kyra had been growing up, she'd had the "cool" mom. She could stay up as late as she wanted, and there were no restrictions on her TV viewing, what she wore, or what she ate. And what other mom would drive her teenage daughter and her friends around the neighborhood on Halloween so they could TP their neighbors' front yards? "But I can't trust you. Anything I tell you will be on a need-to-know basis."

"Can't I at least have your number?"

"No, and don't try calling me back at this number. Your call won't go through."

"What, you're working for the CIA now?"

"As far as you're concerned."

"What if it's an emergency?"

"Call 911."

"What if I was in a coma?"

"Then getting in touch with me would be the least of your problems."

"When did you get to be so cold? I'm your mother!"

"Nice that you remembered. Bye, Mom."

Unsettled by her conversation with her mom, Kyra decided to take a walk after she ended the call, hoping the fresh air and exercise would clear her head. As she walked the tree-lined trail that followed the creek with Ranger, the sun shone and the air smelled of the needles from the fir trees that covered the ground, and more faintly, the cidery tang of the fallen fruit in the apple orchard up the road.

She was passing Coop's house when she heard a gunshot. She froze. It was hunting season, and she'd become accustomed to hearing the occasional crack of a rifle in the distance, but the shot she'd heard had come from the direction of Coop's house. Her heart pounding, she peered through the trees at the white clapboard farmhouse across the field, but saw no sign of a disturbance. The only thing unfamiliar that she noticed was the vehicle parked outside the entrance to Coop's practice, a dark-gray SUV. It might have belonged to one of his clients, or . . .

Was it connected to Rory? Had he discovered her whereabouts and decided to come and appeal to her in person? Had he been somewhere nearby when he emailed her? She imagined a scenario in which he'd showed up at the house and flown into a jealous rage when a man answered his knock. The situation would have escalated from there. And if Rory had refused to leave, Coop might have chased him off with his gun if he owned one, which he probably did. Didn't most cops, even ex-cops? The shot she'd heard might have been fired as a warning. But suppose Rory hadn't heeded the warning? Suppose he was roaming the property in search of her at this very moment?

She felt suddenly chilled and glanced around her, half expecting to see Rory appear from the dense foliage along the creek bank or from behind the deadfall blocking the trail up ahead. She saw no one, nor did Ranger bark like he did at strangers who'd gotten his hackles up. But it didn't assuage her fear. She called to Ranger, who was investigating a beaver dam down at the water's edge. He came racing back. "Time to go, bud." Her voice sounded tight and high-pitched. She was having trouble catching her breath. There was an elephant sitting on her chest. *Oh God. Not now. Of all the times to have a panic attack.* She warbled a laugh at the thought. When else if not when she was panicking?

She hurried back the way she'd come, Ranger trotting at her heels as if he sensed her anxiety. She needed to find a place to hide. Stupidly, she'd left her phone back at the trailer, so she couldn't call for help. She thought about going to Coop, but he might have left the house to look for Rory, and if she were to leave the cover of the trees and cross the field, Rory might spot and intercept her.

Distracted by her thoughts, she wasn't watching where she was going and tripped over an exposed tree root. She was thrown off-balance. Her next step sent her staggering forward, which caused her right foot to come down at an awkward angle. She felt something wrench in her ankle, and a white-hot flare of pain shot up her leg. Gritting her teeth, she continued, moving as fast as her throbbing ankle would allow. She was headed for the old barn at the easternmost edge of the property that she remembered from an earlier excursion. She could hide there. *Don't let him find me. Don't let him find me. Don't let him . . .*

She was brought to an abrupt halt by a startling thought. What if it had been Rory, and not Coop, who'd fired the shot she'd heard? He owned a gun, which he'd acquired after receiving death threats from felons he'd put away in prison, and had a license to carry. Also, she had never known him to walk away from a fight. If he'd mistaken Coop for her lover and they'd tangled . . .

She felt a cold thump in the pit of her stomach, picturing Coop injured from a gunshot wound, lying in a pool of his own blood. She needed to find out if he was okay.

She reversed direction, and then stopped. If he had misread the situation, Rory would feel betrayed, thinking she'd cheated on him. His blood would be up. He wouldn't wait for an explanation. Nor would there be any apologies for his past transgressions if he was to find her. He would lash out at her in his fury. Or shoot her if he was armed. She trembled at the thought.

But she couldn't abandon Coop if he was injured. She had placed him in harm's way by mere virtue of the fact that she was living on his property. She owed it to him, not only as her friend but also as a fellow human being, to see if he needed help. He would have done the same for her in a heartbeat if their roles were reversed. If she couldn't be brave for her own sake, she would have to be for his.

Fear, she was discovering, didn't have to be a deterrent; it could be a motivator. It had gotten her this far, hadn't it? Krystal Stanhope might have run from danger, but Kyra Smith was better than that.

"Change of plans, bud," she said to Ranger. "We need to check on Coop. He might be in trouble."

She headed toward the house, her twisted ankle screaming in protest with each step. Ranger stayed so close that had he walked on two legs, she would've been leaning on him. Winged insects, disturbed by their movements, rose into the air, swarming around them as they moved through the tall grass.

When she reached the house, she peeked through the window into the outer office of Coop's practice and saw him talking with another man, both of them standing and having what appeared to be a tense discussion. The other man looked to be about the same age he was, medium height and physically fit with military-short brown hair. There was no sign of Rory, to her immense relief.

Both men turned to look at her as she entered with Ranger. Coop seemed surprised to see her, while the other man only glanced in her direction. He seemed distracted and disturbed about something.

"I heard a shot," she said, out of breath. "Is everything okay?"

"We had a situation, but everything's under control now," Coop told her. "Are you okay? Why are you limping?"

"I twisted my ankle."

"Sit," he ordered, gesturing toward the sofa and chairs by the window. "If you give me a minute, I'll get you some ice for that ankle. I was just finishing up with my client here." He gestured toward the other man.

Kyra took a seat on the sofa, Ranger settling at her feet. The two men went outside, and a short while later, she heard a car engine. When Coop came back inside, he was alone.

"What was that all about?" she asked.

"We were in the middle of a session when we heard an engine backfire in the driveway. Probably somebody who took a wrong turn, but my client mistook it for a gunshot, and . . ." He trailed off with a short shake of his head. "He served in Afghanistan, two tours," was all he said in explaining why his client had reacted as he had. Coop didn't have to say "PTSD" for Kyra to know that was what he was alluding to. "Unbeknownst to me, he was carrying. When he drew his weapon and I tried to take it from him, it discharged accidentally."

"That was the shot I heard?"

"Yes. Fortunately, no damage was done that a bit of plaster can't fix." He pointed through the door to his private office, where she saw what looked to be a bullet hole in the wall opposite his desk.

Kyra gasped. "Oh my God."

"Thankfully, no one was hurt."

"Is he all right to drive?"

"Probably not, which is why I called my dad. He's giving him a ride home. Now, let's get that ankle of yours iced. Would you like anything else while I'm at it? How about a cup of tea?"

"Water and Tylenol, if you have any. I'll come with." Leaning on Coop, she hobbled into his private office and through the door that led to the main part of the house and into the large country kitchen beyond, Ranger following. Coop pulled out a chair for her at the pine trestle table that stood at one end of the room where there was a picture window, and she sat down, propping her injured leg on the chair next to her. He left her and returned shortly carrying a bag of frozen peas wrapped in a dish towel in one hand and a bottled water and Tylenol container in the other. He handed her the water and Tylenol and placed the bag of frozen peas on her swollen ankle, while she swallowed two Tylenol with water.

He studied her, frowning. "You're pale as a ghost. Why don't I take you to the ER? You should probably get that ankle x-rayed."

"I don't think it's broken. If I'm pale, it's probably from the shock of hearing that gunshot. I thought—" She broke off and, to her horror, unexpectedly burst into tears. Coop dropped onto his haunches so he was eye level with her, taking her hands in his while Ranger pressed up against her leg, eyeing her worriedly. "I—I thought you might be hurt. I thought he'd shot you."

"Who? My client?"

"No. My husband."

"You're married?" He stared at her in shock.

She nodded. "In name only."

"So the 'ex' you mentioned before is your husband?" She nodded again. "Why didn't you tell me?"

"I didn't want to get into it, and I didn't think I needed to. I thought . . . hoped . . . I'd left all that behind when I came here. But today, when I heard the gunshot, I thought he'd tracked me down."

"And that I fired at him to protect you?"

"Yes. At first. You'd chased someone off to protect me, though you didn't actually threaten Scr—that creep Jed who'd tried to pick me up." She managed a weak smile. "But then I remembered that he—my husband— owns a gun. I was afraid he'd shot and wounded *you*."

"So, when you came running, it was to see if I was okay?" She nodded again, and his expression softened. He asked in his cop's voice, "Am I correct in assuming your ex has a history of violence?"

"Yes, although nothing that's on record, as far as I know."

"Was he ever violent toward you?"

"Yes. The last time, he beat me so badly I ended up in the hospital. I almost died."

"The last time? So there were other times before that?"

"Yes," she said in a small voice. Filled with shame, she dropped her gaze to avoid the look of pity, and perhaps disgust, she imagined she would see on his face. When he spoke, she was relieved to hear only compassion in his voice.

"Kyra, I'm so sorry. I suspected you were running from something, and after I determined it wasn't the law, I figured it was *someone* rather than something. When you mentioned your ex, I put two and two together. But I had no idea it was this bad."

"Now you know why I didn't tell you before. I didn't want you to see me as a victim." She choked back another sob, burying her face in her hands.

"Kyra." Gentle fingers pried hers from her face. She brought her head up to meet his gaze, which was as gentle as his touch as he held both her hands. "All I see is someone who was badly treated, and who got away."

"I got away, yes, but we were together for five years before then. I stayed with him long after any normal person would have left." Saying it out loud made it sound even worse. The heat of her shame rose to scorch her cheeks.

"I imagine it was because you didn't feel you had a choice."

"An abused animal doesn't have a choice, but I wasn't caged or chained up." She remembered the pitiful state in which she'd found Ranger when she'd first met him and how outraged she'd been. It had been so clear what was needed, and she'd acted swiftly and aggressively in rescuing him. Why hadn't she acted as swiftly in saving herself? "I could've left at any time. I could've gone to work one day and not come home. So why did I stay for as long as I did? What's wrong with me?"

"Nothing." His hands tightened around hers. "You were traumatized, and that isn't a character flaw—it's simply a fact. You might also have been depressed. It's a common symptom of PTSD, and it can be paralyzing. Kyra, there's no shame in that. No one, I mean no one, has a right to judge you."

She gave a bitter laugh. "I seem to be doing enough of that myself."

"But you got away."

"Yes, but I'm not sure there's anyplace I could go where he wouldn't find me. I changed my name, and I was careful not to leave a paper trail, but . . . he's in law enforcement, so he has resources the average person doesn't."

"He's a cop?"

"Worse. He's the DA of Monroe County in New York. Rory Stanhope. He knows people. People like the investigators who work at the DA's office and the bounty hunters he sometimes uses to track outlaws down."

"I wish you'd told me sooner. I can protect you, but only from a known threat."

"I didn't know who I could trust."

"You can trust me. Has he given any indication that he knows or suspects your whereabouts?"

"No, but I heard from him today. He emailed me. My mom gave him my new email address even though I'd asked her not to."

Coop's gaze sharpened. "What did he want? Did he threaten you?"

"No, nothing like that. He wants us to get back together. He claims he's in therapy now, and that he's a changed man. He begged me to give him another chance."

"Is there any possibility of that? I'm sorry, but I have to ask," he apologized.

"Fair enough. And no, there's zero possibility. But he doesn't give up easily when he wants something."

"I take it you didn't leave a forwarding address with your mom."

"God, no. She doesn't even have my new phone number. She'd sell me out in a heartbeat. She also has a soft spot for Rory." If only Mom cared as much for her own flesh and blood. "But that doesn't mean he won't find me." She felt a fresh stab of anxiety. "Today, when I heard the gunshot, I thought he had. If he'd come here looking for me, the first place he would have gone was the house. I knew you wouldn't tell him anything, but I also knew it wouldn't stop him from making assumptions."

"Such as?"

"He'd have thought . . ." She trailed off, the heat in her cheeks intensifying.

"That I was your boyfriend?" She nodded. His eyes sparkled and his mouth slanted in a smile, suggesting some secret amusement before his expression turned serious again. "Well, just so you know, I've dealt with my share of jealous husbands. Not personally," he added at the quizzical look she gave him. "When I was a cop responding to domestic calls."

"Thanks for clarifying," she said dryly. "Good to know you're not in the habit of sleeping with other men's wives."

"Hardly," he said as if nothing could be further from the truth. "My point is, I can protect myself against threats. You, on the other hand, need protection."

"What kind of protection?"

"This house has an alarm system, but the trailer doesn't. I'll need to secure it. I'll put up additional trail cams around the property, too. You'll also need personal protection. Do you own a gun?"

"Yes, but I've never used it. It was an impulse buy."

"In that case, your first lesson at the gun range is tomorrow. I'll be your instructor."

"Oh. I couldn't ask you to do that."

"You're not asking; I'm offering. In fact, I insist."

She cracked a smile. "One of the benefits of a resident landlord?"

"Something like that."

"Then how can I refuse?"

Nor, as it turned out, could she refuse his offer of a piggyback ride when it was time for her to go. "I feel ridiculous," she said as he carried her on his back across the field to her trailer. He'd insisted over her protests, arguing that she was in no condition to walk, given her injury. "And I probably look even more ridiculous."

"Who's watching?" he said.

"My dog, and he agrees." Ranger ran alongside them, barking excitedly and occasionally leaping up to nip playfully at her dangling feet, like it was a game they were playing.

Coop laughed. "Shut up and enjoy the ride."

It was freeing in one sense, like being a kid again, although there was nothing childlike about the desire stirred in her by the feel of Coop's broad, muscular back beneath her and his strong arms clasping her legs where they were wrapped around him. She felt freer, too, for having unburdened herself to him. He had neither judged her poorly nor made her feel like she was marked "Fragile, Handle with Care." Instead, he'd offered to teach her how to shoot so she could protect herself.

"Thanks for the lift," she said after they'd arrived and he'd lowered her onto the ground.

"Anytime."

For several seconds, neither of them moved. They stood smiling at each other, caught up in the moment. Before she was aware of it, her hand floated up to touch his beard. Soft. So soft. Not bristly like the facial hair on some men. She saw a flash of desire in his eyes and felt an answering tug down below.

He dipped his head to kiss her and . . . *Wham.* Her erogenous zones lit up like a Christmas tree. It had been so long, she'd thought that part of her was dead, or in hibernation. Now it was awake and urging, *Go for it*, and who was she to argue? She parted her lips and let his tongue play over hers.

His kiss deepened, and he tightened his arms around her, causing her pulse to quicken and her knees to weaken. Her hands rode up his back, exploring its contours, and she felt his drop below her waist to cup her ass. As he pulled her against him, she could feel his hardness. When they finally drew apart, they were both breathing hard. Overwhelmed by the emotions battering at her ramparts and the sensations pulsing in her body, making her feel alive again in a way she hadn't in years, she couldn't move or speak. It was as if she were in a trance. She saw a flash of worry in his eyes.

"I'm sorry. I shouldn't have done that," he said. He'd clearly misread her dazed state as a case of regret. Maybe he was worried that he had taken advantage of her when she was emotionally vulnerable.

"It's okay," she said when she recovered her wits.

Okay? Good God, the man just rocked your world, and you act like he apologized for bumping into you.

She opened her mouth to tell him she had wanted it as much as he had, but on second thought decided against it. It would only lead to more kissing, and if they were to take it inside, there would be no turning back. However tempting, a romantic entanglement was the last thing she needed right now.

She didn't know whether to be relieved or disappointed when he said, "Won't happen again."

14

"It's hopeless," said Kyra as she regarded the target into which she'd just emptied her magazine. There were far fewer bullet holes in the figure depicted on the target than in the white space around it.

She blew out a frustrated breath. This was her third lesson at the gun range in as many days, and judging from today's performance, her aim wasn't improving. She was starting to think this was a colossal waste of time.

"You're overcorrecting," Coop said. "Which means you're overthinking."

"How can I not, with my head stuffed full of everything I've learned over the past few days?" Everything from the proper maintenance and handling of a firearm to how to load and safely operate one. She also found Coop's presence distracting. All she could think about was The Kiss, which had become the elephant in the room that neither of them alluded to. She hadn't even confided in her friends, because talking about it would make it a thing. Childishly, she hoped if she ignored it, it would go away.

But it was hard to ignore the attraction that sizzled between them. Impossible with him standing at her elbow, exuding his manly scent mixed with the smell of gun oil. Every time he issued instructions in her ear, or placed his hands on her to correct her stance, it sent an electric jolt to her lady parts. It required all her concentration to keep from grabbing hold of him and kissing him for all she was worth.

Having taught her the basics, Coop was devoting today's lesson to target practice. At which she sucked, apparently. The problem wasn't her choice of weapon. The Smith & Wesson .38 Special she'd purchased in Reno was small enough to fit comfortably in her grip and didn't have the recoil of the bigger guns. *She* was the problem.

"Do it enough times and it becomes instinctual." Coop reeled in the target attached to a movable rack inside the shooting lane, which could be positioned closer or farther away in accordance with the skill level of the shooter. He replaced it with a fresh target set at regulation distance from her position behind the bulletproof barrier enclosing her firing station. No baby steps for her. "Now, reload and rack, and let's try this again."

"It's no use. I'd be a dead woman if he were a real shooter." She motioned toward the gun-wielding figure depicted on the target, who bore an uncanny resemblance to Edward G. Robinson. She used to watch those old G-man movies on TV with her mom, one of her few happy memories from childhood.

"No, you wouldn't, because you've got me as backup." Coop grinned and clapped her on the shoulder, causing her pheromones to send up another smoke signal. He sported his mountain-man look today, dressed in a blue-and-white-checked flannel shirt and jeans. "But you just gave me an idea."

"What?"

"I'll explain in a minute. First, reload your weapon."

She did as instructed and assumed shooting stance. He stepped around behind her to correct her stance. She was acutely aware of his body lightly pressing against her from behind, the tiny hairs on his arms below his rolled-up shirtsleeves brushing against her skin where he held her wrists as he adjusted her grip. He smelled of the coffee and doughnuts they'd picked up at the Country Kitchen Diner on 49 and eaten while driving to the gun range and his own scent. She became momentarily lost in her fantasy of making love with him, which was interrupted by the rumble of his voice against her ear.

"Imagine he's a real shooter who poses a real threat. Now think about how you're going to neutralize that threat."

While she held her stance, he raised her headphones to cover her ears and stepped away. With no sounds to distract her, she was able to visualize the figure depicted on the target in 3D. Except it wasn't Edward G. Robinson she saw; it was Rory. The way he'd looked on that awful day, months earlier, when she'd discovered what the monster inside him was capable of, once unleashed. A monster that knew no limits and showed no mercy. The memory came rushing back: Rory confronting her, after he'd accidentally discovered the birth control pills she'd secretly been taking while they were supposedly trying for a baby. He'd beaten her so savagely, it had been a relief when she'd finally blacked out. She wasn't sure which had been worse: the beating, which had left her with a ruptured spleen and a broken arm among other injuries, or the horror of finding out afterward that he'd staged it to look like an accident, complete with photos of her wrecked car to back up his story.

She froze, her heart pounding, her gun hand shaking. Then her focus sharpened and her hand steadied. She fired, again and again, emptying her magazine into the target. *Take that, you son of a bitch.*

She lowered her headphones to the sound of a low whistle. She turned to find Coop studying the target, now riddled with bullet holes. "Will you look at that?" he said. "All center of mass."

Kyra stared in astonishment at the tight cluster of bullet holes at the center of the target. "I did that? I didn't know I could do that."

"I never doubted it." Coop gave her a sideways hug, and for a second he looked like he wished he could do more before he dropped his arm from her shoulders. These past few days, while The Kiss had been playing on a continuous loop in her memory, she'd sensed he was reliving it, too, and perhaps taking it further in his fantasies, as she had. Fortunately or unfortunately, depending on one's point of view—right now, she was leaning toward the latter—he was respecting her boundaries.

"Damn, woman, that's next level," he said as he went back to admiring her handiwork.

"As in one level up from hopeless?"

"As in certified badass."

She grinned at his assessment, even as she thought, *What if it were a real-life situation?* "Shooting at a stationary target is one thing. Shooting at a moving target is another," she reminded him.

"We'll be working on that next."

"Don't tell me you plan to take me hunting?" she teased. "Because I've never shot at an animal, and I don't intend to start now."

"No live animals involved. You'll be shooting at mechanical targets."

"I'm fine with that, but don't expect a repeat of today's show of marksmanship. It was probably a fluke."

He directed his gaze at her. "Who were you thinking of just now when you fired?"

"I think you know who."

"I rest my case."

"This is a controlled setting. What if it were a real-life situation and I panicked?"

"You have to trust your instincts."

"How can I? Look who I married."

15

The following Thursday was Thanksgiving. Kyra had been invited to dinner by each of the Tattooed Ladies, as well as Shirley, but Frannie had been the first to ask, which was why Kyra found herself standing on Frannie's doorstep with Ranger at three o'clock in the afternoon on Thanksgiving, bearing a bottle of wine from Cask, the wine store down the street from the Shear Delight Salon. Frannie met her at the door, wearing an apron and a welcoming smile.

"Come on in. You can keep us company in the kitchen while we cook."

In the kitchen, Frannie's sister, Vanessa, was stirring something in a saucepan on the stove. Frannie had explained that they traditionally took turns hosting Thanksgiving dinner, and this year it was Frannie's turn, though it was a smaller group than in past years, composed of just her and Vanessa, Hannah, and Kyra. Vanessa's son, Antoine, a marine biologist, was currently conducting field research in the Channel Islands. Her daughter, Cecelia, who'd been named after Vanessa and Frannie's grandmother and who currently lived in Oregon, had planned to come with her husband and children but had had to cancel at the last minute after her youngest came down with strep throat.

"How can I help?" Kyra asked as Ranger, by her side, sniffed the air with all the enticing smells. The turkey was resting, the potatoes boiling. Two kinds of casserole were cooling on the counter.

"Ask Vanessa. She seems to think she's in charge."

Vanessa laughed. "Don't listen to her. I'm the boss only when I'm at work."

"I can cook, you know!" Frannie shook a finger at her sister.

"No one said you couldn't. I merely pointed out that the turkey would be dry if you left it in the oven any longer."

"You also said the green bean casserole needed more salt."

"Just a pinch," Vanessa said, and turned to smile at Kyra. "Welcome to our version of *Family Feud.*"

"I'm not much of a cook," Kyra said. "But I'm good at taking directions if there's anything that needs doing."

"You can chop the walnuts for the cranberry sauce," Frannie said, handing her a bowl of toasted walnuts and a knife.

Hannah popped into the kitchen to greet their guests. "Hi, Kyra! Who's my best boy?" she cooed as she crouched down to pet Ranger while he slathered her face with sloppy kisses. "Can I take him for a walk before dinner?" she asked Kyra. "I'm done setting the table," she told her mom.

"Of course. He'd love it," said Kyra. "How's the new job?"

"It's a job," Hannah replied with a shrug. "But my coworkers are nice, especially this one guy, Darren. He's so funny. You should see his impersonation of our boss. Cracks me up every time." Her eyes sparkled. She looked prettier than usual tonight, wearing a jewel-toned velour top and dressy jeans.

"It makes the job easier when you like the people you work with. Do you ever see any of them outside of work?"

"Darren and I have gone out for coffee a couple times. He also went with me when we collected coats for our store's annual coat drive. He even donated some new coats that he'd bought with his employee discount after noticing none of the ones we'd collected were in kids' sizes."

"He sounds like a good guy."

"He is," she said, a dreamy look coming over her face.

"I think she has feelings for this Darren fellow," Frannie confided after Hannah had left to take Ranger for a walk, which Kyra had already deduced. She didn't look happy about it.

"Is there a problem?" Kyra asked as she got to work chopping the nuts.

"Not with him, as far as I can tell, but Hannah doesn't have the best track record when it comes to men."

"They fall in love with her, and once they get the full picture—as in, what she's like when she's unmedicated—they drop her like a hot potato," Vanessa said with a sorrowful shake of her head. "I adore my niece, but to love her is to love all of her, and her previous boyfriends couldn't hack it."

"To be fair, it's hard being with someone who hears voices in her head," said Frannie as she strained the boiled potatoes and dumped them into a bowl. "You never know which Hannah you're gonna get."

"But she's still taking her medication, isn't she?" asked Kyra.

"Yes, but only because it was a condition of her staying with me." Frannie tossed a chunk of butter into the bowl with the potatoes, then added a dollop of sour cream. "If she becomes involved with this guy . . ." She trailed off with a shake of her head. "Her last boyfriend dumped her after she moved in with him. She was in love and didn't think she needed to be on meds, so she'd stopped taking them."

"Let's not get ahead of ourselves. They haven't even gone out on a proper date yet," Vanessa reminded her.

"Maybe he's different from the other men she's been with." Kyra thought of Coop, who was nothing like Rory. If they'd met earlier in their lives before their hearts had been broken, and in Kyra's case, her trust as well, they might have gotten together and had a shot at their happily ever after. "Any guy who'd buy coats for kids on his salary as a store clerk would have to be pretty special."

"Maybe," Frannie said, but she didn't sound optimistic. She got out the electric beaters and began mashing the potatoes. The whir of the beaters put an end to the discussion.

Hannah returned from her walk with Ranger as Vanessa was pouring the gravy she'd made into the gravy boat. The turkey was carved and set out on a platter on the sideboard in the dining room along with the sides: stuffing, mashed potatoes, two kinds of casserole—green bean and sweet potato—cranberry relish, and homemade orange rolls. The table was set with Frannie's good china and silver, which shone in the candlelight. Ranger was given a rawhide bone to chew on, while the human guests helped themselves to the food and sat down to eat.

Frannie said the blessing while they all joined hands. "Bless us, oh Lord, and these Thy gifts, which we are about to receive from Thy bounty. And this year I would like to give special thanks for the blessing of my daughter and sister, and my friend Kyra, who are sharing this meal with me."

The others each in turn gave thanks for a blessing in her own life. Vanessa was next. "I'm thankful for a meal that someone else cooked. Expertly, I might add," she said with an affectionate glance at Frannie.

"With some help from the real expert," Frannie replied with a laugh.

"I'm thankful for my mom, who's always been there for me, in good times and bad," said Hannah when it was her turn. Frannie beamed at her with shining eyes.

Kyra wished she had a mom about whom she could say the same. But she did have something to be grateful for . . .

"I'm thankful to be among friends," she said.

That reminded her: she'd been invited to the Tattooed Ladies' monthly dinner next week. The last time they'd all been together, at her impromptu wienie roast, she'd allowed the opportunity to come clean about her past slip away. She wouldn't do that with the next opportunity. It was time she told them. Past time, if she was being honest. Still, she worried about how they'd react. She couldn't imagine them being any less kind about it than Sheriff McNally or Coop had been, but they might see her differently once they learned she wasn't who she'd seemed.

Frannie called her an "inspiration." The truth was, hers was a cautionary tale. *Do as I did and you'll live to regret it if you don't die first.*

The food was delicious: the turkey roasted to perfection, the sides all made from scratch. The oyster stuffing from a traditional southern recipe was a nod to the sisters' and Hannah's Creole heritage. For dessert there were two kinds of pie—apple and chocolate pecan—both made by Vanessa.

"This has been the best Thanksgiving ever," Kyra declared two hours later as she was leaving with Ranger, after having stuffed her face and played two games of Scrabble. When she was growing up, holidays had only served to remind her of the traditions other families were observing and that she and her mom weren't. The family dinners she'd hosted on Thanksgiving during her marriage had been tense affairs, with Rory being stiffly polite to his mom while she bent over backward in an effort to please him, the two brothers exchanging subtle digs, and Kyra stuck in the middle. Tonight had been a breath of fresh air in comparison. "Thanks for having me. And thanks for cooking such an amazing meal." She addressed her last remark to both sisters.

"The first of many Thanksgivings you'll celebrate with us, I hope," said Frannie as she helped Kyra with her coat at the door. "Next year we'll be at Vanessa's, but I'm sure she'd love to have you, as would I."

"Absolutely," said Vanessa. "You're always welcome, Kyra."

"You and Ranger can help me keep Aunt Vanessa's grandkids entertained so they don't tear the house apart," Hannah said to Kyra. "Usually, I get stuck with them. They have a *lot* of energy," she warned.

"I'd love to come." Kyra said a little prayer that she'd still be here this time next year.

Frannie handed her the shopping bag filled with the leftovers she'd given Kyra to take home with her, packed in Tupperware containers. "What are your plans for the rest of this weekend?" she asked.

"I'm expecting to be called into work at some point, being as it's a holiday weekend," Kyra replied. The crime rate typically saw a spike during holiday weekends, she'd been forewarned. "I don't have any plans other than my daily lessons at the gun range. Coop is teaching me how to shoot."

"Really." Frannie's eyebrows shot up. "I didn't know you owned a gun."

"I bought one a while ago, but I'd never used it before."

"How long has this been going on?"

"For the past week or so. He, um, thought it'd be a good idea, being as I live alone and he's not always around. I took him up on his offer to teach me." Kyra had advanced from shooting at stationary targets to shooting at moving targets referred to as sliders, drop turners, and whirligigs. It wasn't going so well. She'd missed more than she'd hit. Hopefully, she'd get better with practice.

"Ah, that explains it."

"What?"

"Shirley mentioned you two had been spending a lot of time together. She seems to think you're romantically involved."

"We're not," Kyra said, her face warming. "We're just friends."

"What happened to your relationship being strictly business?"

"Things changed."

"Yes, I can see that," Frannie said, and Kyra had the uncomfortable feeling her friend's sharp eyes saw more than she'd revealed.

Darkness had fallen by the time she pulled into the driveway at Coop's. She waited until Ranger had leaped out, after performing his trick of powering down the window on the passenger side, before she climbed out, carrying the bag of leftovers. They were passing Coop's house when he stepped out onto his porch, shining a flashlight.

"Hold up," he called. "I'll walk you home." He seemed to see it as his duty to escort her to and from her trailer after dark, despite his having secured it with an alarm system and installing additional trail cams around the property. She didn't argue. She felt safer with him by her side, keeping watch.

"How was your Thanksgiving?" she asked as they crossed the field together, Ranger's tail end visible in the beam of Coop's flashlight as he bounded ahead of them down the path.

"My brother Chris and his wife hosted it this year, but it was the usual three-ring circus with the kids and dogs running around, and the adults all talking at once. Oh, and two of my nieces got into an argument over whose turn it was to make a wish on the wishbone. There were tears. How was yours?"

"Great! Frannie and her sister cooked a fabulous meal. I had a wonderful time."

"My mom was disappointed that you couldn't join us."

"I would've come if I hadn't already accepted Frannie's invitation."

"Next time, then."

"I hope she doesn't feel obligated just because I'm living on your property."

"You said the same thing about her bringing you meals. I thought we'd established that my mom doesn't do anything out of a sense of obligation. She likes you. She also likes playing matchmaker."

"Oh." Kyra was glad he couldn't see her burning cheeks in the dark. "Does she know it's not like that with us?"

"I've told her."

Apart from The Kiss and the few times she'd caught him looking at her like he wouldn't mind getting to know her in the biblical sense, Coop had given no indication that he had feelings for her. Still, learning she'd been relegated to the friend zone stung. Why, she couldn't have said. Wasn't it what she wanted?

Neither of them spoke for the rest of the way. Ranger beat them home and was standing at the door to the trailer when they arrived. Coop waited while she let herself in with her key and disarmed the security system, making sure it was in good working order and there was no sign of a forced entry.

"We still on for tomorrow?" she asked.

"You bet. Except we're not going to the gun range tomorrow. We're going to try something different."

"Uh-oh. Should I be worried?"

"Depends on how good a shape you're in. You may have some sore muscles afterward. I'm taking you to my friend Desmond's gym, where I'll be teaching you some self-defense moves."

"Seriously? Isn't it enough that you're teaching me how to shoot?"

"You need to know how to defend yourself against an attack for those times when you're not armed."

"All right, but just don't expect me to get good enough to take you down. You're six inches taller than me and weigh twice what I do."

"Simulated takedown," he corrected. "And you might surprise yourself. With martial arts, it has less to do with your size and strength than it does with how you move and knowing your opponent's vulnerable spots. You could take someone down with a well-aimed head bump, for instance."

"Or give myself a concussion."

"I can teach you how to protect yourself so you don't get hurt."

"If you say so." She wasn't so sure but was willing to give it a try. "Well, good night. Thanks for the escort."

"You're welcome." He lingered a moment longer, his eyes meeting hers in a look that suggested he harbored hidden desires; then he turned to head back to the house. Kyra watched him go until he was swallowed by the surrounding shadows and there was only the beam of his flashlight bobbing in the darkness, feeling things she couldn't name but that were definitely not in the friend zone.

The following morning at the gym, Coop taught her some basic moves with which to defend herself from a frontal assault or if she were grabbed from behind. At one point, he demonstrated how to fend off a frontal assault from a prone position in the event she was knocked down by an assailant.

"Lock your arms around my elbows like so," he instructed when she lay flat on her back on the mat with him straddling her, his hands loosely around her throat. "That's it. Now squeeze with your arms to break my choke hold while wrapping your legs around my hips and pushing me down and off you."

She experienced a moment of panic as memories of other times she'd been down on the floor, overpowered by Rory, rushed in. But she focused on the present and did as instructed, breaking his "choke hold" and pushing him off her. He sat up, grinning. "Textbook. See? That wasn't so hard, was it?"

"It would be if it were an actual attack." She thought again of Rory and shuddered.

"You'll get there."

The problem was the "getting there." Today's lesson had become an exercise in self-control as much as in self-defense, with her picturing them getting hot and sweaty in the bedroom instead of the gym.

"Let's try it again."

Let's not. "Okay," she said. Minutes later, as she lay underneath him with his beard tickling her face and his breath warm against her skin, her lower body pressed between his muscular thighs, she wasn't thinking about fending off an attack but surrendering to her desire. It was sweet torture.

Despite being distracted, she managed to learn some moves. By the end of that day's lesson, she felt more confident in her ability to ward off an attack. "I don't know that I'm Jackie Chan level just yet, but if a sixth grader ever came at me in a dark alley, I could probably kick his ass," she told Coop.

"You wouldn't say that if you'd seen the size of some of the sixth graders I busted when I was a cop. This one kid could've taken *me* down if I hadn't cuffed him before he could try anything. But you did good for a beginner." He grinned and bumped knuckles with her. "You should be proud of yourself."

Kyra couldn't remember when she'd ever won a fight. True, today's had been simulated, but it was still a good feeling knowing she could protect herself even if she wasn't armed with a weapon.

On Friday of the following week, she and Ranger joined the Tattooed Ladies for dinner at Cowboy Coffee, as planned. Normally, she looked forward to spending time with her friends, and tonight was no exception, but she was also nervous. As the women chatted and orders were placed, Kyra waited for the right moment to tell the others about her past and wondered again if they'd be hurt that she hadn't told them sooner, or if it would cause them to see her in a different light. She couldn't bear the thought of losing the easy camaraderie she had with these ladies who had become dear to her.

After their food arrived, the women caught up on each other's news while they ate. Suzy had spent Thanksgiving with her son and his family in Seattle, where her ex-husband had been a surprise dinner guest and "dry for a change." Jo's parents had been in town for Thanksgiving weekend, and she reported that the visit had gone fairly well, meaning they hadn't made any remarks about her "quaint" mountain town or her lifestyle that was unconventional compared to theirs—they lived in the upscale suburb of Houston where Jo had grown up and where the only people of color you saw, according to her, were those of domestic workers, with few exceptions. Marisol had celebrated the holiday with her dad at her aunt's house and gone ice skating with Cal on Saturday, where she'd experienced "more spills than thrills." Kyra spoke of how meaningful it had been celebrating her first Thanksgiving in Gold Creek with Frannie and her family.

"It meant a lot to us that you came. We loved having you," Frannie said. "Which reminds me, there's a piece of club business that we need to attend to." Her gaze traveled around the table. "I propose that we make Kyra an official member of the Tattooed Ladies Club. All in favor say aye."

The motion passed unanimously. Kyra was delighted and deeply touched. It validated her decision to come clean with her friends. They'd shown that they had faith in her, not just by voting to make her a member of their club tonight but in countless ways since she'd met them. Now she needed to have faith in them and trust that they would understand when she told them about her past.

"Thanks, guys. I'm honored, and I'd love nothing more than to be a member of your club," she said, dabbing at her moist eyes with her napkin. "But before I accept, there's something you need to know about me."

"What? Your ex-boyfriend is buried in a shallow grave back home?" Jo joked.

"No. But *I* might have died if I hadn't left. I barely made it out alive."

"Kyra, what are you saying?" Suzy asked.

Kyra, her stomach churning, swallowed hard before she spoke again. "He's not an ex-boyfriend, like I led you to believe. He's my husband. And it wasn't just a 'bad breakup.' He was abusive. I left him because he'd beaten me to within an inch of my life. It wasn't the first time, either."

Her bombshell was met with gasps from the other women. Kyra took a gulp of her iced tea to ease the sudden dryness of her throat before she went on. She told them everything, from her whirlwind romance that led to her honeymoon from hell, and the years of abuse that followed, to the day he'd put her in the hospital—all of it. "When I regained consciousness after my emergency splenectomy, I was told by the surgeon who'd operated on me that it was a miracle I'd survived the accident." She made air quotes around the word "accident." "Rory had told everyone I'd been in a car accident to explain my injuries. He even smashed up my car to back up his story."

"Oh my God. That's horrible!" Jo looked shocked and appalled, as did the others.

"Did you tell the doctor what really happened?" asked Marisol.

"No. I didn't think he or anyone else would believe me. Rory would've suggested that I was confused because of my head injury."

"What about the times he'd beaten you before then?" asked Suzy. She sported what she called her diamond-cowgirl look tonight: a Western-style shirt, silk, in a flattering shade of aqua with pearlized snap buttons, and designer jeans. "Did you ever press charges?"

Kyra told them about her one failed attempt. "I don't know what I was thinking, going to the local police. Not only is he the DA, but he's also the top dog in their jurisdiction. No one would believe he himself was one of the bad guys, like the ones he puts in prison, and of course his loyal soldiers would cover for him, even if they knew better. I suppose I could've gone to the state police or the press, but I was so beaten down by then, it seemed hopeless. I didn't think anyone would listen."

"I hate to think of you going through that alone," Marisol said, shaking her head. She wore sparkly leggings that went with her bedazzled eyeglass frames, and an oversize sweater with a snowman on the front, but other than her attire, she didn't look like her normal cheery self at the moment. Her expression was troubled. "I wish we'd known. I can't help feeling we let you down somehow."

Kyra felt a pang of guilt. "You didn't. I'm the one who let you all down. I should've told you sooner."

"Why didn't you?" Jo asked, not accusingly, but like she was trying to understand.

"At first, I didn't know who I could trust. Later, I kept quiet because I was ashamed."

"Ashamed of what? Honey, you did nothing wrong. *He's* the one who ought to be ashamed," said Frannie indignantly.

"Yes, but I was with him for years. You're probably wondering why I put up with it, why I didn't leave him sooner. I don't have any answers. Unlike the battered wives who feel stuck because they have children or because they lack the means to support themselves, I had a good-paying job and no dependents." Until she'd rescued Ranger, and they took care of each other. Like he was doing now, placing his head on her knee as if he sensed she was stressed. She idly stroked his fur.

"I'm sure you had your reasons," Suzy said loyally.

"In the beginning I stayed because I loved him and believed him when he said he loved me. Each time he beat me, it seemed like a bad dream afterward because the rest of the time he was so good to me. Sometimes it would be months between beatings, but they became more frequent over time. After I stopped loving him, I stayed because . . . I don't know why. Fear? Apathy? Really, I have no excuse." She dropped her gaze as hot shame spilled through her. "What finally did it was him lying about how I had gotten injured and wrecking my car. It was so calculated. I knew then that he could literally get away with murder, and that if I didn't escape, I'd wind up dead in the trunk of his car."

She looked up to see her friends wearing near-identical expressions of horror. Marisol, whom she hadn't known to be a devout Catholic, made the sign of the cross. "Thank God you got away," she said.

"Amen." Jo echoed the sentiment. "And you came to the right place."

"Meeting you guys was the best part." Kyra managed a watery smile. "So do you still want me in your club?"

"More than ever," said Frannie, placing a hand over hers and causing Kyra to grow choked up again.

"You're a hero in my eyes," said Jo. "It took guts to do what you did."

"I'm the last person to judge," said Suzy. "I should've kicked Wayne to the curb when he fell off the wagon after his first rehab. Honey, we've all done things in the name of love that we regretted."

"And we've all made mistakes when we were going through a bad patch and not feeling good about ourselves. No one at this table is judging you. You're our friend, and friends stick up for each other," said Marisol, reaching over to lightly squeeze Kyra's free hand. "Girl, we've got your back."

Kyra dabbed at her eyes again with her napkin, feeling a surge of affection for her friends, mixed with relief at having no more secrets between them. "Thanks, guys," she said in a choked voice.

"Rory. That was the name on your tattoo that I removed, wasn't it?" Frannie asked.

Kyra nodded. "It was his idea for us to get matching tattoos. He had it custom designed. A symbol of our love, he called it. I went along only because I knew if I refused, I'd pay for it later on. I hated it. To me, it wasn't a symbol of love but a mark of ownership."

"Men like that make me sick," Suzy said in disgust.

"He has his own demons, and they twisted him into what he became. But why he is who he is doesn't matter. What matters is that I stay far, far away from him. And I'm not sure if that's possible."

"Does he know where you live?" Jo looked worried suddenly.

"I don't think so, but I heard from him recently. He emailed me after worming my new email address out of my mom."

Marisol's eyes grew wide behind her sparkly glasses. "Did he threaten you?"

"No. He begged me to give him another chance, like he always does. But if I were to go back to him, it would only be a matter of time before he hit me again. Not that I would. I'm never going back. But I'm worried that he'll come after me if he finds out where I live."

"What are the chances?" asked Suzy.

"Let's just say the investigators at the DA's office who take orders from him are very good at what they do. And if they can find wanted criminals, they could probably find me. Unless Rory was to call off the search because he met someone new, or he got hit by a bus."

"It could happen," said Frannie.

"Unlikely." Kyra sighed. "I wish I could erase him like I erased my tattoo."

"You can," said Marisol. "It's called murder. I could help you plot the perfect murder. I've read a ton of mysteries." She speared a cherry tomato in her salad like it was someone's heart she was driving her fork into.

"Prison wasn't what I had in mind when I imagined life without Rory," Kyra said dryly.

"Okay, scratch that. But there are other ways of getting revenge, and not all of them involve criminal acts."

"I don't want revenge. I just want to be free."

"In that case, divorce is your only option."

"The only reason I've held off filing for a divorce is because if I do, he'd know which county and state I'm in. It would narrow his search and make it easier for him to track me down. I might be forced to relocate. I couldn't possibly stay here if it meant placing myself or any of you in danger."

"Does Sheriff McNally know about this?" Suzy asked.

"Yes. I had to tell him when I applied for the job as Gertie's replacement. He told me I was to report directly to him if Rory threatened me, and he'd see that I was protected. But the sheriff's department doesn't have the manpower to provide round-the-clock protection, and even if they did, that's no way to live."

"Where would you go?" asked Jo.

"I don't know. All I know is that I'd hate to leave. I love it here, and I love my job. And I'd miss you guys."

"We'd miss you, too," said Frannie, reaching up to pat Kyra's cheek. "But it won't come to that, not if I can help it. I have an idea. What if you were to do a preemptive strike instead of waiting for him to make the first move?"

"What do you mean?"

"Arrange to meet him."

Kyra gave a squeak of alarm, which prompted Ranger to lift his head from her knee and look up at her with his ears pricked. She stroked his fur, letting him know she was in no immediate danger. Which she might be if she were to act on Frannie's suggestion. "Why on earth would I do that?"

"So you can look him in the eye when you tell him you're divorcing him. Show him you're not scared of him anymore."

"What? I'm terrified!"

"You're not suggesting they meet in private?" Suzy said to Frannie, looking alarmed as well.

"Of course not," Frannie said. "But she wouldn't be in any danger if they met in a public place where there were other people around."

"He'd be angry if I tricked him. He might hurt me, or drag me off to someplace more private, when no one was watching," Kyra said, suppressing a shudder at the thought.

"Not if we were there as backup," said Marisol.

"Your own personal detail," said Jo, jumping on board.

"Like the Secret Service in heels," said Suzy, and grinned.

"Some Secret Service agents do wear heels," Jo reminded her. "Me? I'm wearing sneakers if we're gonna do this."

Suzy's smile faded, and her expression grew thoughtful. "You know, it's not the craziest idea. I mean, I get where Frannie is coming from. You have to confront your demons in order to conquer them."

Kyra was touched by the show of support, but nonetheless questioned the wisdom of the proposed mission. "Do any of you have a secret arsenal or martial arts training I don't know about?"

"Something better." Jo held up her phone. "If he tries anything, we'll make a video of it and post it on YouTube."

"And naturally we'd extract you if it looked like the mission was going sideways," said Marisol.

"Extract me, huh?" Kyra couldn't help smiling at the verbiage. Marisol had read too many spy novels. But she was touched by the show of support from her friends. And she took pleasure in the thought of a caught-in-the-act video of Rory going viral and costing him votes when he ran for reelection. Still . . .

"I don't know," she said.

"He'll be expecting a reconciliation. Instead, he'll get the comeuppance he deserves," said Frannie.

"I told you, I'm not out for revenge."

"I'm not talking about revenge. I'm talking about taking back your power."

Frannie's words resonated. Kyra had felt powerless for too long. Even after reclaiming her life and moving to the other end of the continent, and more recently learning how to shoot and how to defend herself in hand-to-hand combat, she was still at Rory's mercy in one respect: she couldn't go anywhere without looking over her shoulder. *To hell with that.* Frannie was right. It was time she took back her power.

"All right," she said. "Let's do this."

16

The plan was hatched over coffee and dessert. The location for Operation Takeback, as it was dubbed, was the San Francisco International Airport. It was highly trafficked and secured by TSA personnel, law officers, and federal agents. Three hours from Gold Creek, it was also drivable while far enough away for Kyra's comfort level. She didn't want Rory anywhere near her home turf.

When she got home, she emailed Rory before she lost her nerve. *Meet me there this Sunday at noon if you want to talk.* She included the link for the bar/eatery in the international terminal at SFO, which was the chosen rendezvous point. Tapas & Taps was situated outside the TSA security checkpoints, therefore accessible without boarding passes. The plan was foolproof. Executing it was another matter. She thought of the maxim that began with "The best-laid plans . . ." as she hit "Send."

Rory got back to her within the hour with his flight details and the message, You won't regret this, baby.

She was already regretting it. She briefly considered asking Coop to come along as her muscle. But he probably wouldn't approve of the plan and would try to talk her out of it. As would the sheriff if she were to run it by him. But doing the sensible thing wasn't always the right thing to do. She remembered something Suzy had said: *You have to confront your demons in order to conquer them.*

Early Sunday morning, she and her friends set out in Jo's minivan. Weekend traffic was light on the drive to the airport. They crossed the

Bay Bridge by eleven, right on schedule. It was a clear day with temps in the sixties, and none of the fog for which the Bay Area was known. Kyra watched as sailboats cut through the chop out on the water, gulls wheeling in the sky above. In the distance rose the heap of rocks that was Alcatraz Island, topped by the boxy gray buildings of the former penitentiary that had once occupied it, and which operated now as a tourist attraction. It was a reminder of when she'd felt imprisoned in her marriage.

Her courage of earlier had given way to dread, which mounted with each mile that brought her closer to her rendezvous. "I feel like I'm going to be sick," she muttered as they took the exit to the airport.

"I've got you covered." Marisol produced a gallon-size Ziploc bag from her canvas tote, which was one of the items of merchandise sold at Buckboard Books, its logo depicting a horse-drawn wagon piled with books, and handed it to Kyra. "I never go on a road trip without them. You never know when you might get carsick." She wore her retro bell-bottoms and blue-denim jean jacket with her collection of vintage campaign buttons pinned to the front.

"I don't think it's carsickness, more like nerves," Kyra told her. "But thanks."

"Probably a PTSD flashback." Jo looked more like a parent helper on a class field trip than an operative on a covert mission, wearing a Henley underneath bib overalls, her blond head covered by a ball cap.

"Or it's the voice in my head that yells, 'Don't go into the basement!' when I'm watching a horror movie," Kyra said.

"Remember, you're in control. He can't touch you," Frannie said.

"If he lays so much as a finger on you, we'll be on him like a SWAT team," said Marisol.

"Never underestimate a hairdresser who's packing." Suzy, wearing a chic red leather jacket and a black calf-length skirt with a slit up one side, produced a travel-size canister of hair spray from her capacious Coach handbag. "As effective as pepper spray, at a fraction of the cost."

"You've tested it?" Marisol looked dubious.

"Ask the lady who got up in my face because she was unhappy with her haircut."

"You didn't!" Jo called from the driver's seat.

"After she threatened to stab me with my scissors, which she'd gotten hold of? You bet I did. Oh, and FYI, there was nothing wrong with her haircut, even if it wasn't exactly what she'd asked for."

Frannie raised an eyebrow. "Dare I ask?"

"She wanted me to make her look like Gisele Bündchen, which, if you saw this woman, you would know was humanly impossible. I've seen thicker hair on newborns. The haircut I gave her was very flattering, if I do say so myself."

"Even if she didn't agree," said Marisol, laughing.

"Sadly," said Suzy, "most women don't know what looks good on them. I'm thinking of having logo T-shirts made. Mine would read SHE SHOULD BE TOLD. I bet I'd sell a ton."

On the airport access road, they followed the signs to the short-term parking lot for the international terminal. As they walked from there to the terminal, Kyra found herself sorely missing her wingman. She'd left Ranger with Coop, who'd been told only that she was going on a day trip with her friends. She didn't know if dogs other than service animals were allowed in airports. Also, the fewer details Rory learned about her—such as the fact that she owned a dog—the better.

She wondered if he'd even recognize her. She wore the outfit she'd bought at Threads of Distinction, the secondhand clothing store two doors down from Shear Delight, an Armani pantsuit, charcoal with a pinstripe, over a burgundy silk shell. Her long, dark hair was braided in a french twist, courtesy of Suzy. Catching her reflection in a shop window as they passed through the terminal's retail mall, she thought she looked like a CEO in a power suit, plotting a hostile takeover.

She didn't feel powerful. Her heart raced; her palms were sweaty. She gave herself a pep talk. *You can do this. You're not the woman you were.*

Nor was she alone, she was reminded, when Frannie hooked her arm through Kyra's. Frannie wore tan khakis and a teal L.L.Bean fleece. *You can take the girl out of the mountains, but you can't take the mountains out of the girl,* as she put it.

"You've got this," she said, and Kyra gave her a wan smile.

The women split up when they reached the food court. Tapas & Taps, where the meeting was scheduled to take place, was situated between a Dunkin' and a Potrero Grill. Kyra headed there while the others each assumed their positions within the food court. Taking a seat at the bar, she ordered a club soda with lime.

As she sipped her drink, she was thinking she could have used something stronger. She felt like she used to when she'd walked on eggshells around Rory, never knowing when a "wrong" move on her part, or a sudden shift in his mood, might cause him to snap. The only other patron was a balding man in a business suit seated at the other end of the bar nursing a drink, his carry-on parked next to him.

Her phone pinged. She started, and almost spilled her drink as she was sipping it, thinking it was a text from Rory, until she remembered he didn't have her phone number. The text was from Frannie. **We've got your back,** it read. Kyra smiled and felt something coiled tightly inside her loosen.

At 11:40, she checked the status of Rory's flight on her phone and saw that it had arrived on time. It would take him roughly fifteen minutes to deplane and get from his gate to the food court in the same terminal, she estimated. Kyra grew increasingly anxious as she waited. By 12:15, when he still hadn't arrived, she was about ready to jump out of her skin. She wondered what was keeping him. An urgent phone call he'd had to take, or had he stopped to use the restroom?

When he still hadn't shown by 12:20, she suspected he wasn't coming. She couldn't contact him without putting herself at risk—if she were to call or text him, he'd have her phone number—so she was at a loss. At 12:30, she walked to the end of the bar, where she had a full view of the food court beyond. She could see Marisol loitering outside the Potrero Grill. Jo was drinking a coffee outside the Dunkin'. Frannie and Suzy were positioned at the south and north entrances, pretending to look at something on their phones. What Kyra didn't see was any sign of Rory. The suspense was killing her. Now she really needed a drink. Instead, she ordered another club soda when she returned to the bar.

At 12:50, with Rory still a no-show, she texted her friends: I'm calling it.

"Maybe he missed his flight," Frannie said when the women reconvened at the bar.

"Or he never booked it." Suzy scooted onto the barstool next to Kyra with an audible sigh of relief. "Lord, my feet are killing me. Walking in heels is one thing; standing watch in them is another."

"I know he booked the trip because he sent me his flight details." Kyra picked up her phone and reread the email with his flight details. She frowned, noticing something she'd missed before. "Huh. That's weird."

"What?" asked Jo.

"I just noticed it's a travel itinerary, like the ones his assistant prepares, and not a confirmation from the airline."

"Why is that weird?" Jo asked.

"Why would he have bothered his assistant on a weekend when he could've just forwarded me the confirmation?"

"Maybe it wasn't his assistant who prepared it," said Jo, frowning in thought. "Maybe *he* did to fool you into thinking he booked the trip when he didn't."

"Anyone can fake an itinerary," Frannie agreed.

"There's one way to find out. Do you have a number for his assistant?" asked Jo, pulling out her phone.

"Not anymore. It was on my old phone that I ditched. But if you call the DA's office in Rochester, it's on the recorded message on the answering machine. It's the number to call in an emergency."

"What's his assistant's name?"

"Evelyn Porter. She's worked there since Bush Senior was in office."

Jo called the number for the Monroe County District Attorney's Office and jotted down another phone number on a cocktail napkin as she listened to the recorded message. After she hung up, she called the number she'd jotted down. "Hello, this is Jo Myers from the NYPD. To whom am I speaking? Thank you for taking my call, Ms. Porter. Sorry to disturb you on a weekend, but it's urgent that I speak with your boss right away. Is there a number where I can reach him?" She spoke in the authoritative voice Kyra imagined she used with her children when they were acting up, and the bridezillas she encountered in her line of work. "No, I'm afraid I'm not at liberty to say; it's police business . . . I appreciate that, and I appreciate your cooperation." She jotted down another number. "One more thing, do you happen to know if Mr. Stanhope is out of town? I see . . . Thank you, Ms. Porter. You've been very helpful." She ended the call and announced, "According to Ms. Porter, her boss is in town and has no trips planned, as far as she knows. She said she spoke to him not five minutes before I phoned. He told her he'd see her at the office on Monday."

Marisol stared at her as if this was a side of Jo she'd never seen before. Her eyes were wide behind the zebra-striped glasses she wore today. "You do know it's illegal to impersonate an officer of the law?"

"Did you hear me identify myself as a police officer at any point?" Jo countered.

"No, but you implied it when you said you were calling from the NYPD on police business." She made air quotes around the words "police business."

"Okay, so I fudged it, but it was for a good cause." She turned to Kyra. "It appears you were stood up."

Kyra nodded. She didn't know whether to be relieved or worried. "It's not the first time. He used to do it all the time when we were together. We'd make plans and he wouldn't show; then later he'd insist I'd gotten my dates mixed up, among other mind games he played. I'd heard the term 'gaslighting' but never really understood it until it was done to me. But this, I don't get. Why pass up the opportunity to try to persuade me to give him another chance? Unless . . ." She had an unsettling thought and glanced to her right, looking for the man in the business suit whom she'd noticed earlier. He was gone.

"What?" prompted Suzy.

"Did you see the man who was here a minute ago? He was sitting at the other end of the bar."

"Yeah, what about him?"

"He was here the entire time I was waiting for Rory, but he's gone now."

"You think he was tailing you?" Marisol, who was well versed in detective fiction, made the connection.

"I don't know. Maybe." He might be working for Rory. Rory sometimes hired private investigators for what he called his "black ops," jobs of dubious legality that fell outside the purview of the full-time investigators employed by the DA's office. Usually it involved surveillance, either electronic or, in some cases, shadowing someone.

Suzy walked to the end of the bar and scanned the food court. "I don't see him now."

"He was probably just a traveler killing time before his flight." Kyra didn't believe it, though, and felt a slither of unease in her belly even as she spoke.

Making her way through the crowded terminal with her friends, headed for the exit, she kept an eye out for the balding man in the business suit. She didn't see him again. Still, she couldn't shake the suspicion that she was being followed.

17

She emailed Rory when she got home. He didn't respond. She had a restless night, and when she finally fell asleep past midnight, she had a nightmare about being chased by a shadowy figure through a building with endless hallways, scared out of her wits, desperately seeking an exit. She didn't hear from him the next day, either, or the day after that. She didn't know what to make of both his failure to meet her as planned and his present radio silence. He was up to something, she suspected.

She was on edge and distracted when she was at the sheriff's office on Wednesday, interviewing the witness to a shooting. If it hadn't been for Ranger, who'd pawed at her leg or licked her hand whenever he'd sensed her attention wandering, she might have blown the interview.

But even though Operation Takeback had been a bust, she could still take back her power, she realized. She would just have to go about it through the usual channels. She made an appointment with Purvi Kapur, who worked with her attorney, Drew Halliday, at the law firm where they were both partners, and who handled its divorce cases. On Thursday, she went to meet her, leaving Ranger with Suzy at her salon. Kapur, a stylishly dressed woman in her early fifties with a square face framed by a wedge of black hair threaded with gray, was as imposing a figure in person as she'd sounded over the phone.

"What are your expectations in seeking a divorce, Ms. Smith?" she asked straightaway.

"Kyra. I want what everyone who comes to you does: freedom."

"Actually, expectations vary from one client to the next. Some want their freedom. Some say they want it when they really don't. Some want to stick it to their partner. My job is to determine the best plan of action in moving forward, or not, as the case may be. Do you believe reconciliation is possible?"

"No."

The attorney's gaze sharpened at the definitiveness with which Kyra had answered. She leaned forward in her chair and folded her hands on the uncluttered desk in front of her. "Tell me why."

Kyra told her everything, about the abuse and her flight from New York and going into hiding. Hers was a story that would curl the average person's hair, but the seasoned attorney, who'd no doubt heard it all through her years of handling divorces, didn't so much as curl her lip. Only her dark eyes betrayed any emotion. She seemed angered by what she'd heard. For Kyra, the telling of her tale was easier than when she'd told her friends, precisely because she *had* shared it with them. If she'd learned nothing else over the past few months, it was that shame flourished in the dark.

When she was done, the attorney asked, "Did you ever press criminal charges against your husband?"

"I tried to once. It didn't go so well."

"It's not too late."

"It wouldn't do any good. I can't prove my allegations."

"To be clear, are you saying you don't have any photos or medical reports documenting your abuse?"

"That's correct." Kyra felt like an idiot as she said it. Shame had prevented her from seeking medical attention each time after she'd been beaten. But why hadn't she taken photos of her injuries, at the very least? Bruises and black eyes weren't definitive proof, but it would've been something.

"That's unfortunate, but you still have recourse."

"Well, yes, that's why I'm here."

"What I meant was you could threaten to go to the press if he decides to play hardball. I have a contact at the *New York Times*, an old friend from college. This is just the kind of story she'd salivate over. Even if your husband isn't held accountable in a court of law, he would get his in the court of public opinion. The mere threat of exposure might be enough to persuade him to settle."

"I don't want his money."

"Not his money, *your* money. Did you sign a prenup?"

"No."

"Then you're entitled to half of the marital assets, according to the laws of New York State. As your attorney, I'd make sure you get it. You may see me as a country lawyer, but before this, I was a partner at one of the larger firms in San Francisco. I've negotiated multimillion-dollar settlements."

"I don't doubt it, and I would love to have you represent me. There's just one thing . . ." She squirmed in her seat; she hated feeling like a beggar. "I can't afford to pay you a retainer. Would you be willing to accept payment in installments? I'm good for it. Sheriff McNally can vouch for me."

"I know Kurt McNally well. His wife and I are old friends."

"He hired me to take over from Gertie Naylor when she retired."

"Ah yes. How is Gertie? Is she enjoying her retirement?"

"She's on a cruise through the Greek Islands with her husband right now. I got a postcard from her the other day."

"I didn't know people still sent postcards."

"Baby boomers do, apparently. She says she's having the time of her life, and she's learning Greek dancing."

"Is she? Well, that *is* something to write home about," she said with a smile before she got back to business. "Regarding my fee, I normally charge a retainer of ten thousand dollars and bill monthly at an hourly rate of four hundred, but I'll make an exception in your case, Kyra. I'll take a percentage of your settlement instead, not to exceed the amount you would pay in billable hours. How does that sound?"

Kyra's heart lifted as her tight shoulders sagged with relief. "It sounds amazing. But what if the settlement is lower than you expect, and it's not enough to cover your fee?"

"Trust me, that won't happen."

"I don't know what to say. Thank you. That's incredibly generous."

"You're welcome. But I must confess, my offer isn't entirely out of the goodness of my heart. Because, as everyone knows, lawyers have no heart," she added with a wry chuckle. "I also relish the opportunity to give your husband a taste of his own medicine. In the legal sense, that is, though I *do* plan to hit him where it hurts." Kyra didn't doubt that Purvi Kapur would make a formidable opponent.

"I'd settle for my freedom and my fair share of our assets. So what's next?"

"I'll draw up the papers. Once they're signed and filed with the court, your husband will be served. Nine months from now, you'll be a free woman unless he chooses to drag it out. But I don't think he will."

"You don't know him."

"No, but if he's like most public figures, he'll do anything to avoid having his reputation dragged through the mud."

Or stop at nothing. The image of her dead body stuffed in the trunk of his car sent a chill down her spine.

As Kyra walked to her car after her meeting, she passed holiday-themed window displays, lampposts wrapped in red ribbon to resemble peppermint sticks, and rooflines strung with fairy lights. Every storefront sported a wreath. The crystal LED star atop the bell tower on Signal Hill twinkled in the distance.

The jingle of sleigh bells and clopping of hooves announced a horse-drawn stagecoach, decorated with tinsel swags and red bows, before it rolled into view. The driver wore a Santa costume. He waved to her, and she waved back. The festive downtown scene worked its magic on her, even as she kept an eye out for hidden danger, watching for anyone who might be following her.

She stopped at Buckboard Books to pay Marisol a visit. The glass-paned door to the bookshop was hung with an evergreen wreath decorated with miniature felt cats. The window display featured a Christmas tree formed of artfully stacked books. Inside, dwarf firs hung with ornaments and brass bowls filled with clove-studded oranges occupied every surface that wasn't covered in books. The built-in bookshelves were strung with garlands of paper snowflakes, and the endcaps of the free-standing shelves each sported a large tartan bow. Snow globes featuring holiday scenes, and brass bookends in the shapes of elves, reindeer, and other emblems of the season were displayed by the register alongside the literary-themed merchandise that was for sale year-round.

Kyra spied Marisol unloading a carton of books and arranging them on the round table at the front of the store and went over to say hello.

"What do you think?" Marisol asked, gesturing around her.

"It looks amazing. Totally Insta-worthy." The Christmas tree made of books was sure to go viral.

"Christmas is my favorite time of the year. Plus, it's good for business." Marisol was dressed for the season as well, in an oversize knit sweater—white, with a red-nosed reindeer on the front—and dark-green velour leggings. "Would you believe we're sold out of some of our holiday titles already?"

"I can believe it. It looks like Black Friday in here." Usually, business at the bookshop was slow on weekdays, but Kyra counted at least a dozen customers browsing, and every reading nook was occupied. A mother was reading aloud to her young child from a storybook in the children's section.

"Can I interest you in a mystery?" Marisol picked up one of the books stacked on the table, a cozy mystery from its holiday-themed cover and title, *Frankincense and Murder*.

"Thanks, but I see enough crime in my line of work." Kyra loved her work, but her preferred bedtime reading was novels that didn't keep her up at night by reminding her of the darker side of humanity.

Marisol dropped her voice. "Speaking of crime, have you heard from your ex?"

"No, but I have some news." Kyra told her about meeting with Purvi Kapur. "I didn't get the satisfaction of telling him to his face that I'm divorcing him, but he'll find out soon enough."

Marisol grinned and hugged her. "Good for you. I'm proud of you. How do you feel?"

"Relieved. Nervous."

"Nervous about how he'll react?"

"That, and I suspect he's up to something." Assuming Rory's radio silence meant he'd moved on would be as foolish as going into a snake-infested swamp assuming you wouldn't get bit. Just because you can't see the snakes, it doesn't mean they're not there.

"I still don't get it. Why would he stand you up if he was hoping to reconcile?"

"Because he always has to be in control. *He* sets the terms. *He* decides when and where we meet." Her stomach curdled. She should have remembered that about him. What had she been thinking?

"You still think he had you followed when we were at the airport?"

"I don't know. Maybe." She felt a ripple of unease, picturing the man at the bar where she'd waited. "If my hunch is correct, he'd know where I live because the guy he hired would have followed me home."

"If that was the case, wouldn't your ex have come calling by now?"

"Not if his plan is to lull me into a false sense of security first." She'd seen him do it in the courtroom, ripping apart the testimony of a witness for the defense after he'd gotten them to lower their guard. He was more skilled than most trial lawyers in that regard. "If and when he does show, it'll be when I least expect it." Kyra shivered as if a door had been opened, letting in a gust of cold air.

Marisol looked concerned. "Why don't you stay with me until it's safe to go home?"

"Who knows when that'll be? Besides, I'm as safe as anyone can be, with an ex-cop living next door. Coop has the place secured with everything except trip wires, and I'm keeping my gun handy."

"Speaking of which, how are your lessons at the gun range going?"

"I hit more targets than I miss, so I must be making progress. It helps that I have a good instructor."

"Who's also easy on the eyes." Marisol gave her a knowing look, as if she suspected something.

"It's not like that with us."

"Yet the look on your face says otherwise. Spill, girlfriend."

Kyra lowered her voice. "Okay, we kissed. Once."

Marisol clapped a hand over her mouth to stifle the squeal of excitement that erupted from her. "Oh my God, you buried the lede. Why didn't you tell me?"

"Because I knew you'd make a big deal out of it. It was just a kiss." *Which I can't stop thinking about.* "Never to be repeated. I don't do flings, and I'm not ready for a serious relationship."

"That's what I said after my last breakup. That was five years ago. Cal is the first guy I've met since then that I'm interested in. What I'm saying is, it's not like you can just order up the perfect guy when you're ready."

"If I ever am."

"Okay, but if you let this opportunity pass, it might be a while before another one comes along. Maybe you should take your own advice."

"What advice would that be?"

"When you urged me to go for it with Cal. I may be a pathetic cougar throwing myself at a much younger man, but at least I'm in the game, and even if nothing comes of it, we're enjoying each other's company."

"If I hooked up with Coop, it would be awkward with me living on his property after we broke up."

"You make it sound like a breakup is inevitable."

"Isn't it? Speaking for myself, anyway. I seem to have bad karma when it comes to men. And I don't want to have to look for another place to live. I'd never find one that's such a sweet deal. Besides, he isn't looking for anything serious, either."

"He told you that?"

"Not in so many words, but we both have too much baggage."

"Doesn't everyone past a certain age?"

"Maybe, but our combined baggage would fill the cargo hold of a 747."

"Well, at least you've kissed. That's further than I've gotten with Cal." Marisol sighed and pulled the last book from the box, placing it on its end atop the stack on the table where it would catch the eye of shoppers. Since the night Cal had come up to her place for drinks after her book event, they'd gone out for pizza and to the movies a few times, and ice skating once. Cal was also teaching her how to skateboard. "I seem to be stuck in the friend zone, and I can't think of a way to get unstuck that doesn't involve embarrassing myself."

As if on cue, the unmistakable voice of Cal boomed from outside just then. "And here we are at Buckboard Books, the oldest bookstore in Gold Creek, and the second oldest in the state of California . . ."

Through the front window, Kyra could see Cal standing on the sidewalk with a tour group, giving his spiel on Buckboard Books. He entered a few minutes later with his group, and its members, four men and three women, dispersed to browse, while Cal made a beeline for Marisol.

He really is adorable, Kyra thought. Like a cartoon character, with his brushy hair, bright eyes, and dimpled cheeks, as Marisol had once described him.

"Hi, ladies! Love the outfit," he complimented Marisol. "You look like one of Santa's helpers. Should I expect Santa to appear anytime soon?"

"Depends on whether you've been naughty or nice."

"Sometimes naughty is nice." He waggled his eyebrows suggestively.

"I'll put in a good word with the boss, in that case. How's the tour business?"

"I spend my days freezing my butt off, while folks like you stay warm and toasty inside. I think I'm in the wrong business." He pulled his gloves off and blew on his fingers to warm them.

"You should've thought of that before you decided to take a year off from school."

"Yes, Mom," he said, and didn't seem to notice when Marisol winced. The last thing she needed was another reminder that she was a millennial and he a Gen Zer.

"Do you like your job when you're not freezing your butt off?" Kyra asked.

"Sure. What's not to like? I get paid to talk about stuff I'm interested in, and I've met some interesting people." Kyra didn't miss the side-long glance he gave Marisol. "The perks ain't bad, either. They include unlimited access to the ski runs at Timberlake. Speaking of which," he said to Marisol, "my boss told me today I could work part-time as a ski instructor at the resort now that it's open for the season." Cal's boss and the owner of Gold Creek Tours, Marshall Cannaday, also owned Timberlake Lodge, the largest and most popular of the local ski resorts.

"Awesome." Marisol high-fived him. "Does this mean you're staying through the season?"

"Looks that way."

A look of pure joy stole over Marisol's face. "Maybe there's hope for us yet," she said after Cal had left to rejoin his group. "We have time on our side, anyway. If only I can get out of the friend zone."

"He likes you as more than a friend, from the way he was flirting with you."

"He also flirts with the old ladies on his tours."

"You may need to give him more than a nudge. Invite him over for eggnog some evening," Kyra suggested.

"Maybe I will. After I hang the mistletoe." Marisol giggled.

They were interrupted by a woman asking about a book title that she couldn't find. Leaving Marisol to assist her customer, Kyra continued on her way. It was past noon by the time she arrived home. After she took Ranger for a walk, she made herself a grilled cheese sandwich and ate it for lunch.

She was washing up when she heard Ranger bark, followed by a knock at the door. It gave her a start, and she automatically reached for her gun, which she kept near at hand at all times. She was relieved to see that it was Coop when she peeked out the window. Her heart swelled at the sight of him.

"Hey, Coop. What's up?"

"We're having a family dinner at the house tonight. If you don't have other plans, would you like to come?" he asked. "It's my nephew Tim's birthday, but you wouldn't need to bring a present or anything."

"I don't have plans for tonight, but I wouldn't want to intrude."

"Our family isn't clannish that way. Guests are welcome. In fact, my mom will be disappointed if you don't come. She told me to invite you."

She raised an eyebrow at him. "I'm confused. Are you inviting me, or is your mom?"

"Both of us, actually. I'd have invited you sooner, but I was afraid it might be . . ." He trailed off, his cheeks reddening.

"Awkward?"

"Yeah. In the interest of full disclosure, I should warn you, Mom will be wearing her matchmaking hat if you come."

"I think I can handle it." His obvious discomfort made her want to put him out of his misery. "I'd love to come." It would be a welcome change from another evening spent alone with her dire imaginings.

"Great!" He broke into a grin. "Dinner's at six, or whenever you see a bunch of vehicles parked out front."

"Can I bring anything?"

"Nope. We've got the food and beverages covered. Just bring yourself and your buddy here." He glanced down at Ranger, who'd nosed past her, carrying his favorite squeaky toy in his mouth, which he dropped at Coop's feet. Coop bent to retrieve it, and gave it back to him, saying, "Sorry, dude. I don't have time to play with you today. I have to get back to work. See you later," he said to Kyra as he was leaving, flashing her a smile that went through her like a flame through buttercream icing.

She spent the rest of the afternoon doing art projects. She made a card for the birthday boy with a sketch of her dog on the front, then did some painting. She planned to give one to each of her fellow Tattooed Ladies as Christmas gifts. The one she was working on right now was for Marisol, painted from a photo she'd taken of a cat curled up, asleep, on a stack of books at her bookshop.

At five thirty, she showered and dressed for dinner. After trying on and discarding several outfits, she decided on her black jeans with the fitted bottle-green velveteen jacket she'd purchased at Threads of Distinction over a black silk-knit tee. It was dark when she stepped outside, bundled in her parka, and cold enough to have her breath fogging the night air. Lights blazed from every window at the house, and judging from the number of vehicles parked in the driveway, the gang was all there.

As she crossed the field with Ranger, using the flashlight on her phone to light the way, she felt a flutter of nerves. Growing up, she'd spent more time on her own and with her mom than she had socializing, so she wasn't accustomed to large gatherings. What would her role be at this one? Renter, friend, or prospective bride? If Shirley hoped for wedding bells, she would be disappointed.

Coop's mom answered the door wearing an apron with KISS THE CHEF embroidered on the bib. Her rust-gray hair was pulled back in a bun, stray wisps curling around her pixie face. "Kyra. Glad you could make it! You, too, Ranger." She bent to give him a scratch behind his ears, and he wagged his tail.

"These are for you." Kyra handed her the bouquet of flowers she'd picked: black-eyed Susans and purple thistle, the last of this season's wildflowers from the field, mixed with ferns from the creek bank, tied with a ribbon. "I didn't know what else to bring. Coop said there would be enough food."

Shirley beamed at her. "How sweet of you! Thank you. I'll put these in water while you go say hello to the boys. They're in the den. You can join me and the girls in the kitchen when you're ready."

Kyra hung her coat on the row of pegs by the door. She heard blended voices, the sounds of children playing, and a dog barking somewhere in the house. Ranger went to investigate. She was headed down the hall when two little girls, one dark-haired and the other fair, burst from a room at the other end. The dark-haired girl was chasing the blond one, who was squealing with mock fright.

"Kate, Anna!" Shirley called sharply as she intercepted them. "What did I tell you about running in the house?"

Both girls skidded to a halt, wearing guilty looks. "Sorry, Grandma," they chorused.

Shirley gave them each a kiss on the head before continuing down the hall to the kitchen, herding them as she went.

Watching them, Kyra felt a tug, wondering if she would ever have a family of her own: a loving husband, children, and grandchildren someday. It seemed as remote a possibility as her winning the lottery. She cared for Coop, and there was no denying they had chemistry. Something might've come of it if they'd met when they were in their twenties, unencumbered by the baggage they'd accumulated over the years since, but it was too late now. They were both recovering from failed relationships. Coop's had caused him to question whether he was cut out to be a husband. As for Kyra, if at one time she had been cut out to be a wife, she was damaged goods now.

She found the men watching a football game on the TV in the den. Each with a beer bottle in his hand, except for Coop, who was drinking ginger ale from a can. He rose when she entered, and her heart lifted.

"Kyra. I didn't know you were here."

"Your mom let me in."

"You look . . . beautiful." His gaze traveled over her, causing her cheeks to warm. "You remember my dad and my brothers Liam and Declan." She'd met his father, Ed, and his two older brothers in passing on previous occasions. Liam and Declan were both tall and broad-shouldered like Coop, with the same reddish-brown hair, though neither of them had facial hair. "And this sketchy character here"—he gestured toward the man seated in the leather recliner beside him, a younger version of the other Langston men—"is my baby brother, Chris."

Chris stood to shake her hand. "Pleased to meet you, Kyra. You're as lovely as I remember."

He looked familiar. "The bar at the Redbird," she said, remembering where she'd last seen him. "You were waiting for Coop. He pointed you out."

He grinned. "I was watching when he tried to pick you up after chasing off the competition. It's not often I have the pleasure of seeing my big bro get blown off by a lady, so it was a night to remember. Ow!" he cried when Coop punched him in the arm. "Dude, what's your problem?"

"You are," Coop growled.

Chris smirked at him and rubbed his arm. "What? I call it as I see it."

"You'll be seeing stars if you don't shut your trap. Ignore him," Coop said to Kyra. "He hasn't been the same since he was dropped on his head when he was a baby."

Kyra suppressed a smile at the brothers' antics. She wondered if Coop's reaction to his brother's ribbing was an indication that he had feelings for her.

"Boys," their dad chided. He rose and crossed the room to shake Kyra's hand. "You'll have to excuse my sons. They grew up in a houseful of menfolk, and though my wife and I did our best to teach them manners, they don't always know how to behave with a lady." Ed resembled his sons, except his broad shoulders were stooped with age. Blue eyes twinkled from the nests of creases around them. His hair was thick and unruly, like Coop's, with more gray than brown. "Glad you could join us."

She smiled. "I appreciate the invite."

"You settled in okay out there in the north forty?"

"Yes, thank you."

"How are you liking country living?"

"I like it just fine." She darted a glance at Coop. "It's a bit of a commute, but the drive is scenic."

"I'm told you took over from Gertie when she retired. Did you know I used to work at the sheriff's department?"

"Yes, sir. You're a legend at the department."

He look pleased to hear he hadn't been forgotten since his retirement. "I could tell you stories."

"Let me see to our guest before you get going on your war stories, Dad." Coop steered her from the room and into the hallway. The warmth of his fingers, lightly circling her upper arm, spread through the rest of her body, settling just south of her belly. "What can I get you to drink? We have beer, wine, sodas, and sparkling water. There's also some juice boxes if the kids haven't drank them all."

"Wine would be nice."

"Red or white?"

"White."

Coop led the way into the kitchen, where the women were preparing supper. A baby with a mop of dark curls sat in a highchair, gumming a zwieback biscuit. The bouquet of flowers Kyra had brought sat in a vase at the center of the pine trestle table, which was set for fourteen. A triple-layer chocolate cake topped with nine birthday candles stood on the antique oak sideboard, next to a pile of wrapped gifts. The air was redolent of chopped garlic and something heating in the oven. Coop grabbed a wineglass from a cupboard and carried it to the fridge, from which he took a half-full bottle of chardonnay. He poured some wine into the glass, while Shirley made the introductions.

"Kyra, meet my daughters-in-law, Aisha, Danielle, and Deirdre. Girls, this is Coop's friend Kyra." The younger women called out greetings.

"Don't be fooled by the brawn of us Langston men," said Coop as he handed Kyra the wine he'd poured. "The women wear the pants in our family."

"And don't you forget it," said his mom, wagging the spatula in her hand at him.

It was a bit overwhelming, meeting so many people all at once, but Kyra was instantly drawn into the fold and given a task to do, peeling and slicing a cucumber for the salad. Growing up, she'd usually felt like an outsider in large groups. Here, she felt included. It was a nice feeling.

"We do the cooking. The men do the cleanup," said the heavily pregnant Danielle, who worked alongside Kyra, whisking the ingredients for the salad dressing she was making. "Old family tradition."

"More like enforced labor," said Aisha as she stirred minced garlic into softened butter and began spreading the mixture over slices of french bread. She had the same dark eyes and dark curls as the baby in the highchair.

"One year we threatened to go on strike unless the men started doing their share," explained Shirley as she took the first of two pans of lasagna from the oven, bubbling at the edges and evenly browned on top.

"Hey, I resent that! I'm no slacker," Coop protested.

"Dude, you don't get points for taking out the trash," teased the slender, fair-haired Deirdre. She paused to give Coop a hip bump as she passed him carrying a bowl of roasted veggies to the table.

"I also cook and clean."

"If you had a wife, you wouldn't have to do it all," said his mom.

He frowned. "I had one of those, remember?"

"And she left you scarred for life, did she?"

"She walked out on me. I never said I was scarred for life."

"Glad to hear it. Because if you were, you might be too blinded by those scars to see what's right in front of you." Shirley cut a meaningful glance at Kyra. Coop's naturally ruddy face grew even redder.

He looked as uncomfortable as she'd ever seen him. Between his younger brother's ribbing and his mom's meddling, he was in the hot seat tonight. Kyra avoided looking at him so as not to make it any worse.

Dinner was a noisy affair, with everyone talking at once and the baby banging on his high-chair tray with his spoon. Shirley dished out generous servings of lasagna. Bowls of sides and baskets of garlic bread were passed around, along with the salad. Ranger and his new friend, Honey, Chris's golden Lab, dove to gobble up the scraps that fell on the floor. The food was as delicious as it was plentiful.

After they ate, the cake was carried to the table. Everyone sang "Happy Birthday," and the birthday boy blew out the candles on his cake before it was served. He unwrapped his presents—a watch from Grandpa and Grandma, and Nintendo games from his aunts and uncles, except for Uncle Coop, who gave him a GoPro camera for the new bike his parents had given him.

Kyra was touched seeing the boy's face light up when she gave him the card she'd made for him. "That's your dog? Cool," he said, admiring the sketch of Ranger on the card.

After cake and ice cream, the women retired to the living room while the men did the cleanup. Kyra felt an instant bond with them, like she had with the Tattooed Ladies. They wanted to know all about her, where she was from and what it was like working as a forensic artist. She told them a little bit about her work and her background. The only awkward moment was when Danielle asked if she was in a relationship. Kyra answered, "I'm in the process of getting a divorce," and left it at that.

Coop's sisters-in-law all worked outside the home, she learned. Aisha was an OR nurse at Mercy General. Danielle taught fourth grade at the public elementary school. Deirdre worked as a comptroller in the same building as her husband, Chris, who was a California State Highway Patrol officer. They admitted they found it hard to juggle their jobs with the demands of parenting and agreed that the concept of "having it all" was a myth.

In the bosom of the Langston family with her belly full, warmed by the fire crackling on the hearth, Kyra imagined a future in which she was a member of this big, loving family, and this house was her home.

She pushed the thought away. *Not happening.*

When the party was over, the children were rounded up and the leftovers distributed. Coats were collected and goodbyes exchanged at the door. "I hope you weren't overwhelmed," said Shirley as she was leaving with Ed. "We can be a bit much when we're all together."

"A little," Kyra said with a smile. "But I had a wonderful time."

"Does that mean you'll come for Christmas dinner? We're having it here at the house."

"I'd love to, but shouldn't you check with Coop first?" It was his house, after all.

"I'm sure he plans to invite you, but I'll let him know you're coming. What are you doing on Christmas morning? If you don't have other plans, how would you like to help me and Ed dispense cookies and holiday cheer at the nursing home where we volunteer? Some of the residents don't have any visitors on Christmas. We do what we can to make it a special day for them."

"Count me in," she said. Kyra recalled her lonely Christmases when she was a child. Most years, there had been no money for presents or a tree, even. The year she was eight, all she got for Christmas was a stocking full of the hard candies they gave away at the auto dealership where her mom had worked at the time. Anything she could do to brighten someone else's holiday would make her happy.

Then it was just her and Coop after everyone else had left. Kyra was at the door reaching for her coat when she heard Coop say, "Don't go." She stopped and turned around, and then saw something in his eyes that caused her stomach to turn a cartwheel. "Will you stay for another cup of coffee?"

She hesitated. Coffee could lead to other things, and she wasn't prepared to go there. Nor was she ready to call it a night. *Just one cup; then I'll be on my way.* "All right," she said, "but make it decaf, or I'll be up all night."

She followed him into the kitchen, which was spotless. The men had done a good job with the cleanup. She perched on a stool at the breakfast bar, while Ranger, pooped from his activities tonight, settled on the braided rug by the stove for a nap. She watched as Coop poured water into the coffee maker and scooped ground beans from a canister labeled Decaf into the filter, and then switched in on.

"Did you have a good time tonight?" he asked.

"Very much so. I like your family."

"They like you. Especially my mom."

"Hopefully she likes me for myself and not as future daughter-in-law material."

"Ah. So you didn't miss her pointed remark about me needing a wife?"

"How could I?"

"She won't rest until all her sons are married."

"But you were married at one time."

"Unhappily. For the record, I never said I was scarred for life. And I do see what's in front of me." He was looking at her as he said it. She saw some emotion in his eyes that she couldn't read. Yearning, perhaps. It caused her stomach to turn another cartwheel.

"You do?"

"Yeah. And I like what I see."

Her breath caught in her throat as she watched him step from behind the counter and walk toward her. Her heart was racing. In the stillness, the only sound was the burbling of the coffee maker.

He pulled her to her feet and into his arms. Then he was kissing her. He tasted of chocolate and the coffee he'd drank earlier. She felt a sensation like that of warm sand slipping through her fingers, except it involved her entire body. A delicious, silky, falling sensation.

"Is it okay that I kissed you?" he asked when they finally drew apart. He looked like he was worried she would say no.

She smiled at him. Her earlier hesitation seemed to have flown out the window, along with any reservations she'd had about starting something with Coop. "Actually, I was wondering if you'd ever get around to it."

"You were?" His furrowed brow smoothed and he broke into a grin. "I thought I'd blown it after the way you reacted the first time we kissed."

"I'm sorry if I gave you that impression. I wasn't expecting it, is all. I didn't know how to handle it."

"And now?"

"Now I want you to kiss me again."

He didn't waste any time complying. When they finally came up for air, he said in a throaty voice, "You have no idea how much I've wanted to do that. Every morning when we were at the gun range, it was all I could do to keep from ravishing you. And that day at the gym? Oh boy. I had to take a cold shower when I got home."

She was secretly thrilled by his confession. "Ravish me, huh? What does that even mean?"

"I'd tell you, but it might be too much for your delicate ears."

"I can imagine." In fact, she was tempted to suggest they continue this conversation in his bedroom, with their clothes off. It required every ounce of self-control she possessed when she said, "But I think we should take it slow."

"We can take it as slow as you like."

"Where do you see this going?"

"I'm not sure, to be honest, but I'd like to explore it."

"I . . . I'd like that, too, but you need to know that I might never be ready for another relationship. My husband didn't just break my heart, he broke *me*." A wave of emotion surged from some deep place within, catching her off guard and causing her eyes to fill. She blinked back her tears before they could fall.

"I don't see a broken woman." Coop traced the line of her jaw with his fingertip. He held her gaze, his tea-brown eyes as tender as his touch. "I see a woman who was knocked down, but who got up. I see a survivor. Kyra, when I look at you, I feel humbled."

"Humbled?" She eyed him in confusion.

"A lot of the bad stuff that happened to me was self-inflicted, and my marriage wasn't all bad. Angela and I had some good years together. If anyone should be scarred for life, it's you. But you're not."

"Says who?"

"You don't kiss like someone who's given up on love."

She mustered a smile. "Or maybe it's just that you're a good kisser."

"I'm good at other things, too." He drew her close again, his arms tightening around her.

"I don't doubt it, but you won't be showing me tonight." Reluctantly, she withdrew from his embrace and took a step back. "I still have some stuff to work out, so be patient with me. I'm not even divorced yet. Speaking of which, you'll be happy to know I hired a lawyer today."

"You did? That's great." He brightened.

"She's drawing up the divorce papers."

"I'm proud of you, Kyra."

"Thanks, but I still have a pit in my stomach thinking about it. He won't fade away. If anything, getting served with divorce papers will make him even more determined to win me back. He can't stand to lose. With him, it's do or die. Literally in this case, and if either of us wound up dead, it would be me, after he realized I was never coming back. I'm worried, Coop. What if he decides to come after me?"

"He doesn't know where you live."

"Actually, about that . . ." She trailed off, not sure how to break it to him that she'd gone to meet Rory without telling him.

"Did something happen?" Instantly he switched to cop mode. "Did you hear from him again?"

She told him then about Operation Takedown and Rory's failure to show for their planned meeting. "There was a man at the bar while I was waiting for him. I didn't think anything of it at the time—he had a carry-on suitcase and was dressed as if for a business trip—but later I wondered if he'd been sent to tail me."

When she was done, Coop's face was stony. "You suspected you were being followed, and I'm only just now hearing about it? You should've told me sooner—or better yet, before you went through with this cockeyed scheme of yours."

"I didn't think I needed your permission," she said, bristling at his bossy tone. It brought back bad memories from when Rory had used that same tone with her, usually right before he hit her.

"I'm sorry," he said in a gentler voice, his expression softening. "That came out wrong. Of course you don't need my permission. If I sounded angry, it was only because I worry about your safety, Kyra. I can't always be there to protect you."

"No one's asking you to. I can take care of myself."

"I know, but I still wish you'd run your plan by me first."

"You would've tried to talk me out of it."

"Yes, but if you were determined to see it through, I'd have gone with you."

"You're not my bodyguard."

"No, but I was a cop. I can usually spot a tail." He blew out a breath and rolled his shoulders as if to shake off his tension. "So what was your ex's explanation for his failure to show for the meeting?"

"He didn't have one. I haven't heard from him. It's been radio silence."

"Jesus." He pushed a hand distractedly through his hair, causing it to stick up in spots. "That's not a good sign."

Kyra began to shiver, her fears amping up even as she said, "We don't know for a fact I was being tailed. I could be wrong."

"Maybe. But usually when someone has a hunch they're being followed, they're not mistaken. Also, your ex has a history of stalking women."

"What do you mean? What women?"

"I ran a background check on him. Are you aware that he was named in complaints filed by two different women? One was a woman he dated in college. She claimed that he'd gotten rough with her and then stalked her after she broke up with him. The other woman was an associate at the law firm where he interned. She told a similar story."

"I had no idea." Kyra felt the blood leave her face. "Why wasn't any of this made public when Rory was running for office? Isn't that what political opponents do, dig up the dirt on one another?"

"There were no criminal charges in either case. Victim One filed her complaint with the school administration. Victim Two went to HR. Neither complaint was followed up on, from what I could determine."

"Oh God. And I blindly walked into the lion's den."

"You couldn't have known," he said gently, then added, "but I still wish you'd told me before you arranged to meet him." She heard the reproach in his voice and felt a fresh stab of remorse.

"That makes two of us. So what now?"

"We watch and wait."

18

The call came at 2:05 p.m. the following day. Kyra was at Suzy's salon, where she was putting in a few hours every day until the new stylist Suzy had hired could start the following week. Kyra was shampooing a customer's hair when her phone vibrated in the pocket of the pink-and-green smock she wore. She let the call go to voicemail. She saw that it was from the sheriff's department when she pulled her phone from her pocket after dispatching a towel-turbaned Mrs. Cuthbert to Suzy's station.

"I'll be right over," she said after speaking briefly with Deputy Fuentes. She was out the door with Ranger a minute later.

A storm was brewing, the sky leaden and scattered snowflakes falling as she hurried along the sidewalk, headed for the sheriff's office, Ranger trotting at her heels. Fuentes greeted her in reception and escorted her to the conference room where the interview would take place, per usual. "Male victim, seventy-nine, identified as Manuel Rodriguez. He was struck by a speeding car as he was crossing the road. Driver fled the scene. Didn't even bother to call 911." His face tightened with contempt.

"Jesus. Who does that?"

"Someone without a conscience, that's who."

"Any word on the victim? How's he doing?"

"He's listed in critical condition. The crime tech I spoke with estimates the car was traveling at approximately forty miles per hour in a twenty-five-mile-per-hour zone when it struck him."

"Did you get a description of the driver?"

"Caucasian male, blond, between the ages of thirty and forty."

"That really narrows it down," she said dryly.

"Witness reports she saw him for less than a minute, and it was from a distance. She lives next door to Mr. Rodriguez. Inez Santiago is her name. She's in her eighties but seems sharp enough. She witnessed the accident from her porch. By the time she got to Mr. Rodriguez, the driver was in the wind."

"Was she able to describe the car?"

"Silver four-door sedan. She didn't get the plate number and couldn't identify the make or model. We put out a BOLO alert, and the local body shops have been notified to report any vehicle with front-end damage matching that description, but . . ." Chaz shook his head, and the lines bracketing his mouth deepened. "Unless you can pull a rabbit out of a hat, we're looking at an unsolved case."

"I'll do what I can," she promised.

They entered the conference room, where an old woman was seated at the table. She was humpbacked, but her lucid brown eyes were those of one who wasn't missing any of her marbles. She wore pink polyester pants and a powder-blue sweatshirt with a kitten appliquéd on the front. Ranger trotted over to introduce himself, and the old woman's face crinkled in delight as he offered her his paw.

"Ay. Que guapo y amable estas," she said to him as she shook his proffered paw.

Kyra said, *"Gracias, señora. Mi perro tambien dice gracias."*

The old woman looked up at her. *"Tú hablas español?"*

"Más o menos." Growing up in the Southwest, Kyra had become conversant if not fluent in the language, while her mother, who was of Mexican descent, spoke not a word of Spanish. She sat down across

from the old woman, and Fuentes took his usual seat at the head of the table. "Do you speak English, Ms. Santiago?" she asked.

"I should hope so. I taught English at our local night school for years," she said with perfect command of the language.

"My Spanish isn't nearly as good as your English, so we'll conduct the interview in English, if that's okay with you."

"Of course."

"My name is Kyra. I'm the forensic artist who'll be working with you today. Is it okay if I ask you some questions? They won't be like the questions the police might have asked you. It's to help me develop a sketch of the suspect so we have a better chance of catching him," she explained. The old woman nodded, seemingly eager to be of assistance. Good. That was half the battle.

"How is Manny? Is he going to be all right?"

"I don't know, but I can tell you he's in good hands. I'm sure he's getting the best care possible. Would you like anything to drink before we begin? Coffee or tea? We also have bottled water."

"I'll take some water, thank you. Poor Manny." Ms. Santiago shook her head, wearing a pained expression.

Fuentes left the room, and Kyra set up for the interview. By the time the deputy returned with a bottled water, she had her laptop powered on and her art supplies arranged on the table in front of her.

"Can you take me through what happened, Ms. Santiago?" she began.

The old woman uncapped her bottle of water. As she drank from it, Kyra noticed that her hand was shaking. "Manny had gone to get his mail." She explained that the mailboxes for their county road were located at the entrance to the road. "I waited on my porch because he always brings me my mail when he gets his. I don't get around so good anymore." She indicated the cane propped against her chair. "I saw the car coming when Manny was crossing the road on his way back. It was going too fast. I called out to Manny, to warn him. But it was too late." Her voice cracked and her eyes filled with tears.

"Did you see the driver?"

"Briefly. He got out of his car after he hit Manny but left in a hurry when he saw Manny was hurt."

"About how far away were you when you saw him?"

"Thirty feet or so. Too far away to get a good look."

"How old would you say he was?"

"Hard to say. Somewhere between thirty and forty, I'm guessing."

"Was he short, tall, or average height?"

"Tall, I think. I could see his head above the top of his car."

Kyra did a Google search, from which she was able to determine the approximate height of the driver relative to the height of a standard four-door sedan. He stood a little over six feet, according to her calculation.

"How would you describe his build?"

"Lean. Muscular."

"What color was his hair?"

"Blond."

"Straight or curly?"

"Wavy. It came to about here." She raised her hand to a spot just below her ear.

"Did he have any facial hair?"

"No, but I remember thinking he could use a shave."

After showing the witness a series of reference photos and getting feedback, which provided more details about the suspect's appearance, Kyra got busy sketching. As usual, she became lost in the process as the rough image in her mind gradually took shape on paper, becoming more defined as she filled in the features, adding a detail here, a highlight there, shading for depth. When she finally put her pencil down and glanced at the clock on the wall, thirty minutes had elapsed. She sat back to study her finished sketch and gasped, staring at it in shock. It was the face of her husband.

◆　◆　◆

Kyra's head spun as she struggled to make sense of what she was seeing. Was her mind playing tricks on her? She'd been watching for Rory's face in every crowd and listening for his knock at her door. It was possible she had confused him with the suspect, who bore a resemblance to Rory from the witness's description. Both men were around the same age, with lean, muscular builds. Both had wavy, fair hair, even features, and light-colored eyes. How else to explain it? It was preposterous to imagine Rory a suspect in a hit-and-run. He wasn't a criminal. He put criminals in prison for a living.

What he did to you was criminal.

The pieces came together in her mind then. Rory would have had cause to be in the area at the time of the accident if he had come here looking for her. Also, he'd demonstrated that he would stop at nothing to protect his reputation when he'd lied about how she'd gotten injured after putting her in the hospital. Anyone who would stage an accident to preserve his "good" name was also capable of fleeing the scene of an accident he'd caused. Suddenly it made perfect, if horrible, sense.

She was pulled from her thoughts by a wet nose nudging her hand. She glanced down to see Ranger looking up at her with anxious eyes. She stroked his head. Her good boy, always looking out for her. She collected herself and focused on the witness. Turning the pad so the old woman could see her sketch, she asked, "Ms. Santiago, does this look like the man you saw?"

The old woman studied the sketch for no more than ten seconds before her wrinkled face grew animated. "Yes. That's him!"

A positive ID was the goal with any interview, and whenever she achieved her goal, it was gratifying for Kyra. This time it caused her heart to sink. Because it wasn't just a positive ID. It was confirmation of her suspicion that Rory and the suspect in the hit-and-run were one and the same.

"Thank you, Ms. Santiago. You've been very helpful." She was surprised to hear herself speaking in her normal voice. Inside, she was a tornado of emotions. "You can go now, unless Deputy Fuentes has any more questions for you."

"No en este momento. Gracias, señora." Fuentes addressed her in his native tongue. He came to Ms. Santiago's assistance as she struggled to her feet, reaching for her cane.

"What was that all about?" he asked Kyra when he returned from escorting the old woman out. "You looked like you'd seen a ghost."

She handed him her sketch. "He looks like someone I know."

"Who?"

"My husband."

His eyes widened in surprise. "You're married?"

"Separated and in the process of getting a divorce."

If Fuentes had questions about why she hadn't told him this sooner, he didn't ask. Maybe he figured it was none of his business and she was only telling him now because it had become relevant in connection with a crime. "And you think he looks like our suspect?" He studied the sketch.

"I think he *is* our suspect."

Fuentes looked up at her. "Do you know if your husband was in the area at the time of the accident?"

"No, but he had reason to be." She briefly described her situation, leaving out the gory details. If Fuentes was shocked by what she'd told him, he kept it hidden. He was too good a cop, and too good a friend to pass judgment. "I can't be sure he's our man. When I drew the sketch, it's possible I subconsciously confused him with the man the witness described, if he's someone other than Rory."

"But you don't think he is?"

"No."

She pulled out her phone and showed him the most recent photo of Rory on his Instagram page, posted two days ago. It showed Rory dressed in a tuxedo at a black-tie fundraiser. "I don't know if it's the same guy," Fuentes said, peering at it, "but he looks an awful lot like the one Ms. Santiago described. We need to run this by the sheriff."

"I agree," she said.

They found the sheriff in his office down the hall. He was seated at his desk looking at something on his computer when they entered. A half-eaten sandwich sat at his elbow next to an open can of Coke. Ranger eyed the sandwich hopefully, his nose twitching, before he sank onto his haunches beside Kyra. McNally looked up from his computer.

"Must be important to have the two of you in my office. Is this about the hit-and-run?"

"Yes, sir," answered Fuentes. "There's been a development. Frankly, I'm not sure what to make of it." He placed the sketch Kyra had drawn, and which had been logged as evidence, on the desk where the sheriff could see it. "This man was identified as the suspect, and Kyra thinks she might know him."

The sheriff looked at the sketch and then up at Kyra. "You know him how?"

"I think it's my husband."

"How sure are you?"

"Not a hundred percent. I suppose it's possible I got the face I was picturing in my mind mixed up with my husband's when I was drawing it, but it's never happened before, either to me or Gertie." Her mentor would have warned her about that particular pitfall if she herself had ever experienced it. "I think this is a lead worth pursuing. Especially in light of recent events."

His gaze sharpened. "What events would those be?"

She brought him up to date about her aborted mission and her suspicion that she'd been followed home from the airport. "If Rory knows where I live, he would have had reason to be in the area at the time of the accident. I don't think it's a coincidence that a man bearing a strong resemblance to him was identified as the suspect."

"So your theory is that he learned of your whereabouts and came here hoping to reconcile with you, which was when he ran afoul of our victim?"

"Right." She began to tremble as the reality of her situation sank in. A pressure was building in her chest. She felt dizzy. "At first, I thought, 'No way.' He's a prosecutor. It's his job to uphold the law. Then I remembered what he did to me, which makes him a criminal, even though he was never charged. I also know for a fact that he would go to any lengths to protect his reputation."

"So either your ex is a dead ringer for our suspect or we're looking at a criminal prosecutor turned criminal." McNally shook his curly, graying head as he processed it, frowning. "There's one way to rule him out as a suspect. Let's see if he has an alibi." He punched a button on his desk phone and spoke to his assistant. "Sharon, connect me with the Monroe County District Attorney's Office in New York."

A minute later, Sharon's voice announced over the intercom, "Sir, I have the district attorney's office on the line."

"This is Sheriff McNally at the Washburn County Sheriff's Department." He identified himself to the callee. "I need to speak with Mr. Stanhope regarding a police matter. Is he available? He's out of town? Well, is there a number where I can reach him? It's urgent that I speak with him right away." He copied a phone number on his notepad, which Kyra recognized as Rory's cell number. "One more thing. Do you know when he left town? I see. Thank you." After he ended his call, he dialed the number he'd copied, and when the call went to voicemail, he left a message asking Rory to call him.

"Stanhope has been out of town since yesterday, according to his assistant," he said after he'd hung up. "Is it unusual for him to leave town without telling her where he was going or when he planned to return?"

"I've never known him to do so." Kyra felt her gut clench. Evelyn didn't know where he was. But *she* knew. Her suspicion about the man who may or may not have been tailing her at the airport, coupled with Rory's subsequent radio silence and her discovery today that he'd been out of town at the time of the hit-and-run, left her with an incontrovertible conclusion: he'd come for her.

She listened through the blood roaring in her ears as the sheriff went on, addressing Fuentes: "Until he can account for his whereabouts at the time of the accident, we have to consider Stanhope a person of interest. And this case just became priority number one." He glanced at Kyra. "It involves one of our own."

Kyra was moved to tears by his words. *One of our own.* For the first time in her life, she felt protected by the men in blue. Or khaki, in this case.

"Yes, sir," said Fuentes, standing at attention. "I've issued a BOLO, and the auto-body shops in the area have been notified. We've already gotten a call from one about a vehicle with front-end damage that was brought in. But it didn't match the description of the one involved in the hit-and-run."

"If Stanhope's our man, I doubt he'd be careless enough to take his vehicle in for repairs after it had been involved in a hit-and-run. He'd ditch it, more likely. Check with the rental car companies to see if any of their vehicles was recently rented to him, and if so, whether it's been returned."

"I'll get right on it, sir." Fuentes retrieved the sketch. "Will you be making a statement to the press?"

"Let's hold off on that for now. We name Stanhope as a suspect in a criminal investigation without solid evidence to back it up, he and his entire department will be crawling up our asses."

"Have a seat," he said to Kyra after Fuentes had left to carry out his orders. "You look a little shaky." She sank into the visitors' chair opposite the desk. "Not what you were expecting when you came to work today?"

"No, sir."

"I don't suppose you have any idea where your ex might be?"

"No. Even if he was involved in the hit-and-run, he could be miles away by now."

"Does he own a second home?"

"Not that I know of."

"No hideaway like, say, a fishing or a hunting cabin?"

"He doesn't fish or hunt." *Except when he's hunting me.*

"Any friends or relatives he might be staying with?"

"He's estranged from his father, and he isn't close to his mom or his brother, so I can't imagine him going to either of them if he needed a place to hide. A friend might put him up, but I can't think who."

"What about a girlfriend?"

"I wish." Kyra smiled thinly. If Rory had a girlfriend, it would mean he'd moved on, though she wouldn't wish her fate on another woman. "Sir, I believe he's holed up somewhere in the area."

"Because . . . ?"

"Because he hasn't gotten what he came for." She felt her stomach twist, and she automatically reached to thread her fingers through Ranger's collar as he pressed up against her leg. "Me."

When Kyra returned to the salon, Suzy was at her desk in her office crunching numbers on her calculator. She took one look at Kyra's pale face as she entered and said, "Who died?"

"No one. Yet," she added darkly.

Suzy was horrified and worried for her when she learned of the latest development. "Why don't you stay with me?" she said. "There's plenty of room at my house. You can stay as long as you need."

Kyra shook her head. "Thank you, but I can't put you at risk."

"Your ex doesn't know where I live."

"He could easily find out. If anything happened to you, I'd never forgive myself."

"Imagine how *I'd* feel if you got hurt, knowing I could've prevented it?"

"I'll be fine." Kyra's bravado rang false, even to her own ears. "I'm taking every precaution. I keep my gun handy at all times, and Ranger would alert me if there was an intruder. I also have police protection and live next door to an ex-cop." Though the sheriff's department lacked the manpower to have someone stand watch around the clock, the sheriff had ordered patrols. And Coop was close at hand, as well as armed.

Suzy still looked concerned. "Okay, but call me if you see or hear anything out of the ordinary. Even if you think it's nothing. Even if it's the middle of the night. I'll come get you."

"I am absolutely *not* calling you if I hear a bump in the night. It might be dangerous for you to come. I'll call Coop instead."

"Speaking of whom, does he know about this?"

"He knows about Rory, but I haven't told him the latest yet. I will when I get home."

"If you need me for anything, or you just need to talk, call me. I'm here for you. We all are." She stood and stepped from behind her desk, walking over to place her hands on Kyra's shoulders. She wore a peplum jacket, Kelly green with navy piping, over a hot-pink shell and a calf-length black skirt. Her eyelash extensions made her eyes look huge. "We Tattooed Ladies may be few in number, but we're mighty in strength, and we leave no man—er, woman—behind."

Kyra was touched. "I appreciate the sentiment, but hopefully, we won't be putting it to the test."

"Personally, I'd love nothing more than to kick some ass. But if your ex shows up when I'm not around . . ." She returned to her desk and rummaged in her purse, pulling out her travel canister of hair spray. She handed it to Kyra. "Give him a blast of this when you see the whites of his eyes."

Kyra smiled. "Thanks, Suzy. There *is* something you can do for me. Would you let the girls know what's happening? Tell them I'll call them later. Right now, I need to get home and give Coop the 411." There was no time to waste. If her hunch was correct, she was in grave danger. Rory might show up at any minute.

It was after four when she arrived home with Ranger. Coop's truck was parked in the driveway, but when she knocked on the door, no one answered. He was probably in his office at this hour. Rather than disturb him while he was at work, she decided to wait until he was free to speak with her. She let herself in with her key. She'd started a load of laundry earlier, and it had still been in the dryer when she'd left to go to work. She was in the laundry room with Ranger folding her clothes when she heard a door close in the house, followed by footsteps. She froze, and her pulse quickened.

"Kyra, hi. I didn't know you were here."

She relaxed at the sight of Coop filling the doorway. He wore his work uniform of khakis and a button-down underneath a dark-blue merino wool sweater. Ranger gave a happy yip and charged over to greet him, his toenails scrabbling on the slick tile floor. "I came to get my laundry from the dryer." She indicated the piles of folded towels and clothes in the laundry basket on top of the dryer.

"Need a hand?"

"Thanks, but I'm almost done. I'm glad you're home, though. There's something I need to talk to you about."

"Everything okay?"

"No." She felt a lurch in her gut.

Coop's expression turned grim as she brought him up to date. "That's it. You're staying with me," he said when she was done.

She bristled, despite knowing he'd spoken out of concern and not because he was trying to control her. "Was that an invitation or an order?"

"It's not safe for you to be on your own."

Kyra didn't doubt she would be safer staying with Coop than on her own. Safe from harm. But how could she guard against the temptation to jump into bed with him under those circumstances? If there was any possibility of a future together, they'd have to take it slow. Get to know each other first. "Then what was the point of you teaching me how to shoot and showing me those self-defense moves?" she countered.

"Think of me as your first line of defense. If your ex showed up here, he'd have to get past me."

Kyra knew he was right, and he was only trying to protect her, but the part of her that had had enough rebelled. "I'm done running from him. I was forced to flee from my home once before. I won't do it again."

Ranger watched them, his eyes moving back and forth between them as they argued, as if he was watching a Ping-Pong game. He looked like he didn't know which side he was supposed to be on.

"It's only until he's brought in."

"Who knows when that'll be?" She pulled a T-shirt from the dryer and folded it, placing it in the laundry basket. "If he's in the area, he'd have to be an idiot to show his face with every cop in Washburn County looking for him. And while I could use many words to describe him, 'idiot' isn't one of them."

"He can't stay in hiding forever. He's an elected official, for God's sake. Eventually he'll surface. Meanwhile, I'd sleep a whole lot easier if you were here where I could keep an eye on you."

"Actually, I don't think either of us would get much sleep if we were both under one roof," she said dryly.

He smiled at the reference to their kiss on the night of his nephew's birthday party, the memory of which caused her to go all melty inside. "I promise to be the perfect gentleman."

"What if I'm not the perfect lady?"

"Well, now, that's a different situation." His smile broadened.

"Exactly. And I meant what I said about taking it slow. If anything is to come of this—us—it has to happen naturally, as opposed to the romantic equivalent of Stockholm syndrome."

He folded his massive arms across his even more massive chest, leaning into the doorway as he regarded her. "Somehow romance isn't what comes to mind when I think of Stockholm syndrome."

"You know what I meant. We'd be all over each other, and it'd be too much, too soon."

"Tempting though it might be, I do have *some* self-control," he said with a dry twist of his mouth.

I'm not sure how much I have. "It's not as if I'm leaving town. You're two minutes away if there's an emergency."

"One minute and forty seconds," he corrected.

"You timed it?" she said in surprise.

"When I was a cop, one minute could mean the difference between life and death when I was responding to an emergency. I'm not leaving anything to chance where your safety is concerned." His expression grew hard again.

"You've already gone above and beyond. You secured the premises. You taught me how to defend myself. Now it's time I took care of myself." She realized as she spoke that she probably sounded ungrateful, when in fact she was deeply grateful to him. Which was part of the problem. The more he did for her, from his grand gestures to his small courtesies, the more she fell in love with him.

"Do it for me, then. So *I'll* rest easier."

Kyra felt her resolve weaken. She pulled another item of clothing from the dryer, and when she saw what it was—a pair of her panties, the pink ones with the lace trim—it seemed like a sign from the universe. A reminder that she was in danger of losing something besides her life: her heart.

"I'm sorry, Coop. I appreciate your concern, and I don't want you to worry. But the answer is still no."

"Will you stay for dinner, at least? We can discuss it while we eat."

"There's nothing to discuss." She scooped the rest of the clothes from the dryer and tossed them into the laundry basket with the folded clothes. She donned her jacket, announcing, "I have to go. Ranger, come," she called as she headed for the door, carrying her basket of laundry on her hip.

She stepped through the door onto the side porch, Ranger charging past her and down the steps. Snowflakes danced in the air. A layer of fresh snowfall coated the side yard and the field beyond. The forested slopes of the distant mountains appeared draped in white lace. When Kyra reached the bottom of the steps, she heard a door close behind her, followed by the thudding of booted feet on the wooden risers. Coop caught up with her as she was heading down the path to her trailer.

"Let me carry that." He took the laundry basket from her, which annoyed her for some reason, and fell into step beside her. Ranger raced ahead of them. "Fine. Have it your way. If you won't stay with me, I'll stay with you."

"What?" She shot him an incredulous glance. "Don't be ridiculous."

"*I'm* not the one being unreasonable."

"There's barely enough room in the trailer for one person, much less two people and a dog. We'd be on top of each other." *On top of each other. Oh God.* She did not just say that. "No, absolutely not."

"Then don't be surprised when you look out the window and see my tent pitched outside." He took one long stride for each of her two steps, easily keeping pace with her as she hurried across the field.

"Are you nuts? Have you seen the weather forecast? You'd be buried under snow by morning." The forecast was calling for eight to ten inches.

"I'll manage."

"There's no need, because I'm not staying here tonight," she said impulsively.

She'd just thought of the perfect place to stay where no one would find her. Her old haunt, the Pine Ridge Motor Lodge. It was less than a fifteen-minute drive, and the sign posted outside had read VACANCIES when she'd driven past it on her way home earlier. If she left now, she and Ranger could be there before road conditions became hazardous. Coop's next words clinched her decision.

"You're not going anywhere in this weather."

"I wasn't aware I needed your permission," she snapped.

"Dammit, Kyra. This isn't a control thing. It's not safe to be on the road, and it'll be dark soon."

"I don't have far to go."

"Which is where exactly?"

"If I told you, you'd probably follow me there."

"I have a better idea. Why don't I take you? My truck has all-weather tires, and I've driven these roads in snowstorms before. You can call me when you're ready to come home, and I'll pick you up."

"Thank you, but I have new snow tires, and like I said, I don't have far to go."

He blew out an exasperated breath, sending a frosty plume into the air. "Why are you being so stubborn?"

She didn't have an answer. Part of her knew she was being unreasonable. But she couldn't help it. The emotions swirling inside her were like the white mass she'd seen swirling on the weatherman's map earlier. The combination of her fears about Rory, her sexual frustration, and her annoyance at being told what to do collided like the opposing fronts of a storm that was brewing.

She came to a stop at the edge of the clearing and burst out, "What, do you have a Tarzan complex or something? Well, here's a news flash: I'm not Jane. So go swing on your vine and rescue someone else!"

He stared at her with his jaw clenched while snowflakes gathered on his beard and Ranger romped in the fallen snow. Kyra immediately regretted her outburst. She felt even worse when he thrust the laundry basket into her arms and walked away without a word. She started to go after him to apologize but stopped. An apology might lead to a capitulation, and if she stayed, what then?

Better to risk driving on a snowy night than risk getting her heart broken if things didn't work out between them.

19

She called to book accommodations at the Pine Ridge Motor Lodge. Her next call was to the sheriff. She informed him of her change in plans and gave him her new location. He said he'd pass it on to the unit assigned to road patrol in that area and that she shouldn't hesitate to call again if she noticed anything unusual, no matter how seemingly insignificant. After she ended the call, she saw she had texts from Jo and Marisol. They both expressed their concern and promised to call as soon as they had a free moment; Jo was working a bridal shower, and Marisol was hosting a book event. Kyra had packed her suitcase and was throwing together some supplies for Ranger, and enough food to tide them over for the next few days, when Frannie called.

"How are you holding up, sweetie?"

"I'm okay. Or maybe it's just that the shock hasn't fully worn off."

"You got quite a fright today. Goodness, it almost gave *me* a heart attack when Suzy told me your ex was in town. I'll rest easier knowing Coop is looking out for you."

"About that . . ."

"Are you sure that's such a good idea?" Frannie said after Kyra had informed her that she planned to stay at the Pine Ridge until Rory was apprehended. "Why don't you stay with me instead?"

"Thanks, but I couldn't put you at risk. If Rory had me followed, he knows who you are and where you live."

"I have a shotgun and I know how to use it."

"I'd hate for it to come to that."

"You should take Coop up on his offer," Frannie urged. "He can protect you better than anyone."

"I know, but it's complicated."

"Because you have feelings for him?" Frannie guessed correctly.

"Yes." No point in denying it now. "Which is why I can't stay with him. I'm on a slippery slope as it is. One push and I'd be falling in love." She pressed two fingers to her temple, where a headache throbbed. "And I can't. I just can't. If it ended badly, I don't know if I could handle it."

"Why does it have to end badly?"

"Because I've never made good choices when it comes to men, and if by some miracle we do have a shot at happiness, I can't risk ruining it by jumping into the deep end before either of us is ready."

"Sounds like you're coming up with excuses because you're scared to get involved. Which I get. Believe me, no one knows better than I do. After Hannah's dad left me, I didn't date for a long time. And when I did meet someone, I took it so slow, he finally lost patience and moved on. But leaving all that aside, are you sure it's safe to be on the road tonight?"

"It's a short drive, and where I'm going, Rory won't know to look for me. I can't believe I'm saying this, but the Bates Motel is probably the safest place for me to be right now. If I don't get stabbed in the shower."

"Not funny."

"Gallows humor."

"Ack! No talk of hanging, either. Drive safely and text me as soon as you arrive."

"I will. I promise."

Night was falling by the time Kyra set out with Ranger, her bags stowed in the trunk and her gun in the glove compartment. As she drove east on Old Post Road in the gathering darkness, the densely packed trees on either side of the road appeared as impenetrable as canyon walls. The storm that had been brewing had hit, and the snow was falling faster than her windshield wipers could clear. When it got so bad she couldn't see past her headlights, Kyra slowed to a near crawl and considered turning back, but by then she'd gone halfway already; only a few more miles to go. She'd be checking in at the Pine Ridge before conditions worsened, she told herself as she continued.

She was a mile from the crossroads when she saw the headlights in her rearview mirror. Her first thought was that Coop had followed her. She actually hoped it was him because she had grown increasingly nervous that she'd get into an accident and become stranded. But she knew it wasn't Coop when she noticed that the vehicle in her rearview mirror was tailgating her. She'd never known Coop to drive recklessly. She slowed down even more and pulled partway onto the shoulder to allow the vehicle behind her to pass. When it didn't, she felt a prickle of alarm, recalling the horror stories she'd heard at the sheriff's office about female motorists who'd been stranded on isolated stretches of road and met with foul play. Was she being targeted? If so, was it a random predator or someone she knew?

A spike of fear drove into her gut. She groped blindly for her phone, tucked into the cup holder in the center console, and pushed the button to activate Siri so she could place a hands-free call to Coop. Nothing happened. Damn. She must be in one of the dead zones for which that stretch of road was known.

She struggled to tamp down her rising panic.

A minute later, she was blinded by the headlights in her rearview mirror as she was coming out of a sharp turn in the road. She veered off course and overcorrected. Forgetting everything she'd learned in driver's ed when she was sixteen, she hit the brakes and went skidding over the icy road surface across the center line and into the westbound lane. Ranger gave a sharp bark, and in her peripheral vision, she saw him standing with his forepaws planted on the dash and his ears pricked.

Trees loomed in her headlights. That was the last thing she saw before she went off the road and into a ditch.

She was thrown forward with a bone-jarring jolt, and the car's air-bags deployed. The world went gray and swimmy. She didn't know how long she'd sat there in a daze before awareness returned and she felt a furry body wriggle itself in between her inflated airbag and her lap. Ranger. He whined and began licking her face. She put her arms around him, burying her face in his thick fur.

"You okay, bud?" He barked in response. Thankfully, he appeared unhurt. "Me, too. I think." She winced at the sharp pain that shot down her neck when she lifted her head to peer outside. Her headlights shone on a wall of white. The ditch they were in was deep and partially filled with snow. Her car engine was still running, but they weren't going anywhere, not without a tow. "Except we seem to be stuck."

She nudged Ranger off her lap and back into the passenger seat. She fumbled with her seat belt and, when she finally managed to unlatch it, bent to retrieve her phone, which had fallen onto the floorboard below. Her heart sank when she saw she had no signal. She wouldn't be calling for roadside assistance anytime soon. She could only hope a passing motorist would see her and stop to help.

It seemed that her prayers had been answered when, seconds later, she heard the rap of knuckles against the window. Outside, a shadowy figure was bent over, peering in. A man. She couldn't see his face. Suddenly, she was afraid. What if he wasn't a passing motorist who'd stopped to render aid? She was trembling, dread sitting like a block of concrete in her belly, as she rolled the window down a crack.

"Baby, are you okay?"

She froze, hearing the familiar voice. Her heart slammed into her rib cage with the force of the impact when her car went into the ditch. "Rory. What . . . what are you doing here?"

"I saw you go off the road. Are you hurt?"

Was it really him, or was she hallucinating? His face loomed in the window on the driver's side, startling her and causing her to break out in goose bumps from head to toe; it was as if her skin had shrunk and was now a size too small for her body. It was him, all right. He was the driver of the car that had forced her off the road. Now she was trapped. Terror clawed at her throat. His unthreatening demeanor did nothing to alleviate her fear. She knew how quickly his moods could shift.

"I . . . I'm fine." She noticed he hadn't answered her question.

He wore a navy parka—obviously borrowed or stolen, judging by the ski lift ticket dangling from the tab of its zipper. Rory didn't ski. His head was covered by a black knit cap. His face was stubbled with beard growth. "Thank God. Let's get you out of there. The door's stuck, but if you open your window, I can pull you out."

She rolled down the window on the passenger side instead. "Go!" she ordered Ranger. He stared back at her with his head cocked as if to say, *Not without you.* "Go," she repeated. "Get help!"

This time he seemed to understand what was needed and sprang out the window, melting into the trees beyond. She knew she could trust him to get help. The question was whether it would arrive in time.

Rory had disappeared from view, but from the crunch of footsteps in the snow outside, he hadn't left. What was he up to? She powered up the open window and grabbed her gun from the glove compartment. She was shoving it into the waistband of her jeans under her jacket when she heard the banging of a heavy object against one of the rear windows. It was followed seconds later by that of shattering glass. The door locks popped; then she heard the whirr of windows powering down. Frigid air rushed in. The next thing she knew, she was being pulled from the car, kicking and screaming.

She landed butt-first in the snow on the ground. Strong arms pulled her to her feet, and she was steered toward the vehicle that was parked on the roadside a few feet away. Not the silver four-door described by the witness to the hit-and-run, but a black SUV. She couldn't access her gun or execute any of the self-defense moves she'd learned, not with Rory gripping her arm and her feet sliding underneath her on the snow-slick surface. She prayed someone would see what was happening and call 911. But no vehicles passed on the road. Most people, she realized, had the good sense to stay inside during a snowstorm. If only she'd listened to Coop when he'd tried to talk some sense into her.

When they reached the SUV, Rory opened the door to the passenger side. "Hop in." Kyra wasn't fooled by his genial tone.

"No, thanks. I'll call for a tow truck." She pulled out her phone, praying it would magically show a signal, only to have it snatched from her hand.

Rory pocketed it, saying, "You won't be needing that."

"Give it back," she demanded, thrusting her hand out.

"I will, but not just yet."

"When?"

"After we've talked. We're overdue for a chat, don't you think?"

He gave her a boost into the passenger seat that felt more like a push. When they were both inside, he pulled something from the center console. Cold fingers of panic wrapped around her throat when she saw it was a roll of duct tape. She batted his hand away when he reached for her. "No."

"It's for your own good," he said, like someone reasoning with a fractious toddler. "Believe me, I don't like this any more than you do, but I can't have you pulling any stunts while I'm driving. Now, hold your hands out, because I really don't want to *make* you, and I'm sure you don't want that, either. Please. I'm not going to hurt you, I promise. It's just until we get where we're going."

She reluctantly extended her arms, fearing that if their standoff got physical, he would find her gun and confiscate it. "Where are you taking me?" she demanded after he started the engine.

"You'll see when we get there." He shot her a coy glance, as if this was a guessing game they were playing. I Spy, or "name that license plate."

She suddenly felt sick to her stomach.

"Was that your dog?" he asked in a tone of mild interest, as if making conversation with a hitchhiker he'd picked up.

"No," she lied.

"I didn't think so. I never knew you to be a dog person." Kyra had, in fact, always loved dogs, but she'd been afraid if she got one, he would hurt it like he hurt her. "Why'd you turn him loose?"

"He belongs to a friend. She lives down the road, and he knows his way home," she said to throw him off track.

Rory was driving east in the direction of the highway. The road ahead of them and behind was empty. The surrounding landscape was dark and still except for the snow that was falling.

"I don't blame you for not trusting me, but I swear I'm not going to hurt you, Krystal."

"I've heard that before. And I don't go by the name Krystal anymore."

"I suspected as much when my calls and texts didn't go through and the email I'd sent to your old address bounced. Your social media accounts are gone, too, I noticed. Anyone might have thought you'd vanished without a trace. But *I* knew better. So what are you calling yourself these days?"

"None of your business."

"Okay, I guess I deserved that. But, baby, it's gonna be different from now on."

"Then why did you blow off our meeting? Why did you have me followed?"

"You make it sound like some sinister plot. It wasn't like that. I just wanted to know where you lived so I could come see you and we could talk in private. I've missed you."

He'd had her followed and then stalked her, and now he was kidnapping her, but from the way he talked, his were the acts of a loving husband driven to desperation. He spoke in the same tone he had when he was gaslighting her, when he'd sounded so reasonable she hadn't trusted her own reality. But now she knew better than to fall for it. She also knew him to be dangerous. The steel band around her chest tightened. Her breaths grew shallow. She concentrated on her breathing to forestall another panic attack.

She changed the subject. "They're looking for you, you know. The police."

He frowned and darted a narrow glance at her. "What are you talking about?"

"The hit-and-run you were involved in."

"How did you know about that?" he asked, confirming her suspicion.

"I recognized you from the police sketch. It was on the news." She didn't mention that it was she who had drawn the sketch, which had been posted on the local news channel's website, along with an article about the hit-and-run and a number to call if anyone had any information about the identity and/or whereabouts of the driver. "You mowed down a pedestrian and left him to die."

"He's not dead. Last I heard, he was hanging in there."

"No thanks to you. If he dies, you'll be charged with manslaughter."

Rory frowned. "It was an accident. I was on my way to see you, and the guy . . . the old man . . . he came out of nowhere. I didn't mean to hit him. I was excited to see you, so yeah, I guess I was driving a tad over the speed limit, but he should have looked both ways before he crossed the road."

"So now it's *his* fault?"

"I didn't say that. It was no one's fault."

"Why didn't you call 911?"

"I should have. I panicked."

"Is that what you'll tell the judge? You left an injured man to die because you panicked?"

"It won't go to court," he said. "There's no evidence against me. I reported the car I was driving as stolen. When they find what's left of it, there won't be any prints or forensic evidence to collect. And if there was any incriminating footage from traffic cams or doorbell cams, I would know about it."

"It's an ongoing investigation. Also, there was an eyewitness."

"An old lady who probably needs glasses. And she only saw me from a distance for all of two seconds. Besides, I know someone who can pull some strings. Guy I know that owes me a favor. His brother's a California State Supreme Court judge. Even if I was charged, it'd never go to court."

"You'll still be charged with kidnapping."

He gave a short laugh. "*Kidnapping?* I found you stranded by the road and rescued you."

"After you forced me off the road."

"You watch too much TV," he said with an amused shake of his head. "Yes, I was following you, but only so we could talk when you got to wherever you were going. Would you rather I'd left you to freeze to death?"

She heard the edge in his voice and knew to back off before he became wound up. If she pretended to go along with his delusion that he was merely giving her a lift, hopefully she could get him to untie her once they arrived at their destination. Wherever it was. She shivered, the tentacles of dread around her throat tightening.

"So talk. I'm listening," she said.

He nodded as if to say, *That's more like it.* His expression softened. "Baby, you have no idea what these past few months have been like for me." A note of self-pity crept into his voice. "I was a wreck after you left. I couldn't eat or sleep. I could barely function at work. I was drinking too much."

"You said in your email that you were seeing a therapist."

"Yes. Sheila. I've been going to her for the past couple months. I got her name from my friend Keith. She helped him through a bad patch, and now she's helping me. She got me to see it was my parents I was angry at, not you—my dad for abusing me and my mom for failing to protect me. Christ, who wouldn't be a mess after the childhood I had? It doesn't excuse my past behavior. I know that, and I'm so, so sorry for the pain and suffering I've caused you." In the glow of the dash lights, his handsome face was the picture of contrition. She might have believed it was genuine if she didn't know better. "I swear I'll make it up to you. I intend to spend the rest of our lives making it up to you. Things'll be different from now on. I'm a changed man."

Kyra, listening to his delusional ramblings, thought he might be right. But if he was a changed man, it was only because he'd become unhinged. She hoped there was enough left of the man who'd once taken pride in his job to see reason. "If you really mean that, turn yourself in," she urged. "We can talk about any future we might have together after you get your . . . situation sorted out."

He shook his head. "I will, but not tonight. Tonight is for us. I've missed you, baby."

It suddenly seemed hopeless. What was the point of fighting him? He'd win. He always won.

She gave herself a mental shake. *You're not helpless.* These past months, she'd discovered she was capable of far more than she'd imagined. Like learning how to shoot, which she was reminded of by the gun pressing against the small of her back. She wouldn't hesitate to use it to defend herself. Krystal Stanhope wouldn't have dared shoot at anyone even if she'd known how to operate a firearm. Kyra Smith was made of stronger stuff, and if she wasn't yet a crack shot, she could shoot straight at close range.

Ten minutes later, they were turning onto the highway, where traffic was light, undoubtedly due to the conditions. When she saw a black-and-white speeding toward them in the northbound lane, its lightbar flashing, her heart leaped and then sank as it passed them. She told herself it was only a matter of time before Coop or one of her friends grew worried when they couldn't reach her and reported her missing. Eventually, her abandoned car and her dog, would be found, but how would anyone know where to find *her*? Her stomach roiled and her heart raced.

Rory took the exit for Brambleberry Lake after they'd driven a few more miles. Kyra was familiar with the route from when she'd visited Frannie. The main road, Lakeshore Drive, provided access to the residences and recreational facilities on the lake. Frannie's cabin was located on the north shore. They were headed in the opposite direction, toward South Lakeshore Drive.

The waters of the lake glinted darkly through the evergreens to her left. No lights shone from any of the buildings they passed, and from the absence of tire tracks in the snow covering the road, it was clear it hadn't been traveled on recently. Apart from a handful of year-round residents like Frannie, most of the cabins on the lake were owned by summer folk and used primarily during the warm-weather months, according to Frannie. The cabins along this stretch appeared to be vacant. There would be no one to hear her scream, no one she could go to for help. She didn't even have her phone. Kyra had never felt more cut off from civilization than she did now. The fear that coiled in her belly snaked up into her throat.

Finally, they pulled into the driveway of a rustic cabin on the southernmost shore, across the road from the lake. It was surrounded by trees, which blocked the nearest neighbors on either side from view.

"Home sweet home," Rory announced.

He guided her up the snow-covered walkway to the cabin, lighting the way with the flashlight on his phone. The front door was unlocked. She stepped into the living room, dimly lit by the embers glowing in the fireplace. She could make out the blocky shapes of furniture, a wood floor with a large braided rug at the center, knotty-pine walls.

"Do the people who own this place know you're using it?" she asked.

"No, but they seem like hospitable folks." He shone his flashlight on the decorative ceramic plaque affixed to the wall to the right of the door, painted with the word "Willkommen" in old-style Bavarian script inside a border of flowers. *Welcome.* Rory chuckled at his own joke. "Besides, they won't even know we were here. Place was buttoned up tight when I found it."

"One of the neighbors might say something."

"No one's home at any of the cabins along this stretch. They all look to be closed for the winter. We won't be disturbed."

Kyra shuddered at his words. How long did he plan to keep her here? Instead of voicing her fear, she said, "You can't stay holed up forever. The police are looking for you. And what will your constituents think?"

"I don't plan on being here for much longer. As soon as I get my ducks in a row, I'll present myself to the authorities like the law-abiding citizen that I am." He seemed confident that his plan was foolproof.

"And what excuse will you give for not coming forward sooner?"

"I was on a fishing trip where there was no cell service or internet." He had it all figured out, except for her. She was the wild card. But he seemed to be betting on his powers of persuasion, honed by the criminal trials he'd prosecuted—in this case, in persuading her to give him another chance. "Meanwhile, this place is habitable. I found the shutoff valve for the water, so there's running water. No electricity, but there's enough firewood and food in the pantry to last the winter."

Rory crossed the room to the fireplace and tossed a piece of firewood from the woodbox at one end onto the embers glowing on the hearth. He then lit the propane lantern on the mantel. It hissed and flared, sending their shadows leaping up the walls. Kyra fought the urge to make a run for it while he was distracted. She wouldn't get far before he caught up to her, and with her hands tied, she was helpless.

"Will you please untie me? I need to use the bathroom," she said.

He regarded her warily. "You're not gonna try anything, are you?"

"You mean like hit you over the head with the poker?" Her gaze shifted to the set of brass fireplace tools next to the woodbox, redirecting his attention so he wouldn't think to frisk her for weapons.

He seemed amused rather than worried, and why not? He had never known her to make a preemptive strike, or even to fight back. Which gave her an advantage. He wouldn't see it coming when she made her move.

"I trust you," he said.

Bad decision.

He removed his cap and parka, hanging them on the coatrack by the door. He wore jeans and a bulky wool sweater—borrowed from a closet in the cabin, judging by the fact that they were both a size too large. She'd never known him to be anything less than impeccably dressed and groomed. He normally got his hair cut every other week at $100 a pop and wore Hugo Boss and Tom Ford suits. Ready to give a statement to a TV reporter on the courthouse steps or flash his pearly whites at a campaign fundraiser. Now his face was scruffy and his hair shaggy.

He drew a jackknife from a front pocket of his jeans, and she tensed, fearing he meant to harm her. She relaxed somewhat when he used the knife to cut the tape binding her at the wrists. He wasn't going to hurt her. Yet.

"Can I take your coat?" he asked when her hands were freed.

"I'll keep it on, thanks. I'm still a little chilled."

"After you." He pointed down the hallway off the living room. She rubbed her wrists where they were chafed from the tape as she walked ahead of him. "Last door on your left."

She stepped through the door into a small bathroom. It was pitch-black. She pulled her gun from her waistband and placed it on the vanity. By the time she'd peed and washed up, her eyes had adjusted to the darkness. She didn't see a means of escape. The lone window was too high to reach without a stepladder and too small for her to squeeze through. She considered coming out with her gun drawn but rejected the idea. She'd have to be prepared to pull the trigger if he jumped her, and if she fired at close range, she might kill him. Could she do it? Take another person's life, even if it was in self-defense? She didn't know for certain and couldn't take any chances. She'd only get one shot.

She slipped the gun into her coat pocket. She emerged to find him waiting outside. She willed him to turn around and present his back to her so she could seize the advantage. She ground her teeth in frustration when he motioned for her to lead the way instead.

"Let's sit by the fire," he said when they were in the living room again. He led her by the hand to the plaid sofa opposite the fireplace, pulling her down beside him. "Isn't this cozy? Just like old times."

20

Kyra fought the urge to scream as she listened to him go on and on. He told her again that he was sorry, but mostly it was about the suffering her sudden departure had caused him. He recounted his therapy sessions, which had led to his realization that his anger at his parents was to blame for his inability to control his temper before he got professional help. Because, of course, it was all about him. He was a narcissist who was good at faking interest in others or turning on the charm when it suited him, as he'd done with her when they were dating. He didn't need her; he needed to win. To lose her would be to fail. Kyra couldn't believe she had ever been so naive as to be taken in by him.

"Please say you'll give me another chance," he said after his outpouring of self-pity in the name of love. Kyra said nothing. Her fingers itched to draw the gun in her pocket, but she needed to wait until she'd gained some distance from him. If she drew on him in such close quarters, it could end badly for her.

She noticed he was becoming visibly impatient as he waited for an answer. "How do I know things would be different?" she asked in an effort to buy more time by making him think she was considering it. To refuse him would make him angry, but if she agreed readily, he would suspect it was a ploy.

"I'll prove it to you if you'll give me the chance. Actions speak louder than words, right? If you come home, I'll move out of the house and get my own place. We can date until you decide whether to take me back. We could also try couples counseling. You'd love Sheila. She's amazing."

Does she know you beat me? Did you tell her that? "I see you've thought this through."

"I've thought of little else since you've been gone. Baby, I've missed you so much."

"I don't know what to say. It's . . . it's a lot to take in. I'm going to need some time."

"Baby, you can take all the time you need. We have the rest of our lives." He smiled as if confident that she would come around. And why not? Hadn't she always in the past? She stifled a hysterical laugh. He claimed he was a changed man. Little did he know she had changed. *I'm not the woman I was.* "Warm enough now?" He moved to help her with her jacket. She jumped to her feet.

"I'm thirsty. May I have a glass of water?"

Using the lantern to light the way, he led her by the hand into the kitchen. Frozen in time since its last remodel, which looked to have been somewhere in the sixties, from its avocado appliances and Formica counters, it was cozy, or would have been if the cabin was heated and she wasn't being held hostage. A red table with chrome trim and four matching chairs dominated the small breakfast nook. The snow falling outside made her think of gauzy curtains billowing in the wind. She seized the moment when Rory had his back turned filling a glass from the tap, and drew on him. When he turned around holding the glass and saw her pointing the gun at him, he looked stunned.

"What the— Where did you get that? Give it to me before somebody gets hurt," he ordered, extending his free hand toward her, as if she were a child who'd unknowingly picked up a dangerous object. When she didn't obey, he set the glass down on the counter and started toward her.

"Don't come any closer," she warned.

"You'd shoot your own husband?"

"Keep walking and you'll find out."

"Do you even know how to shoot?" He spoke in the dismissive tone she recalled from when he used to gaslight her. He'd made her doubt herself then. This time she knew what was what, and what *he* was.

"Give me back my phone," she ordered.

"It's in my coat pocket."

"Then go get it, and don't make any sudden moves."

She was walking him down the hallway at gunpoint when he spun around, startling her. He lunged at her, and she heard a deafening blast. It wasn't until she saw him clutch his left shoulder, grimacing as if in pain, that she realized she'd fired at him. He was injured, apparently, but not incapacitated, as she discovered a second later when he lashed out, slapping her across the face. She staggered backward, hit the wall behind her, and fell forward onto her knees. Her ears rang. The knotty-pine wall in front of her grew fuzzy as if she were seeing it through a fogged-up window. When her vision cleared, she was horrified to find that she was no longer in possession of her gun. *Oh no, no, no.* She crawled in frenzied circles, blindly groping in the surrounding shadows in search of it.

"You shouldn't have done that, Krystal."

She looked up to see Rory holding the gun pointed at her. The fabric of his sweater was stained a dark color where there was a small hole in it, just below his left shoulder. His face was contorted with a mix of pain and fury. Fear loomed inside her like his shadow looming on the wall behind him.

She felt an urge to curl up in a fetal position to protect herself from the blows she anticipated, as she had in the past when she'd been scared to fight back and too defeated to run, but resisted. Instead, she collected herself and rose to her full height. She looked him in the eye. "My name is Kyra."

◆ ◆ ◆

Kyra didn't wait for him to react. She bolted, heading for the nearest exit. She was betting he wouldn't shoot her in the back. Even he wasn't so insane as to murder an unarmed person in cold blood. Or was he? After what she'd seen tonight, she could no longer be sure of either his motives or his sanity.

She darted across the living room and wrenched open the front door, plunging into the swirling white beyond. She heard Rory's voice call, "Don't be an idiot. You'll catch your death!"

Better that than stick around and get shot or beaten to a pulp.

She hurried down the path, slipping and sliding on its snow-slick surface. She paused when she reached the road, not sure which way to go. The cabins they'd driven past had appeared vacant, but maybe someone was home up the road. She headed in that direction. The snow that had accumulated since she'd set out on her journey, what seemed like ages ago but was probably only a couple of hours, was shin deep as she trudged through it. It was slow going even with her putting all she had into it. It seemed forever before she reached the nearest neighbor's cabin, a distance of roughly fifty yards. A two-story log structure built in the style of a hunting lodge, it occupied a prime lakefront lot where it enjoyed water views to the north and views of the mountains to the east and west. Her heart sank when she saw it was dark and buttoned up tight, secured by storm shutters.

Hearing a car engine, she stopped and turned around. Hope flared briefly when she saw the headlights of an approaching vehicle, until she recognized it as the black SUV Rory was driving. Frantically, she looked around for an escape route. To the north lay the ice-cold waters of the lake, and to the south, a snow-covered expanse of open field and densely packed trees beyond. The road ahead wasn't an option; he'd be on her in an instant. She turned south onto the undeveloped tract instead, where he wouldn't be able to follow in the SUV. Panic spurred her on. Her frosty breaths punctuated the frigid air as she plowed through the snow toward the stand of firs ahead. Her feet were blocks of ice in her boots but she was hot and sweaty underneath her jacket from her exertions.

"Krystal, come back! I'm not going to hurt you!" she heard him call.
How stupid does he think I am?

The engine noise ceased, and she heard a car door slam shut. He was coming for her! Oh God. What now? She had nowhere to hide. Wherever she went, her footprints in the snow would betray her location. Nor was she armed. She was at a loss before she remembered something Coop had said once when they were at the gun range. *A firearm is a tool. Your mind is the weapon.* It gave her an idea.

She ducked into the trees where she was hidden from view. She dropped to her knees and began frantically digging through the snow. After she dug several holes, her fingers were frozen, but she'd found what she was looking for: a rock the size of her fist. She hastily removed one of her boots and the sock she wore underneath. She stuffed the rock into the sock to form a slapper like she'd once seen in a movie where it was used to knock out a villain. She straightened and took a couple of practice swings with her makeshift weapon after putting her boot back on. It would do, but only if she aimed true. She would get only one shot, and it would have to be a disabling blow. If she failed . . .

She pushed the thought away. Failure wasn't an option.

She waited, her heart in her throat, listening to the crunch of footsteps in the snow growing louder in the distance, and watching through the dense foliage that screened her from view as Rory approached. She noticed he was listing to one side. *I winged him good.* She smiled at the thought before remembering that a wounded beast is a dangerous beast. Her makeshift weapon suddenly seemed as puny as a pea shooter.

"I can do hard things." She murmured the words like a mantra. Hadn't she proven it? She'd found the courage to leave Rory even in her weakened state after her hospitalization. She'd traveled across the country in her crappy car with only the vaguest idea of where she was going and no clue what might await her when she arrived. She'd been scared then, but she hadn't let her fears paralyze her.

"Krystal!" Rory's voice rang out in the stillness of the snowy woods. She watched, shivering, as he came to a stop roughly a dozen feet from where she was hiding. She ignored her lizard brain, which was screaming at her to run, and held her position, weapon at the ready. "Come out. I won't hurt you."

"Liar!" she called, baiting him.

"I'm sorry I hit you. But dammit, you shot me!"

"Made you mad, didn't it?"

"No, because I know it was an accident."

"How do you know?"

"Because I've seen a million cases of accidental shootings. Nine out of ten of those shootings were caused by an inexperienced operator, which is what you are. Also, because I know you'd never shoot me on purpose."

Then you don't know me at all. "It wasn't an accident when you hit me."

"I didn't mean to. I reacted in the moment."

"That's what you always say."

He expelled a breath. Peering through the foliage, she could see from his expression she was trying his patience. "We can get past this, Krystal. We love each other. And right now, I could use your help."

"With what?"

"My wound needs to be cleaned and dressed. There's a first aid kit at the cabin you can use."

"I'm not a doctor, and I told you, my name isn't Krystal."

"Fine. Just come out where I can see you. I won't hurt you, I swear."

"Prove it. Give me back my gun."

"I don't have it on me. I left it back at the cabin."

"I don't believe you."

"If you come with me, I'll show you."

"Why would I do that?"

"Please, I'm begging you. After tonight, I'll go to the ER. I'll turn myself in to the police. But first I need to make some calls. Once I get everything sorted out, we can put this behind us and start over."

"Not happening."

"Why are you being this way?" A peevish note crept into his voice.

"I don't know. Maybe it has something to do with you beating me unconscious and lying about it, then wrecking my car to make it look like I'd been in an accident."

"You're right, what I did was despicable, and I deeply regret it. But I'm not the man I was. I've changed."

"Please. You haven't changed one bit. But *I* have."

"I can see that." He didn't sound happy about it.

"You want me, come get me."

He continued, and as he drew near, she came out swinging. When she was in school, Kyra had been a better-than-average softball player. She hadn't cared whether her team won or lost. Her team spirit had been lacking in those days. But she used to love hearing the crack of her bat making contact with the ball.

Now the crack of the rock in her sock making contact with Rory's skull was the sweetest sound she'd ever heard. She watched with bated breath as he swayed on his feet like a punch-drunk boxer, his eyes rolling back in his head. When he toppled onto his back in the snow, she cried out in triumph. Yes!

She fought her instinct to flee while he was still unconscious because she knew she wouldn't get far without wheels. Instead, she squatted down and searched his coat pockets. In his right pocket she found his key fob. The bulge in his left pocket confirmed her suspicion that he'd been lying about not having her gun on him. She was pulling it out when she felt steely fingers clamp over her wrist. She gave a startled yelp, and to her shock and horror found herself staring into his open eyes. A second later she was on her back with Rory straddling her, his hands around her throat.

Blood from his head wound dripped onto her face. His features were contorted with fury.

"You *bitch*!" he screamed.

"Let go. You're choking me." Her voice was a strangled rasp. She clawed at the fingers squeezing her throat.

"Why'd you have to go and ruin everything?"

"Can't . . . breathe," she gasped. His blood-smeared face swam in and out of focus as she struggled to suck air into her lungs. Her brain was sounding the alarm to the rest of her body, but she couldn't seem to get it to work. Her muscles were weakening, her struggles increasingly ineffectual.

"I loved you, and you threw it all away."

"Please," she choked out.

"You had your chance. Now it's too late. If I can't have you, no one else will."

She continued to writhe beneath him and claw at the fingers squeezing her throat, but she could feel her remaining strength ebbing. *Oh God. I'm going to die.* It had all been for naught, running away and starting a new life here. She'd thought she'd escaped, but it had been an illusion. Now she would die at his hands, as a part of her had always known, deep down, that she would.

Another part of her refused to surrender. In the murkiness of her oxygen-deprived brain, she dimly remembered a self-defense move that Coop had taught her. She'd been lying on her back then as she was now, Coop instructing her as he straddled her with his hands around her throat in a simulated attack. Something about using her arms to break his choke hold while she—

Her muscle memory took over where her conscious mind left off. Summoning a reserve of strength she hadn't known she possessed, she locked her arms around Rory's to break his hold on her throat while simultaneously using her legs to push him down and off her. Before he could recover, she rolled out from under him and sprang to her feet, as amazed as she was relieved to have pulled it off.

Through the blood roaring in her ears and the whistling of her breath as she sucked in a lungful of air, she heard a dog barking. Ranger! She didn't know how she knew it was him; she just did. Somehow he'd found her, and from the wail of sirens in the distance, he'd brought help. In her peripheral vision she saw a black-and-tan missile streaking toward them across the snow.

"Ranger!" she cried, her voice hoarse.

The next thing she heard was a howl of pain as her dog sank his teeth into Rory's ankle. "Jesus! Call off your dog!"

"Good boy," she said.

"Call him off, or I'll shoot!"

He pulled the gun from his pocket, but he was distracted by the jaws locked around his ankle, and she sent it flying into a snowbank with a well-aimed kick before he could pull the trigger. She snatched it up and pointed it at him. He gave another howl of pain as Ranger continued to pull on his leg, growling and shaking his head from side to side, like he did on his rope toy when playing tug-of-war.

"Get him off me!" he screamed.

"Ask nicely and I might." He uttered a string of curse words. "What was that? Speak up, I didn't hear you."

"I said . . . *argghhhh*. Please."

"Ranger, come."

Ranger obeyed and bounded over to her, looking pleased with himself and happy to be reunited with his partner in crime. She praised him. "You did good, bud."

She studied Rory. He looked different from how she remembered, and not just because his face was streaked with blood and disfigured by the goose egg forming where she'd clobbered him. Then it dawned on her. "You got small," she said.

The sirens grew louder. A look of panic washed over Rory's face. Even he, with all his political juice and skill at working the levers of the justice system, wouldn't be able to wriggle out of the slew of charges he faced, both in the hit-and-run and her kidnapping. He'd be going away for a long time.

Help arrived sooner than expected. "Kyra!" she heard a man's voice call and turned to see a parka-clad figure churning its way toward her through the snow like a human snowplow. Coop. Her heart soared. Ranger gave an excited bark.

"Jesus. Are you okay?" he gasped when he reached them.

"I'm fine," she told him. "I've got this."

21

Soon, the scene was swarming with uniforms and awash with pulsing blue lights. Kyra counted six emergency vehicles—four county units, the fire department's paramedic unit, and an ambulance—and a total of eight responders. Sheriff McNally had neither wasted a moment nor spared any effort in deploying the troops. She'd given her statement and now watched from the ambulance, where one of the paramedics was checking her vitals, as Rory was treated for his injuries after being read his rights.

"If it were up to me, he'd go straight to jail. A night at the ER is too good for him," Coop commented darkly as he watched the handcuffed prisoner being carried on a stretcher to the paramedic unit.

Neither he nor Ranger had left Kyra's side since they'd arrived on the scene. Coop stood next to the gurney where she sat, one hand resting protectively on her shoulder while the paramedic, a dark-haired young woman named Lauren, took her blood pressure. Ranger stood guard outside the open rear doors of the ambulance, letting everyone who came to speak with his mistress know they had to get past him first. Her detail of man and dog was more reassuring to Kyra than an entire battalion.

"He'll probably need surgery," she said, watching as Rory was loaded into the paramedic unit.

"Yeah, and I'm guessing he won't be using that arm for a while after they operate, and maybe not for a long time. Like, say, if he was in prison getting jumped in the shower and couldn't defend himself."

"He's lucky I wasn't aiming when I shot him, or he might be headed for the morgue, not the ER."

"Instead, he'll live to stand trial. But you still deserve credit, even if you didn't shoot him on purpose. That homemade slapper of yours," he said as he shook his head in wonderment, "was ingenious."

"It was something you said that gave me the idea. About how a firearm is a tool and your mind is the weapon."

"I'm glad you were paying attention."

"Me, too. I was also paying attention when you taught me those self-defense moves." When she hadn't been thrown off her game by his manly presence and her smoking pheromones. "Which saved me from being choked to death when he had me on the ground. That, and Ranger's timely arrival."

Hearing his name, Ranger leaped up into the ambulance and onto the gurney where she sat. Kyra put her free arm around him as Lauren unfastened the blood pressure cuff from her other arm after taking her reading, and he licked her cheek. His fur was damp, and he smelled of wet dog.

Her blood pressure was slightly elevated, which was to be expected after her ordeal, but her other vitals were pronounced normal. Lauren advised Kyra to get checked out at the ER, but she declined. Her injuries were minor—the slight swelling on one side of her face where Rory had struck her, and the bruising on her throat where he'd choked her—and she didn't need a doctor to tell her to get some rest and use an ice pack and Tylenol to bring the swelling down.

Coop helped her down from the ambulance and kept his arms around her, pulling her in close and resting his chin on the top of her head. "Thank God you're okay. You gave me quite a scare."

"How'd you know to look for me?" In the midst of all the excitement, he hadn't gotten around to telling her.

"I saw you leave and followed you, to make sure you got to wherever you were going safely. But I had the bad luck of hitting a deer that ran into the road."

"Worse for the deer. Did it survive?"

"Afraid not, and by the time I'd put it out of its misery and cleared the road, you were long gone. I texted you, and when you didn't respond, I got worried. But it wasn't until Frannie phoned to say she hadn't heard from you, either, that I suspected you were in trouble. You might not have texted me back if you were mad at me, but I knew you wouldn't ignore Frannie's texts."

"I'd promised to let her know when I got to the motel."

"She told me you'd booked a cabin at the Pine Ridge. Why didn't you arrange to stay with one of your friends?"

"I couldn't put them in danger. Rory wouldn't have known to look for me at the Pine Ridge. But he must have been lying in wait when I left the house. He followed me and forced me off the road."

Coop made a growling noise, and his arms tightened around her. "You could've been killed when you went into that ditch."

"Fortunately, the one thing in my piece-of-crap car that works properly is the airbags." She shuddered, remembering the harrowing events that had followed, which she almost hadn't survived. "When he brought me here, I was afraid no one would find me. I can't believe you found me."

"First, we found Ranger." He explained that he and Frannie and her other friends had formed a search party. "We were driving the route I figured you would have taken, and we spotted him down the road about half a mile from where I hit the deer, headed our way. We stopped, and I tried to coax him into Frannie's car, but he wouldn't get in. He led us to where your car was stranded instead."

"Good boy." Kyra drew back to glance down at Ranger, sitting at her feet. He wagged his tail and gave a woof. "I sent him for help. I knew he'd come through. I just didn't know if help would arrive in time."

"I suspected foul play when I saw your car's smashed rear window and the two sets of footprints in the snow. I knew if you'd gotten a ride from someone, one of us would've heard from you by then. Which told me you'd been taken against your will. Your ex was the most likely culprit."

"Was that when you notified the sheriff?"

Coop nodded. "He personally oversaw the investigation and issued an all-units alert after declaring it a crime scene."

"How did they know where to look for me?"

"Frannie noticed suspicious activity on the south shore of the lake after she got home. Smoke from a chimney at one of the cabins that was closed for the season, last she'd heard. When she contacted the owners, they told her they weren't using their cabin and hadn't loaned it to anyone. She called me next, and I went to investigate."

"Before or after you notified the sheriff?"

"Might've been a few minutes after."

"That explains how you managed to get here ahead of the deputies."

Just then, they were interrupted by the distant buzzing of engines. She watched as a pair of ant-size dots moving toward them across the snow-covered road, coming from the direction of the north shore, gradually materialized into a pair of snowmobiles. Their two drivers and three passengers were unrecognizable clad in helmets and parkas. "Did somebody call for backup?" she asked.

"Not that I know of."

The mystery was solved when a familiar voice called, "Kyra!"

Frannie. Kyra broke into a grin as the snowmobiles came to a stop in a flurry of blown snow. The riders dismounted, and then they were all descending on her, pulling off their helmets as they came. Frannie, Suzy, Marisol, and Jo were accompanied by Marisol's friend Cal. The women fell on her with cries of joy and relief, engulfing her in a group hug, while Ranger ran in circles around them, barking excitedly, and the two men watched from the sidelines wearing amused expressions.

"We got here as soon as we could," said Jo.

"There was a tree blocking the road, so we had a change of plans," explained Frannie.

"I remembered Cal's parents' cabin, where he's staying, was just up the road from Frannie's," Marisol said. "He'd mentioned they were into cross-country skiing and snowmobiling, so I thought—"

"Luckily I was there when Marisol called," Cal interrupted. "By the time the ladies arrived, I had the Cats fired up, ready to go." He gestured toward the matched set of blue-and-white Arctic Cats.

"You're a knight in shining armor," Kyra told him before she turned to the other women. "As for you guys, you have no idea how glad I am to see you. I didn't know if I'd ever see any of you again."

Frannie put an arm around her. "Thank God you're okay. You *are* okay, aren't you?"

Kyra dropped her head briefly onto her friend's shoulder. "Yeah. I'll probably have nightmares for the rest of my life, but I'm still in one piece, I'm happy to report. Mainly, I'm relieved it's over."

"Her ex is in custody," Coop put in. "And with all the charges he's facing, he'll be going to prison for a long time."

"Oh my God. Did he do that?" asked Jo as she peered at the bruises on Kyra's neck.

"Yes, but I got away before—" She broke off, shuddering at the memory of her close brush with death.

"She had him at gunpoint by the time I arrived on the scene," said Coop.

"Praise the Lord." Marisol raised her eyes and arms heavenward.

"I hope your ex does his time at the *Cool Hand Luke* prison and not one of those cushy minimum-security joints," said Suzy in a hard voice.

"What's a *Cool Hand Luke* prison?" asked Jo.

Suzy sighed and shook her head in despair as if to say, *Kids these days.* "Before your time, dear." To Kyra, she said, "If we'd gotten here sooner, we'd have shown him some serious girl power."

Kyra laughed. "You guys are like the Pony Express. 'Neither snow nor rain nor gloom of night . . .' I can't remember the rest."

"'Stays these couriers from the swift completion of their appointed rounds,'" Jo finished. "I had to memorize it for school when I was in sixth grade. We *are* like the Pony Express, except we're not delivering the mail."

"Even better; you brought yourselves," Kyra said, wiping tears from her eyes.

Frannie, as usual, summed it up best. "That's what friends are for."

It was after midnight by the time Kyra and Coop arrived home with Ranger after giving their formal statements at the sheriff's office. They rode in Coop's truck, which had a dented front bumper from his run-in with the deer. He parked, and they climbed out as Ranger leaped from the back seat.

"Listen, I know it's late and you're probably tired, but would you like to come in for a cup of tea?" Coop asked.

Kyra knew she'd be tired after she crashed, but right now she was still wired from her adrenaline high and loath to be parted from Coop. "I'd love some tea, but first I need to get cleaned up. Does your offer come with a hot shower?" She was chilled to the bone, and covered in dried sweat and blood.

"Even better. I have a tankless water heater, which means unlimited hot water. I'll run to the trailer and get you a change of clothes while you're in the shower."

When she didn't respond right away—she was thinking about how blissful a long hot shower would be—he said, "I assure you, I'm not going to try anything while you're naked in the shower."

She smiled at him. "You had me at 'unlimited hot water.'"

Inside, she headed upstairs to the guest bathroom, while Coop went to the trailer to get her some clean clothes. She stepped from the shower fifteen minutes later to find a certain male had sneaked into the bathroom while she was showering. Ranger, looking like he could use a bath himself, which would have to wait until tomorrow. In the guest bedroom, underwear, sweats, and socks were laid out on the bed, and a pair of her sneakers was on the floor below. She dressed and went downstairs with Ranger, finding Coop seated on the sofa in the living room, looking at something on his phone.

Flames crackled in the fireplace. On the coffee table stood a steaming pot of tea and two mugs, along with a plate of homemade chocolate chip cookies. The live Christmas tree in the window added a festive touch to the cozy scene. Outside, the snowfall had dwindled to scattered snowflakes.

She sank down on the sofa beside Coop while Ranger curled up on the hooked rug by the fire. Coop poured the tea and handed her a mug along with a cookie on a napkin. "Chamomile. It's said to be calming. As for the cookies, Mom made them."

"It would take two Xanax and a shot of whiskey to calm me down after the day I've had, but thanks. And I never say no to your mom's cookies," she said as she took a bite.

"That was the sheriff," he said, glancing down at his phone before setting it aside. "He reports the operation was a success and your ex is expected to make a full recovery. So it seems he'll live to stand trial."

"Which means I'll be testifying against him." Her stomach twisted.

"How do you feel about that?"

She took a sip of her tea and ate the rest of her cookie while she pondered. How did she feel? A readout of her emotions would resemble the EKG of someone having a heart attack. "Nervous," she finally said. "But it's time I spoke my truth. Past time, if I'm being honest. I kept silent for too long."

"No more. It's over."

"I survived, anyway."

"More than that, you triumphed. You didn't give in or give up. You fought back, and you fought strategically. You'd have made a good cop."

"I've been told that once before." By Fuentes.

Coop reached to gently brush his fingers over the bruising on her neck. His expression was a mix of anger and regret. "I could kill that bastard for what he did to you, but I also blame myself. I never should've let you go."

"You tried to stop me, and when I didn't listen, you went after me. It's not your fault you hit a deer. It's my fault for being stubborn."

"You're one determined lady," he agreed.

"I was also scared."

"Of what? Your ex?"

"That, and the prospect of sheltering with you until he was caught."

"Because you were worried I'd take advantage with you sleeping down the hall from me?"

"Or I'd take advantage of you."

"One of the benefits of a resident landlord," he teased, and they both grinned.

Kyra's smile faded. "Seriously, I meant what I said before. I don't know if I'm ready for a relationship, or if I'm even relationship material. Maybe I was at one time, but I'm damaged goods now."

"Damage can be repaired. I'm not giving up on you any more than I would my truck that's dented from my run-in with the deer."

"Oh, so now you're comparing me to your truck?"

"Hey, I happen to love my truck. But my point is, you don't necessarily throw something out because it's damaged. Some things get better with wear. Like string instruments and antique furniture."

"I'm not sure which is less flattering, being compared to a truck or an antique."

He laughed. "Well, you're not old, but you are beautiful, like many antiques." His expression turned serious as he went on. "When I look at you, Kyra, I see a smart, independent woman who's strong enough and brave enough to move forward and not be held back or dragged down by her past."

Her eyes filled up, and she laced her fingers through his. "You're a good man, Coop Langston. I'm lucky to have you in my life."

"As a landlord, friend, or prospective boyfriend?"

"All of the above."

"Come here, you." He beckoned to her. She placed her mug on the coffee table and scooted over to snuggle against him as he draped his arm over her shoulders. "I was like you once. After my wife left me, I felt like my heart had been ripped out and stomped on. I vowed to stick to superficial relationships from that day on. A vow I kept for years. Then one night, I walked into a bar, and there you were—beautiful, prickly, and possibly wanted by the law."

"I may have been wanted by the law, for all I know." She told him the story about rescuing Ranger from his former owner. "For the record, he was a horrible man and cruel to animals. He deserved to have his dog stolen. Or liberated, as I prefer to think of it." Her gaze drifted to Ranger, who was making whimpering sounds in his sleep, his legs moving like he was chasing squirrels in his dreams.

"So you're a dognapper, huh? Now you tell me."

"And if I'd told you the night we met?"

"I would've said you must've had good reason for doing what you did."

"Because you were hoping to get lucky?"

He laughed lowly. "Lady, I didn't think I had a snowball's chance in hell with you. After you took off like you were fleeing a burning building, I figured I'd never see you again. Imagine my surprise and delight when, two weeks later, I returned home from out of town to find you living in my trailer."

"You have your mom to thank for that."

"Yeah, although some would say it was fate," he said on a thoughtful note. "I'm not a churchgoing man, but in AA we believe in a higher power. I like to think my higher power brought you into my life."

Kyra couldn't help but agree. It seemed they had been destined to cross paths again after their first inauspicious meeting, like the meet-cute in a rom-com. "You might get lucky yet," she told him.

"Is that so?" She couldn't see him smiling, but she could hear it in his voice.

"Yeah. But not tonight." She yawned, feeling suddenly drowsy.

Moments later, Kyra was dimly aware of stretching out on the sofa and a soft blanket being pulled over her. Gentle lips brushed over hers, and Coop's voice murmured, "Good night. Sleep tight."

I could get used to this, she thought as she drifted off.

22

It was a scene as enchanting as any of the snow globes sold at Buckboard Books. The glow from inside, combined with the lights strung along the roofline and porch railings of the A-frame, cast a cheery glow over the snowy landscape and dark waters of the lake beyond. Overhead, the evening stars shone against the blue velvet of the deepening twilight, and the ghost of a crescent moon had appeared. From the surrounding forest came the rustle of pine needles and the creak of snow-laden boughs in the breeze that blew as Kyra and Coop climbed out of his truck, Ranger leaping out behind them.

It was the night before Christmas. Frannie had invited her and Coop to the Christmas Eve dinner she hosted every year at her home. Kyra was excited to spend the evening with her friends and see the looks on their faces when she gave them their gifts. It was her first Christmas in Gold Creek, and shaping up to be her best one ever. Tomorrow morning, she planned to visit the Morningside Veterans' Care Home with Coop and his parents to dispense holiday cheer in the form of Shirley's homemade cookies. Later, there would be Christmas dinner with Coop and his family at his house.

She felt blessed, especially in light of recent events. Something good had come from the darkness of that awful night. She'd conquered her demons, both figuratively and literally with Rory in jail, awaiting his preliminary hearing on a slew of charges. She'd also discovered she had hidden strengths. Now she was discovering that her future hadn't been irreparably damaged by her past.

Her friendship with Coop had blossomed into something more. They weren't labeling the "something more" just yet—Kyra because she didn't wish to tempt fate, and Coop because he was letting her set the pace. It was enough for now, in Kyra's opinion, that they were here tonight as a couple.

"It's so peaceful." Coop paused to gaze out over the lake as they were unloading the gifts they'd brought from the bed of his truck. "I wonder if I'll ever see this view without remembering that night."

"I'm grateful I'm still alive to remember. It might have gone badly for me if my backup hadn't arrived in time." Her gaze strayed to her dog, busy marking his territory on every other bush as he explored the yard. "You brought up the rear," she reminded Coop. He and her fellow Tattooed Ladies, along with Cal. She rose on tiptoe to plant a kiss on Coop's cheek before they headed up the front walk.

Frannie, festively attired in black pants and a white sweater sewn with faux pearls, greeted them at the door. "Hi, you two! Merry Christmas!" Delicious cooking smells, mingled with the pleasant aroma of woodsmoke, wafted from inside. "Everyone else is here. What have you got there?" Her gaze dropped to the shopping bags full of presents they carried as they stepped inside.

"We come bearing gifts," said Coop, leaning down to kiss Frannie on the cheek.

"Hi, Kyra! Hi, Ranger!" Two little girls came barreling down the hallway toward them as Frannie was hanging up their coats. Jo's daughters both looked adorable, wearing matching midnight-blue velveteen smocks and white tights. "We brought tweets!" announced three-year-old Emma.

"You did? What kind of treats?" Kyra asked.

"The bacon kind!" Emma pulled something lumpy and brown and smelling vaguely of bacon from a pocket of her smock. She offered it to Ranger, who gobbled it up and then licked her fingers.

Five-year-old Jess produced an identical dog treat and fed it to Ranger, announcing in a superior tone, "He likes mine better."

"No more treats, or he won't be hungry for supper," said Kyra.

"Is he eating with us?" asked Jess hopefully.

"I'll fix him a plate," said Kyra. She'd never eaten at Frannie's without Ranger also enjoying scraps that Frannie had saved for him.

"Can he sit next to me?" Emma asked as she squatted next to Ranger and put her arms around his neck.

Kyra suppressed a smile. "He can eat with us, but not at the table."

She'd become a frequent babysitter of the "twin terrors," as Jo jokingly called her daughters, since their parents' lives had been upended by Sean's cancer diagnosis. Two weeks ago, he'd gone to see a specialist about his persistent headaches. An MRI had been scheduled, which had revealed a mass in his brain, and the subsequent biopsy confirmed their worst fear—that it was malignant. It had been a devastating blow from which he and Jo were still reeling. Frannie, Suzy, Marisol, and Kyra were taking turns bringing them meals, keeping their house clean, and babysitting the girls so Jo could focus on taking care of her husband and driving him to his doctors' appointments. He was scheduled to start his chemo treatments the week after Christmas. Kyra's heart ached for the couple. Theirs would not be the merriest of Christmases, though they were determined to make it so for the sake of their daughters, who'd been told their daddy was sick but didn't know how sick.

"The girls are spoiling my dog rotten," she remarked to Jo now as she came toward them.

Jo laughed. "You've spoiled *them* rotten. First you take them to the movies, then out for pizza, and then to the mall to visit Santa. Life with Mom and Dad is starting to seem boring."

"Never." Kyra put an arm around Jo's waist. The loose sweater dress she wore, in a soft-rose shade that complemented her red-gold hair, didn't hide her recent weight loss. The stress of her husband's illness was taking its toll on her. She'd gone from waifish to practically skeletal. Her smile was bright, however, if determinedly so. "You're the best mom I know, and Sean's the best dad."

Jo's eyes filled up at the mention of Sean. Coop must have noticed, because he distracted Jess and Emma, saying, "Girls, how would you like to open the presents we brought you?" His suggestion was met with enthusiastic nods from both girls. Their eyes grew wide as he pulled two gift-wrapped packages from the bags of presents he and Kyra had brought—the storybooks Marisol had helped Kyra pick out when she'd been shopping at Buckboard Books last week. "Why don't we go into the next room and you can unwrap them while your mommy and Kyra talk?"

The picture they made, the big bear of a man leading the two little girls down the hallway by the hand, one on each side, evoked tender feelings in Kyra. She imagined him with a child of his own—a son or a daughter with his red-brown hair and her hazel eyes—and thought, *He'd make a great dad.*

"How are you doing?" she asked, bringing her attention back to Jo.

"I'm okay." Jo looked anything but. "Keep on keeping on, right? I'm doing my daily affirmations. I can go for minutes at a time thinking this Christmas is no different from last Christmas except the girls are a year older. Then I remember." Her smile wavered, and Kyra gave her arm a sympathetic squeeze.

"How's Sean?" Kyra lowered her voice.

"He's having a good week," Jo reported, her smile fixed into place now. "The medication Dr. Walker prescribed is helping with the head-aches. And we just found out there's a clinical trial he may be eligible for, which is exciting. He'll beat this. I know he will. He's a fighter."

"You both are," said Kyra. "And we're here to help with the fight."

They joined the others in the great room, where a fire blazed in the fireplace, and appetizers were set out on the coffee table. An eight-foot Christmas tree stood in the window, twinkling with miniature white lights and hung with ornaments, many of which looked handmade. Sean waved hello from across the room. He looked cheerful, as always, if a bit pale below his mop of dark curls. Hannah was there with her friend Darren from work, a light-skinned Black man with a receding hairline—who was more than a friend, from the intimate glance they exchanged when he was introduced. Frannie's sister, Vanessa, was also there, along with Suzy and Marisol, accompanied by Cal.

"I don't know whether to shake your hand or salute you," Cal said as he greeted Kyra. He was as festively dressed as Marisol tonight, wearing a red sweater vest with a pattern of holly sprigs that went with the reindeer-themed Christmas sweater Marisol wore. They made a cute couple and seemed well matched despite the nearly twenty-year gap in their ages. "From the rumors I've heard, you shot your way out of a hostage situation, causing serious injury to your kidnapper before you escaped in the middle of a blizzard. Who needs *Mission: Impossible* when they can follow your exploits?"

"Don't believe everything you hear," Kyra told him. "Besides, you were there."

"Yeah, but not until it was over. We missed all the action."

"Cal." Marisol rolled her eyes and gave him an affectionate swat.

The other day, when Kyra had been shopping at Buckboard Books, Marisol had pulled her aside to confide that she and Cal had "done the deed." Which would have been obvious to Kyra even if she hadn't been told. The glow on Marisol's face was brighter than all the Christmas lights combined.

"I heard the same rumors," said Vanessa from her perch on an arm of the sofa. She looked regal tonight in a gorgeous green-velvet tunic top embroidered with gold thread. "I didn't know how much of it was true."

"Shots were fired. And I got away," Kyra said. The last part was all that mattered.

"She's being modest. She's a true hero," said Frannie, handing Kyra a cup of mulled wine.

"I'll drink to that," said Suzy, lifting her own cup. She looked as elegant as ever tonight, wearing a silk top the color of the mulled wine she was drinking and black palazzo pants accessorized with a rope of pearls.

The others joined in the toast.

"Ranger's a hero, too," said his number one fan, Hannah. "He took the guy down, from what I heard. The kidnapper, who's also Kyra's ex," she explained to Darren, who looked completely lost.

"Kyra and Ranger make quite the team," said Coop. He'd left the girls to leaf through their storybooks by the lights of the Christmas tree and had rejoined the adults. Now he stepped up alongside Kyra, placing an arm around her shoulders. Ranger, hanging out with the girls, looked up and wagged his tail upon hearing his name. "They had the situation under control by the time I arrived on the scene."

Dinner was served. They enjoyed a fabulous meal of étouffée, a traditional Creole dish composed of shrimp in a spicy red sauce over rice, which Frannie made every year for her Christmas Eve dinner, with sides of fried okra, stewed collard greens with crispy bacon crumbled on top, and caramelized pearl onions. They ate at the dining room table by the light of the candles burning in the ornate silver candleholders flanking the floral centerpiece, while Ranger enjoyed his meal of plain shrimp and rice off a plate on the floor. Dessert was a delicious cranberry cheesecake made by Vanessa.

"I'd like to thank my mom for cooking this amazing meal," said Hannah, lifting her glass after they'd eaten. Her eyes shone, and her cheeks were rosy with health. It was hard to believe that this was the same woman Kyra had first met after she'd been picked up off the streets by the police, mentally confused. The meds she was taking were clearly working. Mother and daughter exchanged an affectionate glance. "And thank you, Aunt Vanessa, for your equally amazing dessert, which I'll hate you for in the morning when I step on the scale." Everyone laughed, and there was a groan of acknowledgment from Suzy, who'd abandoned her usual calorie counting tonight.

"You helped with the prep," Frannie reminded her daughter.

"If peeling shrimp counts. And I probably ate as many as ended up in the sauce."

"Which is why I always buy extra," said Frannie.

After the dishes were done, Vanessa took her leave, explaining that she had a Zoom chat scheduled with her son, Antoine, and his family. Hannah and Darren took Ranger for a walk. Sean and Cal retired to the den to watch a football game. Coop got roped into playing a game of Candy Land with Jess and Emma. The Tattooed Ladies gathered in the kitchen to drink Irish coffees and exchange their gifts.

The women were delighted with the paintings Kyra had done for them. Marisol's, featuring a cat curled up asleep on a stack of books in her store window, was a hit. Suzy's, of her styling a customer's hair at her salon, was pronounced "a masterpiece." The one of Jo and Sean holding hands, painted from a photo Kyra had taken of them when they weren't watching, brought tears to Jo's eyes. Frannie was also moved by the one of her and Hannah sitting side by side on the dock, looking out at the lake, from her choked voice when she thanked Kyra. By the time the wrapping paper was cleared away, each had the spot picked out in their home where her painting would hang.

"I did one for Coop, too, of his house," Kyra said. "He loved it." They'd decided to exchange their gifts a day early, since Christmas Day with his family was generally a madhouse, according to him.

"What did he give you?" Jo asked.

"The perfect gift." Kyra smiled, remembering her surprise and delight after she'd opened the blue Tiffany box, tied with a white satin ribbon, and had seen what was inside.

"The gifts men give can make or break a relationship," said Suzy as she sipped her Irish coffee. "I know a woman who divorced her husband after he gave her an ironing board for Christmas one year."

"It's not an ironing board," Kyra said as she reached for her purse to show them what Coop had given her.

"Is it a ring?" asked Marisol, ever the romantic.

"Yes, but not the kind you imagine." Kyra pulled out a key ring attached to a silver chain, from which dangled a silver heart. It held the house key Coop had given her after she'd moved into his trailer, so she'd have access to his washer and dryer. "Since I already had a key to his house, he wanted me to have something that made it . . . official."

"It *is* perfect," agreed Frannie, leaning in to get a closer look.

"I was hoping for an engagement ring," said Marisol. "But I suppose it's too soon for that."

"Way. But if we ever get engaged, you guys will be the first to know." Once, Kyra hadn't dared to believe she could have a future with Coop, but it was starting to seem like a real possibility.

The rest of the gifts were exchanged. Suzy gave the others each a set of handmade bath products from Blossom, the fancy bed-and-bath shop down the street from her salon. Marisol gave books from her bookshop that she knew they'd wanted; Kyra's was a cookbook, a copy of Ina Garten's *The Barefoot Contessa*. Jo gave them each a photo she'd taken of them in a pretty pewter frame. Frannie's gift to Kyra was one that couldn't be wrapped, and that she'd given to Kyra the day before. Kyra showed it off now, rolling up her sleeve to reveal the tattoo on her forearm. It depicted the goddess warrior Minerva wearing a winged helmet—from under which flowed her long, curly locks—and carrying a shield. It was greatly admired as each woman took a look at her outstretched arm.

"Minerva is the Roman goddess of wisdom, justice, law, victory, and the sponsor of arts," Frannie informed the others. "I thought it would be fitting for Kyra."

"I love it," Kyra said, admiring it one last time before rolling her sleeve down.

"It's you," declared Suzy.

"Totally," said Marisol.

"It's us," said Jo, looking around the table.

"I guess we're all warriors; each in our own way," agreed Frannie. "And together we can face anything life throws at us. Heartbreak. Disasters. Men and children who disappoint us or hurt us. Even cancer." Her gaze lingered briefly on Jo as she spoke.

"Best day of my life was when I met you guys." Kyra spoke from the heart.

"Don't you mean the second best?" said Marisol, eyeing her key ring.

"The best because none of the rest would've been possible without you. Frannie and Suzy, you've both been like mothers to me. I was short-sheeted at birth with my parents. You've more than made up for it."

"Stop. You're making me cry." Frannie's voice cracked.

"You're ruining my makeup," said Suzy, dabbing at her eyes with a napkin.

"You're beautiful, even with raccoon eyes." Kyra passed her a clean napkin. "You two are the sisters I never had," she said to Jo and Marisol.

"I always wanted a sister." Jo reached across the table to squeeze her hand.

"Me, too," said Marisol, smiling as she took Kyra's other hand. "And if I'm having my Hallmark Channel moment with Cal, I owe it to you. It was your idea that I invite him up to my place for eggnog."

"Serving it to him under the mistletoe was *your* idea," Kyra reminded her.

"Inspired by a book I read, *Christmas at Lonely Hearts Lodge*," said Marisol. "Have any of you read that one?"

"No, but now I'll have to," said Jo.

"What adventures are in store for us next, I wonder?" said Suzy, gazing at the framed group photo of them.

"Whatever happens, we're in it together," said Kyra.

"Through thick and thin," said Frannie.

They joined hands and chorused, "The Tattooed Ladies forever!"

ACKNOWLEDGMENTS

I wrote the first draft of this novel during the pandemic of 2020. It's the first novel I've written for which I hadn't done field research. Most of what I learned about the various professions depicted in *All They Need to Know*, I got from books, podcasts, Zoom calls, and the internet. I also relied heavily on my memories of trips to the gold country of California and my family's annual camping trip to Pinecrest Lake in the Sierra Nevada mountains every summer when I was growing up.

The fictional town of Gold Creek is inspired by my travels in that region, with its gorgeous scenery and rich history and quaint towns, one of which offered stagecoach rides for hire when I visited and perhaps still does. I created a place where I could go in my mind during a time when travel was restricted. It's a place I plan to revisit in future novels, if only so I can enjoy a virtual cup of coffee and a pastry at Cowboy Coffee with my fictional girlfriends.

I owe a huge debt of gratitude to my husband, Sandy Kenyon, with whom I spent the better part of the pandemic lockdown holed up in our 975-square-foot apartment in Manhattan, him working at one end and me working at the other, meeting in the middle for meals and cuddles and binge-watching *Stranger Things*. He's always been my biggest booster, and he kept the faith during those times when my own faith faltered. He's read every one of my books—multiple drafts, in some cases. He gives me ideas and insights when I'm writing about his beat as a TV reporter. He's not only my life partner but also my best friend. If he were a bagel, he'd be an everything bagel.

I'm also enormously grateful for my friend and critique partner, the fabulous Donna Ball. She not only cast her keen writerly eye on multiple drafts of this novel but also kept me entertained when I wasn't working on my book, reading drafts of her various works in progress. I'm both envious and in awe of her, wondering how the heck she manages to produce three books for every one of mine. If you haven't read any of her wonderful novels—her Dogleg Island, Raine Stockton, and Buck Lawson mystery series; or her Ladybug Farm and Hummingbird House series—go immediately to your nearest bookstore, public library, or e-book platform and buy or borrow one. You're in for a treat.

Thanks, too, to my wonderful agent, Paula Munier at Talcott Notch Literary Services. She not only kept the faith and gave me valuable critical input during the process of drafting this novel but also found the perfect home for it. I'm thrilled to be a Lake Union author and to be working with such a talented editorial team. My developmental editors, Melissa Valentine and Tiffany Yates Martin, provided me with reams of editorial notes that brought my vision for this novel into sharper focus and gave it greater depth. Carissa Bluestone was a later addition to the team, and a welcome one. I'd also like to thank those who not only kept the trains running on time but who also caught all the errors and inconsistencies in the manuscript: production managers Angela Elson and Jen Bentham; copyeditors Karen Brown and Tara Whitaker; proofreader Jill Kramer; and CRR reader Malika Whitley. The term "it takes a village," is never truer than when applied to publishing teams, and this one is stellar. Ladies, I'm in your debt.

I want to give a shout-out to my writer friends, the Beach Babes: Jen Tucker, Samantha Bailey, Meredith Schorr, Francine LaSala, Julie Valerie, and Josie Brown. Our friendship and weekly Zoom meets during the pandemic helped us stay connected when we were all missing one another and our annual writers' retreat at the beach. We shared our frustrations and fears; our triumphs in the form of book deals and book releases; and lots of laughs, as always. For what misery or woe cannot be made lighter with laughter? I love you guys, and I'm in awe of what you've achieved, not just professionally but in every aspect of your lives. You remind me that dreams do come true. You inspired the friendship of the Tattooed Ladies depicted in this novel. You also inspire me on a daily basis to do better on my social media.

Last but not least, I wish to thank my loyal readers, many of whom have been with me since I published my first novel, *Garden of Lies*, in 1986. Your praise and encouragement through the years have allowed me to continue writing. You remind me regularly that the best stories are timeless and of universal appeal, ones that can be enjoyed by generations of readers across the globe, as has been the case with my earlier novels.

I hope you enjoyed the story in these pages. If you did, I would greatly appreciate it if you would take a moment to post a review on Amazon or Goodreads or any other platforms you use. I have an ironic T-shirt that reads I WRITE FOR FOOD. It's no joke, in one sense. Our daily bread as writers depends on readers like you. So thank you in advance for taking the time to let me and others know if you enjoyed this book, and for making it possible for me to continue writing.

ABOUT THE AUTHOR

Photo © Sandy Kenyon

Eileen Goudge is the *New York Times* bestselling author of more than twenty novels, including *Garden of Lies*, *One Last Dance*, and *The Diary*. Together, they have sold over six million copies worldwide. Eileen draws from her own experiences in writing women's fiction, exploring recurring themes of sisterhood/friendship bonds, the joys and heartaches of romance, and reversals of fortune. Eileen got her start as a ghostwriter for the popular teen series Sweet Valley High, which spawned multiple spin-offs and a TV series. Between cooking up plots for her novels, Eileen can often be found in her kitchen kneading bread or rolling out pie dough. In 2005 she published a cookbook, *Something Warm from the Oven*, filled with family recipes and recipes contributed by readers. She lives with her husband, Sandy Kenyon, the former entertainment reporter and film critic for WABC-TV in New York City, in the 1940s home they remodeled in Sacramento, California. For more information, visit www.eileengoudge.com.